## PRAISE FOR

# THE ETERNAL WORLD

"Excellent fantasy thriller . . . The realistic approach is one of this inventive novel's major strengths."

*Publishers Weekly* (★Starred Review★)

"A fantastical witch's brew of Spanish conquistadors, biotechnology, and hubris . . . with cinematic pacing and colorful action cenes, Farnsworth blends a unique premise nto fun summer reading . . . entertainingly explores the border where science fantasy meets reality."

*Kirkus Reviews*

"I've been a fan of Christopher Farnsworth ever since his first book, and he just keeps getting better. *The Eternal World* has exactly what I look for in great adventure fiction: a compelling plot, memorable characters, top-notch action scenes, and heart-stopping twists. Put the coffee on, because you won't want to stop reading this until the very last page."

Boyd Morrison, author of *The Ark* and *Piranha* (with Clive Cussler)

## MORE PRAISE FOR

# CHRISTOPHER FARNSWORTH

"Christopher Farnsworth's taut thriller *Blood Oath* is an irresistible page-turner. . . . Farnsworth summons his talents as a script-writer and journalist to spin a complex and unnervingly realistic tale. . . . The supernatural elements here are dazzlingly clever."

*Washington Post*

"*Blood Oath* is exactly how I like my Presidential thrillers. With vampires."

Brad Meltzer, bestselling author of *The Book of Fate* and *Identity Crisis*

"A fast-paced thriller with supernatural flair . . . For pure entertainment purposes, it's hard to beat Cade and company riding to the rescue."

*Kirkus Reviews* on *The President's Vampire*

"Lovecraftian monsters pale in the context of human terrorism and war. . . . Events build to a cinematic showdown. . . . The conclusion will leave the reader breathless and wondering what horrors the future holds."

*Publishers Weekly* on *The President's Vampire*

**By Christopher Farnsworth**

THE ETERNAL WORLD
THE BURNING MEN
RED, WHITE, AND BLOOD
THE PRESIDENT'S VAMPIRE
BLOOD OATH

*Coming Soon in Hardcover*
KILLFILE

# THE ETERNAL WORLD

CHRISTOPHER FARNSWORTH

WILLIAM MORROW
An Imprint of *HarperCollins*Publishers

This book is a work of fiction. References to real people, events, establishments, organizations, or locales are intended only to provide a sense of authenticity, and are used fictitiously. All other characters, and all incidents and dialogue, are drawn from the author's imagination and are not to be construed as real.



First William Morrow premium printing: July 2016
First William Morrow special paperback printing: August 2015
First William Morrow hardcover printing: August 2015

ISBN 978-0-06-228294-1



10 9 8 7 6 5 4 3 2 1

*For Jean,*
*forever*

*. . . and, as they were an ignorant people, they all set out in search of this river, which was supposed to possess the powers of rejuvenating old men and women. So eager were they in their search, that they did not pass a river, a brook, a lake, or even a swamp, without bathing in it; and even to this day they have not ceased to look for it, but always without success.*

—HERNANDO D'ESCALANTE FONTANEDA,
*On the Country and Ancient Indian Tribes of Florida*, 1575

## AUTHOR'S NOTE

*The Eternal World* is based on the story and ideas by Monnie Willis and Tom Jacobson. I'd like to thank them for letting me play in their sandbox.

# THE
# ETERNAL WORLD

# PROLOGUE

FLORIDA
1527

THE CONQUISTADOR WAS DYING.

They had set upon his men without warning, their fire-hardened arrows and spears punching through Spanish armor like paper. Their heavy wooden clubs, studded with shark teeth, crushed skulls and tore flesh and muscle from bone.

His men panicked. His commands were lost in the sudden screams of pain and fear. He was knocked from his horse and thrown to the ground. There was no strategy, no order of battle, only pitched and desperate fighting.

Within moments, he was separated, surrounded by the endless green and the echoing screams of his men.

Something struck his leg, and he looked down and saw the arrow buried there. He saw a flash of copper-colored skin at the edge of his vision.

He'd thought he was lucky to be hit only in the

thigh. He pulled the arrow out by its shaft, and saw the savage who had shot him disappear into the heavy green of the forest at the side of the trail.

Half-mad with rage, he crashed into the trees on foot, determined to make at least one of his enemies pay for this.

First he had run, then he had limped, and now he dragged the leg along behind him.

He realized now the arrow was poisoned. Sweat stung his eyes. Insects crawled on his face, under his armor, in his hair. Pus spilled from the wound like warm egg yolk.

He removed his armor, piece by piece, leaving it behind like fragments of shell on a beach. His rifle was gone, left behind at the scene of the fight. His pistol was empty and useless in his belt. His provisions had been carried by the men at the back of the line, who were surely dead now.

All he had left was his sword. He used it to swat at the branches as he tried to hack a path through the jungle.

He did not know where he was going. He thought he heard water, and he thought a drink might cool the fever that was raging in him now. But even though he was ankle-deep in mud, he could not find the source of the water. He tried to follow the sun, which seemed only to stick in place, blazing above his head.

It was growing difficult to breathe. He lost the sword somewhere along the way. He didn't remember dropping it.

The soldier stumbled upon a trail—narrow and

partially overgrown, but he could see fresh footprints in the mud. He moved forward as best he could, supporting himself by leaning on the trees between steps.

Finally, he staggered into a clearing. The sun was even more cruel without the canopy of shade in the forest.

He saw a cave: a dark opening in an overgrown hill rising out of the ground. He heard the trickle of water again, echoing from within the hole.

He could no longer swallow, his tongue was so dry and his throat so raw. But it would be nice to get out of the heat.

He fell inside the mouth of the cavern and dragged his body out of the sun with the last of his strength. He knew he would never find the water. This was where he would die. It was a good enough place, he thought. He had spanned an ocean and crossed the world and found only death. He did not need to get any farther from home.

Here, he could rest.

His eyes closed. He heard the voices of his mother and his father. He saw his childhood home. Smelled bread baking in the kitchen. He smiled.

He felt a cool hand on his cheek. He opened his eyes.

There was an angel looking down at him. She was the most beautiful thing he'd ever seen.

His smile grew wider. She looked troubled, and she spoke in the tongue of angels, trying to tell him something mere human ears could not understand. It didn't matter. He wanted to tell her it was all right. He was prepared for judgment. His soul and his conscience were clear.

He closed his eyes again. Wherever she would take him, he was ready.

# CHAPTER 1

CIUDAD JUÁREZ, MEXICO
TWO WEEKS AGO

THE BUTCHER CROSSED the bridge on foot at El Paso. With a few days in the sun, he was dark enough to pass as one of the many day laborers on their way home to Juárez for the evening after long hours cleaning, cooking, and mowing the lawns of white people.

He wore sagging dad jeans and a T-shirt that said Metallica and a sweat-stained trucker cap, all fished out of a Goodwill bin. His face was still unlined, his body strong and young. One woman glanced in his direction and gave him a friendly smile. He smiled back, showing all his fine white teeth. She looked away quickly, and surreptitiously crossed herself.

He tried not to laugh. It wasn't easy. He wanted to tell her that he'd believed once, too. Now he knew better.

Now he was God, or as close as any of these people would ever see.

Once, he had been Juan de Aznar y Sandoval. For a while, he'd variously been known as the Moonlight Murderer, the Servant Girl Annihilator, Bible John, and the Torso Killer. Now he was known best as El Carnicero, El Verdugo, El Sanguinario—the Butcher of Juárez.

Juárez was a city regularly drenched in blood. People died every day in the relentless drug war between the cartels and the military. So many died that the government was unable—or unwilling—to keep an accurate body count. The usual estimate was about eight murders a day. In a city where life was so cheap, it was easy to lose track.

It took real effort to rise above the usual background noise of gunfire. But over the years, people began to notice: young women—girls, really—who worked at the maquiladoras, the factories that straddled the border, were turning up dead.

In 1993, seventeen women were found slashed, strangled, mutilated, and, in one case, burned. They all suffered similar cuts to their breasts. The next year, at least eleven were killed. Eighteen the year after that, and more the year after that, and after that.

The victims, all girls, were drawn to Juárez from their villages in the country with the promise of good jobs. Their pictures began to appear in the newspapers, the faces beaming right next to graphic descriptions of the rape and mutilation their bodies had endured.

People finally began to count all those faces, and all the bodies found in fields or vacant lots or back alleys. Some people got as high as four hundred over a ten-year span.

The police said that was impossible. They said no one man could be responsible for so many deaths. When the outrage over their inaction became too much, they would arrest someone and try to pin all the murders on him.

But the girls kept dying, no matter what the police did or said.

Now most people, if they thought of him at all, believed he was an urban legend. There was even a song about him. He heard it played on a cheap portable stereo as he was walking over the bridge one night. It took him a moment to realize that someone had composed a *narcocorrido* about him:

*Oh little girl,*
*watch where you walk tonight,*
*Oh little girl,*
*watch where you go,*
*Don't you know the Butcher is waiting for you,*
*Stay here with me tonight,*
*Or the Butcher will claim your soul.*

Idiots, he thought. Singing hymns to the man who was slaughtering them. The *narcocorridos* were full of praise for the lords of the cartels, or their gunmen—he'd even heard one about Osama bin Laden. It only confirmed his belief that these people were in love with death, a whole culture bent on suicide, like a herd of cattle running over a cliff.

But he had to admit he found himself humming the tune. It was catchy.

Aznar was not stupid. He was careful. He changed his signature style every other victim now, so that he could not be tracked by the slashing of breasts or a particular weapon or method of murder. He could control the urge for months at a time, staying in his cheap little hovel on the Texas side of the border, keeping quiet, keeping to himself.

But eventually, he would realize, why bother?

He had passed from reality into folklore. No one would ever catch him, because he was like the weather now: simply a condition of life, inevitable and uncontrollable. The police would not even try to stop him, because that would be admitting he existed. The citizens would simply accept him, and every time another body turned up, they would shrug and move on. People still had to go to work, go shopping, and raise their kids. They had their own problems. That was Juárez: proof that people could get used to anything.

This is why he loved the walk across the bridge. For him, Juárez was a playground, and every time, it made him giddy as a child.

Tonight, the Butcher was back.

THE GIRLS FILED OUT of the factory like an offering made just for him. He scanned their faces, looking for the right one for tonight as they hurried back to their little shacks. They would get some food or some sleep or change into their good clothes and hit the clubs that stayed open into the early morning to cater to them.

No one heeded the warning in the song about the Butcher. There was simply no way for women to stay off the streets in Juárez after dark. The factories worked around the clock, manufacturing plastic toys and gadgets to fill the shelves of the stores up north.

Every night, he had his choice of targets. A seemingly endless supply.

That's not to say he didn't have a type. He did. Anyone looking at the photos of his victims would see the common threads binding them all together. All were young, late teens or not far into their twenties, attractive, and, at least superficially, resembled one another. They could all have been sisters, or cousins, from a very large and very unlucky family.

But no one would know the real reason he chose them all. They all looked like her. He would never get tired of killing her. He thought of it as practice for the day when he'd finally get his chance at the real thing.

For tonight, he'd have to be satisfied with another stand-in.

He waited outside the gates of the factory—this one assembled toys from plastic components made in Taiwan and then shipped them back across the Pacific. Many of the girls on the line weren't much older than the children who'd play with the finished products.

He ignored them. It wasn't that he valued them or thought them innocent—none of these mongrels were innocent, in his mind—but they did not look enough like her.

Then he caught a glimpse of an older girl, already turning in a different direction from the stream of night-shift workers.

He caught himself. She looked so much like her,

he had to be careful not to stare too hard. He didn't want anyone to notice him.

But the resemblance—it was too close to let her go. She would be perfect.

He waited an appropriate length of time, and then was drawn after her down the same dark streets.

JUÁREZ WAS BOTH TOO poor and too corrupt for streetlights or sidewalks off the main avenues. The shadows were deep enough for him to hide every time the girl looked over her shoulder. She knew he was there, but she couldn't see him.

She must have lived in the cheapest possible rentals—the slapped-together houses on the far end of the city, parallel to the river and near the railroad tracks. Quite literally, the wrong side of the tracks: bodies were dumped here all the time, along with whatever trash and waste that couldn't be recycled by the countless scavengers and pickers. The shacks were often just four walls and a roof put up over a dirt floor, without water or heat or electricity. The people who lived there were either new to Juárez or had simply given up.

She looked new. Her dress still had some white in it, and there was still some life in her movements.

Aznar was happy; she was going to be worth his effort.

She abruptly turned into an alley between the shells of two buildings near the tracks that had been burned out in a recent dispute between the cartels and the military.

It was time for him to show himself.

He moved out of the shadows, almost gliding over the dirt and broken concrete. He'd try to take his time with her, but he knew it was going to be over quick. The first one of the night always was. And anyway, he could still catch at least two more before morning.

Aznar entered the mouth of the alley and deliberately knocked over a pile of trash. Old cardboard slithered to the ground, taking several wads of plastic bags with it. It sounded nicely ominous to him.

He already had his knife in his hand. He'd planned on gutting his victims tonight, pulling out their entrails and showing them off in the moonlight. It was a cheap, handmade thing—once a kitchen knife, now wrapped with duct tape for a handle, sharpened to a razor's edge. It was ugly and mean and perfect.

He wanted her to turn and see him. He wanted to see the fear in her eyes.

She wasn't there.

Impossible, he thought. He was faster than her, faster than anyone could be, and there was nothing big enough for her to hide behind here.

He ran to the end of the alley, frantic with disappointment.

He saw a soiled dress, still white in places, in the corner of his eye. She dropped on him from above, leaping from one of the dead windows in the empty building.

It was a twenty-foot fall from the window to the alley. No ordinary girl could have made the leap without breaking bones.

But then, no ordinary man could have taken the force of her landing without breaking his neck.

He fell and rolled away from her, and regained his feet instantly. They stood and faced each other.

It wasn't a girl who looked like her.

It was her.

In disbelief, he said her name: "Shako."

She returned his greeting. "Aznar," she said.

Then they went for each other.

SHE WOULD HAVE LIKED to be able to deal with Aznar from a distance. He was dangerous. But she had to be sure it was him. She had to see him face-to-face.

He was good with the knife. He turned it expertly in his hands as he advanced on her, alternating between short, stabbing thrusts and wide slashes that drove her back. He moved so fast the blade seemed to flow like water in the dim light.

But she'd seen it before. He'd changed nothing, apparently learned nothing, since their last encounter.

And she was not defenseless.

She took a flat wedge from the holster she wore like a garter on her thigh. With the press of a button, it sprang a telescoping handle. She took the grip in her left hand, and then, when Aznar stabbed at her again, swung hard for his skull.

He barely dodged in time, the metal ax coming within millimeters of his eyes. It was crafted of a titanium alloy, a high-tech re-creation of a tomahawk.

She was not above using guns or bombs or even missile strikes if it came to that. But it was important to her that all of the Council see her face before they died. Given the chance, she would stick with the old ways.

Aznar fell on his back, his feet sliding out from under him in his sudden retreat. She slashed downward, and realized her mistake. This was a feint, meant to get her overextended and off-balance. He stabbed upward, coming out of a crouch.

She pulled back and caught his knife with her ax hard enough to send sparks flying, but not hard enough to knock it from his grip.

She didn't let up. Didn't let him up. He was still kneeling, still slashing desperately at her. She swung for his head again, and, when he ducked, drove her foot into the bridge of his nose. There was a sharp cracking noise and Aznar flipped over onto his back.

He thrashed wildly, scrambling on the ground on all fours. She realized Aznar was going to run.

No. Not this time. She thought she'd had him in Serbia; she wasn't going to let him get away again.

She leaped forward and sliced through the meat of one of his legs with a stroke that almost looked like a golf swing.

He screamed and bucked as if electrocuted. He never could handle pain. Not at all, she remembered.

Before she could lift her ax again, however, he turned and threw his knife at her.

It buried itself in her left shoulder, up to the hilt. Her arm went numb: he'd taken out the nerve cluster there as deftly as a surgeon.

He struggled up from the ground and gave her a lupine grin.

"Don't look so pleased," she snarled. Wincing,

she yanked the knife from her body. A fresh gout of blood ran freely, soaking the top of her dress. "I've got your knife."

She held the knife in her near-dead hand and clumsily transferred her ax to her right.

His grin grew even wider. "Keep it," he said. "I'll use this one."

And he drew another, just as large and ugly as the first, from under his jacket.

She staggered back a few steps.

He came after her, limping.

He adjusted the rhythm of his attack now, putting his weight on his good leg as he stabbed at her, then dancing back, favoring the bad one, when he dodged.

She clumsily parried his blade with the ax, but he broke through her defense easily. She thought he might have nicked her lung. Breathing was becoming difficult.

Within a few more seconds, he'd opened shallow slashes on her arms, her breasts, and her legs.

He was enjoying himself now. She could see it in the orgasmic light in his eyes, his smile now almost serene. This was what he lived for; he was toying with her.

She wasn't worried. The cuts Aznar had inflicted were superficial. They would have closed instantly if her body were not already trying to heal the major wound in her shoulder. Even the nerves would knit themselves back together, good as new, in a matter of hours.

After all, it wasn't like Aznar had dipped his blades in poison.

She had.

A little of the light went out of his eyes at first. A string of drool fell from his lips, and he began to look confused. He redoubled his efforts, pushing harder, stabbing, trying to close in for the deathblow.

He couldn't do it. He was getting slower. His leg still dragged, when it should have healed as fast as she could. Sweat drenched his face for the first time, despite the warmth of the night.

The next time he brought up his knife, she swung and knocked it away easily. He looked shocked, and then it finally occurred to him what had happened.

She saw it then, in his eyes. The hate was still there. The rage, and the sense of wounded vanity. He never believed he was subject to the rules, even when they were all still mortal.

But above all, she saw the helplessness.

The poison was only slightly weaker than the one she used on the tips of her arrows. It paralyzed before it killed. But that only meant it worked slower. It was still working, implacably shutting down the connections between Aznar's brain and his body, like turning off light switches in a house one by one, until the entire structure was completely dark.

It was almost over.

Aznar knew it, too. He was many things. But he was not stupid.

He ran away from her.

She was caught flat-footed, her weight still on her back leg, ready to parry his next attack. Even with the drug in him, he took off like a shot.

Damn it. All this time, and he could still surprise her.

She raced after him. She would not let him get away. She still wanted answers before he died. Forever, this time.

AZNAR FELT SURPRISINGLY CALM, even as his breath hitched and his legs went numb. He did not expect it to end like this, in the ass end of a diseased slum.

But he always knew it would end somewhere. And he knew, with unshakable faith, that nothing waited for him. There would be blackness, and then, whatever he was, whatever he had been, would be gone.

It occurred to him that he had nothing to fear. That his faith had always been much more about suffering through Hell than embracing the joy of Heaven.

Shako was right on top of him now. He turned to look at her, could see the triumph and determination in her eyes.

Then he tripped and went down hard.

His skull rang against metal. He realized he'd fallen on the railroad tracks. He got to his knees and brought up his knife again, just in time to keep her from leaping atop him and finishing this.

She stood back, wary. He kept the knife up. She could afford to wait. His arm already felt heavy. The poison was still working in him. Soon he'd be helpless.

He could see that she had something to say. Of course, she would want to talk first.

"Where do you keep your source?" she demanded.

He almost felt cheated. She wanted to collect the Water. How boring. She was speaking in the formal, correct Spanish of the old days. It sounded almost like a foreign language in this debased time and place.

He did not return the courtesy. "Go fuck yourself," he said.

She grinned and danced forward, blurring quick, and sliced open his cheek with his own knife.

He hadn't seen it. He was too dull now. The pain burned as if his skin was etched with acid.

He screamed. Blood and tears poured down his cheeks.

"It's amazing how the poison paralyzes but doesn't numb, isn't it? You can still feel everything. At least, that's what I'm told."

He unleashed another stream of obscenities at her.

"Such language," she said. "They used to call you the Saint, behind your back. Saint Juan. Did you know that?"

He nodded. He knew. He could still hear the jealousy and bitterness in their whispers, even now.

"You were always so pious. So correct. And look at what you've become." She glanced around the alley and then back at him. "I can't say I'm surprised. I always knew what you were, deep inside. I always knew what you said about me to Simon. How he should not defile himself, laying down with the lower creatures."

Aznar wheezed, as close as he could come to a laugh. "If only he would have listened."

Another quick slice with the knife, and the tip of his nose was gone. He growled rather than screamed this time. The indignity of this was beginning to gall him.

"Yes," she said. "If only. But he didn't. Now we're here. Now you only have a few moments left to live."

She showed him the knife again.

"If you want to live them as a man, Saint Juan, you should tell me where you keep your supply."

Aznar felt his first stab of genuine fear. He would not allow himself to be violated like that. In all his years, he'd never allowed that.

He tried to stall. "You must know. You must have been following me."

"I've been watching you for weeks. I've seen you come in and out of that little hole where you hide. I know there is some there, but you need more. You couldn't hold enough there to survive for this long. Where do you go when you need more?"

The world was growing dim, but something still clicked in Aznar's brain. He felt a vibration in the tracks. She'd just given him the key. With that one word.

"Weeks?" he asked.

She seemed to realize her mistake. She ignored the question. "Where is it, Aznar?"

"You've been following me for weeks?" He wheezed, laughing again. "Then you must have seen. You must have watched."

He saw the shame in her eyes and wanted to get up and dance.

In the distance, the sound of the train whistle. She heard it, too, but she was distracted.

Because he had taken another girl, only last week. She had seen. She must have known. That's how she knew his patterns, how she put it all together, and how she set this trap.

And she did nothing to stop him. She let him kill an innocent, just to see if she could find out where he kept the Water.

"You let me kill her. Her blood is on your hands."

"I didn't—"

"That's right. You did nothing. Nothing at all. Oh, Shako. Perhaps I was wrong. Perhaps there is a Hell after all. And I will be so happy to see you when you join me there."

Her face went dark. He'd seen that look before—just before she killed him the last time, in Serbia.

The ground shook under them both. The train was hurtling toward them. Those Walmarts up north were hungry. They needed to be filled. The trains had to run on time.

Now or never.

With all his might, Aznar flung his second knife at her.

This time her shoulder wound and her distraction made the difference. She had to fall over backward to avoid the blade plunging into her throat.

Aznar forced his nerveless limbs to move.

He flopped off the tracks just as the freight train barreled between him and Shako.

With his last bit of strength, he reached out and caught one of the cars. He only barely felt his legs bouncing and dragging on the gravel as the train pulled him up and away.

His blood ran onto the dirt. His body was filled with toxins and he labored for every breath as he rolled himself into a filthy boxcar.

None of it mattered. His long, happy life would continue.

He had beaten her again.

SHAKO WATCHED ALL THE cars of the train pass along the tracks. Grit and dirt blew into her eyes. He was gone. But she had to be sure.

She found his blood on the other side of the tracks. She followed it for a mile, until the splatters became drops, then the trail ended completely.

He was gone. This time, unlike Serbia, she didn't even have the satisfaction of killing him temporarily.

Shako walked back toward the city center, where she had a hotel room waiting with a change of clothes and identity so she could get out of this place.

She did not feel any guilt. She told herself that, over and over. It was not her fault, or her responsibility, what the men of the Council chose to do.

What mattered was making them pay. That was enough for Shako. She had her mission, and if there were innocents who died along the way, then so be it.

She had her mission. That was enough.

It had to be.

## FROM THE *NEW YORK TIMES* BUSINESS SECTION, PAGE ONE:

### CONQUEST BIOTECH'S STOCK PLUMMETS AFTER SON STEPS INTO FATHER'S JOB

Simon Oliver III, the chief executive officer and chairman of the leading biotechnology firm Conquest Biotech, passed away unexpectedly late Sunday night, according to company officials.

The same press release also announced that his son, Simon Oliver IV, was elected to the chief executive's position in an emergency board meeting convened via telephone.

The news hit just before stocks began trading on Monday. By noon, Conquest had lost nearly thirty percent of its value.

Although the stock price stabilized before the end of the day, analysts said that the reason is obvious: Mr. Oliver is not ready for his father's job.

Mr. Oliver, 23, is better known for his activities outside of work hours. He has been linked romantically to everyone from supermodels and porn stars to reality-TV mainstays such as Kim Kardashian. (A representative of Ms. Kardashian said that she and Mr. Oliver were simply good friends.) His only previous attempt to involve himself in Conquest was a disastrous attempt to diversify the company in movies and music videos, which ended in several lawsuits. A 2009 drug charge against him was dropped after he agreed to enter a rehabilitation program.

Conquest, best known for its series of anti-aging pharmaceuticals, has met or beaten earning expectations every quarter for the past five years.

But it is facing an expiration on the patent for Revita, its most popular—and profitable—drug, which is used to increase cell vitality and spur synapse growth in elderly patients.

This, plus the selection of Mr. Oliver, has big investors looking for the exits, said Irfan Khan, an analyst with Bank of America Securities.

"Right now, Conquest needs another home run, and they've brought up a kid from the minors who's basically incapable of finding a bat, let alone hitting it out of the park," he said.

But the investors are essentially powerless to change the selection, no matter how far the stock drops. While anyone can buy common stock in Conquest, the Oliver family, which founded the company in 1946 as a manufacturer of pharmaceuticals for the U.S. military and other customers, still controls the majority of special voting stock—giving them a 3-to-1 advantage over other voters. Every member of the board is either related to the Oliver family or one of the original employees of the company.

Until now, investors have been willing to trade their lack of control for the exorbitant profits and dividends that Conquest has always delivered, Mr. Khan said. But with someone like Mr. Oliver at the helm, the big financial firms have decided the trade-off is no longer worth it.

Through a representative, Mr. Oliver and Conquest declined to comment for this article.

# CHAPTER 2

CAMBRIDGE, MASSACHUSETTS
TODAY

DAVID ROBINTON WATCHED the screen carefully. This was a crucial moment. The scanning tunneling microscope was fixed on his latest batch of test cells, and he needed to see the precise moment of division to know if this would work. If he'd actually been able to adjust the length of the telomeres, he could—

He realized he wasn't alone in the lab. Someone was standing at the door, watching him. Then he realized he had no idea how long she'd been standing there.

He dragged his eyes away from the screen and saw Bethany waiting.

David looked at his watch. Past 3:00 A.M. A pang of guilt went through him. He knew they were supposed to have done something tonight, before his trip. But his grant was over, his time at the grad school was done, and very soon he wouldn't have access to this lab anymore.

Damn it. He looked back at the screen just in time. The cells began to divide rapidly. Too rapidly. He'd failed. All he'd done was create tumor cells, and frankly, the human body didn't need any help getting cancer.

She saw the disappointment on his face as she crossed the room to him.

"Another misfire?" she asked.

"Yeah," he said.

"I'm sorry."

"No, I'm sorry," he said, and he meant it. "I know we had plans. I just really thought that this time, I might have hit on the solution. And no one had anything scheduled for the lab at night."

"It's all right."

"No, it isn't. I'll make it up to you. After I get back from Florida, we'll get away for a couple of days—"

He stopped himself. She'd taken something from her pocket and slid it across the lab table toward him.

The key to his apartment.

"No," she said. "We won't."

David didn't know what to say. "Did I miss something here?"

Bethany laughed, but didn't sound all that amused. "My birthday. Meeting my parents. Two out of three of our dates. I could go on."

It was true. David was one of the most gifted—perhaps the most gifted—students to come through Harvard's School of Biological and Biomedical Sciences. At twenty-five, he'd stunned his professors and the other students alike with his sudden, almost intuitive leaps in altering cellular DNA to increase longevity. He had picked up two Ph.D.'s in the time it took most people to earn one. And now that his latest research fellowship was over, there were a dozen big corporations chasing him, from Pfizer to Merck to Aperture and everyone in between, all convinced he would be the one to develop the next multibillion-dollar medicine or treatment.

But all of that came at a cost. Sure, he was smart—but he had to work, and work hard. He taught classes, authored papers, and still made time for his own experiments. He'd seen 3:00 A.M. in this lab many times.

Thinking about it rationally, David was surprised Bethany had put up with him for this long.

She had met him when he was a guest speaker for her biology class. She was a med student, and pretty damned smart in her own right. With her previous boyfriends, she had been the one who had the busy schedule; that earned him some slack at first. But eventually she had learned that David was not just busy. He was driven. No one required him to be in the lab until dawn. There was something inside him that wouldn't let him quit.

She argued that he should be able to choose to spend time with her, the same way he chose to work. He agreed with her, but only to avoid the argument. In his heart, he knew that most of the time, he wouldn't be around, and he hoped she'd just live with it.

Still, he tried to mount some kind of defense for himself. "I don't know any other way to do what I do," he said. "You knew the kind of schedule I kept when we met."

She gave him a hard stare. "You don't get to be the angry one here, David. I know you want someone around when you get lonely. But that is not just a one-way street."

She was right, and he knew it. But he felt some obligation to try to make her see. This wasn't about getting a good grade or even a good job; it was a search for answers.

"This isn't about what I want," he said. "This is about what I can do. We're talking about finding a cure for everything. I mean everything. Cancer. Dementia. Alzheimer's. Heart disease. If I get this right, I could turn back the clock on everything that makes us get old and sick. Do you know how many lives that would save?"

"And you're the only one who can do it," Bethany said flatly.

"Yes," David said. "I know how arrogant it sounds. But it's true. There's maybe ten people in the world who are working at my level, and none of them have made the progress I have. Nobody else is even close. I could really do it. I could find the answer to everything that goes bad or rotten inside our bodies and I could actually fix it. That's what I can do. And I will not apologize for trying."

"I wasn't being sarcastic, David. I know how smart you are. I believe you could find it. But you should really think about this: You can carry all that weight on your shoulders. But do you really have to? What kind of life do you get, while you're busy finding a solution for death?"

David shrugged. "This is what I have to do. I don't know what else to tell you."

"No," she said. "I think there's more to it. You never told me what it was, but I know there's more."

David didn't reply. He wasn't about to open that wound again. Not here. Not now.

Bethany was done waiting for him. "I hope you do find someone who can share this with you. But it's not going to be me."

David understood, finally, that this wasn't an argument. Bethany wasn't asking him to fix something or fight his way back to her side. She was reporting on something that had already happened.

He picked up the spare key to his apartment and put it in his pocket.

"I'm sorry," he said. "Maybe when I get back, we could—"

Bethany shook her head. "It would end the same way."

"You don't know that."

"Yes, I do. You know why I'm telling you this, David? Because I have to. I don't think you would have even noticed I was gone otherwise."

"That's not fair," he said.

She gave him a sad smile. "But is it true?"

David looked away from her. And then couldn't help himself. He looked at the cells on the screen again.

"That's what I thought," she said. "You're a good guy, David. I hope you find whatever it is you're looking for."

Then she left.

David checked his watch again. His flight to

Miami wasn't until later in the afternoon, and the lab was free until eight, when the first students would come in.

He might as well work straight through.

It wasn't like anyone was waiting for him now.

DAVID SAT ON THE plane in the deep leather seat in first class and reviewed the package of materials the company had sent him. Lots of glossy pictures, lots of quietly assured boasting, couched in the usual corporate terms. "Unprecedented innovation," "world-class facilities," "global leader in the industry," and so on.

Well, he thought. At least they didn't use the phrase "fountain of youth." That would have put them right into late-night infomercial territory.

That was the problem with working in this field, David thought, not for the first time. People were desperate to turn back the clock, and sometimes it felt like all of the advances being offered were nothing more than twenty-first-century versions of health tonics and patent medicines. It smelled a lot like a con game.

Which was not to say that Conquest didn't have anything to brag about. Its research had led to Revita, a drug that did some of what David was trying to accomplish in the lab: physical rejuvenation of the human body at the cellular level.

Aging was a hugely complicated process. It might have looked like one long, steady decline—aches and pains, wrinkles, hair loss, memory loss, slowing reflexes, weakening muscles—but it was, in reality, a combination of multiple processes all affecting the body at once.

The search for eternal youth—the idea of holding a person at an ideal age, perfectly balancing maturity and optimum health—had been the obsession of humanity almost since Paleolithic times. The Egyptians believed in a combination of spiritual and actual physical immortality: mummies were preserved in an effort to keep them ready for the souls of their owners on the other side. Early Chinese cultures had believed something similar, to the extent that some emperors had whole courts of followers—wives, soldiers, advisers—killed and buried along with them. Christianity promised the return of the Messiah and a Kingdom of Heaven on Earth within their lifetimes. Only when Jesus failed to show up did the idea begin to morph into the resurrection of the soul.

Every culture had its myth or legend about eternal youth and immortality. But there were some hard-and-fast obstacles to actually pulling it off in real life.

The easiest way to increase human lifespan, of course, was to simply stop so many people from dying. And this had been the great work of the twentieth century, with advances in sanitation, food, and vaccines. Everyone was already living longer because there were fewer things in the world killing them.

But even with outside forces more or less controlled, there were still all the things that could go wrong inside a person. Sometimes when David looked at the body, he saw nothing but millions of little betrayals—everything from genes to major organs all on the edge of failure. Everything from heart attacks to rare diseases were hidden inside people, waiting to pop out like an obscene jack-in-the-box.

This was the undying frustration of David's life. Every one of the problems of aging was like that, and they all had to be cured at the same time, or any one of the solutions was useless. It wasn't much of a miracle to be a person with perfect, unwrinkled skin if you died of a massive brain tumor at forty.

This was why the attempt to create a single cure-all for aging never worked: there was simply too much going on for a single solution. It was like trying to bring down a whole flock of birds with one bullet.

But Revita was fairly effective at the one bird it did target: the aging of cells.

As cells died, they divided and replaced themselves—but after a while, it was like making copies of a copy. Errors began to pile up in the DNA. The cells became filled with junk and waste as they broke down over time.

Revita, however, fixed that. It discouraged the buildup of transcription errors and waste products in cells. Patients who took it, over time, found their overall health improved as new cells made better copies of themselves.

There were side effects, of course. But the demand for the drug was so high that the FDA put it on the market anyway. The baby boom generation wanted to stay young even as they were facing retirement age. Sales of Revita were incredible, despite its high price tag.

That was why David was interviewing with them, even though he'd already gotten better offers from bigger companies. The other Big Pharma players wanted him to work on the next Viagra or the next Rogaine—something that would generate billions of dollars while dealing with one small part of the aging process.

David wasn't really interested in helping a bunch of old men keep their hair or their erections. He wanted to save lives. For all its hype, Conquest was the only company that had been willing to let him pursue whatever research he wanted.

At least, that had been the case up until a couple of weeks ago. The company had been in turmoil since its CEO had died of a sudden massive coronary. His son, Simon Oliver IV, took the top position.

The younger Oliver had used his family fortune to pay for an endless series of parties around the globe while his father worked himself into an early grave. TMZ recently caught him smashing a Lamborghini into a semi, then offering the other driver all the cash in his wallet to take the blame. David felt irrationally, personally insulted at that; he didn't like drunk drivers.

Wall Street didn't take the news well, either. Conquest's stock was down twenty percent, and analysts were on the business-chat shows telling anyone who'd listen it was time to sell.

David wasn't sure he wanted to work for someone like Simon Oliver IV.

But the word on Wall Street was that Simon had

no interest in the company as anything more than a no-limit ATM. David figured he'd never even get so much as a glimpse of the new CEO.

"DAVID."

Simon Oliver called to him from baggage claim. He looked just like his paparazzi shots, which inevitably showed him falling out of a limo, a bottle in one hand, a B-list starlet or wannabe model in the other. Behind him was a full entourage, composed in equal parts of hangers-on, eye candy, and security personnel.

Simon wore a conservatively cut dark gray suit. It made him look even younger, like a kid playing in his dad's clothes. His eyes were hidden behind sunglasses, but he smiled brightly.

He offered his hand. David took it. Simon pulled him into a back-slapping man-hug. "Glad to meet you," he said, pounding David hard between the shoulder blades.

Before David could say anything, Simon spun him around to face the entourage. "Guys, this is David. He's the one. He's going to put us over the top. He's my new MVP, so I want all of you pricks to treat him like you would me."

Another guy, about Simon's age—sharp-featured, wearing a suit that could have been done by the same tailor—smirked. "So we have to pretend he's not an asshole?"

Simon barked a laugh. "Hilarious, Max. I nearly ruptured a bowel. Come on. Let's get a drink in this guy's hand."

Simon still had his arm around David. One of the girls peeled away from the scrum of people and produced, seemingly out of nowhere, a can of beer.

"Beer? *Light* beer?" Simon said in horror. "Oh, Tiffani. Good thing I didn't hire you for your taste."

Other people in the baggage claim area gawked at them. Simon's crowd had formed an island in the stream of people trying to get to their luggage or trying to get out to the taxi stands. A few bystanders even took pictures; they didn't know who Simon was, but anyone with that many security guards had to be famous.

A TSA employee heaved himself from a stool at the nearest doorway and stalked over to them.

"Sir," he said loudly. "You're gonna have to move along. Can't have you blocking traffic."

The smile vanished from Simon's face.

"Or else what, McGruff? You gonna shoot me?"

The security guards flanked their boss with practiced moves. David might have been imagining it, but they seemed annoyed and bored. Not the first time this sort of thing has happened, clearly.

"Just move along, sir," the TSA agent said, waving them off.

"Are you shitting me?" Simon laughed. "I could put this whole airport on my AmEx Black just to fire your ass if I felt like it. I pay more for a decent meal than you earn in a week. In case you still don't get it, I am the One Percent, asshole, and we own people like you."

The agent scowled and reached for his belt. It looked as if this conversation was about to end with

Simon getting Tased. Then Simon seemed to remember David was still at his side.

"Why are we waiting around here?" he said, the smile reappearing, the sun beaming from behind a sudden storm cloud. "We have a lot of sights and sensations to show our new boy. Come on, bro."

He grabbed David's arm again and half-dragged him toward the doors.

The entourage whooped in delight, the security guards looked slightly relieved, and the TSA agent was already lumbering back to his stool.

Within moments, David was inside a limo, Tiffani on his lap, a drink in his hand.

He was just able to see Simon in the farthest seat—the only light came from a video screen and neon tubing on the floor and ceiling—hoisting a glass to him.

"Welcome to Miami, David. I think you're going to enjoy it."

Then he vanished behind a very well-toned, very bleached blonde.

This was a new experience for David. He had never been one of the guys before in his life. He was always too serious, too busy. He wasn't sure he liked it.

But he had to admit, this was a lot more interesting than the other job interviews so far.

---

THREE HOURS LATER, DAVID'S head felt like it was made of foam rubber. He almost never drank, and the beer he'd accepted to be polite somehow led to tequila shots.

This was their third club of the night, and like at all the others, Simon's security had cut an effortless path through the crowd, escorting them to a booth in a prime position. Within moments, more beautiful women joined them, and the tables were covered in bottles.

David wondered if wherever Simon went, people simply waited to meet his needs. Then he realized that was probably what being a twenty-three-year-old billionaire meant.

In the limo, Simon had introduced him to the other young men in suits: there was Max, who sat almost as close to Simon as the girl on his thigh; Sebastian, ridiculously handsome and too bored with everything for a guy in his early twenties; and Peter, thick with gym-built muscle and whose first response to everything was an argument.

They began to get loud enough that David could hear them, despite the thumping bass of the speakers. David was surprised they didn't text one another like everyone else in the club. They were in some kind of political discussion.

"I keep telling you, it's time to get out of Afghanistan, Iraq, the whole Middle East. We'll be lucky if there's anything left there but corpses in the sand in a few years," Sebastian said.

Peter disagreed, loudly. "That's where all the oil is, dumbass. How you going to drive that Mercedes of yours with no gasoline?"

"Of course you'd say that," Sebastian shot back. "You were the one who wanted us in downtown Kabul."

The others laughed, but Peter looked insulted.

"I still say the only thing separating Afghanistan from Arizona is the right kind of investment and air-conditioning."

Max chose that moment to jump in: "And maybe something like Ebola to clear out the locals."

They all clinked glasses to that. David thought it was weird. He knew not everyone took politics as seriously as the students he'd met in Cambridge—because, really, who could?—but they talked like they were discussing investments.

Simon watched them with a smirk, as if he'd heard this before. They finished each other's jokes and sentences, hinted at past idiocies and embarrassments, utterly familiar with one another, as if they had been together since birth.

David felt a pang of jealousy at that.

Simon seemed to notice. Or, at least, he turned his attention to David. He waved, and one of the girls handed David a new drink.

"So, how do you like the job so far?" Simon said.

"I don't work for you yet."

"Oh, come on. I bet none of your other prospects met you with girls. At least not girls like these. I mean, seriously, you should see what Tiffani can do with a banana and a martini glass."

David lost a moment trying to picture that, then shook it off. "I'm sure that's impressive," David said, "and yeah, this is fun and all, but it's not really my world."

"True," Simon said. "But it could be."

"I don't think so. Nobody really gets into science expecting lap dances and body glitter. No offense, but I've got a serious problem I want to solve."

"Not having a whole lot of luck, though, are you?" Simon asked. "I understand you're still working on telomeres. And by 'working,' I mean 'failing spectacularly.' "

David felt his face get hot. Telomeres were the sequences at the ends of chromosomes that kept the cells dividing properly. When the cell ran out of telomeres, it got old and eventually died. David had been trying to increase the length of telomeres and increase the life of the cells.

Unfortunately, lengthening telomeres in a cell was also one of the first steps in the cell dividing out of control. Increasing the lifespan of a cell was also opening the door to cancer. That's why David's current experiments had all failed.

David wasn't sure how Simon knew that—his latest research wasn't published yet—but he was more surprised that Simon even knew what a telomere was.

Simon could see it on his face. "You weren't expecting that question in this club, were you?"

All right, David thought. Let's see how much the boy billionaire learned from whoever gave him the CliffsNotes version of DNA manipulation. "Telomeres are the most efficient way to increase cell life," he said. "Highest reward, least amount of risk. If we can increase error-free replication, the entire body lives longer."

"But the body will still age. Cellular breakdown and disease will still be a problem, maybe even more so," Simon shot back. "What about other solutions? Like, say, boosting mitochondrial life, as suggested by de Grey?"

"Altering the mitochondria?" David asked. "The problem there is the genes identified by de Grey can't survive outside the mitochondria. Move them, and you end up killing them."

"Then why not decrease cell toxicity by improving the cell's ability to remove waste products?" Simon asked, not letting up. "Engineer a tiny little DNA garbageman who takes out the trash."

"Where does the waste go, then? You shuffle it outside of the cell, it can build up in other places and do more damage there. You cure a guy's wrinkles and give him amyloid plaques in the brain and Alzheimer's."

"So we use specific cleansing enzymes, like hydrolases. Regular injections to go after the stuff between the cells and clean it out. You could even apply a modified variant of the same thing to clean up the extracellular cross-links and break them down before they start collecting and causing problems."

David shook his head. "Which could start to erode cellular material indiscriminately if the genetic delivery system mutates. It would make Ebola look like a bad flu."

"Exactly," Simon said, as if David had just made his point for him. "That's why Revita works on transcription errors," Simon said. "Zero defects. Perfect cellular copies. That's the key. Not telomeres."

"Your own research trials show that Revita doesn't fix all the errors. It's more like bleach in the laundry—you erase the stains, but most of the color, too. And that's why you're getting such a high incidence of brain tumors. You've wiped out one of the gene sequences that prevents cancerous cells from forming in nerve tissue."

"None of our other researchers have said that."

"Probably because they're too scared. Like I said, I don't work for you yet. I bet your next set of lawsuits comes from people developing spinal-cord cancer."

Simon gave David a cold look.

Just when it seemed like this job might be interesting, David thought.

Then Simon smiled. "You're right. We're getting some feedback from the FDA about that already. It's probably going to be a class-action suit by Christmas."

Simon didn't appear too worried. In fact, he looked pleased that David had just found a flaw in the company's most lucrative product.

"I think you've got to combine our transcription approach and your telomerase research to find the answer," he said. "What if I told you—"

He was about to continue when the bodyguards shifted from background scenery into sudden, violent movement.

David saw a girl, dark-haired and dark-eyed, approach Simon's table. She didn't look that much different from the other random women who'd joined the entourage.

But the bodyguards must have seen something they didn't like.

They formed a wall, blocking her out completely. The guard in the lead shoved her and sent her flying. He was six-four and easily 240 pounds; she was maybe 110 after a full meal. She landed hard on her ass and went skating backward on the dance floor. Another of the guards put his hand in his jacket as if he were going to take out a gun.

David didn't realize he was on his feet until he was right in front of the bodyguard. "Hey," he shouted. "What the hell is wrong with you?"

The bodyguard raised his hand to knock David aside, but David was quicker than the man expected. He slipped under the guard's arm and pushed him back.

Another guard was on him in a second, wrapping him up and immobilizing him in a complicated armlock. It felt like being inside a very small steel cage.

The guards had a clear sight of the girl again, who was still on the floor, stunned.

There was a moment, strung out like a high wire. Impossible as it seemed, they looked ready to shoot her.

David struggled. He saw the lead bodyguard look at Simon.

Simon gave a quick shake of his head.

And the tension evaporated. The bodyguards relaxed as the young woman hopped up and began screaming about a lawsuit. The guards released David, and Simon approached the girl. A few moments later, she stopped screaming and accepted a thick wad of cash and a drink from him.

David was still buzzing with adrenaline. Simon's friends didn't say anything, just watched him. Then Simon returned from soothing the girl, who was smiling and giggling at whatever he'd said.

They all looked at David, gauging his reaction.

"What the hell was that?" David asked, his voice tight.

Simon shrugged and looked at David. "It's a curse to be so attractive, you know?"

"You need a guy with a gun to protect you from a girl in a miniskirt?"

"They got a little overzealous. It happens." He turned to the lead bodyguard. "Mr. Perkins. Would you please apologize to Dr. Robinton?"

The big man looked at David like a machine scanning a bar code. "Sorry," he said flatly.

"There," Simon said. "All better?"

David shook his head. "You're that scared of random club girls?"

Simon didn't respond. The music thudded, heavy on the bass.

Max broke the silence. "He's that scared of being served with a paternity suit."

They laughed, but it seemed forced. Simon smiled and got David another drink. David calmed down after a few more sips. Then they went back to other topics. That was apparently all the explanation David was going to get.

Maybe this happened all the time in Simon's world. David decided he needed a break from all the fun. He made an excuse about going to the bathroom and looked for a way to get some fresh air.

FORTUNATELY, THIS CLUB HAD a patio that was open to the sky and stars. David felt better once he got out of the noise inside. The patio was almost deserted, aside from a few people keeping to the shadows at the far edges. He found a comfortable cushioned seat. He leaned his head back and drew in a deep breath.

"Tired of the high life already?"

David's eyes snapped open. She'd taken the chair opposite him, was watching him with a bemused smile on her face. He started to reply, and then found he didn't have any idea what to say.

He was looking at the most beautiful woman he'd ever seen in his life.

Her hair was dark and long, and her skin was a deep, burnished copper, the same shade that other women spent hours in the sun trying to achieve. Her eyes were dark, with flecks of gold reflecting back at him in the dim light.

He'd heard the words "breathtaking" and "stunning" before, of course, and seen his share of beautiful young women at all the campuses where he'd studied and taught.

But this was the first time he'd ever had his breath actually taken away. This was the first time he'd ever actually been stunned.

She had to be accustomed to getting stares from men. (And women, too, probably.) She just let him gape at her for another moment, then laughed.

Despite the fact that her laugh was just as distracting—her face lighting up with amusement, her perfect white teeth revealed in a brilliant smile—it was enough to snap him out of his stupor.

"Ah, sorry," he said, just managing not to stammer. "I was taking a quick break. I'm not used to this."

"Yeah," she said. "I could tell. Don't worry. Nobody's as good at celebrating as Simon. I think it's his true calling."

"Oh. Are you—I mean, you know Simon?"

"Sure," she said. She didn't elaborate. David hadn't seen her in the entourage earlier that night, and he would have noticed. Maybe she'd joined the party later, while he was doing body shots off Tiffani. He hoped, suddenly and fiercely, that she hadn't seen that.

And she didn't strike him as one of the party girls. They were almost frantic in their desire to have a good time. The stranger sitting across from him radiated calm—even serenity—despite all the decadence and noise on all sides of them.

The others were girls. She was a woman, even though she had to be the same age as he was.

David realized he was staring at her again.

"I'm sorry," he said, though he wasn't sure why he was apologizing. He offered his hand. "I'm David."

"I know," she said. Her grip was warm and surprisingly strong. "You're here to save Simon's company. Solve all his problems. Change the whole world. Have I got that right?"

David laughed. "I don't know if I can live up to that."

"Simon thinks you will. He's very impressed."

David shrugged, embarrassed and pleased to have someone bragging about him to her.

Suddenly, the woman's tone turned brisk and businesslike. "He'll offer you a million to start."

"A million?"

"Dollars," she said. "It's a big round number and he thinks you'll be impressed by it. He knows you don't come from money. You've got student loans and you've been living on grants and scholarships. He knows you're smart, but he also knows you're naive. He doesn't believe you can use your intellect when it comes to money."

David's feeling of pride evaporated. He hated it when people made assumptions about him because of his background. She was right—he'd never had much money, not since his father died. He could remember wearing clothes that had other kids' names in them. It was still a sore spot.

"Simon doesn't think you'll figure it out. That he needs you more than you need him. You can hold out for two."

David's head spun again, and not from the drinks this time. "Two million dollars a year."

"Plus incentives. A car, a house, all that. Believe me, he'll be happy to give them to you."

"How do you know this?"

She smiled. "I've known Simon for a long time."

David felt a sudden, irrational stab of jealousy. He tried to tamp it down and think of something smarter, or at least charming, to say.

But even with the alcohol fizzing in his blood, he felt like he'd missed a vital piece of the script. There had to be a reason this woman sat down and started talking to him about Conquest's job offer. He just didn't get that lucky.

He decided, after a split second considering all his options, to ask the obvious—and most useful—question: "Who are you?"

She smiled again and stood up. "See you around, David," she said.

Then she walked away without another word.

David was about to go after her, but then Tiffani dumped herself onto his lap.

"There you are," she said, giggling happily. She kissed him hard on the mouth, blocking his vision.

He pulled away, trying to get a glimpse of the other woman again.

She was gone.

# CHAPTER 3

THE NEXT MORNING—afternoon, actually—David shoved Tiffani's legs off his body and rolled out of the hotel bed. She flipped over and resumed snoring. Her expensive dress was wrinkled and discarded on the floor like old wrapping paper. She'd thrown him down on the bed when they got back to the suite, then abruptly stood and ran for the bathroom, where she began an Olympian session of vomiting.

David held her hair, then gave her some water and some privacy. At some point, he must have passed out on the bed, and she joined him whenever she was finished.

David tried to shake off the dull throbbing behind his eyes and realized he was hungover. He knew one thing: you could sweat out a hangover. He immediately dropped to the floor and began doing push-ups.

A few minutes and a hundred push-ups later, he went down onto the thick carpet, face-first. His sweat stung his eyes, and he stank like something left out in the sun too long.

A night to remember, but probably not in the way Simon had intended. He hauled himself into the bathroom to clean up.

David winced at the glare from the fixtures when he turned on the light. The bathroom alone was as big as his apartment back in Boston, done in marble and tile that had to be a thousand bucks per square foot. Like the rest of the suite, it was as if someone poured a thick layer of money over everything and then buffed it to a high shine. Simon had done some damage to the corporate account.

Tiffani was still snoring when David got out of the shower. He couldn't help being relieved. He'd never been that good at one-night stands. Still wasn't, judging by the evidence.

Suddenly, he remembered the woman. He felt a strange pang of regret. Maybe if he'd had more time with her . . .

Someone knocked loudly, shaking David out of his haze. He wrapped himself in a robe and hurried to the door.

It was Simon, with two paper cups of coffee, looking impossibly fresh and rested.

"I got a mocha and a latte. Didn't know which one you wanted."

David took one from Simon's hand. "Doesn't matter."

"Good, because they're both black coffee. I can't stand that frothy garbage." Simon walked past him without waiting for an invitation. "How was your night?"

He looked into the bedroom, where the door was still open, and saw the wreckage of Tiffani there.

"David. You animal."

"It's not like that," David said, unsure of why he cared what Simon thought. He crossed the room and closed the door.

"You don't have to explain to me. We're both men of the world."

He stretched himself out on the couch. Behind him, the big picture window framed the blue of the sky and the ocean and the already brilliant sun. In the middle of it all was Simon, like he'd arranged it just to have something to pose against.

"Sit down. Please," Simon said. "Let's get this over with, then we can get breakfast."

David sat, squinting into the glare from the window. He realized that Simon had not taken off his sunglasses. It now seemed like a smart idea.

Simon swung his feet off the coffee table and leaned forward. Standard negotiating posture. Getting down to business.

"Look," he said. "I don't like to dick around. You know what you're worth. I know what you're worth. Believe me when I say I've talked to everyone in the field. We've checked your references, your dissertation, your grade-school progress reports. There's nobody else who can do what we need to do."

David took a sip of his coffee, hoping the caffeine would kick in fast. "What exactly is that, anyway, Simon? Nobody has ever mentioned any specifics."

"I can't tell you everything. You know that. A single leak, our competitors would be all over us. They find out what we're working on, it could cost billions. That's right, with a *B*. That's real money."

"So you expect me to take the job without knowing what I'll do?"

"Head of research on our most important project. Unlimited budget. You answer only to me, and I'm not going to tell you how to do your job. You're a brilliant guy, David. I wouldn't insult you with something that wasn't worth your time."

"Unlimited budget?"

Simon smiled. "Zeroed right in on the key words. Let me put it this way: if the amount is anything less than eight digits, don't bother asking for approval. Just buy it."

"That's a lot of money."

"Yes, it is."

"Seems like you'd be willing to spend a good amount in salary, then, too."

Simon's smile only got wider. "Right, where are my manners? Of course we'd pay you appropriately. Million-dollar annual base salary. Company buys you a home, a car—and not a fucking Hyundai, I mean a car—that are yours to keep, from day one. One hundred percent pension, for life, vested fully after one year. Health package, annual bonus, plus performance incentives. And perks. You've already experienced some of them."

Simon gave a significant look at the closed bedroom door. David chose to ignore it.

"A million a year?"

"That's right."

David decided to test just how well the mysterious woman knew Simon. "Two."

That slowed Simon down. "Beg your pardon?"

"Two million annual salary. Double that if I reach mutually agreed benchmarks in the first three years. And twenty percent profit participation on anything you manage to sell out of my research."

Simon opened his mouth, then laughed. "That's a pretty big chunk. What's left for us?"

"More than you'd get if I wasn't there to make it happen."

Simon laughed again, as if he'd just put down a winning hand in poker. "Done," he said.

David was surprised. He had the distinct feeling he could have asked for more.

Simon had his hand out, ready to shake on the deal.

David hesitated.

He had a healthy respect for his own intellect, but he wasn't so arrogant as to believe he knew everything. One of the first things that propelled him on the path he'd taken was a moment when he was a little boy, looking up at the sky. Trying to count the stars. He must have been three or four, on a family camping trip. And he couldn't number them all. He got a good way across the big, dark bowl of the night sky before he'd lost his place. It was then he knew—on an instinctive level—that the world was much, much bigger than he could ever possibly understand.

He resolved to understand it all. But he never forgot that there was so much he didn't know. He would have to work hard. He'd have to learn.

Right here, right now, Simon was presenting him with a deal he'd have to be an idiot not to take. And everything inside him said that there was more to this. Maybe too much more.

He didn't trust Simon, he realized in a flash. This had all been designed to shock and awe him, to overwhelm him with money and power. Even the woman last night. She'd been part of the manipulation. To set him off-balance. To keep him from thinking.

David didn't respond well to being played. They thought he was a puppet. It was time to yank himself free from the strings.

David didn't take Simon's hand. Instead, he put the coffee down and said, simply, "No."

Simon laughed again, as if David was joking. Then he looked at David's face. "No?"

"No," David said. "I don't know what you're doing. I'm pretty sure you don't, either. So I'm not going to waste any more time on this. What I do could save lives. Millions of them. And yeah, you have a lot of money. But you haven't the first clue how important this work is. I think you see it as a quick way to make more cash. When you don't get the results you want immediately, you'll get bored and move on. You don't see anything here but a shiny toy, and you'll throw it away eventually."

Simon's smile shut down. The expression that passed over his baby-faced features made him appear, for just a moment, much older—and much colder.

"I know a lot more than you think, David. About this field, about what's at stake, and about you. You should reconsider. Believe me when I tell you: you and I should be on the same side."

David wasn't impressed or intimidated easily. "And if we're not?"

"Then you're walking away from everything you've ever wanted."

"It's a lot of money, but that's not why I do this."

"No," Simon said. "You do it because of your sister."

The words hit David like a blow. "What do you mean?"

"David. Come on. Give me a little credit. I can tell you think I'm a moron. But I am in charge of a multibillion-dollar company. You think I wouldn't have people looking into your past?"

"We never told people."

"Doesn't take much to get medical records. Or a death certificate. Even ones that are supposed to be protected by privacy laws."

David realized he was clenching his fists. "That's none of your business."

"I think it's exactly my business. Because what happened to your sister is what drove you to become the world-class scientist you are today."

"You—you had no right." He realized he sounded like a little kid. But by mentioning his sister, that's exactly where Simon had dragged him: back into the past.

SHE WAS YOUNGER THAN he was. And then she was so much older.

At first, Sarah was the typical pink, pudgy, gurgling little baby that his mom and dad had promised. David was five. He didn't pay a lot of attention to her, but he had to admit she was cute. She crawled around the house after him and subjected his toys to drool and teeth marks, and hugged his knees fiercely until she finally stood up on her own.

She gave him kisses all the time, and sometimes, it was just too much. She'd still laugh and giggle, even when he pushed her away. He would go into his room and close the door so she couldn't toddle after him. He figured she'd get more interesting later.

But then, one day, he noticed she wasn't getting any bigger. He mentioned it to his mom. She said something about all babies being different, and growing at different times, but he noticed: she looked worried.

His father always took his observations more seriously. He knew that David was smart—very smart. And so that began a series of trips. First to one doctor, then another. And another. Sarah came home with lots of stuffed animals and different brightly colored Band-Aids on all her fingers and toes from the needle sticks.

The disease became evident in those months. Her skin, once soft and pliant, bunched and wrinkled. Her face became stretched and birdlike. When she smiled, people no longer smiled back. Adults looked away. Other children stared.

It was about this time David became interested in medicine. A therapist would make a big deal of that, but it seemed logical to him. He spent a lot of time with his mom and Sarah at a lot of different hospitals and clinics. There wasn't much else to pay attention to. So he began soaking up as much information as he could on those visits.

His father, on the other hand, spent more time away from the house. At first that struck David as strange, because he knew his dad was some kind of doctor. But his father explained, as patiently as he could, that he was a doctor who looked at very small parts of a person: their genes. And if he could find the genes that were going wrong in Sarah, he might be able to help her.

Sarah kept getting older. She had a hard time walking. David slowed down so she could keep up. Kids who made fun of her at school quickly found that David could fight. It rarely came to blows after Sarah's first year in elementary school, however. David was, even then, a golden-blond picture of the perfect kid. Everyone, students and teachers alike, wanted his approval. So they treated Sarah with the same respect he did.

Which isn't to say it was always easy on David. There were many times he got sick of Sarah being sick. Got tired of her endlessly cheerful demeanor, that toothless smile in her face as she went through treatment after treatment. None of them worked and she never complained, never got angry. It made him feel cheap and stupid somehow. He could never whine about a test or a bad day, because she was always there to remind him how much worse he could have it.

He felt a little relief when she could no longer go to school with him. Her condition worsened. Her bones became too brittle for any kind of sustained activity outside the house. He was free to be himself, to be someone other than Sarah's protective big brother. He could go a whole day at school without thinking about her. And it nearly choked him with shame on his way home, when he suddenly remembered her.

So he did everything he could to bring the outside world to her. He read to her from his books; he drew her pictures; he watched TV with her in bed when she could not manage to do much more than stay awake. The shades were always drawn—light hurt Sarah's eyes and her skin. She couldn't eat much, either; her teeth had fallen out, and her stomach couldn't handle much of the bland blended mixes he and his mother spooned into her mouth. He gave her ice cream once and the resulting vomiting and diarrhea nearly drove her into seizures. His mother slapped him for that, and he didn't blame her.

His father was barely ever home in those days. His mother would go into the bathroom and turn on the fan and cry. She didn't think David could hear it. Sarah couldn't. She was partially deaf by then; they had to turn the volume all the way up on *Rugrats* just so she could hear. But David's ears were fine.

He had the sense something huge and awful was coming down on the whole house. He could almost feel it placing a large, clawed hand on them all.

Then one morning, Sarah died.

His mother wouldn't let him into her room. She was crying and wouldn't stop. His father told him, in clinical terms, what had happened. He talked like a robot. The words "heart failure" and "pneumonia" were the only ones that really came through.

His sister was dead. She was seven years old.

"COCKAYNE SYNDROME, TYPE TWO VARIANT," Simon said. "It must have been terribly hard for your father. That's probably when the drinking started, wasn't it?"

David felt numb for a moment. It was a couple of years after Sarah. He remembered the police coming to the door the morning after his parents went out. There had been a car accident, the officer said. It wasn't until the funeral that he heard the words "driving drunk."

He went from having a family to being an orphan before he was fifteen. He spent a few years with an aunt and uncle he barely knew, then escaped to college and a series of dorm rooms and cheap apartments.

"Congratulations," he said. "You dug up the worst time in my life. Brilliant recruiting strategy."

"David—"

David was suddenly on his feet, his finger in Simon's face. "You want to be really careful about what you say next."

Simon opened his mouth and then closed it. "I'm sorry." It almost sounded genuine. "I didn't bring up your sister to insult you. Or upset you. Really."

"So why did you?"

The party-boy facade seemed to drop from Simon then. He sagged on the couch. He looked almost apologetic. No, David thought. Not apologetic. Humble.

"I wanted you to know that I get it. That I've lost people, too."

David felt a sudden pang of guilt. "Your father. Right. I'm sorry."

Simon smirked, as if David had made a joke—but the expression vanished almost immediately. "Not just that. I've lost more people than you can count. And you might not believe me, but I feel every one. You are the first candidate I've seen in a long, long time who might understand that. Who wants the same things from this as I do. I know you don't really give a shit about the money. I know you can turn that down. When you strip away everything else, you're just that kid who never wants anyone else to die."

After the sudden rush of anger, David simply felt drained. All he wanted to do was get Simon out of here. He sounded sincere, but David wasn't ready to buy it. "Thanks. But I've heard it already, from better therapists than you. I know the drill: It wasn't my fault. Everyone dies. That's how the world works. No matter how hard I work, no matter what I do, I can never change that."

"But what if you could?"

"What?"

Simon smiled. It was calm. Peaceful. A different kind of smile from his usual shit-eating grin. "This is what I'm offering you, David. This is a chance to change the world. I'm talking about an end to human misery in our lifetimes. I'm talking about the end of disease. I'm talking about a cure for cancer, for AIDS, for everything. I'm talking about the greatest discovery since Jesus Christ rolled out of bed three days after being nailed to a hunk of wood."

David hated to admit it, but he was curious. This sounded like something much bigger than the drugs and stem-cell treatments Conquest bragged about in its annual reports. "What exactly do you mean? What are you working on?"

Simon seemed to sense him wavering. "You've got to see it. It's the only way you'll ever believe me."

David turned away. Simon grabbed his arm.

"Just let me show you this one thing," he said. "If you still think I'm an asshole who's wasting your time, well, great. *Vaya con Dios.* I'll drive you to the airport myself. But I know you won't. I know you're going to take the job."

David looked at Simon for what seemed like a long, long time.

"All right," David said. "Where are we going?"

"To see the future," Simon said. "So you'd better get some pants on."

# CHAPTER 4

CONQUEST'S MIAMI CAMPUS was nowhere near as big as the Tampa headquarters David had seen in the publicity materials, but it was still impressive. An armed guard let them through a gate into the parking lot. Another one issued David a badge with a computer chip and an RFID tag at the front desk. Simon used his own badge to get them past the first set of doors, and from there put his eye to a retinal scanner to unlock more passageways, deeper into the facility.

If this was all for show, David thought, at least they were putting some effort into it.

They stepped past another locked door. David could feel the slight puff of air that came from a negative-pressure seal. They were entering a biologically secure zone. So he wasn't surprised when Simon pointed to a side door and said, "Strip down and shower. There will be a set of scrubs for you."

It was the first thing he'd said to David in a while. In the limo on the way over, Simon had tried to strike up a conversation. It didn't go well.

"Did you know that the early Christians believed in the actual, physical resurrection of the body?" he'd said. "Not just the soul. They believed that we'd actually crawl up out of the ground on Judgment Day. Like zombies."

David had just stared at him.

"Saw it on the Discovery Channel."

David hadn't replied, and since then, they'd mostly ignored each other.

David's head pounded and the coffee burned in his stomach. He wondered if he should have taken a cab to the airport. But since he was here, he might as well see it through.

He put on the scrubs and stepped through another air lock. He looked around and saw a fully equipped diagnostics lab. Everything from chemical testing equipment to a portable MRI to a table of centrifuges and analytical tools. Once again, Conquest had not gone cheap.

David turned and saw Simon. He was on the other side of a thick observation window. It made David a little nervous.

"You're not coming in?" David asked.

"I already showered once this morning," Simon said, pressing a button to speak through an intercom. "Messes with my skin regimen. Besides, I don't want you saying I tried to influence you or what you're going to see."

David sighed. Whatever. His patience was nearing the bottom of the tank.

Then a door on the other side of the lab opened, and a nurse pushed an old man in a wheelchair through.

David was not a medical doctor, but he'd done plenty of research in hospitals and med schools. He recognized the symptoms immediately. Vacant stare. Eyes covered with milky-white cataracts. Unkempt hair. Open-mouthed breathing and muscular degeneration. And, of course, the smell of human waste from a soiled diaper. The patient had an IV hooked to one arm, probably running fluids, since he could not feed or hydrate himself properly.

Severe dementia. Most likely late-stage Alzheimer's.

Wordlessly, he looked at Simon through the plate glass.

"Check his chart," Simon said through the intercom. "I'm not holding anything back from you."

The nurse handed over a metal clipboard. David flipped through it. It said everything he thought it would. Buildup of amyloid plaques in the brain. Steady loss of memories and physical abilities. The man's name was Robert Mueller, but that hardly mattered anymore. David was looking at a dead man, a body that was simply waiting for his brain to forget everything, even how to breathe.

He handed the chart back to the nurse, who took it without a word. All of this passed over Mr. Mueller's head without the patient noticing a thing.

"Why?" David asked. "Why is he here? Shouldn't he be with family? He doesn't have much time left. You must know that."

"You think he'd even notice? He's gone already,"

Simon said. "Besides, he has no family. We pulled him out of a homeless shelter."

"So that gives you the right to experiment on him? That's pretty sick."

"Check the file before you get all righteous on me, please. Back when he still had some marbles, he signed up with us. Free medical care in exchange for a few tests. It's all ethical and legal. We take better care of him than anyone ever has in this life."

"Great," David said. "Good for you. Now, what did you want me to see? I'm ready to be done with this."

Simon looked at the nurse and nodded to her. She took out a syringe, tapped the needle, and, before David could object, injected the contents directly into the patient's IV.

"What was that?"

The nurse didn't answer. Simon didn't, either. They both stared at Mueller.

"I said, what was that?" David asked again. Still no answer.

David marched over to the glass and got as close to Simon's face as he could.

"Hey. I'm talking to you. Whatever forms he signed when he was competent, that doesn't mean you can do whatever you want—"

"David," Simon said, as gently as possible through the intercom. "Shut up and look."

David turned around.

Mr. Mueller was blinking and moving his head. He stared and stretched, as if waking from a long nap.

"What happened?" he said. "Where am I?"

Then he stood up, out of the chair.

Impossible, David thought. Even if Simon had hired an actor, there was no way to fake the degraded muscle tone, the loss of motor ability that David had witnessed just a second before.

The man in that chair did not have the self-control to keep from crapping his pants, let alone stand.

Now he was walking.

David noticed more changes in Mueller. Muscle tone. Skin texture. Even the old man's hair seemed to be thicker. He looked a decade younger in every way. At least a decade. Maybe two.

The nurse finally spoke, since David was gaping in silence.

"Mr. Mueller, you're in a long-term care facility. Do you remember coming here?"

"Oh," he said. "Right. It just seems like it's been a long time." He looked down at himself. "Have I been sick?"

Simon's voice came over the intercom again. "You were, Mr. Mueller. But I think you're going to feel a lot better from now on."

"I feel pretty good already," Mueller said.

"Well, why don't you let our doctor here check you out," Simon said. "Just to be sure."

He meant David. And David was ready. Whatever kind of hoax this was, whatever kind of sick joke, he was sure it would take him only a moment to unravel it. He wasn't a medical doctor, but he knew there was no way to undo the damage he'd seen in this man.

To Mueller—if that was the man's real name—David was achingly polite. He smiled so hard it hurt his face.

"Just have a seat on this table over here, Mr. Mueller," he said. "I'd like to run a few tests."

"Whatever you say, doc," the patient said. "It's just, uh, you think I could have a fresh change of drawers? I seem to have messed these ones up pretty bad."

Mueller smiled at David. Jesus Christ, did the man suddenly have more teeth? No. That had to be David's memory playing tricks on him.

"Of course," David said, and the nurse led Mueller to a changing room. David accompanied him the entire way, to make sure no one played any more tricks he couldn't see.

When Mueller was freshly cleaned, David guided the suddenly quite limber older man to the exam table, still playing the dedicated M.D.

He spared a moment to glance through the window at Simon. Simon looked peaceful.

David had no idea what was going on. But he would find out. He didn't like being played. He was sure this whole joke would collapse once he got to work.

SIX HOURS LATER, Mr. Mueller was not smiling anymore. He'd become cranky and bored as David ran every test he could. The old man was clearly getting tired of having his blood drawn and sitting his ass on a cold metal table.

But he was still healthy. Still vital. Still a completely different patient, in every way, from the end-stage Alzheimer's case that had been wheeled into the room.

David had put Mueller through an MRI, a CAT scan, and a PET scan. He compared the resulting images with scans taken just a week before, according to the charts. Dark spots from miniature strokes in the man's brain had disappeared. Cerebral tissues that had once been clotted with Alzheimer's plaques were now free and clear.

David assumed, of course, that the earlier scans were fakes, planted in the file for just that purpose. But the recovery wasn't just internal, either.

The cataracts over Mueller's eyes that David had clearly observed were gone. Mueller's vision was back to 20/20, unassisted. "Haven't seen that well since Nixon was in office," the old man joked after David and the nurse ran the eye exam.

Muscle tone and skin elasticity were improved as well—Mueller appeared to have the flesh of a man twenty years younger. Gum recession had been reversed. And David hadn't been imagining it—Mueller now had white, cavity-free replacements for his missing teeth.

Jesus Christ, he grew new *teeth.*

The only way this could be possible was if they'd switched patients on him. But he'd never turned his back on Mueller, not for a second, and even the best magician would need a momentary distraction to pull that off.

What's more, he'd seen it happen. And it kept happening. The man's arterial blockage shrank by twenty percent between two different tests. Capillary circulation improved, and kept improving every time David measured it. David suspected stimulants, or adrenaline, so he rechecked the old man's reflexes. Motor response improved, hour over hour. He put Mueller on a treadmill and the patient's cardiovascular function improved each time. Liver, kidneys, colon, all healing from years of abuse and neglect. Mueller was getting healthier—no, go ahead, say it, *younger*—as David watched.

David's hangover was gone, his fatigue burned away as he worked. Every now and then, he checked the window, but Simon was there only some of the time. Apparently, he felt so sure of his trick that he didn't feel the need to stick around and monitor the whole ordeal.

Surreptitiously, David checked his own blood for the presence of hallucinogens or other drugs. Maybe there was something in that coffee that Simon gave him.

Nothing. Not a thing.

David was at a loss. It was simply impossible.

But the evidence was all in front of him. In charts, computer readouts, and chemical analysis. Not to mention the living, breathing man sitting nearby.

Whatever they'd injected Mueller with, it had stripped at least twenty years of aging away.

David felt numb. It sounded odd, echoing around in his skull. He found he was having trouble saying the obvious.

But there it was, right in front of him.

He was looking at something that made people younger.

An honest-to-God fountain of youth.

"Well?" The angry voice of Mr. Mueller woke David from his reverie.

"I'm sorry, sir," David said. "You're in perfect

health for a man your age." David was aware of the irony in his words, even as he said them.

"Does that mean I can go?"

David nodded dumbly.

"About damn time," he said. The nurse, who had been nothing but quiet and helpful throughout the whole day, took Mueller's arm and led him into another room.

David heard the seal on the outer door hiss. He didn't look up until Simon, freshly dressed in new clothes, came into the lab and sat down across the steel table from him.

Once again, he brought coffee. David didn't care if it was drugged. He might even prefer it that way. He gulped it gratefully.

They sat together in silence for a moment.

"I don't understand," David finally said.

"Give yourself a little more credit," Simon replied. "Sure you do. You just don't want to believe it."

"How did you do it?"

Simon smiled. "Ah. Well. That is the trillion-dollar question, isn't it?"

For a moment, David again felt like punching Simon. He was in no mood for riddles.

"That man was dying of Alzheimer's when he came in here," David said. "You cannot fake that kind of late-stage deterioration. And in two minutes, he was twenty years younger. Now you tell me how the hell that was possible."

"That's just the problem," Simon said. "I can't."

David stood up. Now he was pretty sure he *was* going to punch Simon.

"I'm not playing around, David," Simon said.

"We have, for lack of a better word, a compound. This compound can do everything you just saw. And more. That was a diluted sample. At full strength, it can reverse the aging process altogether, not just stop it or slow it down. It can grant years of life to terminal patients. This compound is exactly what you saw. It's the answer to all our prayers. It is eternal life in a bottle."

David sat down again. It was ludicrous. But he believed Simon. He trusted his own intellect, and his own instincts, that much. There were ways he could be fooled, sure. But not inside a lab. And not like this.

There was only one answer. Simon was telling the truth.

"So why do you need me?" he asked.

"Because we can't duplicate it," Simon said. "We know it works. But we don't know how. We've got the cure for aging, the cure for almost every disease, right at our fingertips—but we're not smart enough to crack the code."

"And you think I can?"

"I know you can. Not just because of your credentials. Or all the letters behind your name. But because you have to. This is your chance. Your whole life, you've wished you could save your sister. And I swear to God, I wish I had found you then so that this would have been available for her. But it's too late for her. It will always be too late for her."

David winced a little, hearing it said so baldly like that.

Simon grabbed his arm, forced him to meet his gaze again.

"But that's why we need you. Without that loss, you wouldn't be able to do this. Because you know what's at stake, you can save others. You can spare them the pain that she endured. We need you to figure out how it works. So together, we can save everyone."

The relentlessly logical side of David's brain argued that it was too good to be true. The world did not dispense candy and free beer in response to wishes. There was always a hidden cost.

"What is it?" he asked, almost to himself.

Simon raised his eyebrows.

"The catch," David said. "What's the catch?"

Simon smiled. "Ah. Well. Here's the part you're not going to like. You cannot test the compound itself. You may have access to every one of our subjects, every bit of data we've got, every page of our research. You get bloodwork, DNA, MRIs, chemical analysis, every possible test we've ever run. But the compound itself is off-limits."

The logical part of David said, There it is. The catch.

Out loud, he asked, "Why?"

"Think it through. This is the greatest discovery in history, and the supply is limited. I'm not going to give you a chance to waste any or, worse, steal a sample. It's not just my ass on the line here, David. I have responsibilities to other people as well. I will not lose so much as a single drop. This isn't a negotiating tactic. This is the one hard-and-fast rule. Take it or leave it."

"Where did you get it?"

"I found it under a four-leaf clover."

"Seriously."

"Oh, seriously?" Simon smiled. "In that case, I got it from an alien who needed new parts for his flying saucer after he crashed at Roswell. No, seriously, I got it from a gnome after I guessed his name. No, wait, actually—"

"I get your point. But without the original sample, what you're asking is impossible."

"Not for you," Simon said. "I have faith in you. If anyone can do it, it's you. And you know it."

David sat there for what seemed like a long, long time. It was probably only a few moments. But it felt like hours.

He had always felt his sister's death was like a guiding star, pulling him in the direction of what was right. And now here was this person—this kid, really—telling him that it was all possible. That he could really do it. Save everyone.

But what he had seen was impossible. The fact that Simon would not share the actual compound—that sounded all kinds of alarms in David's head. That was the gimmick: the part of the magic trick that the performer never reveals.

There was no way this was genuine. It was all much too good to be true.

That's what the cautious, careful voice in his head told him.

But for the first time in his life, David stopped listening to that side of himself. He didn't care.

He had to know what was in that vial. No matter what.

He looked back at Simon, who was waiting.

"I'll take the job," he said.

"Thank you," Simon said. He leaned over the table and dragged David into an awkward hug, releasing him only after a long moment.

"Thank you," he said again. "Together, we are going to save the world."

David pulled away, slightly embarrassed. "I should get back to the hotel. Get some sleep before my flight."

"Oh no," Simon said, suddenly clownish again. "You are going to shower and get dressed and then we are going out."

"I appreciate it, really. But I am exhausted."

Simon's grin turned mean. "Hey, you better have some fun tonight. Because on Monday, I am your boss, and you are not going to see anything but the inside of a lab until you get me what I want."

David laughed.

"I'm not joking," Simon said. "You're going to earn that two million a year. Never thought you would have such solid negotiating skills."

David was momentarily confused. "Really? I thought you sent that woman to give me that advice last night."

Now it was Simon's turn to look confused. "Tiffani told you to hold out for two million? Wow. Smarter than she looks."

David was about to correct Simon, to tell him about the woman in the club. Then he stopped himself. He realized that Simon did not know about the woman, even if the woman did say she knew about Simon.

That was interesting. He didn't know what it meant. But he was smart enough to keep it to himself.

Simon had been holding on to all the secrets. It wouldn't hurt to have a few of his own, David decided.

ON THEIR WAY OUT of the building, Simon ducked into a side office. "Just wait a second," he told David. "Got to sign a couple things, then you and me, we're going to tear this town a new one."

David smiled at him wearily. "Sure. Whatever."

Simon's expression changed as soon as he was through the door. David was exhausted. Simon was grateful. David was smarter than he'd guessed, and having him tired and off-balance made it easier to fix the little details around the edges.

He walked through another door, into what looked like a medical exam room.

Mueller was there, dressed in a new set of clothes, fresh from the men's section of the local Target.

"Mr. Mueller," Simon said. "You look like a new man."

"Yeah, well," Mueller said. "That's why I wanted to talk to you."

"That's what I was told. How can I help you?"

"Seems to me you might have taken advantage of me when I came into this place."

Simon closed his eyes. Unbelievable. You give someone the gift. The most precious gift possible. And they immediately want more.

"You believe we cheated you?"

"Look, I'm not stupid," Mueller said. "What you did to me. I'm pretty sure it wasn't legal. Now, if you don't want me to bring the cops around, it's going to cost you."

Simon didn't respond. He let the silence linger. Mueller shifted from foot to foot. Just before Mueller opened his mouth again, Simon spoke.

"I was prepared to let you go with my blessing," Simon said. "I assumed you would spend the limited time we'd given you as you did before we found you: drinking paint thinner, facedown in a gutter. You might tell someone what happened to you, but who'd believe a waste of flesh like yourself?"

"Hey, now," Mueller said, trying to work up the nerve to be insulted.

"But as you've shown, we can't trust you for even that. I apologize, Mr. Mueller. I apologize for thinking you might rise above your sorry, pathetic excuse for an existence."

Mueller had no response to that. Probably because he was choking to death on his own blood.

From inside his pocket, Simon had drawn a short-handled dagger and shoved it deep into the old man's chest. He'd driven it through the left lung on its way to the heart. It was a completely silent death stroke, expertly delivered.

Simon had many, many years of practice.

He withdrew the blade. Mueller dropped to the floor. Simon pressed an intercom button, and the nurse reappeared a moment later.

"Put this thing in the incinerator," Simon ordered her. He gestured for her to step closer. She hesitated but complied. He wiped the blade on the hem of her scrubs, carefully checking to make sure he'd gotten all the blood. He'd had this dagger for years. He'd actually lost count of all the times he'd replaced the handle, then the blade, then the handle again. It raised the old question: was it really the same knife anymore?

He liked to think so. It was reliable. Faithful. That was why he always kept it by his side.

When the dagger was clean, he put it back inside his pocket.

Simon was smiling again when he rejoined David in the hall.

"What was that about?" David asked.

"Just the usual," Simon said. "There's always someone who thinks he's more important than anyone else. And he's always wrong."

# CHAPTER 5

TAMPA, FLORIDA

SIMON ARRIVED AT the board meeting last. It was his prerogative as chairman and CEO, but it was also in keeping with his character. He slouched into the boardroom twenty minutes late, sunglasses on, head bopping to the music blaring through his earbuds.

The door closed behind him, sealing the room like a vault. It had been constructed to demanding specifications. Completely soundproofed, it was a reinforced steel box wrapped in concrete and framed inside the girders on the top floor of Conquest's office tower. It was impervious to any kind of radio wave, and used sophisticated jamming and baffling devices to prevent electronic eavesdropping. No one was going to get interrupted by a call on their cell phone while inside the boardroom. The only signal coming in or out was over a broadband cable with military-grade encryption.

The boardroom also served as a panic room, with storage tanks under the floor containing its own air and water supply, if it ever became necessary to lock out the entire outside world.

As soon as the door was shut, Simon stood straighter and yanked the earbuds out of his ears. Of all the tiresome requirements of his public face, the music was the worst. Call him old-fashioned, but he did not find repetitive shouting of obscenities at all entertaining or restful.

The other members were already at the table. There were four of them. Conquest's board had more members than that, of course. Twenty-six at last count, not including the various subcommittees and part-time advisers. But that was the public board. They met in a different room.

This was the place where the real owners met. This was the Council.

Max was in his place, immediately to the left of Simon's chair. Sebastian and Peter flanked him. Antonio sat alone on the other side of the table.

Each of them had a glass. In front of Simon's empty chair was a crystal pitcher, filled with water, next to his own glass.

"Gentlemen," Simon said, signaling that it was all right for the others to speak. In these meetings, they always used formal, Castilian Spanish. Despite everything, they held fast to some traditions.

"Simon," Antonio said. "You look well." He was currently stuck in his midforties, and they all knew he hated it.

They learned they aged faster the more time passed, if they didn't have the Water. None of them knew how long they might last without a regular drink.

But they had to get older, just a little, or the world would discover what they were. They had to perform a balancing act. So Simon and the others had been succeeding themselves as father to son for generations now.

It was, frankly, exhausting. And painful. The interim period was the hardest. Carefully measuring the dosage, waiting for the change to be complete, and handling the physical pain as one advanced and retreated over several decades in the space of a few hours. Simon no longer remembered what real aging was like. Every time he was cut off from the Water—even willingly, even to advance the deception—a piece of his mind worried that he would never get his youth back, that this would be the time the miracle didn't work.

It lasted for only a few seconds, but it was still terrifying. Simon suspected that they would all dry up and blow away if they tried to live like normal men again. The accumulated weight of centuries would crush them to dust.

In earlier times, even thirty or forty years before, it was easier. The press didn't care as much about the private lives of the rich, and there was a certain distance enforced by wealth. The last time Simon had succeeded himself—gone from Simon Oliver II to Simon Oliver III—there had been a discreet funeral notice and a few faked pictures. These days, he had to contend with amateur paparazzi hunting for cell-phone videos, demands for childhood photos from supposedly respectable publications, and coroners and authorities who were increasingly difficult to bribe. He'd been forced to create a whole separate identity for himself, a celebrity image shiny enough to distract attention away from the fact that the supposed father and son were never seen in the same time zone, let alone the same room.

On the West Coast, he played the idiot boy, spending money, wrecking cars, chasing whores. On the East Coast, he'd played the disapproving father, managing the day-to-day affairs of Conquest—which grew only more challenging over time—and letting himself age.

The others didn't have to be quite as careful, or take such elaborate measures. They weren't the public faces of the company. The last time they had "died" had been in a faked plane crash during a corporate retreat in the Bahamas.

Antonio had been in Europe at the time, and felt left out. He couldn't act as part of the group in public anymore. It would have looked too suspicious—and foolish—for the boys to be out partying with a friend of their fathers'. "I wish we could find some way to make the change all at the same time," he said. "This sort of imbalance breeds division, and we cannot afford that, with our numbers so few."

"Perhaps we can arrange for you to be murdered, Antonio," Simon said as he took his seat. "Would that satisfy you?"

"What? Who? Who was murdered?"

The voice came from a speakerphone placed at the seat next to Antonio and hooked into the room's hard line for the occasion. Carlos had not appeared in person at a meeting in nearly twenty years. He moved constantly, from stronghold to stronghold throughout Latin America. Simon honestly had no idea where he was right now.

Simon held back a sigh of frustration. The line was capable of carrying an ocean of data. A phone call was a mere trickle compared to that. It was Carlos's hearing—or his attention—that was the problem.

"I was making a joke," Simon said. "We're all here now, Carlos."

"We need to talk," Max said. "Antonio has some disturbing news. And we need to discuss the Robinton decision—"

Simon gave him a hard look. There were rules. Protocol had to be observed.

"My apologies," he said.

Simon nodded.

"Calling this meeting to order," Max said. He opened a beautifully bound leather journal on the table in front of him. "Simón de Oliveras y Seixas, presiding. Also present, Maximillian de Cortez y Anquilles, Sebastian de Hernandez y Quinto, Pedro de Alvarez y Fonseca, Antonio de Ortega Montez, and Carlos Gaspar de Valenzuela."

Simon stood and took the pitcher from its place. He filled his own glass first, then carefully filled the others', with movements like a surgeon's in their precision. He did not spill a drop.

They all stood. Each man raised his glass solemnly. The water inside appeared completely ordinary—save, perhaps, the slightest blue tinge. But that could have been a trick of the light.

"*El agua es vida*," Simon said.

"The water is life," the others repeated.

They all drank, draining their glasses.

It was a maintenance dose, nothing more. Still, they all shuddered slightly, as if downing eighty-proof vodka.

They waited in silence for a moment.

The moment was shattered by Carlos. "What happened? Did we lose the feed again?"

This time, Simon had to restrain himself from laughing. He couldn't help it. He was in a good mood today.

"You didn't lose the feed, Carlos. Are you drinking with us?"

"Yes, yes, yes," Carlos snapped. "As much as you'll send me, anyway."

Simon doubted that. Carlos sounded peevish and irritable. Old. He'd have to send someone to check on him in person.

He sat in his chair again. The others took their seats as well.

"First," he said. "Any old business?"

Max's patience, however, was at an end. "There's always old business. Too much of it. You need to listen to Antonio."

Simon nodded. The mark of a good leader was allowing his subordinates some leeway. He turned in his chair. "Antonio, what has Max so upset on such a fine day?"

"Shako."

The word. The name. Two syllables. And such a terrible weight they carried, Simon thought. He could feel it, coming down over the entire room.

For a moment, it felt as if they were in a tomb together, not safe but trapped.

"What about her?" he said as carefully as he could.

"She tried to kill Aznar two weeks ago," Antonio said.

"Good," Simon said. "He should have died a long time ago."

The others did not take that well. They expected shock or outrage. Or at least an attempt to feign concern. They scowled at him, their dissatisfaction plain.

Antonio was the only one to say it out loud, however. With the difference in their appearances, he looked like an uncle scolding an unruly nephew. "That is not right," he said. "Whatever you think of him—"

"He is a pig and a rapist and a murderer," Simon cut in.

"Whatever you think of him," Antonio continued, not hearing Simon or not caring, "he was one of us. We owe him some loyalty."

"We owe him nothing. Aznar lost his place at this table a long time ago," Simon said. "The worms can have him, if they don't gag on his flesh."

"She found him," Carlos interrupted, over the speaker. "However distasteful you thought he was, we should worry about that. She's getting closer to all of us."

"She already knows where to find us," Peter said. "The only one in hiding is you, Carlos."

"That seems like a wise decision now, doesn't it?" Carlos shot back.

Antonio would not be deterred. He stabbed a finger at Simon. "We should have eliminated her as a threat long ago and taken her supply of the Water, wherever she hides it."

Simon rubbed his eyes. "You're a genius, Antonio."

That derailed his growing outrage. "What?"

"Find her and kill her. And take her supply of the Water as well. My God. What a strategy. What a plan. You must play chess. Why didn't I think of that? It's as brilliant as it is simple."

Antonio scowled. "Mock me all you want—"

"Oh, I will, thank you. You know we have tried." He pointed at all of the men around the table. "All of you know we have tried. We have tracked her every time she has appeared. We have followed her. We have sent our best men. And we have never seen them again. It's not that we cannot find her; we cannot even find the bodies. Tell me, what would you do differently? What would you have me do, Antonio? What is your plan, aside from find her and kill her?"

Silence around the table. Antonio looked away. The other men would not meet his eyes, either.

"We could always go back to the original source," Antonio said, much quieter now.

"The original source? Not this again. It's gone. I know—believe me, I know—how much you want to believe that it's still there, buried somewhere. But that is a dream. We lost it long ago, and we will never get it back. You know we've tried. You know we have attempted to purchase the land, to buy our way into the good graces of the Seminoles. It has never worked. They remember us. She makes sure of that."

"Simon," Max said, his voice pitched to soothe, "we are not questioning your efforts. We know how hard you have worked. We have been there, all of us. But perhaps there is someplace else, some other source that we've missed."

"Max, we have looked all over the planet. We have only found the one source. You know this."

Max said, "Then perhaps this is a good time for you to tell the others about—"

Something occurred to Simon. He raised a hand for Max to be silent. "How did you know?" he asked Antonio.

"How did I know what?" Antonio said.

"How did you know that she tried to kill Aznar? How would you even know he was still alive?"

There was a long silence.

Carlos, over the speaker, sounded mocking: "This is a terrible connection today."

"Shut up," Simon said. "Answer the question, Antonio."

Antonio shrugged. "It only makes sense. If any of us goes missing or dies, it has to be her. She's the only one capable of doing it."

Simon ignored the challenge in Antonio's voice. "No," he said. "As far as any of us were aware, Aznar died in Serbia in 1993. Now, how do you know any different?"

Antonio slumped in his chair, all fight gone out of him. "He has been in contact with me. I've sent him money, when he asked. Arranged travel and sanctuary when he needed it," Antonio said. He regained a little of his dignity. "Like it or not, we are brothers. We are the only ones in the world who understand each other. That forgives all manner of sins. You remembered that once. You never should have turned your back on Juan."

Outwardly, Simon's face was as blank as an empty slate. Inside, however, he felt a quickly building rage. But he wouldn't allow himself to show any loss of self-control. It was how he ruled.

"And what else?"

"What?"

"What else have you sent him?"

Antonio went pale. "Nothing."

"You've been sending him the Water."

Panic made Antonio's face go white. "Simon, I would never do that. I barely have enough for myself. You see to that. You all know that! We have too little as it is!" He looked around the table for support. No one would meet his eyes.

"This is why you've aged," Simon said. "You have been dividing your allowance. Sharing it with him. How else would Aznar even be alive? You know what happens without the Water. How is he still breathing?"

Antonio was sweating now, squirming in his seat. "It is not me. I swear."

"Yes," Simon said. "You swear. You swore an oath. Over and over, I've heard you swear. But you broke it when you helped him."

Simon stood up. Every man at the table held his breath. They could even hear Carlos do the same, over the phone. He walked around the table and stood over Antonio.

"You have forgotten the rules," Simon said.

Antonio refused to look up at him.

"Let me remind you, then. We agreed to forsake family and children. We are not bound to this world, and we have no heirs. This Council is our only family. We do not make the mistake of looking to our offspring for immortality. Until we have perfected this world, we do not lower ourselves to become common men. We have to be able to see beyond our immediate futures. We have to be able to make the sacrifices beyond the requirements of blood, kinship, family, tribe, and race. In return, we received—you received—the greatest gift any man could ever know. And you have betrayed us."

Antonio looked like a whipped dog, mean and ready to bite. He seemed to curl into himself as he spoke. "Aznar is one of us, Simon," he said. "We do not always get to choose our family. But only a coward deserts them."

Simon picked up the glass in front of Antonio.

"I see," he said. "So you chose to share your Water with him. Perhaps you can make do with less, then. Perhaps you don't need any more at all."

Then he smashed the glass onto the surface of the table, shattering the heavy crystal.

The other men froze in pure horror.

"You are over five hundred years old, Antonio," Simon said. "Without the Water, how long do you think you'll last?"

Only Carlos, thousands of miles away over the phone line, protested. "Simon," he said. "Antonio made a mistake. You cannot—"

"Does this seem like the time to tell me what I can and cannot do, Carlos?" Simon asked, his voice dangerously soft.

The phone line went quiet again.

"Anyone else?"

No one in the room would look at him. Or Antonio.

When Antonio spoke, his voice was close to breaking. "No. Simon. Please. I apologize."

"Shut up," Simon said again. "All I want to hear from you is the latest location of Aznar, and where you've been sending his shipments. Max will make arrangements to deal with him and clean up this mess."

"Yes, Simon," Antonio said. "Aznar is in Juárez."

"Of course he is," Simon said, barking a short, unamused laugh. "Of course. Wherever you find corpses, you will find a maggot."

Max wrote the information down on a separate piece of paper—this sorry affair was not going in the beautiful notebook. "I will handle it, Simon," he said.

"Good. Antonio, you will not receive another drop of the Water—"

Antonio looked stricken.

"—until I have decided you have fully repented for your stupidity. You're going to age, Antonio. It will not be pleasant. I hope you retain enough of your wits to remember why you are being punished."

He glared at the others. "Are there any more matters of honor I should know about?"

They all looked away quickly. But Sebastian cleared his throat.

"What?"

Sebastian would not meet his eyes. "Antonio was

wrong. We all know that. But he is right that Shako is still a threat. Perhaps we should consider . . ."

He left it hanging there.

Simon refused to pick it up. "Consider what?"

"Perhaps you should tell us where you have hidden our supply. In case she does finally kill you."

"No." He said it flatly. This was not up for debate or a vote. This was the cornerstone of his empire. He would not ever give it up.

He knew they had to ask, of course. It was the polite version of the desperation they'd all heard in Antonio's voice. No matter how much was given to them, there was always that greed for more.

Simon could not really blame them. He was guilty of that same greed himself.

Max sighed heavily. He was the only one not impressed with the dramatics. "Now can we tell them?"

Simon nodded. It would give them something to cheer after all the bad news.

"Tell us what?" Sebastian asked.

"We've hired David Robinton."

There were smiles. Not exactly the applause Simon had hoped for.

"Well," Sebastian said into the silence at the center of the room. "Let's hope he succeeds."

"He will," Simon said. "We've tried for years to duplicate the Water. This time, we have someone who will succeed. He is the one. I know it."

Again, there was no response.

"I'll believe it when I see it," Carlos finally said over the speaker.

Simon frowned. Carlos spoke because he was

a safe distance away. But he had no doubt they all thought the same thing.

He knew it was only self-preservation—basic fear—that made them surly and suspicious. He'd been dealing with these men so long that he doubted anything they did would ever surprise him again. But he found their lack of faith disturbing.

Max, embarrassed, tried to cover by going back to the agenda. "Moving on, then, we should probably discuss the next cash infusion from Carlos—"

"I have had enough for today," Simon said. "Get out. Go about your business."

Antonio almost ran out of the room. Peter and Sebastian hurried out, keeping a respectable distance from their disgraced colleague. Carlos hung up.

Max stayed. As soon as the door to the room closed again, Max asked him, "What in the name of God is wrong with you, Simon?"

Of all of the original Council, Simon had never once doubted Max's loyalty. And only Max would speak to him like this.

That didn't mean Simon liked it. "Careful, Max," he said.

"Or you'll cut me off as well?"

"Antonio deserves it. I gave an order. After Berlin, Aznar was to be shunned. I will not be disobeyed."

"We are supposed to be equals, Simon. You treat us like servants, this is what you get. Antonio feared coming to you about Aznar, and so he has risked himself by dividing his supply."

"Let him. It hurts only him."

"No. It doesn't. You heard the tone in Carlos's voice. He thinks you'll treat him the same way. And with our stock price taking the hit it has recently, we need Carlos's revenue streams more than ever."

"When did you turn from a warrior into an accountant?"

"Perhaps when you began spending money like a drunk in a whorehouse. Two million a year for Robinton? That money could be going to more exploration. Further searches for the Water."

"Where do you imagine we'll find it? We've looked everywhere. There isn't a tribe in the rainforest that we haven't contacted or a cave in Siberia we haven't surveyed. We had our source. And we lost it. If you're so worried about money, empty one of the Cayman accounts."

"I have. And the Swiss accounts. We need Carlos, and not just for his money. We all need each other. There are few enough of us, and every time we've tried to add to our ranks, it has been a disaster. If this Council cannot work together, you risk everything we are still working toward."

Simon said nothing.

"And for what? A flea like Aznar? Since when did you get so squeamish? We've put more bodies in the ground than Aznar ever could, in a century of trying."

"We are nothing like Aznar."

Max scowled at him. "At least he did his butchering personally."

Simon slammed his fist down on the table. The sound reverberated in the perfectly quiet room.

"Enough," Simon said. He began walking toward the door, but Max stood in his way.

"What is it, Max?" he asked.

Max looked conflicted. But he plunged ahead. "What are you doing, Simon?"

"What?"

"You were the one who told me, 'We cannot afford illusions about anything—least of all, ourselves.' What are you really trying to do?"

Simon sighed. This was growing tiresome.

"My goals—*our* goals—are the same as they have always been. I am trying to save this miserable, fallen world from itself. I am trying to put the right people in the right positions of power. I am trying to save the greatest number of lives. I am doing everything I can to ensure the greatest good for the greatest number."

"I know the speech, Simon. I still believe in it. But I want to know if you do. I can accept you acting maliciously, or spitefully, even against one of us—but you cannot act stupidly. I will not allow you to hide your motivations."

"Oh, you won't?" A superior little smile twisted Simon's lips. "Thank God I have you here to guide me, Max."

Max ignored the sarcasm. "Why is Shako still alive, Simon?"

That wiped the smile right off Simon's face. "What?"

"This is not about Aznar. Or Antonio. Or your authority. You are not thinking clearly because this is about her."

"I'm not that sentimental, Max. I would think you'd want her alive, too, so she can lead us to her source of the Water."

"I'm not sure she has one. It takes far less to keep

one person alive than it does six of us—or seven, if you want to count Aznar. I suspect she's growing as desperate as we are. Which makes her even more dangerous to us. You've let her live too long."

"You think I haven't tried to kill her?"

Max weighed his next words carefully. "I don't think you're displeased that she is still breathing."

"Perhaps I simply find her useful."

"My friend, she will bury us all if she gets the chance."

Simon made a dismissive noise. "You have always been too afraid of her."

Max seemed tired as he shook his head at Simon. "How many times do I have to say this? She is not the woman you knew all those years ago. She has had a long time to become someone else entirely. We all have. You want to remember the girl she was, and you forget everything she's done since. For your sake, I hope she is as sentimental as you the next time she has your head in her sights. At your age, nostalgia can be fatal."

"Well," Simon said, "no one lives forever."

He crossed the boardroom to the door. After a moment, Max followed.

# CHAPTER 6

DAVID COULD FEEL the heat of the asphalt under his running shoes. With the humidity, it was like trying to breathe through a wet sponge. Drivers in their air-conditioned cars looked at him as if he were an escaped lunatic.

He kept running anyway. He was trying to punish himself, force his mind to work harder. Because there was no way around it: he was stuck.

The weeks after accepting Simon's offer had been one long blur for him. True to his word, Simon put him to work immediately. He had just a day to go back to Boston and pick up a few changes of clothes, and then he was expected immediately at the Conquest headquarters in Tampa.

(When David asked Simon why Conquest was based in Tampa, rather than Miami or any of the biotech hubs, such as San Diego, he'd just grinned and said, "Strip club capital of the world, baby!")

His credentials waited for him at the front desk, and security escorted him into a lab stocked with everything he could ever want for diagnostic equipment.

For the first few days, he lived in a hotel room he barely saw, except to use the bed for a couple of hours at a time. After that, Conquest moved his stuff into a new condo for him. (He'd given an assistant the same key that Bethany had given back to him for the movers.) The first time he came home to the place, he found all his things neatly boxed and waiting. In one plastic bag, he discovered old take-out containers and the remains of a sandwich. They'd packed and moved his trash.

His double bed and small pieces of furniture were dwarfed in the cavernous spaces of his new place. He made a mental note to buy new things as soon as he got a chance, then promptly forgot about it and went back to the lab.

He'd checked Mueller's samples again. He compared genetic markers, made certain there was no possible fraud, and then established that there was nothing superhuman or unique about Mueller himself.

There was nothing that made him reconsider his earlier findings, as fantastic as they seemed. Mueller had regained twenty years of youth, at a minimum.

David had been going through the results of application of the liquid—or serum, or cure, whatever you wanted to call it. Mueller wasn't the only test subject. The outcome was always the same: immediate rejuvenation of the patient, despite life-threatening conditions in some cases.

The test subjects had not only recovered, they'd *improved* in every single way. Strength, reflexes, immune response, cardiovascular capacity—they were all markedly better, all the way down the line.

Even baseline IQ increased in the before-and-after testing. Subjects who had trouble with basic spelling on the intake forms were scoring ten to twenty points higher after they took the cure. Part of that was surely due to the fact that many of these people were homeless and drug addicted—Simon seemed to have a deal with one of the local shelters to sign up people like Mueller—and they were getting regular nutrition and medical care while in the trials.

But part of it was physical as well. EEG and MRI showed increased brain activity and regrowth of damaged neurons. (Which was a whole other level of impossible, but David was getting used to that.) The test subjects were not more knowledgeable—they hadn't picked up any new facts after taking the cure—but they were able to recall and use their own memories and experiences better.

Actually, that last result calmed David down a bit. There was no biological way for the treatment to impart new skills and information, unless it was magic, and that was something David was never going to buy. He didn't even read his horoscope.

Whatever the cure was, it was based in science. He was sure of it. That meant it could be duplicated. It could be cracked.

The problem was, in every patient, in every case, the liquid did not leave a trace, not a single clue.

Nothing David tried worked. He was no closer now than when Simon had first shown him the miracle cure.

So he went back to his mostly empty condo, put on his shoes, and started running. This was how he broke down problems when they wouldn't break any other way. He ran.

And, he admitted to himself, it gave him a place to put his anger, gave him a physical pain to drown out any other kind of pain.

The day after his parents' funeral, he'd started running and didn't stop until his legs were shaky and he couldn't see for the sweat in his eyes. When he finally caught his breath, he realized he'd run almost twenty miles and barely had an idea of where he was. He had to call a relative to get a ride home.

Today wasn't like that. Today was just another run.

He hit Morgan Street and kept going south past the Forum, headed for the bay, his pace steady.

He'd tried everything. He had examined the blood samples of the "cured" test subjects—the ones who were now, inarguably, certifiably younger—all the way down to their DNA: three billion letters of genetic code, six feet of proteins packed into a space a thousand times smaller than the eye of a needle. He'd run them through a sequencer, comparing the subjects' DNA before the cure and after. The only difference was that after the treatment, the DNA no longer had the usual errors and missing sequences that came with aging. The same sequence, only cleaner.

But damned if he could figure out why.

Maybe he was looking at it too closely. After all, he was primarily a molecular biologist. His inclination and training led him to look at the very smallest part of the picture. Maybe there was something affecting the entire organism that was only then expressed in the DNA. He had the feeling he was missing something vital. How was it possible to reverse the damage done to the DNA *over time*—

David broke off his train of thought when he realized someone was coming up behind him. Fast.

That surprised him. He wasn't a world-class runner, but he hadn't seen many people in Tampa who could keep pace with him. He suspected the heat and humidity kept them on treadmills, inside the climate-controlled fitness clubs. He wasn't used to having someone right on his heels.

He picked up the pace a little, trying to gain some room.

Behind him, he heard the other runner do the same, matching him stride for stride.

David accelerated again. He could see the bay from the end of the street now. He was about to make his usual left turn and follow the shoreline along the greenbelt.

Then, without warning, the runner behind him shot out and passed him.

He saw dark hair tied in a ponytail. She looked over her shoulder at him, and he could have sworn he saw the hint of a mocking smile before she smoothly accelerated away.

It was her. The woman from the club.

He ran after her.

She remained just ahead of him, not looking back again, but never getting more than a dozen feet away. She led him down past the marina, through the park, and off his usual route. She just kept going, beautiful and unstoppable, legs carrying her effortlessly over the ground.

David, for his part, was struggling. He wasn't in marathon shape, and they were running at a sprinter's pace. He felt like he was being dragged along in her wake. His mouth was open and he was sucking wind hard. He imagined he must look like a stereotypical pervert chasing a pretty girl, tongue hanging out and sweating from every pore.

She ran even faster.

She took a sharp turn on a path that led down to the shoreline. It wasn't much of a beach—mostly rocks and dirt, a lot of uneven ground.

He found some hidden reserve of strength and followed. His feet nearly went out from under him on the downhill slope and she got farther away. He recovered quickly. If he was this wrecked, she had to be feeling it, too, at least a little.

Trouble was, she didn't seem to be breathing hard.

They splashed along the waterline. She vaulted a few large rocks and then ran out onto the breakwater, a large promontory built to protect the shore from the constant erosion of the waves.

David hauled himself up, stumbled, nearly fell again, and kept chasing her. He might not be able to find any answers in the lab, but he was going to get her name. He could at least catch her long enough to ask the question.

She came to the end of the breakwater. There was nowhere to go, unless she dove in and started swimming.

For an instant, he was afraid she was going to do just that.

Instead, she turned and stopped.

David stopped, too, barely able to keep himself from colliding with her.

The falling sun lit her up from the west. Her skin shone. She was drawing deep breaths, evenly, mouth only slightly open.

She looked magnificent.

David put his hands on his knees and wheezed. Spots danced in his vision. He couldn't speak, which was probably not a bad thing, since he had no idea what he would say.

When he recovered enough to look up, she was still there. He hadn't imagined her. And she was watching him with a smile that went all the way up to her eyes.

"Hello, David," she said. "So how do you like the new job so far?"

HER NAME WAS SHY Walker. She bought him a bad cup of coffee at a Starbucks a few blocks inland. The air was chilled just above freezing by the air-conditioning. He tried not to show how grateful he was for the chance to sit down.

She didn't look tired. Too much time in the lab was turning him soft, David thought. Or he was getting old.

He shoved the thought away and focused on Shy.

"So," he said. "I think you owe me at least some explanation."

Her expression was carefully blank over the rim of her coffee cup. "You think so?"

"You come out of nowhere, give me the best career advice of my life, and then vanish."

"I'm a busy girl," she said. "I was out of town."

"Vacation?"

"I travel a lot. Business."

"So then you show up again and run me half to death through the streets of Tampa."

She shrugged. "You were following me. You could have dropped out anytime."

"That's not really me."

"I know."

"You know a lot about me."

She stared at him, still dreadfully calm. Then she said, "Well, David. That's because I'm about to recruit you for the most dangerous mission of your life. The fate of the world rests on your shoulders."

She held his gaze long enough that David thought he might be looking at the world's most beautiful lunatic.

Then she burst into laughter. "Sorry," she said. "I couldn't resist. You're a very serious guy."

Oh thank God, David thought.

As it turned out, there was nothing terribly mysterious about Shy. She was a corporate headhunter for the pharmaceutical and biotech industry. Everyone in her field knew David, because everyone wanted to bag him for their clients. She knew Conquest was especially interested, and she'd assembled a profile of David for them. When she saw David in the club, it wasn't much of a leap to figure out what was going on.

"You work for Conquest?"

"I work for myself," she corrected. "But I did some freelance consulting for Simon Oliver."

"Simon didn't seem to know you."

She rolled her eyes. "Not the perpetual adolescent. His father. I'm sure his son never even read my report."

"He's not a real detail-oriented guy," David admitted.

They talked for an hour. She seemed to know a little bit about everything, but David had never felt so comfortable with someone. It was hard to believe she was a stranger. She was already finishing his sentences when she looked at her watch—the women's version of his own Casio G-Shock—and said that she had to get moving.

"I've got to see you again," David said. He blurted it out and immediately regretted it.

Fortunately, Shy laughed and smiled. "That could be arranged," she said. They headed out of the air-conditioned store, back into the unforgiving heat.

David didn't enjoy the idea of running back to his condo. Shy looked as fresh as ever.

She took out her cell and they exchanged numbers. Then, unexpectedly, she kissed him lightly on the cheek before she turned and ran away.

He couldn't stop grinning, even though his legs hurt and his side cramped all the way home.

# CHAPTER 7

SIMON WAS INSIDE the VIP lounge at some club inside a Vegas casino when the past caught up with him.

He and a dozen other people were drinking and watching a young woman, perhaps nineteen, as she danced alone, very drunk. She'd been hired for some bachelor party, which Simon remembered was the reason he was here. Some other wealthy young idiot. Like he was supposed to be. The girl began removing what little clothing she wore, and everyone cheered. She smiled at him, caught his eye, and revealed a little more of her tanned and sculpted flesh. Suddenly, it hit him just how old he was, just how vast the gulf of years between them was.

When he was this girl's age, no European had ever stepped this far into the interior of the American continent. This was empty desert. Perhaps a few thousand humans at most had passed over this ground in centuries, always on their way to someplace else. And a young woman who took off her clothes in public would be branded a whore or a witch. A death sentence, either way.

Now he stood inside a building taller than the biggest cathedral of his youth, next to a man-made lake, surrounded by five times as many people as had lived in Rome at the height of its empire. Within hours, he would step aboard a plane and travel a distance that once took years and cost lives. But first he would see this young woman naked, bathing in electric lights, unaware of how many disasters she had dodged just to get to this point. The vaccinations against the diseases that killed so many children. The clean water and plentiful food that gave her long legs and clear skin and just the right amount of body fat and muscle. The synthetic fabrics that no longer covered her. She danced to notes clearer than any human choir could produce, with a pill under her tongue that would have been considered a revelation direct from God Himself once upon a time. And all the while, she remained completely ignorant of the miracles that surrounded her.

Perhaps she was stripping her way through college.

He couldn't see her anymore. Couldn't see anything but the indisputable fact: everyone he knew as a boy was dead, had been dust for longer than this city had existed.

For a second, it was difficult for Simon to breathe. The weight of the years felt like it would crush him, drown him in time.

This kind of extreme dislocation had happened

before. It was the opposite of what he supposed other people called déjà vu. They had the impression they were seeing something that had happened before. Simon, by contrast, had seen almost everything before. He breathed deeply and let it wash over him, and rode it out. He suspected it was one more symptom of his long use of the Water. Men were not meant to live as long as he had.

He took a breath. Then another. He breathed. He was still alive. Despite everything, the world had not been able to kill him yet. And it would not.

Simon stood and walked away from the naked dancer.

The host of the party, the bachelor himself, stepped in front of Simon and placed a hand on Simon's chest. "Hey, man, where you going? Party's just getting started."

It took every bit of restraint Simon owned to keep from grabbing that hand, twisting it, snapping the bone, spinning the man to expose his chest for the sword—

No. That was a different time.

Men did not touch each other so casually then. This was not a challenge. This was what passed for sociability.

He remembered to smile. "Gotta get a little space."

The other man looked disturbed. Simon did not manage to get the tone quite right. Sometimes it leaked out. The age. The difference. Especially at moments like this.

He finally got himself under control by the time he reached the back booths of the club. They were mostly deserted, everyone's eyes on the hired girl now, clustering around. In another moment, more women from the crowd would begin to strip—spontaneously joining the party, just as they'd been instructed and paid to do.

He'd seen it before. He'd seen it all before.

This was worse than usual, Simon had to admit. He had weak moments. Usually after he heard about Shako.

How long since he'd last seen her? Really seen her, not just a blurry surveillance photo passed along by the CIA or some other top-secret government agency?

Centuries. More time than these people thought possible.

He flattered himself that she still thought of him, too. Of course she did. She intended to kill him.

There were moments—like this one—where he considered offering himself as a target. Let her get it over with. Max would say that he had this suicidal impulse all the time, but Max didn't understand. He wasn't there for the true beginning.

Simon put the drink down. It was not going to help.

Perhaps he was feeling nostalgic, as Max had said. He was so close to—well, there was no better word—to winning.

The others didn't understand, because all they wanted was for their lives to continue. And he couldn't blame them, not really. He'd made them comfortable and powerful and rich beyond the imagining of their mortal lives.

But in truth, they'd advanced only to the point

of that stripper: happy and protected and safe in the knowledge that her youth was eternal. The difference was, for her that was the standard illusion of the young. For Simon and the other members of the Council, it was truth.

But Simon had always wanted it to mean more. The others didn't always see the plan. They didn't see how difficult it was to maintain all the spinning plates, to keep the wheels within wheels turning.

He thought of his plan, in his private moments, as a great wall, assembled stone by stone. The end result would be the world as he envisioned it: safer, better, stronger. Everything perfect and eternal.

But for every stone he moved into his wall, another rolled out of place. It was incredibly frustrating. He spent all his time putting the world back together, and it just kept falling apart.

Time had a way of changing everything.

Vegas, for example. What was once a Mormon outpost along a desert road became a modern-day El Dorado, exactly like the legend, because the Mob needed a place to launder money. They gave the mandate to build a casino to Bugsy Siegel, who took it as a license to create a dream. They killed him for it, but it was too late. The dream grew huge and became reality.

(Simon had met Ben several times back then. He'd liked him, even though the man was deeply unstable.)

You couldn't control everything.

When he'd started, Simon believed it was possible to unite the world under a single crown, and the Water would give him the power to manipulate the crown. He and his men would control the resources of the New World, and they would force the old one to be better. He'd planned to lift all men up, one at a time, if necessary, to see the glory that was possible in this world. He would share the wealth he'd found, once they were ready. His original idea had been a happy and united population, all following his ideals. They seemed grandiose at the time: cleaner water; food for all; schools open to every child, not just those of position or wealth; and an end to slaughter and war by the simple method of having the biggest and most powerful army on the planet.

But first, to do that, he had to secure his position. Amass enough wealth and power to make his voice strong enough so he could not be ignored. Then he'd use the power of the Spanish monarchy to begin changing the world for the better.

The English were the first to destroy that illusion for him. They destroyed Spain's armada and began their decades of influence over the world.

So Simon and the Council had to adapt, had to use their riches to adjust to the new reality of an English-dominated world. Simon made the moves he could. He financed alchemists, then scientists, and other thinkers. He tried to overthrow England's monarchy by supporting a fringe group of religious extremists, and they even succeeded for a time.

Then they fell apart, and the monarchy was restored. Simon had adapted to that, as he did everything else.

His grandiose goals became the status quo, bit by bit. And yet, somehow, the better world always remained just out of reach. People still, stubbornly, refused to behave in their best interests. Children were still starving and men and women still dying of pointless diseases and slaughtering one another in pointless wars.

Simon no longer believed in God, but he believed in sin. One sin in particular. He knew pride. He saw how it corrupted everything. How it kept people from knowing their place. How much better the world would be, he often thought, if only it would behave, and listen to someone who truly knew how it should work.

And yet they all insisted on following their own whims, even when they led straight into Hell.

At moments like this, especially, Simon could easily fall into despair. He controlled vast fortunes. He held the fate of powerful men in his hands. He'd seen empires rise and fall, and buried more enemies than could fit in a hundred graveyards.

And the world wasn't perfect yet. Despite everything he'd done.

But he would not surrender.

Above all, he survived. Almost everyone and everything else he'd ever known was dust and rot, but he remained.

The dream was still good. And he'd see it come to life. No matter how long it took.

Now, with the possibility of an unlimited supply of the Water—of a true cure for death—he was closer than he ever thought possible. No more games. No more hiding behind the scenes. A man who could offer a cure for death could have anything. There was no one on Earth who would fight him then. They would all finally have to do as they were told. And then he would have the world as he had always dreamed it, made perfect and eternal.

He heard a noise behind him. It served to wake him from his dreams of the past. His mask fully in place, a modern man once more, he turned and looked.

The girl stood there, wearing nothing but a thong.

"Hey," she said. "Never had that reaction before. You really didn't like my dancing?"

He smiled. She wouldn't take rejection. It was as foreign as the past to her.

"Maybe I just wanted a private show," he said.

She smiled, back in a familiar script, and moved closer to him. Simon put his arms around her as she settled onto his lap and began to writhe.

Men were not meant to live as long as he did, he reminded himself. But that didn't mean he was going to give it up anytime soon.

# CHAPTER 8

DAVID COULDN'T RECALL being nervous like this before a date. In fact, he couldn't recall *ever* being nervous before a date.

As arrogant as it might have sounded, he'd simply never cared this much before. Even in high school, it had seemed immature to drown in the drama of pursuit and rejection. He was always working on other things that took precedence.

Most of that, he did not need a therapist to tell him, was because of the losses he'd suffered. His sister's death was like a bullet from a random drive-by cracking the drywall of his family's home. It taught him that nothing was ever as solid or safe as he thought before.

He'd decided to fix it. He would make sure that it never happened again, to anyone. A childish hope, sure, but hey, he'd been fourteen, and in all honesty, he was smart enough. So he already had a quest.

Dating and girls, and then relationships and love, were distractions at best. Other people were capable of finding love. Only David was capable of finding what he was looking for.

And if that meant putting his own life on hold for a while—well, he was young. There would always be time to catch up later.

Those thoughts melted when he knocked on the door of her condo overlooking the bay and Shy opened it and smiled at him.

She wore a simple and elegant black sheath, held at one shoulder with a silver clasp that gleamed against the dark tan of her skin. He had to kick-start his brain into supplying the standard greetings.

This is what normal people do, David told himself, handing over the bouquet of flowers he'd agonized about bringing. (Corny or romantic? Endearing or childish?)

Shy took the flowers and thanked him, then invited him inside, the black silk clinging to her tightly.

David stood at the threshold for a moment longer. Then he shook his head and stepped in.

Christ, get a grip. It's just a date. People do it all the time. It doesn't mean anything.

SHE MADE HIM DINNER, and they ate in front of a window that seemed to frame the entire horizon as it met the water. It was beautiful. The food was perfect.

He looked at the view twice and barely tasted what was on his fork. Instead, he stared. A lot. And struggled to find something to talk about with her.

You are blowing this, he told himself.

She threw him a lifeline and asked about work, which was the only thing he really had. "So, what does Conquest have you doing?"

Unfortunately, he also had a very strict nondisclosure agreement. "I'm really not supposed to talk about it."

She smiled. "Come on. Surely you can avoid slipping out any corporate secrets."

David laughed, relaxing a little. "Ah, it's probably dull as hell to you. I'm stuck on some complicated DNA stuff. You don't need me droning on about that."

"Oh, I see. You don't think I'm smart enough."

"No, no," David said, rushing the words out. "It's just—you know, technical."

"Oh. Technical. I see. That clears it right up."

He had the distinct feeling she was laughing at him. Still blowing this, David. Come on, bring it back around.

"All right," he said. "I warned you. Ready?"

She put on a serious expression, her eyes lit up with mockery. "Ready," she said. Then she leaned forward, inadvertently revealing a distracting slice of her cleavage.

David forced himself to keep his eyes level. "Okay. No secret that Conquest is working on antiaging approaches, right? The trick is, which approach do you take? Aging is so fantastically complex. The body breaks down in all sorts of ways. It's like the story of Hercules and the Hydra. Cut off one head, another two take its place. Deal with one problem, another one pops up. The idea of a single magic bullet to target them all, that's got to be a fantasy, right?"

"Except you don't think so."

He smiled. She was fast. And he reminded himself, she didn't work for Conquest, so he'd have to be careful.

"The basic problem is in our DNA. Humans have never lived as long as we do now. So we're running into the unintended consequences of our success. Evolution didn't come up with solutions for all the problems of aging because it's not crucial to our survival. As long as our species can still breed, evolution doesn't care. Sexual maturity comes when we're in our teens. But we survive long after that. It's like we outlive our warranties by fifty or sixty years. The longer we live, the more wear and tear we get. Our cells get corrupted, too, so our most basic building blocks start to fall apart. We get tumors, we get slower, our hair falls out, our cuts don't heal as fast, our skin gets thinner and sags. That all starts way down in our DNA."

"Right," Shy said. To David's ears, it sounded very much like *Duh.* He wasn't breaking any new ground here, and she seemed on the verge of boredom. "So, how do you fix that?"

"I think there has to be a way to address all the problems all at once. A truly holistic solution, instead of trying to chop off another head of the Hydra every time it appears. There are self-repairing mechanisms already in DNA."

"You mean nucleotide excision repair," Shy said.

"Right," David said, reminding himself he wasn't lecturing a hall of Biology 101 students right now. "Those sequences get old and wear out and start picking up errors, too. But if we fix them—get them to repair themselves perfectly, with zero errors every time—we could have an autocorrect for the human genome."

Shy smiled. She saw it now. "If the repair mechanisms are perfect—"

"They can repair the DNA in every cell and make them perfect, too. Think of it as a massive software upgrade for the entire human body. A way to reboot DNA without any flaws."

"So you're going to fix something that's gone unaddressed by millions of years of evolution."

"I can do it," he said.

"You seem pretty sure."

David knew it sounded impossible. But he had an advantage over Shy, over everyone in his field, in fact. He knew it was possible. He'd seen it firsthand.

But Shy hadn't. He worried he'd said too much and started talking rapidly to cover it up.

"There's got to be a way to train and shape the DNA-repair sequences," he said. "We've created custom genes. We have the tools. Hell, it might even be there already, somewhere in the junk DNA that hangs out in the cell, just waiting for the right circumstances to activate it. I've been looking into the Johns Hopkins research on hydrogels, which can be turned into self-activating, self-assembling proteins. They could create a cluster of the right kind of amino acids. But that raises its own interesting questions. The delivery method alone . . ."

David had been talking uninterrupted for a while before he realized Shy had stood up from the table and was standing over him.

He blinked and looked up at her. She had that enigmatic half smile on her face again.

"Sorry," he said. "I can get carried away."

"Perfectly all right," she said. Her voice was throaty, as if she was holding back a laugh. David figured he'd bored her out of her mind. A deep disappointment welled up in him. He'd definitely blown it.

"Sorry," he said again. "It's just, when you think about the implications this has for cancer research alone. The idea of programmable cells—" *Oh my God, you're doing it again, what is wrong with you, for God's sake, why can't you shut up?*

Then Shy touched the clasp of her dress, sending it to the floor in a puddle of silk.

David shut up.

"I'm sorry," she said. "Did I interrupt your train of thought?"

He just stared. Her skin was beautiful. All of it.

"Well," she said when he failed to answer. "Maybe we can find something else to do with your mouth."

She leaned down and kissed him.

It was like the contact between them closed some circuit, reactivated some vital knowledge in him. He kissed her, his body instantly aware of every inch of hers, her warmth and bare flesh only inches away from him.

He stood and ran his hands over her, trying to touch all of her at once. His pulse sang in his veins. He felt clumsy, overeager, like he was in high school again, making out in the backseat of his car.

She let him paw at her for a moment as she effortlessly guided him from his clothes.

He looked at her again. Still could not believe it.

Every inch of her was perfect. Flawless, copper-colored skin smooth over supple muscle. She stood effortlessly, lightly, on the balls of her feet, watching him watch her, eyes still smiling, amused by him and his awe. He felt like he was in the presence of great art, inside a cathedral, his head buzzing with the impulse to worship, to kneel.

So he did.

He hiked her right leg over his left shoulder, supporting her as he lapped at her, unable to show any restraint. She ran her fingers through his hair and tugged occasionally, pulling and guiding him.

Then as her back began to arch and she started to push against his mouth, she suddenly broke contact and yanked him to his feet.

She took him in her hand and pulled him along, leading him quickly to the bedroom.

He was suddenly on his back, in her mouth, feeling like he would explode in seconds. But she held him off, working him expertly, bringing him to the edge and no further.

When he thought he could not take it anymore, she released him. He was gasping for air when she swung a leg over him, straddling his hips, drawing him deep inside her.

He thrust upward and felt a kind of savage pride as he saw the look on her face, her eyes rolling under her closed lids. Her mouth was open, a small triangle of skin flushed red, right under her throat, above her breasts.

There had been other times with other women, but at this moment, they seemed like dim matchsticks in the dark against a blazing incandescence. She pulled something from him, something stronger than he'd ever felt before.

He'd never felt so hard, so sure, so right. This was different. She was different.

He pushed against her and she held him down with her hips, pushing back.

She cried out as she shuddered, and it was more than enough to put him over the edge. He thrust again and again, his strength draining, his muscles going liquid even as she kept on building and building, her cries reaching a high pitch before she collapsed on his chest.

David felt as if he'd ridden lightning to the ground. He felt as though he'd been broken. He felt an unaccustomed surge of peace.

He looked at her face and saw her eyes open, watching him.

She smiled, and he saw something predatory there, something triumphant.

He did not care. He felt that, too.

They curled into each other, side by side. David did not feel as if he'd ever need to move again.

But within a few moments, he felt himself stirring. So did Shy. She looked at him over her shoulder, both a challenge and invitation in her eyes.

That was all he needed, and he was lost again.

Just a date, he reminded himself. People do it all the time. It doesn't mean anything.

# CHAPTER 9

DAVID WALKED QUICKLY from the building, unshaven, wearing the previous day's clothes. It was still early, but this would be the latest he'd gotten to the lab in a week. That's how long the man named Mathis had been following him.

Mathis stretched and yawned. He'd been up most of the night, parked in a nearby garage, watching the front of the building, waiting for David to emerge. The woman's condo opened onto a shopping plaza filled with shops and restaurants. When the coffee place opened, he set up camp at a table outside with the biggest cup they had.

He let David go without following. There was no real urgency. The only places the geek seemed to go were the lab, his home, and, occasionally, some hospital where he volunteered. He'd pick up David at Conquest's offices later. Right now, he wanted to find out more about the woman.

Mathis's employer had told him to trail David and find out who he was seeing. It had been mind-numbingly dull so far. Then, finally, a date. Hallelujah, some kind of break in the routine.

Mathis knew he shouldn't complain. He could have ended up like the other guys in his unit, since returning from Afghanistan: one a part-time bouncer at a strip club, one in the VA learning how to walk again, one wait-listed for the police academy, one doing construction, and one who'd put his gun in his mouth and eaten a bullet.

Boredom should have looked pretty decent by comparison. But he couldn't help searching for the same rush he got when he was an MP at Bagram.

At least he had a diversion today. He'd run the condo's address through a real-estate database on a laptop in his car, trying to get the name of David's hookup. Turned out it was rented through a holding company. Not that unusual. But not at all helpful. Similar searches through utilities and credit bureaus based on the address were dead ends as well.

He figured he should follow her to work. From there, it would be a five-minute search on the Internet to get her identity. Take a couple of pics with his phone for the file, run her background, make sure she wasn't working for one of Conquest's competitors. Most likely, she was just a one-night stand. But she had to be more interesting than another day spent waiting for the geek to hang up his lab coat.

He was about to go inside for a refill when he saw her walk from the building, wearing workout clothes and carrying a gym bag. He committed the rookie mistake of staring. He had not really gotten a good look before, and she was incredible. His bullshit meter immediately pinged. There was no way someone this hot would go out with a science nerd. Not when there were so many tanned and gym-buffed guys—like himself, he'd be the first to say—on the market.

This was definitely getting interesting.

She fixed a pair of headphones in her ears and walked away. There was a twenty-four-hour fitness place not too far away, Mathis remembered. That was probably where she was headed. He'd have to leave his car and follow on foot.

No problem. She was off in her own little world. He waited for a moment, let her get around the corner of the building, and then crossed the plaza after her. He dropped his empty cup in a trash can on the way.

He rounded the corner as she disappeared from sight again. She was quicker than he thought. He saw her ponytail bounce as she took a shortcut in an alleyway between two buildings.

He picked up the pace. Mathis made sure that his jacket was buttoned—all employees of his firm were required to wear jackets and slacks, partly for the company's image, and partly to hide the guns they wore in belt-mounted holsters.

He walked into the alley, which turned out to be a little access passage for the restaurants and shops to put out their garbage and take deliveries.

She was gone. He didn't see her anywhere.

Shit, he thought. She might have started running. He should have been quicker. He didn't think she'd seen him. She hadn't glanced in his direction.

He was going to have to hustle, catch up with her at the gym.

Mathis had broken into a jog when she stepped out from behind one of the plastic garbage bins. They could have been standing side by side, in line for a movie. His mouth opened and he struggled to think of an excuse for chasing her down the alley.

Then she swung her leg in a roundhouse kick that connected with his head and knocked him completely off his feet.

He had a small moment of disbelief before the back of his head hit the pavement and he went completely unconscious.

THOMAS PICKFORD SAT BEHIND his desk in his office near the top floor of a tower overlooking Tampa's downtown, booting up his computer. Outside his window, he could already hear the sirens as the city woke up and began killing itself. Music to his ears. He never said it out loud, but he thought it all the time: the decline of civilization was great for business.

Pickford had been in Iraq on the first go-round, way back in the nineties, in Special Forces and intelligence. When he was done, he discovered that his skills were more highly valued by Saudi businessmen. He worked in private security overseas until 9/11, when he decided it was time to go home.

He didn't return out of any great sense of patriotism, but he could smell the opportunities opening up. The massive reduction in troops after Gulf War I created a lot of vacancies for guys with résumés like his. In Iraq and Afghanistan, military contractors were used to fill in every vacant space. In the States, every guy with a seven-figure bank account suddenly decided he was a target for Al Qaeda and wanted his own private army.

So Pickford took his savings and a federal loan and opened his own firm: OpSec. (His clients loved the name; it sounded like authentic Jack Bauer badassery to middle-aged businessmen who'd never been closer to the military than TV and movies.)

The paranoia after 9/11 died down—more or less—and even the demand for contractors was easing as the politicians tried to sneak the military out of Iraq and Afghanistan with as much dignity as possible.

But OpSec had flourished and expanded. Crime was rising again. Local governments couldn't pay for more cops. And the news, especially in Florida, was 24/7 fear and tragedy. Between meth-heads and the remnants of the drug wars and the usual urban horror stories, it never took much selling on Pickford's part to convince his clients they needed protection.

Currently, he had his guys in Mexico, escorting businessmen on a deal there; in a private jet on its way to the Dominican Republic, acting as security for a party of old men loaded on Viagra and Scotch and looking for teenage hookers; and all over the suburbs, bored as they made a bunch of millionaires feel safe at night in their gated communities.

OpSec also did jobs for corporate clients, such as Conquest Biotech. He'd never put their name down as a reference, but Conquest had used his services since he'd started business, from background checks to bodyguarding to the occasional B&E job in the lab of a rival firm. If he had any loyalty, it was to the steady stream of income Conquest had always supplied OpSec.

So when Max asked Pickford to follow around a new hire named David Robinton, Pickford didn't think much of it. Guys like Robinton were loaded with intellectual property. It made sense to keep an eye on an investment like that. OpSec did it all the time. This was a ten-grand handjob at the most.

The War on Terror provided Pickford with plenty of young guys loaded with testosterone and lethal skills, fresh out of war zones and with few job opportunities. He sent one of them, a kid named Mathis, to shadow Conquest's pet geek and come back with a report.

Then Mathis entered his office without knocking, hands up and behind his head. Directly in front of a woman who held a gun.

She wore tights and a workout bra and held a gym bag in her other hand. Mathis had a rapidly swelling bruise and an embarrassed look on his face.

"Had a bit of a problem, sir," he said.

"Yeah, I can see that," Pickford said. He kept his hands where the woman could see them, and waited.

"This boy belongs to you," the woman said.

"He works for me, yes," Pickford said. "Can I ask why you're holding a gun on him?"

As he spoke, he gestured with his left hand. It was meant to distract her while he reached for the silent alarm under his desk with his right.

It didn't work. She pivoted on the balls of her feet and brought the bag against Mathis's skull in a single move. Mathis's eyes rolled up and he went down as though he was hit by a tree branch. Before Pickford could draw another breath, the gun was pointed directly at him.

He had to admit, a beautiful woman in spandex holding a gun on him slotted into some of his more specific fantasies. But she was disturbingly calm, as if she did this sort of thing every day. He doubted her pulse was much above sixty.

Her gun hand didn't waver. He gave all of his employees nine-millimeter Berettas loaded with hollow-point rounds. He could see the red dot on the side of the gun that meant the safety was off. If he didn't want this to end with massive hemorrhaging, he realized he was going to have to be very, very careful now.

One hopeful sign. Neither he nor Mathis was dead already. If she meant to kill them, she'd had her chance. Keeping them alive was only increasing her risk at this point.

He might get out of this yet.

He put up his hands.

"Who hired you?" she asked.

He considered lying, or at least stalling. But she'd seen Mathis following her, taken him out, and forced him to lead her back here. That wasn't easy, even if Mathis was still young. There were a dozen ways it could have gone bad on her, and she still made it to his office.

That put his odds of bullshitting into the unfavorably low range.

He decided to go with the truth and see where it led.

"Conquest Biotech," he said.

The look on her face scared him. It was there for only a split second, but it was equal parts disgust and anger. It motivated him to tell her something that might keep her from pulling the trigger.

"We weren't hired to follow you, exactly. I assigned Mathis to David Robinton. He's supposed to keep an eye on him. Make notes of who he sees. Where he goes. That sort of thing."

She considered that.

"It's really a compliment, if you think about it," Pickford said. "He's very valuable to Conquest. It's more a formality, for his protection, more than anything else."

She raised the gun to center on his forehead.

"Have you told them anything about me yet?"

Pickford got the distinct sense his life might depend on the answer. He decided, again, the best course of action was the truth.

"No," he said. "We report once a week. I didn't even know you existed until you walked into this room."

He held his breath.

She nodded. She seemed to be thinking.

"Is he your boyfriend, or are you—"

"Quiet now," she said. He shut up.

She looked at him carefully for another moment, and then seemed to come to a decision.

"I believe you," she said. "Here's your problem. I don't want Conquest to know I've been near David. I don't want them to have any idea anything is wrong with their pet genius."

"You're working your own angle," Pickford said.

She was an operator. She had to be. High-level industrial espionage, with those skills.

She didn't confirm or deny, which he expected.

"Your problem," she continued, "is that I need to believe you won't report any of this back to Conquest once I leave this room."

Pickford swallowed. Once again, he decided honesty was the best policy.

"Well, I hate to say it, but there's only one way to be sure of that." He looked at the gun.

She smiled, and it was so brilliant that for an instant he forgot how much trouble he was in.

"No," she said. "Fortunately for you, I thought of another way."

She put the gym bag on his desk. It landed with a surprisingly heavy thud. He wondered if she kept weights in there.

She gestured him back with the gun, and he complied. Without taking her eyes off him, she reached into the bag and lifted out what was inside, placing it on the desk blotter right next to his computer.

Pickford drew in a sharp, short breath.

It was small, shaped like a tiny loaf of bread. There was an ornate character stamped into its side. And it was the most beautiful thing he'd ever seen.

It was a gold ingot.

He'd never seen real gold before, but he had no doubt that was what he was looking at now. It took in the overhead light and doubled it, pouring it in rich waves back into the room.

He couldn't stop staring at it. Until she took out another, and another, and another, from her bag.

He looked at the ingots and tried to do the math

in his head. They had to weigh at least three pounds each. He listened to Glenn Beck, and though he didn't think of himself as a Doomsday Prepper, he did keep an eye on the price of gold. It was going for around $1,300 an ounce right now. Three pounds was forty-eight ounces was $62,400 per ingot.

That was almost a quarter of a million dollars, right there on his desk.

"That would be a down payment," she said. "I would like to buy out your interest in David Robinton. And I'd expect a few more favors, here and there. Unless, of course, you feel some great loyalty toward Conquest."

Pickford wanted to touch the gold so badly he felt it in his chest. She still had the gun on him. But it didn't matter anymore.

He liked to believe he had a code. But looking at the gleam of the little bricks, he knew definitively that he'd left those sorts of ideals behind with his uniform. He was a mercenary, and mercenaries did not have a code. Mercenaries only had a price.

He couldn't keep the smile off his face when he looked back at her.

"I think we can see our way clear to taking you on as a client," he said.

She smiled back at him.

"I thought you would," she said.

Only then did she lower the gun.

# CHAPTER 10

DAVID WALKED DOWN the hall to Max's office.

They'd met only briefly when David had first gone to Miami, but he and Max had spent a lot of time together since then. Max, David learned, was Simon's right-hand man, the guy who kept tabs on everything so Simon could spend his time chasing models or getting thrown out of bars.

Max's executive assistant—a blonde packed into a tight outfit who seemed to have come straight from a naughty-librarian fantasy—escorted him in, and then left them alone.

As always, the office seemed almost unused. There was never a coffee cup on the desk, or even any papers. It was like he came in only for these weekly progress reports with David.

Unfortunately, there was no progress to report.

David was explaining that he had found nothing

in the latest round of DNA testing when he noticed that Max wasn't paying attention.

"Hey," he said. "Are you listening to any of this?"

Max focused in on him again and gave him a sharp smile. "Not really," he said. "I sort of lose focus after you tell me you've failed again."

David was never sure exactly how much of the work Max understood. He was the same age as Simon and, like Simon, always dressed in an impeccable suit. But where Simon was unrestrained, Max spoke as though each word cost him money. He waited for others to step out of line, and then knocked them back into line with a cold, well-chosen sentence.

David was in no mood for it. He was exhausted. "This isn't like mixing a drink," David told Max. "There are millions—billions—of factors that play into what we're trying to do."

"Oh God, spare me. I don't need to hear again how complicated it all is."

"Then we should probably skip these meetings altogether. I could get more done in the lab."

"You sure?" Max shot back. "Doesn't seem like it. We've handed you a solution, David. All you have to do is copy it. Are we not paying you enough?"

David took a deep breath, trying to hold on to his temper. He reminded himself that he was here to ask Max for a favor.

"Listen to me," he said. "I've looked everywhere. I've eliminated the possible causes and agents inside the human body. Whatever this is, it's in your serum. I've done what I can from the results. I cannot go forward without a sample. I need the liquid, Max."

"You can't have it," he said flatly.

"I want to talk to Simon about this."

"You think he'll give you a different answer?"

"He said anything I wanted—"

"Except that," Max shot back. "You just started working for us, and you want a sample of the greatest medical breakthrough in history?"

"You think I'm going to steal it?"

Max smiled at him. "I believe people are fallible. No one is above temptation. No one knows that better than Simon. That's why there are rules. You were given the rules. I'm not going to break them for you."

"Let's ask Simon, then."

"Well, unfortunately, he's out of town."

"They don't have phones where he is?"

"I'm sure they do, but it's hard to hear when you've got your head between someone's thighs. Probably difficult to speak clearly, too."

The whole time they'd been talking, Max had been staring at his computer screen and occasionally tapping his keyboard. David assumed Max was checking his email. Now he shifted in his seat and got a good look at Max's monitor.

It was running a screen saver. Max wasn't even playing a video game.

David's fists clenched. He stood. It was probably a good idea to end a meeting before you punched your immediate superior in the face. "Great. Well, then you're paying me a lot of money to waste all of our time."

Max finally looked away from his computer. He seemed to relent a little bit. "I'll pass on the message. In the meantime, you keep trying."

"I need that sample," David said. "Without it, I'm just running in place."

Max went back to pretending to check his email. He spoke without looking up. "You're a smart guy, David," he said. "I'm sure you'll figure something out."

AFTER THE WHORE LEFT, Max sat alone in his darkened apartment, thinking about his meeting with David that morning.

The lights around the bay looked like a small galaxy from the patio of his high-rise apartment. He didn't really see them on a conscious level anymore. Instead, he noticed the streaks on the glass of his floor-to-ceiling windows, the layer of dust on everything in the apartment, despite the money he paid to a white-glove cleaning service to visit twice a week. He ran his finger over the stereo, which he'd bought only six months before. Like the one it replaced, he'd never even switched it on. He didn't really care for music.

So much of his life was like that: repetitive maintenance, time and money spent keeping up appearances, the constant polishing of his disguise.

Even the whore tonight had been something barely felt, a response to a small tug of lust, a minor itch easily scratched.

Max tried to remember when he last actually felt something deeply, but abandoned the effort after a moment. Simon needed to be told his latest savior was failing.

He picked up his phone from the side table, struggled to remember how to work the damned thing, and then pressed the button. It was not actually a button, of course. It was a mirage, a trick of light on glass. There was a time he would have thought something like this was witchcraft. Now he simply found it infuriating. He hated these toys. He and the others could barely work them. They were one of the things that made him feel truly old.

He tried to put his irritation aside as Simon answered, after the usual delay. Simon wasn't good at working his phone, either.

"What?"

"Where are you?"

"Beijing," Simon said. "Some of our creditors here are a bit nervous about parking any more dollars with us."

"I don't blame them."

There was a deep sigh over the line. "Max, I hope you have more important things for me than your attempts at humor."

"It's David. He's requesting a sample of the pure, undiluted Water. Again."

Simon hesitated. "I'd hoped he would make more headway with what we'd given him. Tell him to work harder."

"He works fourteen hours a day."

"What's he doing with the other ten?"

"Nothing that we don't know about. I have one of our security contractors shadowing him at all times. He works, and he goes home, and he runs. He talks to no one outside the labs. Oh, he does do some volunteer work."

"Where?"

"All Children's Hospital. He reads to the sick children. I suspect it's his way of being with his dead sister again. Aside from that, all he does is work. He's quite obsessed."

"And that's why he is the one who will find the answer. He views death as a personal enemy. He will deliver a solution for us. I am sure of it."

"I know you believe that."

"You don't like him, do you?"

"Quite the contrary. He is decent and responsible and moral. And that's the problem. I worry he might actually believe in something greater than his own needs. A man with principles is dangerous."

"Fortunately, there aren't many of them."

"This isn't a joke, Simon. What happens if he does find the answer? Do you plan to take another member into the Council?"

Another pause. "I haven't decided."

After all these years together, Simon still thought he could get a lie past Max. Max smiled.

"What are you doing, Simon? What is your plan?"

"The same as always. To save the world. In spite of itself."

"I was talking about your more immediate goals."

"We need him, Max. We need someone more comfortable with this era. We need someone smarter. We need new blood. And most of all, we need a solution. Do you honestly think I chose poorly?"

Max looked at the lights again, and again did not really see them at all.

"I wish I could say yes," he said. "But no. He is brilliant. Truly. He's burned through all the false paths it took the others years to discover. I've done everything I can to stall him. I believe he is right. The answer is in the Water itself. Not in anything it touches. And that is why he's doomed to fail. We cannot give him what he asks. Not without revealing ourselves."

Simon brooded about it for a moment. "We might not have a choice. This is about our survival, after all."

"You're not seriously considering—"

"No, of course not. Give him more time. He will surprise himself. And you."

"May I ask one favor?"

"You know that's a ridiculous question."

"I'm not so sure these days."

"Max. It's late. Ask your favor."

"Please tell me before you extend your offer to David. Before you reveal us to him. He might react badly. As I said, he's more ethical than our previous candidates. He might surprise us badly."

"You're wrong," Simon said flatly. "In the end, all he cares about is solving the problem. That is the only principle he really has. If we give him a way to do that, he will not care about the morality behind the mystery."

"I hope you're right."

"I've gotten us this far, haven't I?" Simon said. "You just need a woman."

"I just had one."

"Have another." Simon hung up.

Max considered throwing the phone against the window, then remembered that meant he'd have to go through the torture of learning to use a new one. He set it back on the side table.

He knew what he needed. More of the Water. He needed to bathe in it, soak in it, let it saturate him and fill him.

They all needed this, but he was the only one who knew it. He wasn't sure when he'd realized it, but it became increasingly obvious with every passing year: they were slowly petrifying, becoming stiff parodies of the people they'd used to be.

Pedro—Max could not call him "Peter" without a bad taste in his mouth—was still a child, desperately fascinated by the latest toys, buying cars and computers and boats and planes and anything else that was shiny and made interesting noises. He still longed for the chance to play war, even though soldiers had been surpassed by drone strikes and cruise missiles. Sebastian had never been a complex man, and time had refined him down to a few points. He was accustomed to being worshipped for his physical beauty, and that was enough. Max sometimes wondered if everyone who was born with such genetic gifts was the same way, if they just accepted the world as it was, because for them it was nothing but pleasant attention. Carlos was hidden away somewhere in South America, a prisoner of his own paranoia. And Aznar—well, Aznar had become even more like himself.

They were all clinging to being human, when they should have been reaching for the next step, evolving into something more.

If a sip of the Water could do so much, what would happen if they drowned in it? What would happen if they gave up the idea of all limits? What would they become then?

Simon wouldn't hear of this. Max tried to tell him, but Simon was content to play his games and dance around the real problems. He was still enamored of the idea that this world was perfectible. He still believed that this gift—all the additional years the Water had given them—was meant to allow him to push the rest of humanity into some kind of order.

That was truly frustrating, for of all of the Council, Simon was—had always been—the most brilliant, the most perceptive. It was maddening that an intellect, a spirit, like his should be so chained by nostalgia.

In their lives, they had already redrawn the maps of the world several times. They'd toppled governments and moved behind the scenes of history. They controlled entire economies of wealth. They were the secret chiefs of the Earth.

And what had they really changed?

Not a damned thing.

There was always an excuse, always an inherent barrier to the changes Simon wanted.

The truth was, people did not want to change.

Take, for instance, their efforts to finally sever their homeland from the inbred and antiquated monarchy that was suffocating it. They'd backed a movement they thought would unite the country and would force it to fulfill its potential, to retake Spain's place as a world power.

But sentimental loyalists, malcontents, and opportunists saw their own chance at power. The ensuing chaos forced them into an alliance with foreign powers who were hell-bent on war with the entire world. It took years to recover from their tactical error in joining with the Axis, and years more to accept the fact that Spain would never again be the empire of their youth.

Since then, every one of their efforts in the world, while profitable, had become tediously predictable to Max. They would plan and strategize, and carefully shift money and influence and people. And inevitably some little bastard would undo all their hard work with greed and incompetence.

It was like trying to play chess with toddlers: every time you set up the board, they knocked all the pieces onto the floor and covered them with snot.

Now Simon thought he'd found someone who'd find an answer. This boy David.

Simon believed if he could find the secret of the Water, then he'd finally be free of all limits. He could force the world to behave by giving the gift of endless years to his followers and punish those who dissented with their natural lifespan. Eventually, the only survivors would be the ones who obeyed.

Max smiled. Because it's worked so well in our little group.

Max wasn't so blinded by hindsight. He could see that the Council was afraid. They were still thinking like men. They didn't know what they would be without their old habits. But he was chained to them, his ability to move forward limited by Simon's stubborn refusal to give up any more of the Water than absolutely necessary.

So his life became a holding pattern.

Simon didn't seem to realize—or perhaps did not

want to realize—that it didn't matter why the Water worked. They had been given a gift. They'd been given a chance to surpass their mere humanity. To pursue anything else was a waste of time.

And despite all appearances, their time was not unlimited.

Max knew what had to be done. He'd known it since before David Robinton was born, in fact. But he'd hoped Simon would wake up.

Now he saw the truth. If Simon believed he could find the secret of the Water—or if, by some miracle, David actually succeeded—it would be more wasted years at best. At worst, it would be the end of their lives, because there was no way they could share the secret and survive.

If they were going to make the leap, if they were going to transcend their humanity, then they had to leave Simon's dreams behind. The world would not tolerate men like them, if it knew they existed. Once the secret was out, their days were numbered, no matter how much of the Water they had.

Simon had to be made to face reality. One way or the other. Yes, they needed a replacement for the Water. But once they had it, they wouldn't need David Robinton anymore.

# CHAPTER 11

DAVID AND SHY were at dinner, even though it was past eight. In this part of Florida, that was late. Most of the restaurant was empty, and the staff stood around, waiting for them to finish.

It didn't help David's mood any. It had been another maddening day in the lab, one false lead after another. After his meeting with Max, it seemed idiotic to run the same pointless tests again. He had never been this stuck before, and he wasn't good at dealing with the frustration. He spent most of the meal in silence, pushing his food around on his plate.

"Is it the food or is it the company?" Shy asked, breaking him out of his reverie.

Shy was usually patient with him when he went off into his own head. But her smile always brought him back to her, in a way that felt like sitting in an airplane as it climbed off the tarmac.

They had been spending almost all of David's free time together. He didn't have much, but she had her own things going on as well, and she didn't press him. For the first time in his life, he found himself making time to see her, actually breaking away from the lab in order to go by her place, or go for a run, or simply share a meal.

She would have him whenever she could—and that went for the sex, too. Shy wasn't about to wait around for their schedules to allow them to sleep in the same bed. He learned this the second time they met, after their first date. She would put her arms around him, or grab his head and pull him in for a hard kiss, and then it was happening, no matter where they were. They would tumble into a bathroom in a five-star restaurant, her legs wrapped around him, her back up against the wall. She bent over on her desk naked in her office and told him to hurry, she had clients arriving soon. On one early-morning run, she grabbed him and pulled him off the path behind a row of hedges, pushing him to the ground. He almost felt like he'd been mugged, but he had trouble wiping the grin off his face for the rest of the day.

David was not a complete idiot. He knew there was an excellent chance that Shy was not a corporate recruiter but a corporate spy, sent by Conquest's competitors. It was entirely possible she was using him.

He could rationalize that by telling himself he was using her, too. That he was being smart and worldly about the whole thing.

But on a deeper level, he knew that was crap.

Something in him sang when she was around.

The pressure he'd always felt behind him, the constant feeling that he had to run to stay ahead, lessened when she was there.

Spy or not, he was surprised to find he didn't really care. He was idiotically happy. And he wanted to hang on to that for as long as he could.

"Such a deep scowl on your face," she said. "Is it that bad?"

"No more than usual," he said.

"Work?"

"Yeah."

"You put too much pressure on yourself, David. It's not like the whole company depends on you. Conquest has a product that deals with this already."

David shook his head. "Revita has problems. Serious problems."

"Really? What kind of problems?"

"Cancer. The FDA has opened an investigation. I told Simon it was going to happen," David said, and then realized he'd just spilled a huge corporate secret. He looked around, suddenly glad that they were the only people in the restaurant. "Um. Please don't repeat that. It's not public knowledge."

Shy waved it off. "Who am I going to tell? Anyway, that's not the point. You shouldn't feel so responsible."

"That is the point," David shot back. The anxiety balled up in his chest. "I *am* responsible. This is what I've always wanted to do. This is my life's work. And now that I have the chance to make it happen, I honestly don't know if I can pull it off."

It was the first time he'd ever said it out loud. The first time he'd ever considered it, really. He was used to solving the problem, used to success, used to winning. And it wasn't happening this time. He could hardly believe he was saying it to Shy. He trusted her, he realized suddenly. More than lust or love, he had faith in her.

Her reaction, however, wasn't what he expected.

"Maybe you shouldn't," she said while casually scooping a bite of the tiramisu into her perfect mouth.

"What?"

"Maybe this is so hard because what you're doing was never meant to be done," she said.

David was actually rendered speechless for a moment. Old-fashioned terms like "flabbergasted" and "struck dumb" bounced around his skull for a moment, while he tried to come up with an answer.

All he could say was "Are you serious?"

Shy gave him The Look, which once again made him feel like he was in junior high and she was the senior prom queen. Of course. She was always serious.

But David felt like he was on pretty solid ground here, for a change. This wasn't about which restaurant to go to or what color tie to wear. This was his life's work.

"I don't think you understand," he finally said. "I'm talking about an end to suffering. An end to senility, to pain, to loss . . ."

"To death," Shy said. "Yes. I understand. I don't think you do."

Now David started to get angry. "Right. Because I've only spent a decade working on DNA, cell structure, and senescence. How could I possibly understand?"

Her face remained calm. "Sarcasm is a waste of time, David. Say what you mean. You think you understand the problem better because you think you're smarter than me."

"I didn't say that."

"No, but you meant it. And maybe you are."

Damned right I am, David thought. Three Harvard degrees beats a corporate recruiter in Florida.

"But I don't think you've ever considered the larger implications of what you've been seeking all this time. You've attacked the problem without knowing what, exactly, you're solving. Answer me this: what happens if you succeed?"

"I'm talking about giving people back their health. No more cancers. No more heart disease. No more random, pointless illnesses. All the stupid, preventable things that happen to our bodies, all the little twists in our DNA that evolution hasn't gotten around to fixing yet. How is that a bad thing?"

"You're going to keep people alive."

"Yes."

"Forever?" Shy asked.

"Of course not. Don't be ridiculous."

"Are you sure? Isn't that what you're offering with this? A way out of the rules? A way to cheat death?"

"There are no rules," David said. "There's what we can do, and what we can't. That's all. And I'm saying that I can do this. I know it's possible."

"And I'm just saying, again, that because it's possible doesn't mean it's right. There are limits on what we do. What happens to the population when all those people start living longer? What happens to the planet if they keep on consuming resources indefinitely? More important, what happens to them? What will it do to their souls? Did you ever consider that maybe we only live a certain amount of time for a reason? That maybe death is a part of life?"

David resisted saying something about New Age bullshit. But just barely. His voice was tight when he said, "Talk to me when you've lost someone close to you."

Shy reached across the table, her eyes full of sympathy. She touched his cheek. He tried not to flinch. He was furious, and she seemed completely calm. It made him even angrier.

"We all lose someone eventually."

David grabbed her hand, too quickly. He saw a brief flash of surprise—maybe even pain—in her eyes, and immediately regretted it. But he was still angry. Shy was too perfect, too unscarred, too young, to know exactly what was at stake here.

He stood up and opened his wallet, throwing some bills on the table.

Shy remained seated. "Are you leaving?" she asked.

"We're both leaving," he said. "I want you to meet someone."

WHEN THEY ENTERED THE hospital, the aging security guard at the reception desk didn't even make them sign in. He smiled and waved at David. "Good to see you again, son," he said.

Shy looked at David, a little amused, a little perplexed. "You come here often?"

They were in the lobby of All Children's Hospital. David was still angry at her. He muttered something in return.

Shy kept her face calm, because she knew that if she smiled at him, he'd think he was being mocked. He was so very serious.

She let him lead her to the elevator.

They got out on the seventh floor, in the Pediatric Cancer Center.

Again, the nurses and doctors all waved at him. One pretty nurse, a blonde, gave her a sharp look before turning a radiant smile on David. "We haven't seen you for a while, David. I wondered if you'd forgotten us."

He gave her a distracted smile back. "Busy at work, that's all. Is she up?"

The nurse rolled her eyes. "Constantly."

"Okay if we head on back?"

"She'll be delighted to see you." With another unfriendly look at Shy, the nurse turned and went on her way.

David led her down another corridor, to a patient's room. Shy felt an artificial wind as he opened another set of doors. The area maintained a negative-pressure environment, to keep germs and other contaminants out.

Shy was unprepared for the pain seeping from the rooms as they passed. Through the open doors, she got glimpses of the patients and heard snatches of the cartoons on their TV sets. Their parents sat in chairs by the beds, doing their best to smile, to put on their bravest faces.

What was worse were the kids themselves, most

not yet ten years old. They had been scalded down to pale echoes of themselves by the toxic soup of chemicals pumped into their bodies in an effort to kill their diseases. They were bald and hollow eyed and thin, their skin pale and translucent.

Almost all of them were doing the same thing: smiling in an attempt to reassure their parents, to look brave.

It reminded her that she did not have any monopoly on pain. But life was pain, she knew. She didn't need a reminder of that, if that's what David was trying to do.

David knocked on an open door. A young female voice answered.

"No," she said. "No more blood today! Vampires! Go suck on someone else!"

David laughed, and she saw the anger evaporate from him. He moved aside the curtain around the patient's bed and revealed a young girl, maybe nine or eleven years old. It was hard to tell because of the shrinking effect of the chemotherapy.

But her smile and eyes shone, and she wore a multicolored scarf over her bald head, along with insanely bright Powerpuff Girls pajamas.

"David!" she squealed. She couldn't quite rise up. Her IV tethered her to the bed.

David came to her and leaned in for a hug.

Over his shoulder, the girl's eyes locked onto Shy.

"Oh, you finally got a girlfriend. About time, loser."

She punched him, surprisingly hard, in the arm as he pulled away.

"Ow," David said. "What was that for?"

"I haven't seen you in a week. Don't you know that my time is limited?"

His smile vanished. "Don't talk like that."

"Wimp," she said, dismissing him instantly and turning to Shy. "Hi. I'm Elizabeth. David's apparently too rude to introduce us."

"I'm Shy," she said, and shook hands. The girl's fingers were like a bundle of straws and radiated a fever heat. She was right, whether she knew it or not. She did not have much time left. Shy could feel it.

David tried to smile and reclaim some good cheer. "I wanted you two to meet," he said. "Shy didn't know I volunteered here."

"Yeah. When you can spare the time," Elizabeth said sourly.

"Work has been busy. But you're right. That's no excuse. I'll make more of an effort."

She made a face. "I'm only teasing." She turned to Shy again. "So. Is he a good boyfriend? Does he take you nice places? Has he asked you to marry him?"

"Elizabeth."

Shy laughed. "It's all right, David. Yes, he's a good boyfriend. We don't go out much."

"Oooooh," Elizabeth said.

David flushed a little bit red.

"And no, he hasn't asked me to marry him. It's still very early for that."

"Has he bought you anything yet?"

"No."

"Ha! He's bought me stuff."

She pointed to a stack of books on the bedside table. "Mostly books, though."

David looked offended. "What else could you want?"

"How about something pretty, dummy?" she shot back. "Girls like that stuff. Didn't you know?" She gave Shy a look that said, Can you believe this guy? "So, how did you two meet?"

"Through work, sort of," David said.

"I didn't ask you," Elizabeth said. "Be a dear and go get me a soda, will you?"

"Cancer loves sugar."

"Then a diet soda."

"Pretty sure you're not allowed to have anything but ice chips when you're on the IV."

"Fine," Elizabeth growled. "Ice chips. Don't hurry back."

David squeezed Shy's hand on his way out of the room, his mood softened now.

"He's cute, isn't he?" Elizabeth said.

Shy laughed. "How old are you?"

"Eleven. I'll be twelve in two months."

Then a shadow passed over her face. As if she were actually considering the chance of seeing her twelfth birthday.

"How do you know David?" Shy asked.

The shadow flitted away and the brightness returned. "He comes by and helps out every now and then. I guess he's a doctor, too, but not a medical doctor. I mean, they don't let him do procedures or needles or anything. But he sits with the kids here when their parents need to get a shower, or something to eat, or sleep. He holds our hands when we puke and brings books and toys and stuff."

"But not enough pretty things."

"I know, right? I'm in here a lot, so we've spent some time together." She looked around, then leaned in, as if imparting a deep secret. "Don't worry. I won't steal him from you. He's too old for me."

"Thank you," she said. "I appreciate that."

Shy laughed again. A chrysalis, she thought. A rosebud, about to bloom and flourish, already showing signs of the magnificence and color she'd display, given just a little more time.

Time she was not, Shy could see already, going to be lucky enough to get.

"So, what do you do?" Elizabeth asked.

"Executive recruiter," she said.

"Oh, a headhunter."

Shy smiled. "Some people call me that."

"Is it fun?"

"It has its moments."

"Sounds boring to me," Elizabeth said. "All that sitting around in offices, talking on the phone. I've spent enough time indoors already in my life."

"So what are you going to do?"

"Aquatic paleontologist."

"I've never heard of that."

"It's because I invented it," Elizabeth said proudly. "I figure there have to be a ton of dinosaur bones we haven't found yet because they're underwater. So I'm going to learn to be a marine biologist and a paleontologist, and set up digs on the ocean floor."

Then she seemed to remember where she was. She looked at the hospital room and her bed and the tubes in her arms. "At least, that's the plan," she said.

There was an awkward silence. Shy didn't know what else to say to the girl.

"It's all right," Elizabeth said. "I know this probably isn't your idea of a fun date."

"I've been on worse."

Elizabeth's eyes lit up again. "Really? Tell me all about it."

"Let's just say I've had some very awful boyfriends in the past."

"Oh, come on. You can't keep me hanging like that."

David returned with the ice chips then, rescuing her.

"Here you go, Your Majesty," he said. "Ice chips. With lemon flavor."

"Aw, he really does care," Elizabeth said. She took the paper cup from David's hand and poured some of the ice into her mouth, crunching it between her teeth.

"You ever want to lose weight, Shy," she said, "let me tell you, there's nothing like the chemo diet."

A pretty, but haggard, young woman entered the room. She stiffened, but then smiled when she saw David.

"Oh, hi, David," she said. "Elizabeth was wondering where you've been."

"Hi, Amber," David said. He introduced Shy to her. She was Elizabeth's mother. She tried to smile and exchange pleasantries, but Shy could see that none of it was really touching her. All of her thoughts were focused on the girl in the bed. She practically hummed with anxiety.

Elizabeth seemed to fade then, too, her energy dimming as if someone had flipped a switch.

"Tired," she said in a croaky voice.

"We're going to go," David said. "I'm sorry for the interruption. I've got a shift coming up this week. I'll be here for sure."

"Right. Sure," Elizabeth said, turning on her side.

"It's the chemo," her mother explained, half apologizing. Whispering: "She doesn't want you to see her, you know . . . throw up."

"Shut up, Mom. Jeez."

David and Shy made their good-byes. Elizabeth barely responded. But on their way out, she found the energy to call after them.

"You'd better buy her something pretty, David," she said. "That is, if you want her to stay your girlfriend."

"I will," he said.

She didn't respond. Her mother waved at them, then went back to stroking her daughter's scalp where there used to be hair.

SOME OF THE ANGER seemed to find its way back to David as they rode down in the elevator. He was stiff and held himself away from her.

They were outside, walking back to the car, before she tried speaking to him.

"She's a lovely girl," Shy offered.

"Yeah. She is. And she's dying. Acute lymphocytic leukemia. Recurrent. There's usually a better than fifty percent chance of a cure, but she's on the other side of the coin flip. This is her fifth round of chemo. It's failing. She's got maybe three more months at the outside."

He was fuming now, frustration and helplessness

curdled to anger, searching for someplace to vent. "So, you tell me again about your larger plan and the balance between life and death. You tell me how that girl deserves to die."

She stopped and took his hands in hers. He did not pull away, but she could see that he wanted to.

"She doesn't," Shy said. "A lot of people don't. But we all have to face it. People are still going to die. There will still be car accidents. People will still fall down stairs. There will still be madmen with guns opening fire on crowds of complete strangers. Little girls will still die, even if you succeed. There will still be evil in the world. Even more of it, in some cases."

David looked baffled. "You think what I'm doing is evil?"

"I don't think you can see the end of the path you're choosing."

"No. You just don't see what I'm trying to do. I don't care about getting rich off a wonder drug. I want to keep people alive. Sure, there will be some rich assholes who try to hoard this for themselves. That's the way with every medical advance. But eventually everyone benefits. It's like vaccination. Or protease inhibitors for AIDS patients. Eventually, everyone will get access."

"You think Conquest will really allow that?"

He took his hands away from hers. "Enough. I'm not arguing this with you anymore. This is pointless, and I have work to do."

"Right," she said. "You have to save the world, after all."

"Look," he said, taking a deep breath, clearly

trying to calm himself. "This is science, not magic. The way this has been going, I may never get an answer. I could spend years on this and never come close to succeeding. And even if I succeed, it doesn't mean the end of death."

"Now you're lying to yourself," Shy said. "I believe you will succeed, if you keep trying. And you know it's going to mean much more than a cure-all for a few diseases. You're doing something unnatural. You're severing a connection between life and death. You're going to give people a way to put off dying for years. Even decades. Or longer."

David looked at her, utterly bewildered.

"How is that a bad thing?"

She gave him a sad smile. "I suspect you're going to find out."

## FROM THE *NEW YORK TIMES* BUSINESS SECTION, PAGE ONE:

### WONDER DRUG UNDER INVESTIGATION BY FDA FOR LINK TO CANCER

Revita, the massively popular antiaging drug from Conquest Biotech, is under investigation by the federal Food and Drug Administration for potentially causing tumors of the spinal cord and brain, the *Times* has learned.

The FDA, through a spokesperson, confirmed Revita was the subject of an active investigation, but declined to comment further. However, sources both within the FDA and close to Conquest gave details about the investigation to the *Times* on condition of anonymity.

Dozens of patients who have used Revita have contracted cancer, the sources said. The drug, which is supposed to encourage healthy cell growth, apparently has damaged the cells' reproductive process in some cases, leading to runaway cell division in nervous system tissue, causing tumors.

The sources within the FDA stressed that these findings are preliminary. But sources close to the company said that Conquest is aware of the complications caused by the drug, and may have even hidden these problems from federal investigators.

If true, these charges would be a massive blow to Conquest's bottom line. Sales of Revita were responsible for 70 percent of Conquest's revenues in the past year.

Legal experts say that this scandal could mean

a class-action lawsuit or worse against the company. "Liability for something like this could be in the billion-dollar range," said Michael Bartlett, a trial attorney specializing in high-stakes liability cases. "If it's true that the company knew the risks but put the drug on the market anyway, they could be looking at enormous punitive damages."

A spokesperson for Conquest declined to comment. Efforts to reach Simon Oliver IV, the company's recently installed chief executive, were unsuccessful.

# CHAPTER 12

DAVID STOOD UNDER the cold spray of his shower. The hot water ran out a while ago. He barely felt it.

He was trying. God knew, he was trying his best. And he was failing. There was no answer in the cells of any of the test subjects. Whatever miracle whipped through them and cleaned them up and rebuilt them, as if they were fresh off an assembly line, did not leave a trace.

At least, not one he could see. He'd tried everything. Computer modeling. Genetic sequencing. Tests for foreign matter. Nuclear resonance imaging.

None of it worked. He found nothing.

Failure.

On his last visit to the hospital, he found Elizabeth had checked in again. He'd had a stupid, desperate hope that he would crack the code of the miracle cure in time to get her into clinical trials.

But he hadn't been fast enough. She was not going to make it. It was a matter of weeks, if not days.

Failure.

Things were even bad between him and Shy. True, he was still seeing her almost every night. In his paranoid moments, he suspected that she was keeping him exhausted to keep him from focusing completely on his work. It was an insane theory, but it would explain the distance that had grown between them since they'd fought.

He looked down into the drain of the shower. He was having a hard time finding the energy to get out, dry off, and head to the lab to fail again.

He noticed something. Hair. More than usual at the drain.

Terrific. On top of everything else, male-pattern baldness. It almost made him laugh. Here he was, trying to cure old age and disease, and he'd have to get a prescription for Propecia himself.

He got out of the shower, toweled off, and began to shave. A scrape and a sting on his chin told him that he'd pushed one too many days out of the razor blade. Either that or his skin was getting thinner, too.

Everything falls apart. Everything ages. Everything dies. Failure.

Of all people, he should have known this was inevitable. Somewhere in his cells, a tipping point had been reached, and the downward slide had begun. Free radicals ricocheting around his body, breaking things up like a drunk in a bar. Mutation erupting in his genes as ultraviolet light and transcription errors piled on top of one another. And the never-ending strain of breathing, eating, and bleeding, every day. We are not built for long-term success, David remembered. Aging was constant and unstoppable, the continual erosion of the body against time. Over time, we are all dead.

Failure.

Wait. *Over time.*

Intuition pulled something together at the back of his mind. It had been there almost since day one. He'd truly witnessed the process of the cure in action only once, when Simon showed him Mueller. But he hadn't seen it at the cellular level.

Since then, he'd spent all his time on tissue samples, cell slices, and DNA markers.

But his tests had all been static—examinations of one moment or a single result. He'd never watched the process in action. He'd never seen how it behaved in the human body, over time.

It couldn't be that simple, could it?

Only one way to find out. But he had to have an actual sample of the original cure. Otherwise it was useless. He had to convince Simon any way he could.

He wiped the shaving cream from his face, got dressed in record time, then ran two red lights on his way to Conquest.

There might be a solution lurking behind all this failure after all.

# CHAPTER 13

DAVID HAD NEVER been on a private jet before, but he suspected he could get used to it very quickly. Instead of being groped by a TSA agent—there was no way on Earth he'd allow one of those radiation-leaking scanners to mess with his genes—he'd walked in his own shoes up a rolling staircase before he sat down in a comfortable leather armchair.

Because this was Simon's plane, of course there was a model-level beautiful stewardess handing out drinks. David had been up all night in the lab, and he felt a buzz behind his eyes after just a few sips.

He put the drink down before they took off.

Aside from the stewardess and the pilots, they were the only ones on board. Simon said this was the only time they'd have to talk.

"Where are we going?" David asked. Nobody

had bothered to tell him the itinerary. His instructions included only the time of departure.

Simon rubbed his eyes. He wore yesterday's clothes and smelled like body spray and club girls. There was a small patch of body glitter stuck to one of his cheeks.

"Washington, D.C.," he said. "See an old friend about this." He took a sheet of paper from a folder on the seat next to him and tossed it over to David.

It was another letter from the FDA, demanding more information for the investigation into possible side effects from Revita.

Simon crunched the ice from his drink between his teeth. "Wish I knew who tipped those bastards off," he said when David had finished reading.

David looked up at him, saw Simon eying him carefully.

"It wasn't me," David said. "But I did warn you. You should have pulled it."

"Saying 'I told you so' is not the way to convince me that you didn't call the *New York Times*."

David shrugged. "Maybe I should have. Those patients wanted a new outlook on life, not cancer."

Simon sighed. "They took their chances. Way down in the small print of the warning label, we put in a clause about everything possible. We included everything from rickets to STDs. We can beat them in court. But it's still a huge pain in my ass. Stock is tanking. Feds are sniffing around. We can't have that. That's why we're headed to Washington now."

"Maybe you can do something for the people who did get cancer. Offer to pay for their care."

Simon laughed. "Yeah. And why don't I just hand over the keys to my Porsche while I'm at it? No. We're going to stall this out in court. Most of those geezers will be in the ground long before it ever goes to trial."

"How humanitarian of you."

Simon scowled at him. "I don't pay you for your legal advice. You're so concerned about these coffin cases, why don't you give me another miracle cure to sell them? Isn't that what we're supposed to talk about? Why don't you have a solution for me yet?"

"I told Max—"

"Max is not here. I am. Tell me."

"I need the original sample. Whatever it is. I've done everything I can with what I've been given, and I'm at a dead end. I have to see the original compound if I'm going to duplicate its effects."

Simon sat with that for a long moment, just looking at David.

"And here I thought you were smart," he finally said.

David felt himself flush a little. "I'm on the right track now. It's a process that has to be observed, in real time. Without getting too technical, I need to see how it works if I'm going to know how it works."

Simon gritted his teeth in what was definitely not a smile. "I told you from the start. I gave you everything else. But I told you, there was only one thing, *one thing*, you couldn't have. And now, of course, you want it."

"You've asked me to re-create a unicorn just from hoofprints. I've come closer than anyone else you've ever had on this. And yes. Now I need more. I'm asking you—no, I'm telling you—I need the original sample. Or we're done."

Simon didn't appear to hear him. He stared at the bottom of his glass for a long time, then looked up again.

"Oh, you're telling me, are you?" Simon said. His voice was different. There was no mocking tone, no trace of the usual twist of irony that usually punctuated every sentence out of Simon's mouth.

"One thing," Simon said. "And now, of course, you have to have it. You goddamn *child*. You think you can make demands of me? If you were as brilliant as you thought you were, we wouldn't be having this conversation. But you're not. You're not the man you think you are. You are simply not on my level. If you were, you wouldn't need to ask me for favors."

David would have replied, but Simon got up and walked to the bedroom in the back of the plane.

"You disappoint me, David," he said. "I expected more from you."

He slammed the door behind him and did not come out until the pilot announced they would be landing soon.

EVEN THOUGH SIMON WAS freshly shaved, showered, and dressed, his mood hadn't improved. He'd communicated to David mostly in grunts since they left the plane.

"Nice suit," David said.

"Piece of crap," Simon shot back. "I've had this one six months and the stitching's already falling out. I've got a Savile Row in my closet that was sewn in 1953, still looks brand-new."

"From your father," David said.

Simon gave him a face. "Right. From my father."

They waited in the lobby of Senator Anthony De la Cruz's office. The senator was "on an important conference call," according to his assistant. This didn't help Simon's attitude, either.

De la Cruz was a rising star. Even David watched enough CNN to know that. He was the fourth member of his family to enter politics: his grandfather had been a state legislator, his father a governor, and his uncle a well-known congressman. But none of them had reached the heights he had. His blandly handsome features, vague ethnicity, and carefully crafted media image made him a valuable property with both parties recruiting the Latino vote.

Even so, he'd barely squeaked into office in the last election. He'd been up against a well-financed and well-liked incumbent, and voters weren't certain they wanted to take a chance on a new guy, no matter how inoffensive and polite he seemed. A last-minute blitz of phone calls trashing his opponent pushed enough voters to pick him.

Looking at him, David would have thought De la Cruz had been elected by a landslide. He practically bounced through the office door to shake Simon's hand. The smile barely dimmed when he offered Simon condolences on the death of his father. "He was quite a guy," De la Cruz said.

"Yeah, he was a prince," Simon said. "Can we take this inside, please?"

They went into De la Cruz's office. It was surprisingly small, but everything about it screamed money: the thick carpet, the richly polished furniture, the butter-smooth leather on the chairs.

The three of them sat down in a conversation area in a corner away from the desk. De la Cruz took a chair under a wall of pictures from his career, a halo made of images of himself.

De la Cruz read through the same FDA letter that Simon had shown to David. He frowned and nodded. Then he put it down on his desk.

"I am sorry for your trouble, Simon. But I'm not sure what you expect me to do."

"It's pretty simple. I want you to make this go away."

De la Cruz looked uncomfortable. "You know I can't do that."

"You're on the Finance Committee. You hold the purse strings for the FDA. I'm pretty sure you can."

Senator De la Cruz ran a hand through his thinning hair and sighed. "I would like to help you, Simon. I really would. But this is going to get into the media. A lot of my constituents are elderly, and they pay attention to things like this. They know all about medications that don't work as promised."

"Not the point," Simon said. "The drug isn't the problem. It's the FDA investigation. We'll pull it. Let the supply work its way through the pipeline, take it back for more testing. But it has to be voluntary."

Another hapless smile from De la Cruz. "Again. I wish we could work out a solution like that. If we'd had the results we wanted the last election, we'd be facing a friendlier FDA. We didn't. It means we've got to work harder, of course. That's why we need contributions from you and your company, to carry on the fight."

Simon stood up and loomed over the senator. He appeared to be struggling to hold himself in check.

"You are not seriously asking for money right now."

"Now? No, of course not. But in 2016, who knows? With a better president, businesses like yours will not be in situations like this."

"You're saying you don't want to risk getting your hands dirty when you've got a possible shot at the Oval Office."

De la Cruz stood up to look Simon directly in the eye.

"I'm saying I am sorry I can't help you. Maybe this is a hit you have to take. The regulatory agencies, you know, they need a scalp now and then."

Simon's face grew even darker. "Don't talk to me about scalps."

De la Cruz smirked. "Simon. Look. I knew your dad. Our families have been very successful together over the years. You'll survive this. And if I do make a run at the White House, well, you know, I won't forget those who were there with me at the start."

Simon stared at him coldly. "That's all you have to say for yourself? After everything I've done for you? That's really how you want to respond to me?"

De la Cruz choked out a laugh. "Look. I owed your dad. Not you. You're not your father, and this isn't *The Godfather*. This is reality. You can't just come in here and dictate—"

Whatever else he was going to say was lost in the sudden contact between Simon's fist and his face.

David was stunned. Simon just punched a U.S. senator. He half rose out of his chair. Simon gave him a warning look and turned back to De la Cruz.

It wasn't a particularly hard punch, but it was enough to rock De la Cruz. He sat down in his office chair and then touched his nose, which started to bleed.

He looked at the blood and then at Simon in a kind of horrible fascination.

"You—you can't—" The senator gulped like a goldfish violently spilled from its bowl. "You've got to be crazy. I'm going to have you arrested—"

Simon raised his fist again, and De la Cruz immediately shut up and covered his head with both arms.

"Jesus, Simon," David blurted out. He couldn't believe he was seeing this.

Simon turned on him, suddenly furious. "You *shut up*," he ordered David. Then he wheeled back on the senator.

De la Cruz peeked out from between his fingers again. Simon unclenched his fist and simply pointed at the senator.

"Don't interrupt me," he warned. "You want to talk about reality, Senator? Then allow me to reintroduce you to reality. I know you've been spending a lot of time on CNN and Fox lately. I know there are a lot of people filling your head with grand plans for the future. And I don't blame you for liking those plans. It's easy to get your head caught up in big dreams.

"But you should never forget your past. My grandfather owned your grandfather. Everything your family has, you owe to me. You think you owe my father? You owe me. I paid for your diapers, whether you know it or not. You are my employee. And when I tell an employee what to do, I expect him to say nothing more complicated than 'Yes, sir.' "

De la Cruz almost spoke up, but a warning look from Simon was all it took to close his mouth again.

"If you're still having trouble with the concept, I'll put it in plain terms. I know about the slush funds, the bundling of contributions, and the PAC money that paid for the last-minute ad blitz that saved your ass in the last election. I have the records. And I also know where the cameras were in your hotel suite in Miami last fall. I know who else was in the room. And, unlike my father, I know people who can have that video up on YouTube in fifteen minutes."

David noticed the senator's face turn very pale against the blood from his nose.

"This is not a negotiation. This is me with your life in my hands, and you begging me to do whatever it takes to keep it safe and undisturbed. And so far you're doing a piss-poor job of convincing me."

De la Cruz looked up, eyes filled with panic. Simon gave him the slightest nod in permission to speak.

"Please," he said. "I'll make it happen. I'll do whatever you want. I'll—"

Simon looked bored again. "You call that begging?"

De la Cruz gave a spastic jerk of his head, and then looked back up at Simon. His expression seemed to ask a question, but he found the answer in Simon's eyes.

Quickly, clumsily, the junior senator from the state of Florida slid out of his chair and kneeled. Then he put his forehead on the carpet in front of Simon's feet and begged.

FOR AT LEAST TWO minutes, they walked through the Capitol halls in silence, the sound of their shoes echoing from the marble walls and floors.

David watched Simon, unbelieving. "What the hell was that?"

"You try to be polite with some people. It never pays," Simon said. His mood had improved dramatically. He seemed almost joyful now that he had the senator's blood on his knuckles.

"No, seriously, Simon, what the hell were you doing in there?"

Simon stopped and looked at David. "He forgot who signs his checks. I reminded him."

David wondered if he should push it, but decided he had to know.

"What did he do in that hotel room?" David asked.

"What?"

"Nobody behaves like that unless they're terrified. He would have kissed your feet if you'd asked him. So what did he do in that hotel room that made him so afraid you'd release the video?"

Simon smirked and took his time answering.

"There are a lot of trade-offs involved in making a better world, David. I've known it for a long time."

"From your father," David said.

Simon gave him a suspicious look. "Yes, from him. But also from watching the way the world works. You have no right to be this naive. You should know better than anyone by now that there are very few people willing to be good on their own. Most of them are scared, selfish, and horny, and they'll step on their own grandmothers' necks to get what they want. That makes our task—yours and mine—more difficult in many ways. But it's better for us in at least one way. Because all those scared, selfish, and horny bastards are predictable. We can use them because we know how they will respond. They will never surprise us with a sudden burst of conscience. And that means that sometimes we have to dip our hands down into the sewer where they live."

"Simon. What did he do?"

"He followed his nature, David. That's all I'm going to tell you. And he will always follow his nature. That's why he's useful. I'm glad you saw this. Now you know: the world doesn't behave unless you force it."

They were outside the Capitol now, walking to the spot where the limo would pick them up. David was considering how to respond when Simon stopped suddenly.

He thought for a moment, then appeared to come to a decision.

"You can have the sample," he said.

He held out his hand for David to shake. David took it. He started to thank Simon—out of polite reflex, if nothing else—when Simon cut him off.

"I expect you to solve the problem. But if you can't, then we're going to have a problem. And I don't think you'll like my solution. Do you understand?"

Simon would not let go of his hand. Even though Simon was smiling, there was a coldness that David had never felt from him before.

It was like meeting a different person, hiding underneath the surface of Simon's party-boy facade. Someone stronger. Older. A purer version of Simon, undiluted by concern with anything but his own agenda. With a shock, David realized that man had been there all along.

For an instant, David reeled as his mind struggled to reject what his intuition was telling him.

Simon still waited for an answer. David didn't know what to say. Then it came to him. He'd already been told his lines.

"Yes, sir," he said. "I understand, sir."

Simon kept his smile and hard grip on David's hand. "Yes," he said after a moment. "Yes, I think you do."

# CHAPTER 14

EVEN WITH THE SAMPLE, it was not easy.

The Water—as David came to think of it—had a slight blue tinge but was otherwise unremarkable. It had no obvious chemical components different from regular $H_2O$. The trace elements and minerals were common to any natural spring water.

He didn't waste time trying to figure out the Water itself. He had less than a cupful. He had to see what the Water would do.

David locked himself in the lab. Shy called. He didn't answer the phone. Max summoned him to his office. David ignored him.

He worked. He went as long as he could without sleep, running every test himself. He didn't trust any of his assistants with a single one. He took his own blood and skin samples and used them for the tests. He monitored the results under a scanning tunneling microscope, watching the chains of molecules dance and twist themselves into new shapes.

And he saw it.

As he'd suspected, it was there in the self-repair sequence, a total reorganization of the base proteins. They rearranged themselves from the usual human chaos into something almost crystalline in their order and perfection. And then they ran up and down the strands of DNA, incredibly, impossibly fast, plucking out imperfections and errors and excising whole sequences of damage and decay.

It took only seconds, but in the aftermath there was an entirely perfected chain of DNA. From this basic set of instructions, all new cells would be rebuilt without junk or cancer or waste. They would be born again, whole and pure.

Now all he had to do was duplicate the process.

FOUR DAYS LATER, DAVID looked at the sample hydrogel, now containing the synthesized DNA repair strands.

The hydrogel was really just a delivery system, mostly purified water contained in a network of polymers at a molecular level. It bonded together in unexpected ways; the self-healing properties of the gel base acted as a kind of catalyst for the proteins, and the molecular structures replicated themselves throughout the liquid. It turned out to be incredibly stable, maintaining integrity and viability at room temperature. It would not require refrigeration or even special handling.

Just like water.

But inside, it was more like a DNA-charged biological machine. It told cells how to rebuild themselves without flaw or disease.

At least, that was what his computer models said.

Out in the real world, David had no idea if it would really work. If he was forced, right now, to give an estimate of his chances of success, he'd say seventy to seventy-five percent. Maybe even eighty percent.

Animal testing would be useless. It was designed only for human DNA. When he'd injected some into a lab mouse, it simply refused to spread through the cells. It was inert.

He considered trying it on himself. Then stopped. He was healthy, near peak physical condition, and he had only a small sample. How would he actually know it had worked? There was nothing to cure in him. It could be a waste of all his time and effort.

He realized he might be scared, too. He tried to tell himself that wasn't entirely selfish. If the hydrogel killed him, there would be no one equipped to carry on his work. He wasn't being arrogant; even with his detailed notes and research material, it would take another researcher enormous leaps to catch up to where David had started.

Ordinarily, this would be the beginning of a long series of tests. He would finally give all those other scientists working for Conquest something to do. There would be lab testing, the publication of a paper in a peer-reviewed journal, a patent application, and then, finally, clinical trials on humans.

That would be the safe, ethical, and completely sane course of action.

Instead, David loaded the sample into a syringe and left the lab.

When he got into his car, he spent a good ten minutes sitting there, trying to talk himself out of what he was going to do. It didn't work.

He started the car and began driving toward All Children's Hospital.

AMBER, ELIZABETH'S MOTHER, WAS dozing in a chair when he arrived. She snapped awake and looked vaguely guilty, as if she could act like some sort of watchdog against her daughter's cancer.

But there was nothing that was going to save Elizabeth. David could tell just by looking at her. She was curled onto her side, burned down to almost nothing by the drugs, bones sharp and pronounced through her pale and papery skin.

"It's good of you to come," Amber said. "She really liked you."

Maybe it was her accidental use of the past tense, or perhaps she was simply too full of misery, but that was all it took before she began sobbing. David hugged her and tried to mouth some comforting words, but he felt like a liar and a fake. Only part of his mind was even conscious of her body in his arms. Instead, he felt the syringe in his jacket pocket, as if it weighed twenty pounds.

He offered to stay by Elizabeth's bedside while Amber went and got something to eat. Amber resisted, of course—he'd known she would—but it took only a little convincing. He'd been in this situation so many times before as a volunteer. The parents needed a little air, a little space, that wasn't infused with so much dread. They needed a minute or two to feel normal and catch their breath before returning to the place where their children were dying.

Amber was no different. There was no mistaking the guilty relief in her eyes when she paused at the door before she left. David had her cell number and promised to call if Elizabeth woke.

She wouldn't. She'd just had her latest hit of pain medication before David arrived. There wouldn't be a nurse around to check on her or draw blood for another hour at least, David guessed.

This was the right thing, he kept telling himself. It was her only chance.

So why did he feel like some kind of predator, hovering over the young girl as if waiting for a chance to cull her from the herd?

There were a hundred ethical reasons not to do this: uninformed consent, human testing, the very real chance it would kill her.

But she was dying. There was no other choice.

David kept telling himself that.

He tried not to think of Mengele and the other butchers who experimented on their victims in the Nazi concentration camps. They said that was for science, to advance the cause of human knowledge, too.

This was different. He was going to save her, not kill her.

At least, he sure hoped so.

He stood and removed the syringe from his coat. It would work. It had to work.

Just before he plunged the needle into her IV,

David froze. His conscience seemed to be screaming at him. What if he was wrong? What if he had made a mistake somewhere along the line?

Then what he'd invented was no cure. It would probably tear through the girl's body like a tank through tissue paper, replicating itself madly. It could unwind her DNA at the cellular level, practically melting her body's organs as it tore apart the protein chains that made up the building blocks of life.

If he'd screwed up, she would die horribly, quickly, and in pain.

He could feel himself at the threshold, like a man standing in the door of an airplane, wearing a chute and preparing to jump. Take this step, and there was no going back.

He had to wonder if he was doing this to save her or because he simply had to have an answer, one way or another. If he simply needed to solve the puzzle that badly.

Are you really willing to do this? he asked himself. Are you willing to sacrifice another human being for your own reasons?

He looked down at Elizabeth. She was still and fragile.

No. He would not sacrifice her.

He would *save* her.

He pressed down on the plunger and sent his sample into the tube leading directly into her veins.

He heard someone at the door just in time. He slipped the syringe back into his pocket while keeping the motion hidden with his body.

Amber had returned.

"I forgot my purse," she said. "Got all the way to the cafeteria before I . . ." She looked at him strangely. "What are you doing, David?"

"I thought the IV might be clogging," he said. He was both amazed and horrified how quickly and easily the lie came to him. But something must have shown in his face, because Amber was suddenly wary.

"Was that something in your hand?"

"No," David said, too fast.

She stepped closer to him, eyes narrowed. David wasn't sure what she was going to say.

They both jumped as the alarms on all of Elizabeth's monitors went off at once.

The machines screamed in electric panic. Her heart rate shot up to 176. Her blood pressure skyrocketed. Elizabeth's body began jerking violently.

Amber's eyes went wide and locked on David. "What did you do?" she demanded. "What did you do?"

She screamed the question at him as nurses and then a doctor ran into the room. They pushed both David and Amber back to get at the girl. David positioned himself at the foot of the bed. He wanted to see. He had to see.

Amber kept yelling at him. The nurses, as busy as they were, looked at them both, wondering what the hell was going on.

The doctor was too busy. "Get me Ativan," she said. "The girl's seizing."

"What did you do?" Amber yelled again, and this time she hit him, hard, aiming for his face. He turned in time to catch it on the shoulder.

God, he thought. What did I do?

Then, suddenly, the machines stopped wailing. "Wait," the doctor snapped at a nurse, just before she put a needle of drugs into the girl.

It was like the electric current going through the room was cut off. The frenzied motion, the tense commands, they all went silent. Everyone watched.

The monitors told the story in quiet pings and blips across their screens. Elizabeth's pulse, blood pressure, and breathing all returned to normal.

And Elizabeth blinked slowly, and sat up.

She looked around at all of them gathered by her bed. "Mom?" she said uncertainly.

Amber pushed past the medical staff and put her arms around her daughter.

The doctor was still looking at the machines, baffled.

David didn't move. He didn't even want to breathe, for fear of breaking the sudden peace and sending the room into chaos again.

"Honey," Amber said. "Elizabeth, sweetie, are you okay?"

Elizabeth blinked more rapidly, still confused. "Yeah," she said.

Amber started crying.

"Mom," Elizabeth said, drawing out the word as only an embarrassed daughter could. "What are you doing? I'm fine."

"Elizabeth. How do you feel?" the doctor asked.

For a moment, Elizabeth said nothing. Then she smiled over her mother's shoulder.

"Honestly," she said. "I feel *great*."

DAVID WAS EVENTUALLY HUSTLED out of the hospital room, as more and more doctors and staff began to crowd inside. He hung around long enough to overhear one of the nurses use the term "miracle" before she was shushed.

As he left, Elizabeth said, in a strong, clear voice, "Really, I feel *fine*."

He went back to his car and looked at his hands. They were shaking slightly as the depth of what he had done began to sink in. It was past midnight by now. He put his hands on the wheel, and they stopped shaking.

He went back to work.

IN THE LAB AT Conquest, he engaged in busywork—the soothing kind of pointless cleanup and straightening that usually came after he was finished with any big project. He organized his notes, backed up his data, and even cleaned the gunk out of the DNA synthesizer. Sometime in the early-morning hours, he went to the atrium at Conquest's entrance and found a chair. The night sky was clear through the giant glass windows. He was too keyed up to sleep, despite his exhaustion. He stayed there, almost motionless, for hours, just thinking.

He talked to Amber shortly before 3:00 A.M. She apologized for the late hour, apologized for striking him, apologized for everything, really.

"I don't know what I was thinking," she said over and over. He told her not to worry about it. Stress, exhaustion, and the natural instinct of a mother to protect her child—it all came together.

"Yes, but to think you were hurting her, I must have been insane," she said.

No, you weren't, he thought. But he didn't correct her. He could hear the release of so much weight in her voice, the joy of actual hope returning.

"The doctors are saying something about total spontaneous remission. Have you ever heard of that?" she asked.

Yes, he had. It was incredibly rare. But it happened sometimes.

"It's like a miracle," she said.

Yes, it was.

She hung up. Elizabeth was cured. There would be more work to do, of course. But David was sure of it. Even without access to her charts or blood samples, he could see it. It was the same glow of life and health that Mueller had suddenly exhibited after receiving Simon's cure.

When the sun began to rise above the horizon, he decided it was time.

Time to change the world.

He took his phone out of his pocket and made the call.

Simon's voice was thick with sleep. "What is it?" he demanded.

"I think you'd better come to work today," David said. "I did it."

# CHAPTER 15

SIMON WAS LITERALLY dancing in his office. On top of his desk.

"Come on, David," he said. "This is worth a little victory celebration."

David just watched. "Seems a little premature to me." He held up the invitation that had been in his company mailbox when he arrived that morning. "We're not even in clinical trials yet, and you're having a party?"

The invite was beautiful: thick embossed paper, trimmed with gold, asking the recipient to attend Conquest Biotech's "latest breakthrough on the frontiers of medicine." There had been a press release emailed companywide that morning as well.

Simon gave David a scolding look and kept on dancing. "Are you worried your discovery isn't going to hold up?"

"No, but—"

"There you go. You know it works, and I know it works. We need the stock jump and the good news after the Revita mess. So what's the problem?"

Simon had already tested David's formula. Personally. He'd taken the next available sample of the hydrogel and, before David could stop him, drank it down in a single gulp. For a split second, David had worried he'd just killed his boss. But then Simon had sucked in a deep breath and said, "Oh yeah. That's the stuff."

A battery of tests on Simon confirmed it. As young as Simon was, he'd done a lot of hard living. But all the damage to his liver and pancreas was healed in an instant. David even saw regrowth of hair and the disappearance of a few tiny crow's-feet around Simon's eyes.

That was all the proof Simon needed. So he was throwing a party. Perfectly in character, David figured.

But something kept nagging at him. That was why he was here; it wasn't just the party. Something had occurred to him, late at night, while Shy slept beside him. Now he had to know if he was right.

David took a small vial from his pocket and tossed it to Simon. Simon caught it one-handed without missing a beat.

"What's this?"

"What's left of the original sample of the Water. I don't need it anymore."

"You call it the Water?"

"Yeah. Seemed like the most fitting name. Why?"

Simon smiled like he'd just heard a dirty joke. "No reason. You should hang on to this. Like a souvenir."

"I don't need it. My formula works, remember? And I'm healthy enough. I don't need to use either of them."

"You're going to be in a minority in a very short while, then," Simon said. "Once we hit the market with this, people are going to pay any price for it. Youth in a bottle. Perfect health, available with a prescription. Ask your doctor about it today. That reminds me, I've got to get marketing on the line about names for this. What do you think? Genesis? Too biblical? Well. Whatever we call it, people are going to mortgage their children to pay for this stuff, David."

"No. No, they're not."

Simon stopped dancing. "Excuse me?"

David took a deep breath. Then he asked the question. "How long have you been using the Water yourself, Simon?"

Simon stopped cold. The smile, the dancing, every piece of the happy-little-party-animal act he liked to display to the world—it all froze up like a defective ride at Disneyland.

David could practically see the calculations running behind Simon's eyes, weighing the chances of effectively denying it, of lying his way out of this.

Evidently, the odds weren't good. Simon hopped down from the desk and straightened up, ironing the slouch out of his shoulders and the smirk off his face. He relaxed and seemed, in an instant, a more solemn and impressive man.

"I suppose I should have realized you would work it out," he said. Even his voice had dropped half an octave. "I must be getting complacent in my old age."

"Just how old is that?"

Simon smiled. "More than you need to know right now, David. But yes. I have been using the Water for some time now."

"The others, too. Max, Peter, Sebastian?"

"Of course. How long have you known?"

"I'm actually a little ashamed it took me this long to figure it out," David said. "All those comments about your father. But I thought because the Water was scarce, it would be too valuable to waste without a viable replacement. That's backward. The reason it's scarce is because you've been using it. And when you began to run out, that's when you came to me for a replacement. Isn't that right?"

"More or less. Don't feel bad, though. Only a few people have guessed before you did."

"I still should have seen it. Of course you've been using the Water yourself. Who wouldn't want to be young and healthy all the time?"

"Better than Viagra and Rogaine combined," Simon agreed. "The question now is, what do you intend to do about it?"

David took a deep breath. Now or never.

"Everyone gets the cure," he said. "Everyone. When it's ready and cleared for market, you agree to make my discovery available on a discounted basis, worldwide."

"You're serious."

David nodded.

"Such an idealist. What if I say no? What then?"

"I'm the only one who knows how my cure works. If you want it, you'll do what I say. Or you can age, just like the rest of us. How old are you, anyway, Simon?"

"How old do you think?"

David shrugged. It had never really occurred to him to guess. He didn't care that much. "I don't know. A hundred?"

"Interesting guess. Why a hundred?"

"I don't know," David admitted. "I guess it's because you're still so good at being childish. I figure if you were much older, you'd have grown up a little more."

Simon's smile went cold. "That's one perspective," he said, then changed the subject. "What if I take you to court? You've got a contract."

"Go ahead. The courts are slow. How long can you wait without my cure?"

"I could do considerably worse than sue you. I'm sure it hasn't escaped your attention that I have a lot of men with guns around here."

"You can't risk hurting me. If I die, you die. Eventually."

The tension between the two of them stretched and sang for a long moment.

Then Simon laughed. "You really believe you've got this all figured out."

David couldn't be sure if Simon was mocking him or not. He decided it didn't matter. "Well, not to brag, but I am a pretty smart guy."

"All right," Simon said. "I'll do it. On one condition. You sign away any rights you have to profit from your work."

Now it was David's turn to freeze up. "What?"

"Ah, there it is," Simon said. "I'm offering you exactly what you want. But you have to return the house, the car, everything we bought you. And whatever meager profits we get after curing the world remain ours alone. Nothing for you. Are you willing to pay the price for your ideals, David?"

David hesitated for only a second longer. Simon had just threatened his life, after all. He handled that. He could handle being poor again.

"Fine," he said. "Draw up whatever papers you need. I'll give up my profits as long as everyone gets a fair shot at this. Maybe you were just looking for a way for you and your friends to keep living like young morons for many more years to come. You might have been bullshitting me about saving the world. But you're going to do it anyway. I'm going to make sure of it."

Simon spoke slowly, as though to an idiot or a child. "David. You are giving up literally billions of dollars."

"In the end, more people are going to live. That's enough for me."

"And what about our little secret?"

David shrugged. "You mean the fact that you took something amazing, something that could have benefited humanity, and used it selfishly, kept it hidden, and exploited it? That's going to have to be between you and your conscience. Who'd even believe me if I told them? Simon, you're going to mass-produce a cure for almost all disease in the world. I can live with whatever it's taken you to get here."

"You seem fairly sure about that."

"I can live with it. I'm sure."

Simon shook his head in disbelief. "All right. I'll make your deal. The cure will be made available to all. And you will not see a penny of it. You get to be a saint. I promise."

"I'm not interested in sainthood, Simon. I just want to do the right thing."

Simon looked at him. "Yes," he said. "I believe you do."

David had heard that before. He turned to go.

Simon stopped him.

"David, for the party: you might want to buy a new suit. You're not poor yet."

# CHAPTER 16

At this moment, Max was experiencing a peculiar, singing pain behind his eyes; a tight, gritty texture inside his skull that he could not quite place.

Then it came to him: he had a headache.

He tried to remember the last time this had happened, and could not. Decades, at least.

This disturbed him for a number of reasons. It meant that either the Water was becoming less effective or his present troubles were serious enough to tear through the usual wrapping of perfect health he'd come to expect. He found that the more he thought about either possibility, the worse the headache became.

Jesus Christ, he thought. Imagine living like this all the time.

He sat alone in a cheap coffeehouse, a desperate attempt to cash in on the absence of any Starbucks in a six-block radius, located in a dying strip mall. The bored teenager behind the counter watched the screen of her phone and nothing else. He was the only customer. In fact, his was the only car in the entire parking lot. This was as close to being invisible as Max could come.

Then another man entered. He didn't look like much. The only unusual thing about him was the tip of his nose. It was bright red, the skin tender and raw, as if it had just come out from under scar tissue. But that wasn't terribly unusual in Florida, where people had skin cancers and plastic surgery in about equal measure.

The girl behind the counter didn't look twice.

The man got a huge, frothy, whipped-cream-covered drink and walked directly over to Max, then sat down next to him. The girl went back to her phone.

They sat in silence for a few moments and drank.

Max spoke first. "Took you long enough to get here."

"The bitch nearly killed me," Aznar snapped back. "If you wanted me on my feet, you should have sent more Water."

"Simon's being stingy these days."

"When is he not?" Aznar sucked from his straw and gave a huge sigh of pleasure. "I tell you, the Frappuccino might just be mankind's crowning achievement."

"Not the smallpox vaccine? Or penicillin? Or the atomic bomb?"

"Overrated. Well, except for the bomb. That, at

least, is useful. In fact, it's the one that's been used the least, and should be used more."

Max smiled. Aznar was the only one of them whose sense of humor had improved in the past five hundred years.

Except he wasn't really joking, of course. Aznar was never really joking. It was important to remember that.

It had been this way between them since Berlin. Unlike Carlos, Max had never thought of it as a matter of honor between the original holders of the covenant. He simply had not seen the logic in removing a useful and effective player from their game.

Aznar had never particularly liked Max, but he was not so nihilistic that he was willing to throw away his long life over a matter of personal distaste. So, over the past sixty-odd years, they had formed a comfortable working relationship.

Max used Aznar to clean up the Council's messes. He sent Aznar to war zones where his work would be lost in the background noise of atrocities and corpses. He disappeared problems like stubborn labor leaders in Chile, an outspoken priest in El Salvador, a reluctant colonel in Nicaragua, a brilliant militia leader in Chechnya. In return, Max gave Aznar the Water, and he overlooked Aznar's more vicious hobbies.

Neither of them went into it with any illusions of friendship or affection. Max was Aznar's boss. He gave orders, and Aznar followed them, or he was truly dead.

Aznar sighed and finished his drink. "Tell me

what you want," he said. He rubbed his eyes. Perhaps he was having headaches, too. His supply of the Water was irregular at best. It had to be, to avoid Simon discovering the siphoning from their very limited personal supplies. Max's emergency flask was only half-full now. And Antonio had stopped contributing to the flow. Max wondered if this constant back-and-forth, aging and then being made young again, bouncing across the years, had contributed to Aznar's madness.

Ultimately, however, it didn't matter. Aznar was a weapon. Max pulled the trigger.

"Robinton," Max said. "He's going to be a problem."

"Can you afford to lose him already?"

"Not immediately, no," Max admitted. "But soon. He says he's cracked the secret of the Water. He will have to transcribe all his research. Put together patent applications and create a design that others can follow. Once that is done, Simon will want to extend a place at the table to him. Reveal the whole truth."

"And you would never want another man coming between you and Simon," Aznar said.

Max ignored Aznar's insult. "Even with an unlimited supply of the Water, the world is still too small for too many like us. But for now, he's safe. We need him to complete his work."

Aznar grunted agreement. "So, what do you want from me?"

Max opened his suit jacket, extracted a piece of paper from his pocket, and handed it to Aznar.

Aznar unfolded it and saw the headline: "MIRACLE" GIRL SUDDENLY CURED OF CANCER.

Aznar read it and frowned. "And I keep hearing newspapers are dying."

"Everything is dying. Except us."

"True enough. How did you hear about this?"

"I have an assistant who searches for things like 'miracle cures.'"

"You have someone who does nothing but read, looking for stories like this?" Aznar seemed shocked, his old piousness emerging at the sheer luxury and waste of resources.

"She does it with a computer. It's something called a Google search."

"Computers," Aznar said suspiciously. "Did they also tell you that Robinton was connected to this? I don't see his name anywhere."

"He volunteers at that hospital. He's quite sentimental about such things. But he's also quite obsessed with his work. I suspect he had to know if his solution would work before he would take it to Simon. If that's true, then this girl's veins contain traces that will lead back to us. It's not a risk I am willing to take. I want you to deal with it."

Aznar looked at the printout again. There was a photo of the "miracle girl." Even in grainy black-and-white on standard office paper, her smile beamed.

"Max," he said, suddenly cheerful. "For me? And it's not even my birthday."

"EXCUSE ME, BUT WHERE can I find Elizabeth Saunders?"

Anjelica Reeves, the nurse at the duty station at All Children's Pediatric Cancer Center, was immediately suspicious. The man asking the question wore a white coat and a smile that reminded her of clowns and party magicians. She couldn't see a name badge, either. There had been several reporters—she wouldn't call them journalists—who had tried to sneak in and interview Elizabeth since the "miracle cure" story broke. She personally wanted to wring the necks of the idiots in the public relations department who told the media. The little girl needed rest and privacy more than the evening news needed a feel-good story.

Of course, no one ever asked her.

Anjelica gave the man in the white coat a fake smile right back. "I'm sorry, sir, I'll need to see your ID badge before I can give you that information."

He showed her a badge. She had to admit, it looked legit. Still, she'd never seen the guy before, and he wasn't about to go tromping around on her floor without a little more than that.

"Can I ask why you want to see the patient, Dr. Cortés?"

The smile didn't waver. "I've been asked to do a consult."

That, at least, made a little sense. Every department in the hospital wanted a piece of Elizabeth—quite literally. They'd all sent representatives to get tissue and blood samples in an effort to learn how she'd managed to avoid dying. If her spontaneous remission from leukemia could be duplicated, then being anywhere in the same zip code as the answer could be a massive career boost.

"Does it have to be right now? She's sleeping."

His smile tightened. "Well. Now is when I'm here."

She picked up the phone. "At least let me call ahead."

"Oh, that's really not necessary."

Anjelica put an edge in her voice. "It's no trouble at all."

His face became as inflexible as a doll's sculpted features. "I don't have time for this," he said. "Tell me which room."

Anjelica felt a small, guilty pleasure. She'd get to send this guy packing, and she could protect the girl's sleep for a few hours. She might get chewed out for it, but it would be worth it.

"I don't have to tell you a thing, Doctor, and furthermore—"

His eyes looked up and to the left. The smile returned. "Oh," he said. "Never mind."

She looked to the side and saw that he'd finally noticed the patients' names and room numbers on the whiteboard. Well, she'd tried.

She reached across the desk for the phone. She wanted, at least, to give the girl some warning.

Something sliced through the air. She felt a deep burn across the top of her throat.

It quickly became painful, then intolerable. She tried to scream but couldn't breathe.

She looked up and saw the arrogant doctor grinning down at her, the bloody scalpel still in his hand.

Then everything went dark as she watched him turn and walk down the corridor toward Elizabeth's room.

"—KEEP TELLING YOU, I want to go home." Aznar heard her voice from around the corner. It was the unmistakable whine of a young girl, a sound that had always put Aznar on edge.

"Honey, the doctors just want to do a few more tests," an older woman's voice answered. So the girl's mother was in the room, too. That didn't present a problem to Aznar. He played his thumb over the blade of the scalpel with just enough pressure to keep from cutting his own flesh. He could be in and out in seconds, before either of them had a chance to scream.

He only had to get close enough.

He went into the room smiling, the hand with the scalpel concealed in his white coat.

"Good evening, ladies," he said. "Or should I say morning? It's well past your bedtime."

The girl didn't laugh. "What do you want?" she snapped.

"Elizabeth," her mother scolded, her voice sharp. "Sorry, Doctor. She's had a rough few days."

"No problem," Aznar said, smile fixed in place. "I understand. All these tests and procedures, they can get pretty boring, I bet."

Elizabeth wouldn't look at him, her face in full-on sulk. "Yeah. So why don't you stop doing them?"

"Well, your suffering is almost at an end," Aznar said. He took a step toward the bed, within arm's reach of the mother and girl both. "There's just one more thing I've got to do . . ."

The girl suddenly lost her sulk and stared at him. "Is that blood on your coat?"

Aznar looked down and cursed himself. Of course

it was blood. The sow behind the counter had splattered down the front of him.

He kept trying to smile. "Yes," he said. "A bad experience with a patient. Nothing to worry about."

The girl shrank away from him. The mother did, too. It didn't seem like anything conscious. But why, why, *why* did they always do that?

"What sort of tests are you here to do?" the mother asked sharply.

The hell with this. He brought out the scalpel.

The girl opened her mouth to scream. Her mother sucked in a deep breath.

Aznar felt his face stretch in a wide grin.

Then the lights went out. Aznar froze despite himself as the room went black.

Something—someone—hit him hard at the base of his spine. It felt like a kick from a horse, and it sent him tumbling over the end of the bed. He didn't stop moving until he hit the wall beneath the room's window.

The only light came from the screens of the girl's medical equipment and the hallway. He saw the outlines of the girl and her mother, and another shadow coming at him fast—

Another kick, this time aimed for his skull. He managed to deflect it with his arm, but he lost the scalpel. It hit the tile floor with a ringing noise.

The next kick caught him full in the face, and he heard the snap of his nose—his brand-new nose—breaking even as his head bounced against the wall again.

Enough. Enough of this.

He used both arms to block the next kick he knew

was coming and pushed back, hard, using his own legs to launch himself at his attacker.

He felt her give way, almost fall to the ground, even as he regained his feet, and he started smiling again.

He saw her outline clearly against the light from the hall now. He knew her, knew the way she moved. No mistaking that shape.

Shako.

She was right here. It was too good to be true, she was right here in front of him.

He threw a punch at her head, followed with another, and another, keeping her down and dodging. He suddenly changed tactics and turned, putting his left fist into her stomach, a devastating uppercut that lifted her off her feet.

He heard her grunt in pain and spun to grab the scalpel. It shone in the reflected light only a few feet away. He bent over and picked it up.

Only when he turned back did he realize he'd been played. The shadows of the girl and her mother appeared before the door as they ran out of the room. Shako was moving them along, her body shielding them from him.

A fire alarm went off. Flashing emergency lights. Someone must have found the corpse he'd left at the desk now. A voice was yelling over the PA system, but he couldn't make out what it said.

Damn her, she had robbed him of his prey.

He could feel his options closing by the second. There would be security and then police skittering through the building like ants when their hill was disturbed. He might have to take a hostage, one of the little sick brats on this floor, just to get to the door.

But first, by God, he could kill the Uzita witch. He had a knife. She was unarmed. He could spare the time for that.

He charged, slashing with the knife, missing by wide margins. She was too fast. But she was on the defensive. And she did not seem to want to let him leave the room. Perhaps she thought to protect all the little dying boys and girls nearby.

That would kill her. He could corner her and drive the blade into her, again and again and again . . .

He lunged once more, she dodged again, and suddenly, she had the large, plate-glass window at her back. She had no place to run.

"Long time coming, *salvaje*," he said, his breath coming in ragged gulps now, more from excitement than effort.

"Too long," Shako said back, her teeth gleaming white in the semidarkness. "No more children, Aznar. No more little girls."

Aznar had just enough time to wonder, Why was she smiling?

Then he realized: He had not maneuvered her. She had maneuvered *him*. There was nothing behind her but the window.

And they were on the seventh floor.

It was too late to check his lunge. He was off-balance and leaning forward.

She came up underneath him, and picked him off the floor bodily, grunting under the sudden strain.

He slashed at her arms, but he wasn't in them for long.

There was a brief moment of uninterrupted flight.

The glass shattered at his back and parted like a curtain.

Then he was falling, flailing, trying to swim in midair, his arms and legs pinwheeling around him.

He bounced off the lip of the roof of the parking garage, and again off the edge of a stairwell.

But when he hit the ground, he didn't move at all.

# CHAPTER 17

IN HER CONDO, Shako trembled a little as she picked up the necklace to loop it around her neck. Then she put it back down, angry at herself.

With minimal effort, she willed her hands to be calm again.

How long had it been since her body had betrayed her like that? When was the last time she had ever shown a genuine, unplanned emotion or gesture?

But tonight was different. Tonight it would end. Probably for her. Definitely for Simon.

David might survive. He might not.

She'd tried to warn him, but not seriously. To be honest, she had not wanted him to stop his work. If he did, she'd likely never get inside Conquest, or close enough to Simon to finally finish this.

Simon would have to be careless. He would have to believe he was invulnerable again. He would have to think he could not lose. She'd known Simon a long time, and she knew he was most careless right when he believed he had won everything that mattered.

Those were the times when he was almost human again, too.

Shako did the clasp on the necklace. It was worth roughly half what she'd paid for the condo, and it was stunning. If anyone doubted what a woman of her color was doing at the party, one glance at her jewelry should prove she at least belonged in the same tax bracket.

Or perhaps they'd just assume she was a very well-paid whore.

Over the years, her gender and her skin color had been Simon's greatest allies in keeping her away. Not too long ago—less than fifty years, so, for her, not very long ago at all—she could not have walked some of the streets of this city without someone questioning her. While Simon and his friends could stroll into any building or boardroom and work their influence directly, she had to be much craftier. For years, her money had been hidden in the names of fictitious fathers, brothers, and husbands. She'd dressed as a maid or cook or waitress more times than she could count, because someone like her was never supposed to be anything but a servant. In secret, she'd seduced politicians and bankers and real-estate barons and moved them like chess pieces, always playing the long game. Simon moved across the world, across the years, in bold strokes, smashing opposition and braying his name loudly to anyone who'd listen.

She had hidden her true self and worked in the

shadows. She wondered if Simon had any idea that she was the source of his current woes with his Chinese bankers, or the sudden pressure from the FDA. Of course not. A good spy never lets anyone know she exists.

And she was sick to death of it. All of it. The lying, the mewing and bowing and faking, the necessity of standing behind men to accomplish her goals.

Men like David.

No, not like him. David was, to his credit, kind and decent, intelligent and driven. He had a natural arrogance, but, truth be told, she'd always liked that in a man. First in Simon, all that time ago, then in Drake, and then in perhaps a half dozen other lovers she'd taken. There had been a precious few like that, the ones she truly mourned now. They were the ones she allowed to touch her heart, not just her body.

She left them all behind, of course. Because she would not make any more monsters like Simon. None of them, no matter how good they seemed, could be trusted with her greatest secret.

Everyone had to die. Eventually.

Even David. If his time came tonight, then all it meant was that he was no exception to the rule.

She had done him one last favor with the girl, Elizabeth. And she'd managed to remove that tick Aznar from her hide once and for all. She supposed she owed David for that, at least. But either way, it would not change what she had to do tonight.

Some people died too soon. And others had already lived too damned long.

Her hands were shaking again.

That was all right, Shako told herself. It was only natural. She'd waited a long, long time for this. She could be a little nervous—a little human—before it happened. It was a reminder of how much she wanted this, how long and how hard the journey had been to reach this point.

Her hands would be steady when it counted.

PARKER WESTON SMILED POLITELY and waved the woman through the metal detector, then instructed her to leave her rings in the tray when it squawked at her. She scowled but complied.

Her husband—or boyfriend or whoever—in a tux, waited impatiently on the other side of the gate that OpSec had set up in front of the hotel's grand ballroom. He'd clearly had a few pregame drinks. "I didn't realize we'd have to deal with the goddamn TSA tonight," he muttered, just loud enough.

Weston kept the polite smile. "We apologize for the inconvenience," he said, as he'd been trained.

"You think Al Qaeda's going to attack us tonight?" the woman asked sharply as she retrieved her rings. The jewels were huge, and her dress looked to be worth more than Parker's car, but her accent was pure Florida trailer park.

"Just a precaution," Weston said.

She snorted and walked into the ballroom with her husband, both of them radiating indignation.

It had been like that all night, one well-dressed asshole after another, complaining about being made to walk through a security line like some shoplifter trying to sneak a couple of DVDs out of Best Buy.

In truth, Weston sort of agreed with them. He had no idea why Conquest had hired OpSec for what looked like a staggeringly boring gathering of rich people.

But he'd learned back in the army that orders didn't have to make sense; they just had to be orders. Whoever was running this gig wanted to make sure that only the right people were inside the room.

Weston could handle that. He'd had three tours in Iraq and one in Afghanistan, had managed not to get himself blown up, and was even decorated for bravery when his armored column was attacked after hitting an IED. Back home in Florida, however, he had a hard time finding a job where courage was one of the requirements listed in the ads. Fortunately, OpSec needed guys exactly like him, and he joined the private security business. Most of the time, he wore a suit instead of Kevlar as he protected men who had more money than real enemies. It paid much better than dodging bullets in downtown Sadr City.

The party tonight was a celebration of some new advance in medicine, if Weston read the signs outside the ballroom right. There was only one special request from Conquest: an artist's sketch of a woman, done up with several different hairstyles and looks, with explicit instructions to stop her and detain her if she showed up anywhere near the hotel.

The head of Conquest's internal security detail handed out the photocopies to Weston and his fellow guards personally. Weston had studied the pics carefully, memorized the face, and then folded the paper and put it in his inside pocket. She didn't look especially dangerous to him, but OpSec also did a lot of industrial espionage work. Maybe she was a spy for a rival company. Or a journalist looking for a story to embarrass the company. Or maybe she was a process server or she was the angry ex-wife of one of the directors on the board.

Didn't matter, really. She wasn't going to get past him.

Just then, a couple came through the line, drawing more than their share of attention.

The guy was young—about the same age as Weston—and escorted an incredibly beautiful woman wearing a gown that seemed to have been poured over her. People were stepping out of line for them, stopping him to shake his hand, and simply gawking at her.

The guy didn't look famous to Weston, but even if he was, he put them through the same routine as the other celebrities who'd already shown up: he put her clutch on the conveyor belt and had them step through the metal detector.

Without his phone, the guy went through clean.

The woman, however, set the detector off. She removed a pair of earrings and went through a second time. Another squawk from the detector. She smiled prettily at Weston—he felt it all the way down to his groin—and leaned in close to him.

"This is embarrassing," she said. "It might be the underwire on my bra."

Weston was no expert on lingerie, but he'd call himself an enthusiastic amateur when it came to breasts. And he had a hard time believing hers were contained by any bra at all.

But he didn't think staring down her cleavage was the way to advance his career. All he said was "Not a problem, ma'am." He directed her over to the side, pulled out the handheld scanner, and passed it over her.

It didn't beep near her chest. He continued down her legs—again, trying not to leer—and got a beep at her thighs.

Weston gave her a questioning look.

"Sorry," she said. "I have a little secret."

She opened her gown where it was slit nearly to her waist, and showed him. Around her upper thigh was a garter with a slim silver flask tucked snugly beneath it. "I keep a little something close by. Just for emergencies," she said in a stage whisper, like she was letting him in on a personal joke.

Decision time: pat her down and look like a pervert or send her away entirely. The guy was clearly important, but Weston had his instructions. In fact, now that he thought of it, she did look a little like the sketch of the woman he'd been given.

Pickford came over. He'd been lurking around the entrance all night. He usually let his people do their jobs without interference. But not now, for some reason.

He stepped neatly between Weston and the couple, as if shielding them, and smiled at them. "Dr. Robinton. A pleasure to see you and your guest."

The guy looked a little confused. He'd never met Pickford before, Weston could tell. But he was obviously used to VIP treatment, which meant a lot of strangers greeting you as if you were an old friend.

"Sorry, we didn't mean to hold up the line," the guy said.

"Not at all," Pickford said. He turned to Weston, face suddenly cold: "Let them through."

"She set off the detector, sir."

Pickford gave him the boss voice. "This is Dr. David Robinton. He's the guest of honor. I don't want him delayed any longer. Are we clear?"

Weston felt the need to defend himself. "Sir, I was just looking at this message from Conquest—" Weston said as he held up the paper for Pickford to see.

Pickford snatched it from his hand and crumpled it into a ball.

"Why are you still talking? Let them through."

The other guests in line were starting to make noise. Some of them were enjoying the show of the employee being chewed out by his boss.

Weston screwed his polite smile into place and waved Robinton and his date through. "My apologies, Doctor. Miss."

Robinton, to his credit, looked embarrassed. "No worries," he said. "You're just doing your job." The woman gave him another radiant smile that made him forget how pissed his boss was at that moment.

They walked off, and Pickford, with another glare at Weston, went after them.

Weston took a last look at Robinton and the woman before they entered the room. They walked hand in hand, and unlike some of the couples he'd seen that night, seemed genuinely happy.

Screw it, Weston decided. After all, it wasn't like she was going to cause any trouble.

"Next in line," he said, and the slow march into the ballroom continued.

PEOPLE SWARMED AROUND DAVID and Shy, smiling at them, shaking his hand, complimenting her on her dress, congratulating him. There were wealthy shareholders and politicians and celebrities in the crowd. And they all wanted to talk to him, to get a little bit of his attention.

They don't even know what I've done yet, David thought, but they're ready to celebrate it anyway. Simon had kept a tight lid on the actual reason for the party tonight. All the guests knew was that Conquest was about to announce another breakthrough, and that its star employee, David Robinton, was the reason.

He had not been sure Shy would want to come with him. "I didn't think you approved of my research," he told her. She'd smiled and kissed him and said, "I'd never miss your big moment."

He had not told her what he'd learned about Simon. He didn't know how. It was too strange, and too big. What would she have to say about that? What would she think if she learned that his discovery wasn't even the first time someone was breaking the rules of nature?

It felt like an actual weight in his gut. It took him a while to realize that was guilt. He did not want to have secrets from Shy. He wanted her to share everything.

Until now, he'd had the excuse of work to put off these feelings. But that excuse was dead. This party was where they would bury it. Starting tomorrow, he would have to find a way to tell her how he felt. There was a good chance she might leave him over it. He might lose her, and that caused another, almost physical pain for him. But he couldn't keep anything from her anymore, he'd decided. Not if he really wanted them to be together. Starting tomorrow, he'd have to put all secrets behind them.

Starting tomorrow. Tonight, he wanted her here, and wanted to believe she was proud of him.

One of the guests, an older man with white hair, stumbled into them, nearly spilling his drink.

With a start, David recognized him. Antonio Ortega, one of the board members. They'd met, only a few months before. But he seemed to have aged years. His hair was white, and his face was lined with wrinkles. He looked confused.

"I know you," he said. "Don't I?"

Drunk. Or stoned on some kind of prescription meds, David guessed. "We've met, Mr. Ortega," he said. "I'm David Robinton. I was hired by Simon, remember?"

Ortega still looked confused. David realized he was staring at Shy, not at him. "No," he said. "I know you. We've met, I'm sure of it."

Shy gave him a radiant smile. "I've done some consulting for the company in the past. Maybe that's it."

Ortega's face screwed up with frustration. "No," he insisted. "It was something else. Someone else. I know it."

He tried to grab her arm. She caught his hand

and returned it gently but firmly to his side before David could even move.

"I'm sure you're right," she said. "It's nice to see you again."

Ortega's determination fled just as quickly as his anger had arrived. He looked as if he was about to weep. "Sorry," he said. "So much to remember. So many things."

He wandered back to the bar, still muttering.

David laughed, more out of discomfort than anything else. "Someone needs to cut him off," he said.

Shy made a face at him. "Relax," she said. "It's a party. Eat, drink, and be merry, for tomorrow we may die."

"Not tomorrow," David said. "Not for a long, long time. Not anymore."

She laughed. "Yes, David. We all know you're very smart. You've cured all our ills and saved the world. That's why we're celebrating."

"No," he said, holding her hand tighter, looking into her eyes. He wanted her to understand this. "That's why I did it. I know you don't approve, I know you've got . . . misgivings, you think it's all mad science and bullshit, but this is why: because I want more tomorrows. For me and you. And for everyone else. I want more people to have a chance to feel this."

It all came out in a rush. And then he felt deeply embarrassed.

She looked at him for a long moment. Something crossed her face. A look almost like pain.

"What's wrong?"

"Nothing." She kissed him then, so intensely that some of the onlookers made comments.

When she broke away, she looked him in the eyes again. "You are a remarkable man, David Robinton," she said.

He didn't know what to say to that. She stepped back, as if embarrassed herself.

More people came from the bar at that moment, putting themselves between Shy and David. They were all talking at once.

Shy shrugged at him and smiled. "I have to powder my nose. I'll be right back."

David watched her go before he could say anything else, and in moments, she was swallowed by the crowd.

The men around him were still talking at him, and he tried to follow Shy's advice. Relax. Enjoy yourself. After all, it's your party.

SIMON AND MAX WERE going to be late. Their limo was a mile away from the hotel. They weren't worried. It was expected of Simon.

Simon had his head back against the seat, his eyes closed. Max had not seen him look so peaceful in a long time.

That only made Max worry more.

"This seems premature," he said.

"You and David are more alike than you know," Simon replied. "He said the same thing. In a few months, we will have the formula running from the taps if we want. Will that be enough for you then?"

"It's not exactly the same as the Water. You've

said so yourself. His cure works for now, but in fifty years? A hundred? What then? Will it break down and fail?"

"True. It feels different, somehow. It's not as powerful. I can't quite explain it. David admits there are properties of the Water that have eluded him. But this is as close as we're likely to get. We have David's formula. We will begin FDA trials soon, but we know it works. There's no earthly reason to wait any longer."

"Then we don't need David anymore," Max said. "It's time to ease him out of our lives."

Simon smirked. "You've really never liked him."

"I don't like anyone getting too close to the truth. You've given him enough clues, Simon. He's not an idiot. He could figure out our secret, and then what—"

"Max. He knows."

Max remained very still for a moment. Then he turned and nearly spat venom at Simon.

"You *told* him?"

Simon decided to let him have his moment of pique. "No. You're right. He's very smart. He put the pieces together himself."

"Jesus Christ, Simon! And I suppose you told him everything else!"

Simon couldn't help laughing at Max. Just a little. "Don't be ridiculous. Most people cannot fathom what we are, even when it's right in front of them. Even someone as intelligent as David. He believes we're old men who use the Water to keep ourselves stiff and virile. Senior citizens at most. He literally cannot conceive of anything older."

Max breathed deeply, trying to calm down. "That's small comfort. We've worked for years to maintain our secret. You know this. You know why. They would kill us for what we have. What we are."

There was no question who Max meant by "they." He meant ordinary humans. The ones who had to face death every day.

Simon was impatient with Max's old fears, however. "The world has changed, Max. You don't see it yet. But we have changed it, with David's help. The old rules no longer apply."

Max clenched and unclenched his fist. "You have still risked us all, Simon. You have gambled our lives."

"You're being dramatic, Max. You should be grateful that we have a way to survive now. You know, David told me he wants to give up his profits in order to make sure everyone gets a chance at the cure. Wants us to offer it for free to the starving and the poor."

"You must be joking."

Simon sighed. "I'm not going to do it, Max. Don't worry. David will see the light."

"Once you offer him a place on the Council, you mean."

"That's right. I think he's earned it."

Max was literally shaking with fury, but he kept his voice low. "That is a mistake. You allow him inside, and he will use that leverage to tear us down. He's already got far too much power over us by controlling this new cure."

"You think someone like him, given the chance to see the future happen, would turn it down? No.

He will grapple with himself, and then he will realize: he cares more about knowledge than anything else. He will want to keep living if only to keep finding answers. And after a few decades, or a century at most, he will come to understand that this is the way of the world: there are rulers and there are servants. I know which side he will choose."

"He won't. I told you, he clings to his own morality. He really believes he's a better man than we are. He will follow his conscience, no matter what the cost."

Simon smiled at that. "Maybe we need a conscience like that. To remind us of what we once were."

"This is not a joke," Max snapped. "It's a massive risk. You are undoing everything we have, everything we've ever done, with your faith in someone you barely know."

"We owe him our lives. I think that earns him a little gratitude. I don't believe we have a choice."

"There's always a choice," Max said. He felt a twinge of triumph amid the burning anger. He knew Simon would make this error. He knew Simon better than anyone.

The limo came to a halt. The driver stepped out and opened the door for them.

"You might be right, Max," Simon said, yawning hugely. "But sometimes the choice is so uneven that it's no choice at all. I'm comfortable with my decision. If you're not . . . Well, then, find a way to deal with it. The matter is closed."

Simon got out of the car and walked toward the front entrance.

Max sat for a moment longer, his face still hot. He bit back several replies. Simon wouldn't have cared about any of them.

Simon didn't care about anything else, as long as he got what he wanted.

Well, it was Max's job to protect Simon—to protect all of them—from Simon's worst impulses.

Max was glad he had Aznar nearby. David Robinton didn't know it, but tonight was the beginning of the end of his life.

He took a few deep breaths and then followed Simon, jogging to catch up.

# CHAPTER 18

SHE FOUND ORTEGA wandering around near the restrooms on the far side of the ballroom. There were only a few people around, and they didn't pay attention when she went to his side and took his arm.

She drew him around a corner and stood close. If anyone was watching, they looked away politely. An older man and a much younger woman. It was a fairly common sight in Florida.

He looked right at her and, again, completely failed to recognize her.

She looked into his eyes. She recognized the loss and confusion there. He'd been cut off. Now he was drowning in his past, the years washing over him. He was clinging to his most recent memories as if they were a raft that would save him.

It was cruel, when viewed from the outside, but it wasn't enough.

For a moment, she wondered why Ortega was being punished like this. If Ortega was still here, then in his more lucid moments he must have believed that Simon would take pity on him and give him a drink, restoring him.

Whatever Ortega had done to anger Simon, it had been good luck for her. She would have been recognized otherwise, and that might have meant failure.

She was done hesitating. No more good-bye kisses. It was time for an end to all of this.

"I *know* I know you," he said.

"You know me," she agreed. "Do you remember?"

He tried. He struggled to bring it back up to the surface.

She helped.

"You had a sword. My family was all around you, running. One man tried to stop you, barehanded, and you slashed open his throat. The women screamed. The children cried. And you were laughing."

There it was. Finally. A spark of recognition.

"No," he said. "That wasn't— It was a different time. It was so long ago."

"Not long enough," she said, and slid her dagger—the one she'd strapped to her other thigh—up under his ribs and into his heart.

"Shako," he said.

She set him down more gently than he deserved and left him there. If anyone found the body, it wouldn't matter now.

This was where it ended. And she'd already begun.

SIMON TOOK THE LECTERN on the stage at the front of the ballroom.

The gabble of conversation immediately quieted down.

David stood on the floor, in front of the stage. Here we go, he thought. This is the last moment of your normal life. This is where it starts. This is where you finally begin to save everyone.

Once the announcement was made, there would be frenzy and skepticism, praise and scorn, a million Internet headlines, ignorant people talking knowledgeably about it on every TV channel.

There would be millions of people clamoring for a spot in the clinical trials, and millions more who would want to use his formula the same way Simon had, to look and feel twenty years old again.

But eventually, there would be acceptance. Eventually, it would get to the right people.

This was where everything changed, but it would be worth it in the end.

"FRIENDS," SIMON SAID. "THANK you all for coming tonight. Even those of you who are just here for the free booze."

Polite laughter.

"People always asked my father, 'Why is the company called Conquest?' I mean, it doesn't make sense, does it? We've always been a medical firm. We've made vaccines, drugs, and devices that are all about keeping people alive. So, why Conquest? Why name the company after something that sounds like blood and war and death?"

Simon smiled and leaned forward. "This is what my father and his father always said: 'Because Conquest is what we do. We conquer markets. We conquer our rivals. We conquer diseases and human frailty and age and sickness of every kind. That is what we do, and that is why it is our name.' "

Spontaneous applause. Simon could really work a crowd.

"But today, that name is more fitting than at any time in our history. Today, we are announcing a new product, developed exclusively for our company by Dr. David Robinton, who is here with us tonight. Take a bow, David."

David did not bow. He got a round of applause anyway. People near him patted him on the back and smiled.

"Today, we announce a product that is nothing less than revolutionary. And I don't mean in the usual bullshit marketing way. I mean this really is going to change the whole world. You will tell your grandchildren you were here this evening. You will tell your great-grandchildren, and their children. You will tell them in person. Because that is what we have done. Conquest has finally achieved the goal it was built for: we have conquered death itself."

The movie theater–size screen behind Simon lit up with a stylized logo: ReGenesys.

"We have created a drug that reverses the effects of aging."

Simon let that sit there for a moment. The crowd seemed unsure of how to take the news.

"I know what you're thinking. This sounds like

some crazy fountain-of-youth infomercial scheme. But it is the truth. ReGenesys will actually turn back the clock, physically, on every process in your entire body. It will cure almost any disease, and will halt senility and aging. I know it sounds too good to be true, but I would not be telling you this if I had not seen it with my own eyes. This is an actual miracle, made by science. And you get to be a part of it. Now, we cannot release everything yet. We still have enemies out there in the world. But I would not be telling you this if the product did not work, and if we were not ready to begin human trials. In less than a year, you will see this on the market. And everyone in this room will be richer than you ever dreamed possible."

That brought about the loudest applause of the night.

"Ladies and gentlemen, thank you for listening. Now it's time to celebrate. The future is bright—and every one of us will be around to see it. Thank you."

SIMON SHOOK OFF THE dozens of people who wanted to question him, who kept demanding answers. He wanted to see David.

He walked over and embraced the scientist.

"ReGenesys?" David asked.

"Best our marketing people could do on short notice. We didn't give them a lot of time to focus-group it."

"Whatever you want to call it. I don't care. As long as everyone gets a chance at it."

The crowd pressed at them both from all angles.

Simon nodded and smiled. "Just a minute," he told someone. "Be right there."

Then he turned back to David, his eyes serious, the mask of youth gone for a moment. "I keep my word, David. Be sure that you do the same."

David felt cold. Whenever Simon let down his guard like this, David had the feeling that something more dangerous lurked underneath. It reminded him, uncomfortably, of the sound of a gun being cocked.

But he wasn't about to back down. "You've got no reason to doubt me," David said. "I've never lied to you."

If Simon heard the veiled reproach, he gave no indication. Just like that, the grin was back. "That's what I like to hear," he said. "So, you going stag at the biggest party of your life? That's really pathetic."

"My date's in the restroom."

"Of course she is."

Irritation swept over David, displacing any unease he'd felt a moment before. For someone who was actually a senior citizen, Simon could be incredibly immature. Then he caught a glimpse of Shy as she headed toward them. "In fact, here she is now," he said.

Simon turned in the direction David was looking.

Shy was partially blocked by the crowd, but David still felt an absurd pride, the science geek who'd managed to bring the prettiest girl to the prom.

Simon's mouth actually dropped open. David wasn't expecting that much of a reaction, but he wasn't going to say he didn't like it.

Simon kept staring as Shy quickly stepped to David's side. The crowd kept pushing them all together. She moved in close, wrapping her arm around his, her other hand holding her clutch purse. She kissed him quickly on the cheek, but her eyes did not leave Simon's.

"Simon, this is Shy," David said.

"We've met," Shy said.

Simon said, "No."

Then Shy brought up the hand with the clutch purse. The purse dropped. A blade appeared there, as if from nowhere. It was already spotted with blood.

Someone began to scream.

IMPOSSIBLE, SIMON THOUGHT, AND lost a precious few seconds to disbelief.

He was safe. He was surrounded by security and hundreds of his supporters. He had not seen her close-up in more than a hundred years. It had to be some kind of mistake.

But it wasn't. He knew that.

And yet he watched her entwine herself with David, place a kiss on his cheek and smile at him, all while he stared like an idiot.

Shako. Close enough to touch.

Touching David.

She raised her hand, and he saw the knife.

He finally began to move.

THE WOMAN SAW THE man's skinny ankles from behind the potted plant, black socks sagging, revealing a pale stripe of hairy leg.

She'd gone looking for a quiet spot to sneak a cigarette at the back of the ballroom, away from her husband, who still jogged every morning and could quote morbidity statistics for smokers off the top of his head. What she got for marrying a cardiologist.

She wondered if the man was ill, or perhaps drunk, so she stepped around the plant and leaned down to speak to him.

Then she saw the horrible red blood all over his shirt, the horrible second mouth opened in his chest.

She began screaming, and everyone turned to the back of the room to look.

IT WAS ENOUGH TO distract the bodyguards for a crucial second.

They were having a hard enough time keeping an eye on Simon as he moved into the crowd. They thought he was safe in the scrum of expensive suits and dresses. Besides, he liked to have space to do the meet and greet.

Only one of them turned from the commotion at the rear of the ballroom in time to see Simon suddenly dancing backward, knocking people out of his way, a bright red slash across his tuxedo shirtfront.

The woman with the knife went after him.

At this point, people still thought Simon had bumped into them because he was drunk or stoned or simply rude. Their brains had not quite caught up to what their eyes were seeing.

The bodyguard, however, had been trained for this. He didn't hesitate.

He withdrew his gun, a Glock nine-millimeter loaded with wadcutter rounds, and opened fire.

MAX SAW HER AT almost the same time Simon did. From across the room, near the bar. He saw her take David's arm and kiss him.

Then the screaming started a panic, and the gunshots only added to the stampede. The noise went from one woman wailing in the back to a universal screech that filled the air.

Chaos.

Max did not stop to wonder how Shako had gotten this close, or how she'd gotten a knife inside the party. Pointless questions. It was Shako.

He shouted at Peter and Sebastian, who were rooted in place a few dozen yards away, trying to see what was going on.

One word: "Shako!" Then he ran toward the shooting.

The bodyguard was trying to hit Shako. Max was sure he was a good shot under other circumstances. But he would never even get close to her. She was too fast. Max had seen her dance around automatic-weapon fire before.

The bodyguard was putting his bullets every place she had been a moment before. As a result, he was doing a lot of collateral damage.

A clot of people blocked Max's way. Max didn't slow down. He leaped and cleared them all, rising eight feet in the air and covering twenty feet of distance.

The Water had given them all great gifts. He hadn't used his in some time.

Shako spun and dodged the bullets again, and, as she always did, found a way to turn an enemy into an advantage.

She hesitated for a second.

The bodyguard drew a bead on her.

She danced away, just before he pulled the trigger.

Simon was behind her, now directly in the line of fire.

Max reached the bodyguard just in time, hit the man with a full-body block that sent him spiraling across the floor, skidding to a rest against the wall.

He'd dropped his gun. Max scooped it up and began looking for his target.

SHAKO CURSED HERSELF FOR being so dramatic. She had to get close to use a knife, true, but she didn't have to let Simon speak. She didn't have to do anything but cut his throat.

Instead: "We've met." Stupid.

Still, the look on his face.

She saw Max take out the guard who was busy shooting up the room. Then she lost him in the rush of bodies.

She found Simon again, though. He was hurt, not badly, but enough to make him stand out, blood soaked into his shirt, a red flag that let her track him wherever he went. He ran toward the stage.

She moved to pursue him when another body blocked her.

Sebastian.

He snarled something obscene at her in Spanish, his beautiful features made ugly with hate, and threw a punch at her.

She ducked under it and came up with a kick that caught him on the chin.

It snapped his jaw shut and pointed his eyes at the ceiling.

She was about to follow it with another kick to his midsection when Peter caught her arm. He whirled her about and reached for her neck.

She sliced with the blade, missing anything vital but opening a nasty cut across his forehead all the way down to his nose.

The blood welled up from the split flesh and ran into his eyes.

He cursed and let her go.

Sebastian was mostly recovered by then. He unleashed a flying roundhouse kick at her head.

She would have rolled her eyes if she'd had time. Always going for the big, fancy move. He never changed.

She followed him around as he spun, and drove the point of the blade into his back.

It deflected off his shoulder and did not reach his heart, but his sudden roar of pain was a good result in itself.

She yanked the blade free and looked for Simon again.

Two bodyguards got in her way. She hit one and

broke his sternum in three places. The other went down after she punched him in the throat, choking on the wreckage of his hyoid bone and cartilage.

They were soldiers, she reminded herself. They stepped into the battle willingly.

She found Simon again. In the whirlwind of chaos, she saw that he'd stopped running. He was kneeling on the floor. Helping someone up.

It was David.

Simon lifted him from the ground and pulled him toward the door. David limped. He left a trail of blood drops. He'd been hit by a stray round.

There was nothing altruistic in this, Shako knew. Simon needed David. That's why he'd been her ticket inside.

What she couldn't figure out was why *she* still cared what happened to him.

She crossed the distance between them in a matter of steps.

She pulled David away from Simon and sent him spilling to the floor again.

Finally, finally, finally, this was almost done. She would finally be able to rest.

Simon was too off-balance to put up much resistance as she spun him around and got the tip of her knife beneath his ear.

Just one long, even motion, and then he'd be dead. Even if they killed her now, he would finally pay.

She heard someone shout her name.

"Shako!" Max bellowed.

She looked. She saw him.

He stood a yard from David. He held a gun,

aimed at David's chest. There was no way he could miss at that range.

Everything seemed to stop.

MOST OF THE FLOOR was clear. Only a few of the partygoers remained, the ones who had been hurt too badly to run or who hid in the corners.

They peeked out to watch the standoff.

Max kept the gun trained on David, who was kneeling, caught halfway while rising.

"Stay down," Max told him.

Simon gasped, caught in Shako's arms. "Max, don't—" he blurted, before Shako cut him off by poking the tip of the knife into his neck.

"Shut up." To Max, she said, "You think that's going to stop me?"

Max smiled. "Seems like it already has."

David remained kneeling. "So you guys all know each other, I guess," he said.

Shako almost laughed at that. She noticed Sebastian and Peter moving closer. "Back up," she warned them. "I won't tell you again."

They stopped where they were but didn't back off.

"This is where you decide who's worth more," Max said. "Your old lover or your new one."

"He's nothing to me."

"Then why haven't you killed Simon yet?"

Shako hesitated. That was a very good question.

David looked at her, fear mingled with confusion and betrayal. He did not know her. He was her key to a door, that was all. She had learned that sacrifices had to be made. People died. That was the way of the world.

But this . . . As with the girl, Elizabeth. This was not simply letting someone else die.

This was something she caused. This was uncomfortably close to murder.

She'd killed dozens, hundreds of people, to get here. She thought her conscience could take the weight.

The question was, could it handle one more?

The moment stretched like a tightrope, tension drawing out exquisitely as the spectators watched, waiting for the moment when someone dropped, when a human being became a dead body right before their very eyes.

She looked at David and made her decision.

She released Simon.

Max smiled and pulled the trigger anyway.

DAVID FELT A HARD punch against his chest. He'd thought the bullet fragment that caught him in the leg was the worst pain he'd ever known. But this was much worse.

The pain did not subside. It only grew and radiated outward, expanding until it felt like a new form of gravity that was bringing down the whole world on him.

He struggled to breathe. Dimly, he was aware of people moving around him. Max disappearing from the edge of his vision. People running, the clip-clop of high heels as they rushed for the exits. Shouting. He thought he saw Peter go flying through the air at least seven feet over his head, but that was crazy.

Then Shy was there, her face at the end of a dark tunnel. She looked deeply into his eyes, as if searching for something.

He knew, in an abstract way, that her arms were around him, but he could not feel them. He tried to speak but could not catch his breath. Goddamn. This really *hurt*.

"I'm sorry," she said.

The tunnel began to close. Her face was the last thing he saw before everything went black.

FROM CNN:

(THIS IS A RUSH TRANSCRIPT)

**WOLF BLITZER:** I'm sorry, we are breaking into our program with a developing story out of Florida. It seems there is a situation at a party, a corporate event, a possible terrorist attack on a corporate party in Tampa, Florida. Do we have . . . yes, we have video there from the local affiliate, a shot from the news helicopter; you can see the emergency vehicles and the people running out of the building. I'm going to turn it over to the reporter on the scene, Teresa Nazario, from the local station WFLA. Go ahead, Teresa.

**TERESA NAZARIO:** Wolf, as you can see behind me, there is chaos on the ground here tonight at the Grand Regency Hotel in Tampa Bay. People have been shot, the police are still attempting to put up a cordon around the hotel, and a SWAT team is about to storm the building. The situation is still very much in flux. There's a lot we don't know right now.

**BLITZER:** Teresa, can you tell me who was involved in this?

**NAZARIO:** Right now, we are told that this was a corporate event for Conquest Biotech, to announce a new product launch. Then, according to at least one witness, someone began attacking guests with either a knife or a sword, followed by gunfire.

**BLITZER:** Was this a terrorist attack?

**NAZARIO:** Impossible to say right now. At this point, the ballroom in the hotel is still unsecured. So we have not got a statement from the police yet; they are still trying to get the situation contained. We have seen several people being treated by paramedics, and they are being rushed to the local emergency room.

**BLITZER:** Teresa, can you tell me how many people have been wounded or killed?

**NAZARIO:** At this point, we don't know, Wolf. We just don't know.

# CHAPTER 19

FLORIDA
1527

THE WOMAN STALKED through the trees, still furious.

She carried everything she needed to stay away for weeks. Months, if necessary. Her father kept telling her she did not understand. That was the problem. She understood all too well.

The Uzita were under attack. They'd heard from other tribes far south that more and more of the strangely dressed invaders arrived every month. They spilled out of their giant ships on the coastline and moved inland like a river going backward. Some of the other tribes hoped the invaders would leave—there had been visitors before, but they always went away.

Clearly, this was not the case this time. The invaders set up camps, chopped down trees, and began building shelters. They would not be ignored. They were not going away.

Which was why the Uzita needed to be united and strong. They needed to put aside any of their own differences to face the threat.

And she had been chosen by her father as the sacrifice that would bridge the gap between the Water Clan and the Wolf Clan. A marriage between the two most powerful families of the Uzita. Yaha had many sons and grandsons. Despite his age, he was still a fierce warrior, and he was the strength of the tribe. Her own father knew this, because her own father held the wisdom of the Uzita. Yaha had always believed that his strength was greater than her father's brain and heart. They had clashed for years, since they were boys themselves.

Now her father had decided it was time to end the rivalry. So he chose to merge their families. She was promised as a wife to Yaha's oldest son, a thick, dull boy with twice his father's strength and none of his intelligence.

She had protested. Her father, ordinarily tolerant, became a different man in front of her eyes. He raged at her. He commanded her to go along with the marriage for the good of the entire tribe.

She saw the fear in his eyes then, and misunderstood it. She thought he was frightened of Yaha. She felt rage and contempt. He was bargaining with her life to preserve his own power. She had never thought he would be so cold or cruel.

If he cared that little for her, she could show him the same regard. A week before she was supposed to wed Yaha's son, she ran into the woods.

She ran to the one place she knew no one would look, where not even her father would dare follow her, because to do so would be to risk the secret.

She was going to the place that did not exist. She went to the cave.

To her great shock, she discovered someone there. One of the invaders. He was dying. She saw the wound in his leg, the blood gone black. His breath came in ragged gasps. She recognized the poison, and wondered idly if her husband-to-be was the one who had fired the arrow that would kill this man.

He did not look as strange as the stories said. His skin was pale, true, but he was shaped like any other man, now that he was stripped out of the odd shells they wore. His face was different, but somehow familiar to her. As if she had always known it, and was just now remembering him.

It was in her power to save him. She knew what her father would do—what he would order her to do, if he were here. He would tell her that this man was an alien, an invader, a disease infiltrating their land, who would kill everyone with his mere presence if given the chance.

Her father was no coward. She'd seen him fight and, more important, she'd seen him win without fighting, simply by standing his ground. Until the invaders came, she'd never seen him afraid.

And this? This was what he was afraid of? A pale man, sick and dying, unable to even find water when left on his own.

She touched the invader's cheek.

His eyes snapped open. For a moment, she saw his fear and panic and pain. She felt for him. For all his strangeness, he was lost and alone. She thought she understood the feeling.

Then as his eyes latched on to her, he smiled. He said something in a language she didn't understand, barely a whisper.

He touched her hand and brought it back to his cheek. He burned with fever, but his eyes never left hers.

"*Angel*," he said again. "*Angel del Cielo.*"

He closed his eyes again. Peace radiated from his features like the heat from his skin. There was, in that moment, a perfect trust between them. His life was in her hands. She could almost feel him handing it over, like a physical weight had passed to her.

At that moment, she decided.

He would not die.

FOR THE SECOND TIME that day, they sat down outside the cave and the man tried to teach her to speak.

The first time had not ended well. He'd brought over a group of small objects: stones, sticks, some things he'd salvaged from his few possessions. Then he would point at them while speaking very slowly at her. He looked so serious, his young features drawn into such fierce concentration, that she kept laughing.

Eventually he was holding the stone in front of him, barking the same word over and over: "*Piedra, piedra, piedra!*" She couldn't help herself. She fell into a fit of giggles.

He stood up and stomped away.

She felt bad for him. She was young, but she already knew how men treasured their dignity. Laughter was the quickest way to shatter their illusion of controlling the world.

It did not help that he was nearly naked. So was she, but she was accustomed to wearing little in the hot summer months. For him, it was clearly a maddening distraction. When he was sick and dying, she had used her knife to cut the torn and bloody clothing off him. The pile of rags was thick and stank of sweat and piss and blood, and she'd taken it far away from the cave.

After he woke, healed by her, he covered himself with his hands and searched for the stinking pile. He came back with what was left of his pants tied around himself, and the white shirt he'd worn under everything else.

She had decided that where he was from, everyone must have worn that heavy clothing all the time. He stole glances at her and quickly looked away. She wondered briefly if her body was somehow different from those of the women he knew, but quickly dismissed the notion. He turned from her, but she saw his erection rising at those moments. It wasn't that he didn't like how she looked. He'd simply never seen a woman's breasts before.

She took pity on him when he finally came back to her. She wrapped her breasts in a cloth so that he would be able to meet her eyes. This was hard for him. She would have to be kinder.

They sat facing each other again. He pointed to himself. "*Hombre*," he said.

She pointed to herself. "Shako," she said back.

He looked frustrated. Pointed again. "*Hombre,*" he repeated.

"Shako," she said again.

He shook his head, grabbed her hand, used it to poke himself in the chest. "*Hombre,*" he said, even slower now.

She tried not to roll her eyes. "Shako," she said, even slower than him.

He shrugged irritably and moved on to something else. He pointed up at the sun in the sky. "*Sol,*" he said slowly and carefully. "*Sol.*"

"*Haasi,*" she said back.

His eyes narrowed. "*Sol.*"

"*Haasi.*"

"*Sol!*" he insisted. "*Sol. Sol.*"

She tried to keep from laughing, but her mouth quirked into a smile. "*Haasi, haasi, haasi!*"

"*Maldición!*" he spat. Then another string of rapid-fire words. She didn't understand a single one, but she knew the tone.

She took his hand and gently pulled it toward her chest. She placed it on her skin. The sudden contact seemed to shock him out of his tirade. She looked deep into his eyes, trying to will him to understand what was really happening here.

"Shako," she said, tapping his fingers against her chest. She pointed at the sun. "*Haasi. Sol.*"

She picked up the stone and placed it in his hand. "*Cvto,*" she said. Then, mimicking him perfectly, "*Piedra.*"

Understanding dawned in his eyes. He thought he had been teaching her. Now he realized, she was teaching him.

He pointed at the sun. "*Haasi!*" he said.

She smiled back and playfully mimicked him again, repeating the word as slowly as possible, putting a thick look on her face.

He was shocked. For that moment, she saw him struggle with his temper again.

Then he laughed and smiled, suddenly delighted.

She placed her fingers gently on the skin under the remnants of his once-white shirt. "*Hombre?*" she asked.

He understood now. He shook his head. "Simón," he said. He put his hand over hers. "Simón."

She pulled his hand back to her chest. "Shako," she said again.

"Shako," he repeated.

So now they at least knew each other's names: Simón and Shako.

His hand was still on her. She let him keep it there.

ONCE THEY LEARNED HOW to speak to each other, one of the first things he asked her was to show him the way back to his people.

That was something she couldn't do, no matter how much it displeased him. (And to be honest, it hurt her a little, too. She knew it was absurd. If she woke up lost and far from her people, she would expect to go back home as well. Still, she wondered why she felt such a pang at the thought of him leaving.)

Either way, it was irrelevant. She did not know how to find his people. And she wouldn't take him, even if she did. There had been only minimal contact between the Uzita and the invaders now coming to their lands. But her father feared them enough to begin preparing for war. She wasn't as afraid, but that didn't mean she would willingly put herself at their mercy, either.

He was smart enough, at least, to keep from running off into the swamps by himself in search of them. It had been sheer luck that he'd found her the first time. He would, most likely, end up lost and starving or feeding some alligator or panther.

With Shako, he was safe. She could keep him safe. She hunted and caught fish. They cooked over a small fire and slept in peace under the trees.

After a while, he stopped asking how to get back.

# CHAPTER 20

HE'D NEVER BEEN happier. He should have been dead.

Those two thoughts battled in his mind constantly, always pushing their way to the forefront of Simón's thoughts. He was bathing in a creek with Shako, the cool water flowing over both their naked bodies, until he could not hold back any longer, and he took her in his arms as she laughed and smiled at him—and then he remembered, he should have been dead.

Or he would sit, brooding, in front of the fire they made each night, at the end of their foraging and hunting. His belly was full, but his thoughts were troubled, as he wondered what had happened to Narváez's expedition, to the other soldiers, to his friends—and despite all that, Shako would look at him and a grin would break across his face.

She gave him a knife.

It was a small thing but a huge gesture of trust. She had found the broken point of his sword, sharpened it against a stone, and then mounted it in a bone handle for him.

He could finally help with the hunting and the cleaning and dressing of the game. He could defend himself if one of the panthers or bobcats came too close.

And he could slit her throat while she slept.

But she trusted him with it anyway.

It was the first gift he'd ever received that did not feel somehow paid for, either by humiliation or fealty or obligation. His father had given him bruises as a child, and repeated lessons in never trusting a drunk. His mother had died behind her eyes, and had nothing to give him. He had bought his first armor and weaponry himself when he went to war against the Moors, and everything he received since then he'd paid for with an oath to Narváez.

It was the most unselfish thing he had ever seen.

She did not seem to understand why he became so still, so reverent, when she handed it to him. But she looked into his eyes, and seemed to see something there.

They kissed for the first time.

He had been with a woman before. A whore in a brothel the night before his first battle. The older men in his company had taken him, and it seemed like the right thing to do at the time. They did not want to follow a beardless virgin into battle. He wanted to convince them he was a man. It didn't hurt that he was also very drunk.

Fortunately, it didn't last long. She lifted her skirts and he pumped and was done in what seemed like seconds. He felt soiled and angry with himself as he paid her.

The next day he killed for the first time. That didn't make him feel like any more of a man, either, but it felt more honest.

With Shako, it was different.

He'd had nothing but wanton thoughts from the moment he saw her, naked and free in the open air. Guilt kicked at him over and over as he tried to remember his vows as a knight in the king's service and as a saved child of Christ.

It didn't help much.

When they finally fell into each other's arms, he thought he would shatter from how much he wanted her.

But he held back, forced himself to be gentle. There was no hurry. They had nothing but time and each other.

She put him on his back in the soft grass and straddled him. He ran his hands up and down her naked body, unable to look away. She smiled at him and took one hand and guided it, gently, down, helping him find the right place, and moving his fingers for him.

He held on, somehow, as she rocked back and forth, her skin closer and then farther, swaying over him. Then they locked eyes again, he saw her losing herself, and he could not take it anymore, he exploded, arms and legs shaking violently, spasming like a drowning man.

He was gone, far gone, from all the familiar landmarks and signs, lost in an unknown country, and his entire being was filled with happiness.

SIMÓN HAD KNOWN PRECIOUS little happiness in his life so far. He had a noble's name, but a peasant's upbringing.

His family had been given lands in southern Spain by a long-dead king that were overrun and abandoned when the Moors conquered most of the country. By the time Simón came along, the Oliveras were little more than a forgotten coat of arms and a few people living as impoverished guests on the land of another lord in the north.

Perhaps it was this constant reminder of their lack of wealth that made Simón's father a drunk. Or perhaps it had been beaten into him by Simón's grandfather, by all accounts a cruel man. But when Simón came of age, he found there was nothing to his inheritance but debts and empty wine barrels.

All that was left was the name, and whatever talent he possessed.

His talent, fortunately, was in war. He joined King Charles's forces against the rebel Moors still living in Spain after the Reconquista, the long struggle to return the land to Catholic rule. His gift for strategy and an innate charisma inspired men to follow him and trust his judgment, despite his youth.

When the fighting was done, like thousands of other soldiers, Simón wanted to seek his fortune. He wanted to go to the New World, where explorers like Columbus and Cortés reported that gold lay on the ground for anyone to see, and the natives were docile enough to pick it up when ordered.

His record and reputation were enough to win him a command position under Pánfilo de Narváez, who had been granted the right to declare himself *adelantado* of all of the new land of Florida, to govern and collect tribute in the name of the king.

It seemed like destiny to Simón.

Destiny didn't seem to agree, however. Narváez, a rigid, one-eyed man with a strong notion of his own importance, had not met with much success on his first trip to the Americas. He had been sent to rein in Hernán Cortés, who had overthrown the native Aztecs. The crown feared Cortés was setting himself up as a rebel lord half a world away from Spain.

Cortés defeated and humiliated Narváez, meeting him at the shore and forcing his surrender. He kept him prisoner for two years. Cortés then made his own peace with Spain—helped considerably by the vast amounts of Aztec gold he was now shipping back to the king—and was never punished for his treason. Narváez was eventually sent back to Spain in disgrace.

The expedition to Florida, and the wealth that was supposed to be there, was his reward for his suffering and his loyalty.

Things went wrong from the beginning of the journey, however. The king did not offer to pay for the expedition, and Narváez had to call in debts and spend his own fortune. They set sail with eight hundred men in four ships.

A storm in Trinidad sank two of the ships as they stopped for supplies. They were delayed again in

Cuba as Narváez was forced to raise money to purchase two more. While trapped in port, the remaining soldiers and sailors ate their way through all of the expedition's food before roughly half of them deserted the expedition entirely. Narváez was in a constantly foul mood, spitting about treachery and lack of honor.

Since his family came from Cuba, Narváez prevailed on old friends to extend him credit for his adventure. He was able to find two more ships, as well as a pilot named Miruelo, who claimed to know of a harbor almost as big as a sea on the east coast of Florida. Perhaps thinking he'd finally gotten some luck, Narváez made Miruelo the captain of a ship and the expedition's navigator.

They sailed from Havana nearly a year after they'd left Spain, now down to four hundred men.

They were within sight of the Florida coast when a hurricane swept them up, seemingly out of nowhere.

Those few hours were the most terrifying of Simón's life. The winds tossed the ships around like a toddler playing in a puddle. Horses and men screamed below the decks as Miruelo blindly turned up and down the coast, looking for the safe harbor he'd promised.

By the time he finally found it, three of the ships were floating wreckage. Men leaped from the decks with their armor and horses, and swam to shore in the pelting rain. Many never made the sand.

When the storm blew over, Narváez's expedition was down to one barely seaworthy ship, a few provisions, and three hundred hungry and angry men.

They made camp on the beach, where Narváez

read a proclamation on parchment paper, signed by the king himself. Simón wondered how it had managed to stay dry through everything.

He read that these lands were claimed in the name of King Carlos of Spain, and that by the right of God and the king, everything and everyone within it were under his dominion.

He promised mercy to those who would convert to the one, true, and Catholic church, and protection and justice.

"But if you do not do this," Narváez intoned, "then by God, we shall enter your country and make war against you in every way we can. We will take you and your women and your children and make you our slaves. We will take all your property, keep what we can use and what we desire, and destroy and burn the rest. If you refuse to obey us, we will show you no mercy, and any deaths that result are your fault, not our own, for we have given you fair warning, here in the sight of God."

Narváez looked around, as if anyone would challenge him.

Most of the soldiers were still dripping wet in the sand. No one said a word.

THE NEXT DAY, HE and his captains—including Simón—began to make their plans to conquer America.

Miruelo was ordered to repair the one remaining ship from the wreckage now floating in the bay and return to Cuba as fast as possible, to get more supplies and men.

Narváez would begin exploring the interior of the coast, sending men into the jungle to find the treasure they all knew was there.

Simón was given command of a squadron and a mostly blank map, with the order to march inland.

While his friends were still making camp on the shore, he set out with more than one hundred conquistadors, servants, and horses behind him. The trail into the jungle was easy and open, the weather clear and brilliant.

They walked a full day out of sight of the harbor without being assaulted by anything more than the insects that constantly buzzed around their exposed skin.

Then the savages came boiling out from between the trees, dozens of them, hundreds.

That's where Simón knew he should have died.

There was no way around it. He had checked the skin where the arrow had pierced his thigh over and over, and there was not so much as a scar.

That wasn't all. When he woke from his fever to find Shako tending him, he felt a lack of the aches and pains he'd previously thought were a constant part of life. A recurrent toothache that had plagued him for months on the journey across the ocean had disappeared. He'd been skin-and-bones thin when he went into the jungle. He had pains in his legs and a slight tremor in one arm where a Moorish arrow had punched through his armor back in Spain.

All of those old injuries and hurts were gone. He was fit and glowing with life.

And he was stronger. Faster. Better. He could bend the steel plate of his armor with his bare hands, leap a dozen feet from a standing start, and keep pace with the deer that ran through the swamp. He seemed to see and even think more clearly.

Shako would not explain. When he asked Shako about it, she would say only that she gave him medicine. In his limited understanding of the Uzita vocabulary, that could have meant anything from native herbs to sorcery.

She refused to say anything more. If he pressed the issue, it led to the only fights they would ever have. He would shout the only words he knew in her language, over and over. She would answer in monosyllables, in Spanish, which only infuriated him more, as if she was mocking him and his inability to make her obey, or even understand. Then she would simply walk away from him, sometimes for hours. At those times, he felt abandoned and lost in the wilderness.

Only once did she ever reply with more than a simple "No." She said to him, "Isn't it enough that you are alive?"

It should have been. She was right about that. But he wondered if it was true. At times he thought he was actually dead and this was Paradise, but it was nothing like the nuns and priests had described. It felt too real, and the pleasures were all pleasures of the flesh.

Somehow Shako had saved him. Remade him, better than ever.

And the happiness and the guilt were threatening to tear him apart from the inside out.

He had to know what she had done.

SIMÓN SCREAMED, AND SHAKO came running.

When she found him, a short distance away from their camp, he'd already tied a strip of his tattered shirt around his leg.

He didn't have to explain. She sucked in a deep breath when she saw the rock nearby, and the tail of the snake poking out from underneath, the diamond-shaped pattern of its scales running up and down its back.

He looked up at her, a mute pleading in his eyes.

The rattlesnakes in the swamps were huge and fat and entirely deadly. Simón could delay the poison racing toward his heart by binding the wound—Shako had taught him that—but he could not stop it. They both knew he was in for an agonizing death. It might take days, or even weeks, but there was no undoing this.

Not by natural means.

Shako bent to one knee and kissed him hard on the mouth. In their pidgin of Spanish and Uzita, she told him not to move, not to fear. She would save him again.

"I know you will," he said, and kissed her back.

She stood and went racing off into the jungle.

For a moment, Simón admired the way she moved, the muscles under her smooth flesh, her incredible grace as she disappeared behind the trees.

He had to get going if he didn't want to lose her.

He dropped the cloth on the ground. The skin underneath was unmarked. The rattlesnake was real, and dead enough, but it had never come close to him. He'd searched for hours before he found the fat snake sleeping in the sun, and smashed its head with the rock.

Then he'd arranged the scene for Shako, and screamed at the top of his lungs.

He followed her into the jungle.

SIMÓN DIDN'T HAVE TO worry about losing her trail.

Shako ran in a panic, breaking branches and leaving footprints everywhere. He'd never seen her so careless.

She must have been terrified. For him. He shoved down the guilt that came with the thought. He had to know how he was alive. He had to know the secret.

Despite the distance from their camp, things began to look familiar to him. There was a kind of fever-dream quality to his memories. He heard the sound of water, echoing. He knew that sound. He had been here before.

He saw the cave, and it came rushing back. The pain, the confusion, and the surrender to the inevitable. Then the appearance of an angel, who took all the pain and fear away with one drink of water.

He saw her footprints in the soft, damp earth and followed them into the cave.

It took a moment for his eyes to adjust to the gloom after the Florida sun, but the trail inside was worn and marked. He followed it, and a different kind of light began to emerge: a blue glow that grew stronger as he made his way deeper.

Simón was well below ground when he found the

pool. Its eerie blue light glowed off the roof of the cave, casting weird shadows in the rock and along the walls. There was nothing but the sound of the small spring, which flowed up from the cracks in the earth, filling the pool.

Shako kneeled before the pool at a well-worn indentation. She said something in words that sounded nothing like the Uzita she'd already taught him. She took a bowl from a stack. It was richly decorated and covered in gold leaf—the only gold he'd seen in Florida so far.

She filled the bowl, muttered some more, and then stood and turned.

That's when she saw him.

The bowl dropped from her hands.

The shock and betrayal on her face were so sharp he felt them like new arrows into his flesh.

With one part of his mind, he knew he had violated her and fouled the peace they had managed to create together, possibly destroying it forever.

But that barely mattered, as the rest of his mind understood what he had found.

"Mother of God," he whispered. "Bimini."

EVERY CONQUISTADOR KNEW THE legends, ever since the stories Ponce de León brought back with him from Columbus's second voyage. The stories told of a spring that gave water that could cure any illness, heal any wound, and possibly deliver life everlasting.

The waters were supposed to be located in Bimini, a place that ranked second only to El Dorado in its elusiveness. De León had named an island in the Bahamas after the legend, but no one seriously believed the waters actually existed, especially since de León died like any other man a few years later.

But the legend persisted. Even the hardened veterans on Simón's expedition, like Narváez, still spoke with a wistful desire of the Bimini waters.

Simón never believed the stories. He thought fresh, clean water was rare enough. He didn't need to believe in a magic elixir of life.

But he could not deny the evidence of his own eyes, and his own body.

This was the Fountain of Youth. Simón had discovered the greatest treasure the world would ever know.

All it took was betraying the only woman he'd ever loved.

SHE WOULD NOT TOUCH SIMÓN.

There was a new distance between them after they returned from the cave and the Fountain. They spoke. They still hunted and ate and lived side by side, but she never allowed him to get too close again.

He recognized, once more, how limited their vocabulary was, in both number and meaning. So much of what Simón and Shako had was encoded in touch, in a physical language of proximity and feeling. Without that closeness, he now felt as if he was trying to reach a faraway island by throwing stones at it, hurling one empty word after another.

She had explained, slowly, several times, until he

finally understood. Her family was the Water Clan. They had been guardians of what he called Bimini as long as they had been here, generation after generation. While other chiefs of the Uzita were known for their strength, or their skill at war, or hunting, or fishing, the Water Clan was always the protector of the secret. They held the tribe's knowledge, and they kept the legend safe.

The Water was a gift, to be used only sparingly, only on certain occasions. To use it too often, to violate the natural order of birth and life and death, was—she used the Spanish words here—the greatest possible sin known to man.

He could not imagine how that could be, and he could not get her to understand his bewilderment. This was a miracle, not a sin, he told her. He used the Spanish as well, since Uzita didn't have either word.

She shook her head, and he felt the distance between them grow, even though she didn't move. The Water was never supposed to be used selfishly. It gave too much, she said. Those who drank it and lived past their natural lives became corrupt, their souls rotting long before their bodies died. Corpses on the inside, wrapped in fresh skin and flawless beauty.

Simón pitied Shako then. Despite her greater-than-average intelligence, despite her obvious gift with languages, she was still a savage, mired in folklore and superstition. He tried to explain it to her as he would a child. The Water could preserve life, could end suffering and illness. It could be used by the right men, honorable men, to ensure that peace and justice reigned for everyone. A good king would not have to pass his empire on to a wayward or selfish son. Without the fear of death, wars would no longer need to be fought to protect territories and property. The best men could take this gift and use it to forge a new and better world. Surely she had to see that. Surely that was better than letting the Water stew in some forgotten cave next to a primitive swamp.

She did not see that. "You do not know," she told him. "You have never seen it." There were Uzita who'd fallen prey to the same vanity Simón was preaching. Even one of her ancestors, a great chief of the Water Clan, had not been able to resist the temptation. He lived for years past his natural lifespan. He did not grow wiser, even though he was stronger than any of the men and women who came after him. He didn't make the clans any safer, even though he accumulated great wealth and power. He grew only more distant as the sons and daughters he'd had aged and died ahead of him. He severed himself from everything that made him who he was. Death became little more than a joke to him, and he spent the lives of the Uzita on foolish wars against other tribes and clans. Finally, he was exiled. He became a sinister figure, forever lurking near the tribe but no longer of it.

"A story told to children to get them to behave," Simón said.

Her eyes grew cold. She stopped talking to him and went away to find someplace else to sleep. That was the last time they discussed it.

Simón considered begging for her forgiveness

several times, but he didn't believe he'd actually broken her faith. She could have told him about the Bimini waters. She didn't have to keep it a secret from him. And he still believed he could convince her to let him use the Water for the greater good. She could lead him back to the expedition, and with the help of the other men, they could collect and bottle this marvelous resource and make a better world with it.

He didn't want to leave her, however. Even if he lived a thousand years, Simón couldn't imagine living it without her.

He would have to make her see the truth. It would take time. But that was not a problem.

They had nothing but time.

Until, one day, their time ran out.

SIMÓN WAS HUNTING A raccoon—they made a surprisingly filling meal—when he heard a crashing in the brush. He hid behind a tree.

Shako had told him what to do if he ever saw another one of the Uzita, or any other Indian, without her: run.

He put his ego aside and listened, for once. Simón had never been a coward, but he remembered how swiftly his men were destroyed by the Uzita. He remembered almost dying. He didn't want to repeat the experience. He had no armor and no weapon, save the makeshift knife Shako had given him. He could not expect to win if discovered by the Uzita warriors, and there was no guarantee Shako would use the Water to save him.

It wasn't in him to run from a fight, however. So he watched from behind the tree, silently waiting.

Maximillian came stumbling out of the jungle, face red with exertion, boiling in his armor like a shrimp tossed into a pot.

For a moment, Simón was shocked. Did I ever look that sick, that pale? His skin was a deep brown now, tanned by the constant sun. He wore nothing but a breechcloth and sometimes his old tunic. His stomach was always full these days. And he hadn't been sick since Shako gave him the Water.

Maximillian stood there, gasping and squinting at the sun, desperately trying to get his bearings.

For an instant, Simón considered letting Max go crashing and stumbling on his way, his armor rattling with every step. He was happy here. He could die here, and no one would ever know.

Something about that stuck in his throat, however. No one would ever know. He had traveled across the globe and it would not make a bit of difference. He might as well have died on his family's bankrupt estate or at the hands of some Moor. The world would not be changed one bit by his passing. For some reason, he could not live with that.

Simón stepped from behind the tree. He almost laughed as Maximillian's eyes went wide with shock and he fumbled to pull his sword from its sheath again.

"Max," Simón said. "Don't be afraid. It's me."

Recognition dawned slowly on Max's face. His jaw dropped. And then Simón saw sheer joy overcome his stupor.

"Simón," he said. "Mother of God. Look at you. I can't believe it. We found you. We found you!"

He began yelling, and the others came crashing through the grass a few moments later. They grabbed him and embraced him, their armor hot and sharp against his bare skin, clapped him on the back, and laughed with joy.

His friends. They had never given up on him. They'd finally found him.

MAX. FRANCISCO. PEDRO. Sebastian. Antonio. Carlos. Even Juan Aznar, the shy little priest that they had befriended on the long ocean journey from Spain. They all came for him.

They'd gone to war against the Moors, as Simón had, and like him, they were too late to have acquired lands or titles from it. They were young and hungry for glory, and they became inseparable after they joined Narváez.

Until Narváez separated them. Simón had wanted to bring all of them along on his initial foray. Narváez had refused the request, saying that he needed experienced men to lead the fresh recruits. They had all seen battle before, even Aznar, who had served as a priest ministering to soldiers. Narváez would not risk them all on a single errand. In hindsight, Simón had to agree. If they'd come with him, they'd likely be as dead as every other man he'd led.

"We decided it was time to come looking for you," Max said that night, as they sat around the campfire, eating the deer that Shako had killed earlier to feed them.

Simón's friends tore into it as if they hadn't seen meat for weeks. As it turned out, they had not.

The past several months had seen many changes in Narváez's expedition, none of them good. Food was still scarce. The grueling heat made overland marching a slow, painful chore. The native tribes abandoned their villages before the conquistadors could arrive, and they took their food with them. Worst of all, there was no gold to be found anywhere.

"Narváez was probably glad to see us go," Francisco said. "Fewer mouths to feed."

They had not exactly asked permission for their search, either. They had simply left after another long day of fruitless foraging led them to the spot where Simón's troops had been killed.

"I believe you dropped this," Max said, holding up his helmet, now badly rusted and dented. "We followed the pieces of armor as far as we could."

Shako had been watching silently, away from the men and the campfire. She did not share in their laughter, and for the most part, Simón's friends simply ignored her or ordered her around. It seemed completely natural to them that Simón should have found a willing and obedient savage to cook and care for him.

To all of them except Aznar, anyway. When they returned to Simón and Shako's camp, his eyes had gone wide with shock when he saw Shako there. He crossed himself repeatedly and hissed to Simón, "Who is that?" He muttered darkly to himself and gave her suspicious glances, sullen eyes darting back to her repeatedly, running up and down her bare legs. Now Shako wore the cloth that covered her breasts for the first time in several months. Aznar still glared.

The others were less obvious about it, but it clearly bothered them, too. Max was the one to finally bring up the question.

"So, Simón. When you come back with us, are you planning on bringing your new little wife?"

Everyone laughed but Aznar. And Shako.

They thought Shako did not understand Spanish. Neither Simón nor Shako had corrected them.

Simón didn't know what to say. Until that moment, he had not even been sure he would return with the others. But he had to, didn't he? He swore an oath to serve the crown and Narváez. He'd had a pleasant interlude. But it had to end sometime, didn't it?

Simón wondered if he could really stay here. If he could send his friends away and spend the rest of his life with Shako. It might be a very long life, with the Water.

But that was insane, if he really thought it through. He couldn't live here, any more than she could live with him in Spain. They were of two completely different worlds.

Simón looked at her. She was watching him carefully, to see what he'd say.

Before he could answer, Pedro spoke up. "What I want to know is, can she lead us to anything worth having in this godforsaken swamp?"

"What?"

"It's a good question, Simón," Max said. "Do her people have treasure? Food? At this point, anything would help."

"I don't know," Simón said.

"You don't know?" Max was incredulous. "What have you been doing all this time?"

Sebastian laughed. "Oh, I know what he's been doing," he said, and leered at Shako. "Perhaps she has sisters waiting for us."

Shako turned sharply toward him, her sudden anger plain on her face.

Sebastian laughed. "My God, it's almost as if she understands me. You've got her well trained, Simón."

Pedro reached for Shako's arm. "Will she do whatever you say? I've got a couple tricks I could teach her."

Shako slapped his hand away. Simón saw her reach for her knife.

He couldn't let this happen. "Stop," he said.

But Pedro kept on laughing. He still thought it was a joke. Simón knew that Shako could gut him in an instant and then turn on the others. She might even get Max or Francisco, who were nearest after that, but then, certainly, one of the others would find his pistol. "Stop!" he said again, wondering who he was really trying to protect.

Before anything else could happen, however, the grasses shook and men came leaping forward.

They tackled the Spaniards, knocking them all to the ground and wrestling them down in a matter of moments.

Simón felt his hands yanked up behind his back

and felt ropes being tied around him. He was lifted like a child and then kicked in the stomach to take any fight out of him.

He was still watching Shako's eyes. They were wide with surprise. She had not expected this tonight, either.

But they both knew it had to happen sometime.

The Uzita had found them.

THE BONFIRE AT THE center of the Uzita village was so hot that Simón smelled his own hair burning.

They'd been dumped next to the fire by the Uzita, and the whole tribe gathered around them. It was like being in some portrait of Hell. The Spaniards were stripped down to their underclothes. The Uzita jeered at them and threw stones. Little children rushed forward to poke and prod at their strangely colored flesh. A wooden spit was hefted up and over the fire. More dry logs were thrown into the pit, and the heat grew even more intense. The Spaniards were given a good view of the preparations. The Uzita planned to roast them alive.

Aznar was gibbering to himself in panic. The others winced or occasionally cursed as a stone or a blow landed on their heads. They all looked terrified.

Simón had not seen Shako since they'd been carried from the swamp. He wondered, for a brief, absurd moment, if she was safe.

Then the chief arrived, and the Uzita fell silent.

Hirrihigua. Simón had heard his name from Shako, but now he understood the slight tone of awe she used when she spoke of her father. He was a tall, powerful man, his hair still black, his skin as smooth and dark as old leather. The Uzita all made way for him.

He walked to where they lay on the ground. If he felt the burning heat, he gave no indication. Instead, he peered down at each of them, as if weighing and measuring every man.

He did not appear to like what he saw.

He said a few words in Uzita. The warriors grabbed the Spaniards and hauled them up on their feet.

Hirrihigua walked close to Simón and stared deeply into his face. The chief's eyes were unreadable. Simón knew that his life had already been decided. He wondered what the chief was looking for.

"You drank the Water," he said, so quietly that Simón could barely hear him over the roar of the flames.

Simón found he couldn't lie. "Yes," he admitted.

Hirrihigua shook his head a fraction of an inch. Simón saw something in his eyes, then. He saw pain.

"Into the fire," Hirrihigua said, and turned away abruptly.

Simón did not even have time to let that sink in when he heard a shriek of protest from the crowd.

"No," Shako screamed. She shoved her way through the Uzita and ran to Hirrihigua. He barked at her in Uzita, something so rapid and angry that Simón couldn't understand. She screamed back at him, slapping her hands against his arms when he tried to push her away.

One of the warriors, a man even taller and thicker than Hirrihigua, tried to pull her back into the crowd. Shako turned and kicked him in the gut, and he went gray and staggered.

She shouted at her father again. She did not plead. She demanded.

He looked shocked, and then furious. He lifted his hand as if to strike her.

"No," Simón shouted, and somehow found the speed and strength to push past his guards and lunge for Hirrihigua.

He didn't get far. The butt end of a spear smacked his legs and then cracked him hard on the back of the head. He fell facedown into the dirt.

When he looked up, Shako was beside him. She pulled him up, cradling his body, arms around him as if she would never let him go.

Hirrihigua watched them both. He looked as if he'd tasted something foul.

Shako's eyes were filled with tears. She said, "Please."

Hirrihigua sagged. The anger was gone, Simón could see, replaced by a deep and bitter sadness.

"Your knife," he said to one of the warriors. He took the blade when it was offered. He kneeled down to them.

With a quick slash, he cut Simón's bonds.

Then he crossed to the others and did the same for them.

He handed the blade back to the warrior and walked away.

The Uzita stood there, confused, uncertain.

Shako was not. She pulled Simón upright and began pushing him away from the fire. The others followed as quickly as they could.

Muttering and grumbling began as soon as Shako hurried them through the crowd. She didn't stop. She kept moving them past the Uzita's houses, off into the darkness at the edge of the village.

None of them spoke. She kept hustling them along until they found a trail, barely visible in the dark. They could still see the flames and shadows dancing from the center of the village. The muttering of the Uzita had turned to loud argument now.

Shako shoved Simón. Hard. "Run," she said. "Keep running along this trail. Follow the flow of the river when you reach it. It will take you back to your people. Now run."

He clasped her hand and tried to pull her along.

She drew back as if scalded.

"Shako," he said.

"Run," she said again, pain in her voice and on her face. "And don't ever come back."

The shouts of the Uzita grew closer, and Simón heard some of the men moving into the brush after them.

"Simón, we must go *now*," Max said. He and the others were ready to bolt, but they had no idea where they were going.

Simón nodded. He leaned forward and kissed Shako.

Then he turned and ran.

# CHAPTER 21

THERE WERE A few mutters of "traitor" and "deserter" when Narváez took him back into the fold. His friends put a stop to that talk with their own bluster and threats. Simón was surprisingly indifferent. He was back where he was supposed to be, but he felt lost.

Despite this, Narváez gave him used armor and another sword. Perhaps he felt a sense of obligation to Simón after bringing him across the ocean. More likely, it was an acknowledgment that Narváez needed every able-bodied man he had left.

The expedition was now down to about 250. Illness and hunger had killed a couple of dozen while Simón was gone. Raids by the native tribes as the conquistadors blundered through the wilderness had taken the rest. The remaining Spaniards were pale and wormy as something found under a rock.

Simón was now the healthiest and strongest man

among them. Narváez had even commented on it. "You look well for a man kidnapped by savages," he said. Narváez still dreamed of conquering Florida, of taming the land granted him by the crown. And it was becoming increasingly clear he'd never do that without a fight. Simón supposed that made him an asset again.

He certainly had nothing else to offer. His friends could not tell Narváez where the Uzita were located, and Simón feigned ignorance as well. He said he'd seen no treasure in his time in the wilderness. He had betrayed Shako once already. He wouldn't do it again. He knew Narváez would raid the Uzita for their food alone. And if Narváez learned of the Water, then he would stop at nothing to possess it. He would take the glory and become the most powerful man in Spain, perhaps in the world.

Simón would not allow that.

So he kept silent. And he waited for several weeks, until Narváez was distracted by the constant press of foraging for food and keeping his troops satisfied again.

In the meantime, he made a plan.

"WE HAVE TO GO BACK."

"For your whore? For that animal?"

Simón resisted the urge to split Aznar's face open along the lines of his sneer. He tamped his anger down.

He'd gathered his friends at a fire on the edge of the camp, late at night. He'd considered simply leaving without them, but they did not abandon him, and he wouldn't abandon them now. The truth was, they all needed to escape. And he needed all of them if his plan was to work. But he couldn't tell them the truth. They would think he wasn't just smitten but infected, that he'd caught some kind of pox from Shako that was already destroying his brain.

So he gave them a half-truth.

"Because there is treasure there."

They paid attention to that. Simón was reminded of dogs sitting up at the scent of meat.

"Gold?" Francisco asked.

"Where?" Aznar demanded. "Why didn't you tell Narváez?"

"Why should Narváez be the only one who profits from this disaster? We can have it all for ourselves. And believe me: we will be richer than kings. All of us."

"I didn't see anything on your savage girl that looked like gold," Pedro said.

"You were looking at her other charms," Sebastian said.

Again, Simón had to bite down on his bile. He could endure a few insults to his honor if it meant getting Shako back, and getting to the Fountain.

"It's there," Simón said. "Why do you think I spent so long among the savages? I wanted them to trust me. They don't even understand what they have. If you come with me, I can negotiate. I can convince them to let us take the treasure with us."

"You're talking about mutiny," Aznar said. "You should tell Narváez."

"Has anything on this expedition gone as Narváez planned?" Simón shot back. "I was the one who was lost in the wilderness for months, but you are the ones who are filthy and starving. We could be hundreds or thousands of miles away from our destination. It's lucky an ocean separates us from Spain. If the king knew of this, he'd have Narváez beheaded simply to avoid the embarrassment."

There was a grudging silence. Simón knew from experience: hungry men were always angry.

"Do you believe you could do better?" Aznar asked, sullen.

"I believe *we* can do better. History belongs to the man who takes it. If we bring the Uzita's treasure back to the king, I guarantee he will give us anything we want."

They all stood in silence for a moment, considering that.

For a moment, Simón feared they would turn against him. This was treason. But more than that, this was an admission that the power and glory of Spain had its limits. To leave Narváez now would be to concede that the king, in his wisdom, had committed all their lives to the wrong man and the wrong cause. It was far easier to follow along than to sever that last link, that last string of hope that everything would work as planned because God and Kingdom had decreed it would be so. This was more than abandoning the mission; this was taking responsibility for their own destiny.

Finally, Max broke the silence.

"We'll need supplies," he said. Pragmatic as ever.

Just like that, the decision was made. They would follow Simón. This was uncharted territory, and they were trusting him to lead them through it.

Of course, the greed in their eyes had something to do with it as well.

"Gather what you can without attracting too much attention," he said. "We leave the camp tonight."

HIRRIHIGUA STOOD AT THE center of the Uzita village, flanked by nearly a hundred of his warriors. Each one of them looked ready to eat the hearts of Simón and his friends.

At this point, the only thing holding them back was the flag of truce and Hirrihigua's tolerance.

"I'm starting to have doubts about your plan," Max said in a low voice.

Simón tried not to show any fear. He and the others stood in the clearing at the middle of the Uzita's village, circled by the wooden houses and their palm-thatched roofs, much as they had when Shako had begged for their lives.

The rest of the Uzita, all the old men, women, and children, crowded around the edges of the central ground, gawking at them.

Simón desperately hoped they looked more impressive this time. He wanted to negotiate from a position of strength, not beg for his life. They were all wearing armor and carrying their pistols and swords. Simón once more wondered if they'd made the right decision when they chose not to steal an harquebus, one of the cannonlike muskets that required two men to set up and fire. Narváez would have noticed that immediately, and even the lighter rifles would have slowed them down too much.

It was said that a handful of men with Spanish steel were worth a whole army in some battles. Simón hoped it would not be necessary to prove that.

Simón had argued against stealth, and instead walked right up to the village in the bright morning sunlight, carrying a once-white rag as a sign of peace. He spoke to the sentries in their own language, and asked—not demanded—to see Hirrihigua.

The chief must have been intrigued. He agreed to let Simón speak. But he had them face every warrior in the tribe to do so.

Simón had never lacked courage. He wouldn't whimper. This was his chance.

And, to the audible gasps of his fellow soldiers, he kneeled.

"What are you doing?" Max hissed.

Simón ignored him.

"Great Chief," he said, with as much humility as he could muster. "We are here to offer you our apologies."

That caused a murmur among the Uzita. Hirrihigua looked around, and they went quiet again.

"What did you say?" Max asked.

"Quiet," Simón growled, and continued to speak to the chief in Uzita. "We do not have to fight. I believe we can have peace. I believe we can work together. I come to you to ask for a chance to prove this."

Simón searched through the limited vocabulary he'd learned from Shako. There were so few words, but each one had multiple meanings. The phrases seemed to slip away the harder he tried to grasp them.

"We have many things that can help the Uzita. Help with the food. Help with the tools. Medicine. Weapons."

The chief finally spoke. "And what is it you want?"

Simón hesitated, then plunged ahead. "The Water."

There was an audible gasp from the Uzita. Simón was aware he'd just committed the equivalent of blasphemy, so he hurried ahead.

"You know what a treasure this is. It would be worth much to our"—they had no word for king—"chief across the ocean. He would bring you much treasure for this. He would make your tribe stronger than any other."

"From what I have seen of you," Hirrihigua said calmly, "your people can barely feed themselves."

A little of Simón's pride reared up at that. He looked the chief directly in the eyes. "We have conquered greater warriors than yours," he said. "And more of us are coming every day."

The Uzita men bristled at that. There was a general muttering of anger, a readying of weapons.

The chief remained stoic. "Then perhaps we should kill you now, to save ourselves the trouble later."

Max chose that moment to speak up again. "Simón, I can't help but notice this doesn't seem to be going well."

Simón breathed in deeply to remain calm. All he wanted was a few barrels. That's all it would take. He could take those and Shako and return to Spain an impossibly wealthy man. The king would give him anything if he returned with the Bimini waters. He could restore his family's lands and then find a small place far away from everything, where they could live in peace.

He had to make the chief see. He stood up so he could be closer to eye to eye with the man.

"My words . . ." Simón hesitated again. "I need to find the right way to explain. It would help if your daughter was here. To talk for me again."

If Hirrihigua was stone before, now he was ice. Simón realized he'd made a mistake, but he did not know what.

The chief looked at him and did not reply.

Simón tried again. "Where is Shako?"

There was finally something like an expression breaking through the stone of the chief's face. It was barely a grimace, but to Simón it looked like contempt.

He spoke one word in Uzita: "Gone."

Simón felt like the world had dropped out from under him. His head spun. Like most of the Uzita language, the single word had multiple meanings. But there was one he knew best from his lessons with Shako. "Gone" meant "dead."

"You killed her?"

That broke the chief's composure completely. He erupted in rage. "*You* killed her," he shouted back. He lifted the war club above his head. Simón was still frozen and reeling. The others did not even know exactly what had been said. They were hesitant and confused.

The chief roared and the warriors of the Uzita roared with him. At that moment, Simón knew he'd brought his closest friends and allies with him only to die. A single thought filled his mind. Perhaps in Heaven, he would be reunited with Shako.

Then something burned Simón's face. Smoke stung his eyes, and he could no longer hear the bellow of the chief or his warriors.

The chief looked down at his chest, which was a smoking ruin. A musket ball with a heavy charge of black powder had smashed into him, tearing a hole through his ribs and into his heart.

His eyes went dead as the blood began to flow, and his body hit the ground, lifeless.

But we didn't bring the harquebus, Simón thought.

Then he turned and saw the conquistadors. Dozens of men from the expedition, pouring from the overgrown jungle in full armor, with Narváez, the one-eyed demon, leading the charge.

The big harquebus fired again, this time to Simón's left. Someone tackled him to the ground before the next blast took his head off.

Max pulled him from the dirt and hurried him off to the side. "Get out of the way, you idiot," he grunted. The other soldiers of their expedition were already preparing to fire again.

Impossible, Simón thought. How did they find us?

The soldiers came from everywhere. They had surrounded the village completely. The lines of men closed in like a knot being pulled tight.

The guns concentrated their shots on the warriors, who were conveniently lined up where the chief had been standing. They had been caught just as unaware as Simón. The musket balls hit them as they tried to cross the village ground, laying half of them down in the first few moments of the fight. The smoke and noise sent the Uzita scrambling for cover, their defenses broken in second. Then it was nothing but slaughter.

The conquistadors laid into the Uzita with their swords. Everyone in the circle was a target. He saw a woman with a baby at her breast stabbed in the throat. An old woman had her face smashed with a mailed fist. A man took a musket ball to the back of his head a few steps away, his skull shattering under the impact. Those who ran screaming were impaled on a relentlessly advancing wall of pikes. Narváez screamed, "No prisoners! No quarter!"

They followed us, Simón realized. One of his own had told them. They laid in wait, and they surrounded the village, and they took their moment.

Simón felt heat on his face and arms, and saw that someone had set the thatched palm of the roofs on fire. He watched an Uzita woman driven into the flames by two pikemen he'd eaten and drank with. He saw the baby torn from his dying mother's breast.

He closed his eyes, because he did not want to see what happened next.

He wanted nothing more than to wake, screaming, from this nightmare.

THE SUN CLIMBED OVER the scorched earth of the Uzita camp. The burned wooden houses. The plain unpainted pottery, now smashed into fragments everywhere. The bodies, which wore no jewelry or decoration of any kind.

Narváez surveyed it all. The other men were still stacking the corpses in a pile.

Simón and the others were not even given that humiliating duty. They were assembled, on their knees, in the center of the village. Guards had watched them since the battle—or, more accurately, the massacre—was done.

Simón had tried to speak once, and was beaten by the guards for his trouble. His face was now swelling with bruises. The others took the hint and remained silent.

One of Narváez's lieutenants came from the burned huts at the edge of the village. He and Narváez spoke quietly for several minutes. Simón couldn't hear the conversation, but there was no mistaking the anger on Narváez's face.

Narváez then turned on Simón, his one good eye squinting. "Where is the gold?"

Simón was unprepared for Narváez's rage. "There is no gold."

Narváez crossed the ground between them in a few quick steps, his saber at Simón's throat before the younger man could blink. "You told them there was treasure here. You swore to it."

"There is—there is treasure," Simón said, and then stopped. His life was in his commander's hands now. A twitch of that blade and Simón's life would spill out all over the ground.

Along with the lives of every man, woman, and child of the Uzita.

He had never intended this. He felt shame and fear and anger. He thought about Shako.

He looked into Narváez's eye and said, "Find it yourself."

The look on Narváez's face was pure murder. For a moment, Simón was certain he was about to die.

Then Narváez withdrew his sword and stepped away. He called to his second-in-command. "Alvar," he said. "Divide the savages' food among the men. We will continue into the interior on foot." He pointed to Simón and his friends. "The traitors stay here. Strip them of weapons and armor and supplies."

Aznar wailed as if stabbed in the gut. "No," he said. "You cannot abandon me here. I was loyal! I told you! I came to you!"

"You repeated his lies," Narváez spat back. "You gave me nothing."

Aznar began to protest, but the nearest guard clubbed him hard with the hilt of his sword. Aznar went down to the ground, gasping for air.

"Tie them up," Narváez ordered. "If they resist at all, kill them."

He looked at Simón one last time. "You kneel to a savage? Then you can rot here with the rest of them."

FOR THE REST OF the day, Simón and his friends watched, bound and seated on the ground, among the buzzing flies that feasted on the dead bodies of the Uzita. The other conquistadors swept through the remains of the village, gathering what little food remained in the storehouses. They took fresh water from the nearby stream and packed the supplies on the horses.

By midafternoon, the expedition was ready to move on. Narváez ordered every man to march past Simón and the others, both as a torment to the disgraced and a warning to those who remained.

Aznar did not stop wailing the entire time, no matter how often he was kicked or punched. "Please," he screamed to Padre Suárez as the priest passed by. "For the love of God."

Suárez averted his eyes. The other soldiers were stone-faced as they walked away into the jungle. Simón knew they were hungry as well as angry, and eight fewer men meant eight fewer mouths to feed.

The others were stoic, but Simón could feel their fear and tension. They blamed him for this. They were right. This was all his fault.

Despite that, Simón was calm. He had been sitting among corpses for the better part of a day. The fat black flies landed on his face and, unable to brush them away, he no longer even flinched as they bit him.

In his mind, a part of him had already died. A piece of his soul was gone. He had lost everything: the woman he loved, followed shortly by his rank, his position, and his few possessions.

His body, however, went on living. As his mind turned over his new circumstances, he forced himself to see the advantages.

For the first time in his life, he was truly free. Free of expectations, free of obligations, free of the chains of family and honor and duty and loyalty. Free of anything but his ambitions.

As soon as he was certain Narváez and the rest of

the expedition were well away from here, he would make the others see as well.

They had been left alone with the greatest treasure any man had ever known. And Simón would make certain they used it right.

He had intended none of this. But he would take the responsibility.

This was the New World. His world.

IT TOOK SIMÓN THE best part of an hour to squirm out of his bonds. His wrists were slick with blood by the time he got the ropes off. He didn't feel the pain.

He released the others, then convinced them to follow him. He promised food and shelter. They didn't want to move at first, but they had been baking in the sun all day, and whatever anger or misgivings they had, they still got up and walked behind him. At this point, he was their only option.

Aznar never shut up. He implored them to go after Narváez, and then threatened to go himself when no one listened. It was an empty threat. He hurried after them as they kept trudging through the tall grass and among the trees. Finally, he contented himself with cursing Simón, an endless muttering stream of promises of hellfire and damnation and insults.

It made Simón grind his teeth, but he kept on walking, even as the sun began to set. He knew the way from here. He could find it, even in the dark.

They reached the caverns by the light of the moon. The others were tired and hungry, their eyes hollow. The reality of their situation was beginning to impress itself on them, Simón knew. They had been marked as traitors, abandoned an ocean away from home, and left for the savages.

He led them into the cave. They followed, because they had nowhere else to go.

They stopped at the edge of the pool. The blue glow reflected over all their faces, and Simón saw the fear there. Good. They were not dead yet. They were not completely broken, because fear was the only appropriate response for something as otherworldly as this.

Aznar, of course, was the first to find his voice again.

"What is this?" he demanded. "Is this some kind of pagan sorcery? Is this the work of that savage whore? Was she a witch as well? Answer me, Simón! What kind of abomination in the eyes of God—"

Simón hit him in the face.

Aznar fell down hard. He looked up at Simón and struggled to rise.

Simón hit him again. And did not stop. Despite the pain in his arms and the bone-deep exhaustion, he hit him again and again and again.

The others watched. Perhaps they saw the demon lurking behind Simón's eyes then, or perhaps he was simply doing what they'd wanted to do for a long time.

Whatever the reason, Simón stopped beating Aznar only when he could no longer lift his fists.

He looked at the others. They looked back, wary and anxious or dull-eyed and apathetic. It made no difference to him. As long as they were watching.

Aznar lay on the ground, blood bubbling through split lips and broken teeth.

Simón went to the pool and took one of the ceremonial bowls from the stack by the pool, just as he'd seen Shako do. He filled it from the pool and held it to Aznar's lips, almost tenderly.

Aznar struggled slightly, but there was no power to it. He was half-dead.

Simón forced him to swallow.

Then he drank deep from the same bowl himself.

Aznar sputtered. Beneath the congealing blood, the broken bones of his face shifted. The bruises softened, cleared, and then faded. The broken skin closed and healed.

"Holy Christ," one of them whispered.

Now they all looked at him with only one expression: fear. Even Aznar, who sat up, blinking, not comprehending what had just happened. They all feared him.

That was good. That was a start. He needed them to listen.

"This is the treasure I promised you," he said. "This is where our new lives begin. We are reborn here and now. This is the Water. The Water is Life."

Simón's fists and arms no longer hurt. His hands were whole and unbroken when he passed the bowl.

They all drank.

NARVÁEZ NEVER MADE IT back to Spain, or anywhere. He wandered, lost in Florida, until starvation forced him and his soldiers to melt down their weapons and armor to make parts for boats. A hurricane drowned the would-be ruler of Florida somewhere in the Gulf of Mexico. The surviving members of the expedition washed up on an island that would one day be named Galveston. From there, they made their way back to land, before trekking on foot to Spanish settlements in Mexico. Of the eight hundred men who began the expedition, only four survived.

At least, that was the version the history books recorded.

Simón and his conquistadors returned to Tampa Bay, where they found the shipwrecked remains of the two ships. They dragged the timbers onto the beach. They collected rope and damaged sailcloth. They boiled sap from the nearby trees and made pitch.

They worked steadily, morning until night, every day for months.

They made barrels. Hundreds of barrels.

MIRUELO RETURNED WITH THE fifth ship of the expedition, as he promised Narváez he would, and found them waiting on the beach. At first, it seemed as if Simón and the others were to be captured and chained as deserters.

But Simón convinced Miruelo to speak with him privately. He took him to the place in the jungle they had cleared for their camp. Simón gave him a drink of water and made his offer.

From that moment on, Miruelo was another member of the Council.

They sailed back to Cuba and used Narváez's credit to begin their real work.

They found the Water made them stronger. Tougher. Smarter. Faster. They never got sick. It was amazing how much of a difference these advantages made, in a world racked with danger and disease.

They began as scavengers, picking over the world's graveyards. When plagues ran through Valencia, Brazil, and Chile over the next several years, Simón and Sebastian walked through the cities without fear and paid almost nothing for the properties of the dead. When the Thirty Years' War shattered Europe, they were able to amass a fortune selling food at extortionate rates to the millions left starving by the chaos. They even worked for a time as mercenaries, returning to the field despite wounds that would have killed other men.

Then they became bankers. When the Dutch economy collapsed in 1637, they were there, profiting from the speculation as well as the sudden crash. They could lend money at a fraction of the cost, and make investments that would not pay off for decades, if not longer.

At some point, Max began calling them the Council of the Immortals. He twisted it with irony, as he always did, but the others took it seriously. The name stuck, at least among themselves.

Eventually, they became so rich and owned so much that the rulers came to them, seeking advice, approval, and protection, along with the money they always seemed to need. Simón and the Council were always happy to provide what was asked, for a price. Nothing was ever free.

They used their influence to pull levers and

strings behind the curtains of history, to nudge and shove and force the world in the direction they wanted.

It wasn't easy. They backed the wrong men time and time again, and were often blinded by their prejudices to losses that looked inevitable in hindsight. They didn't have any love for the British, but Simón was stunned when an only marginally competent general named Washington managed to scrape out a victory for his colonial rebels. Their belief in the natural superiority of the aristocracy put them on the losing side of the French Revolution as well.

It was not long after that when Simón Anglicized his name and began calling himself Simon Oliver. He learned English, and forced the others to do the same.

He still believed he could make the world behave. He could force it to be the paradise he dreamed, given time.

And they had nothing but time.

At least that was how it seemed for almost two centuries.

MIRUELO WAS THE FIRST of them to die, and the one who taught them the danger of going too long without a drink.

He set out overseas to visit Mexico and manage some of the Council's holdings there. His ship was caught in a hurricane and blown hundreds of miles off course, delaying him by months. He'd left without any of the Water.

Simon received a report from one of his trusted

subordinates a year later that chilled him down to his soul.

By the time Miruelo made port, the letter said, he was barely recognizable. He'd lost all his hair and teeth, his eyes were milky with cataracts, and he was bent nearly in half with arthritis. It had happened within a few weeks on the ship, so quickly that the sailors suspected witchcraft. Miruelo lasted a few more weeks once the ship made land, and then died in his sleep, a shriveled husk of his former self.

But the most frightening thing, to Simon, was what had happened to Miruelo's mind. It was as if all the experiences of the past century had crushed him under their weight. At one moment, his lieutenant wrote, he would speak in the confident tones of a master pilot, barking out orders on a ship. And in the next he would be weeping like a child for his mother. Most of the time, however, he simply reacted to everything and everyone around him as best he could; he'd become a new, third person with no memory at all.

Simon's lieutenant was utterly baffled. Simon was not. He wrote back about mysterious diseases that befell longtime sailors, and dismissed all of Miruelo's desperate pleading for "the Water of Life" as the need of a repentant man to confess his sins before he died.

Simon knew what had really happened. Without the Water, the years they had cheated would come rushing back all at once—and would take their minds as well as their bodies.

From then on, Simon declared that every member of the Council would carry at least a flask of the Water with them at all times. He thought that would be enough.

He didn't know it at the time, but Miruelo was the only member of the Council who would die peacefully. He didn't yet know that someone was hunting them.

# CHAPTER 22

PANAMA CITY, FLORIDA
NOW

DAVID WOKE LIKE a drowning man trying to escape the ocean.

He sucked down air in a huge gasp, kicking and thrashing hard, trying to push himself free of the massive weight that had been crushing him only moments before.

Then he realized, sweating and panting, that he was in a bed.

The details came to him more quickly and sharply than he would have expected. The room was dark but appeared merely gray to his eyes. He felt the high thread count of the sheets; saw the modernist design on the wall; the chunky, faux-custom furniture. Hotel room. Not a cheap one, either.

David saw her in the chair across the hotel room, watching him, her eyes reflecting the dim light like a cat's.

"Take it easy," she told him. "We're in no danger. You're safe. We have plenty of time."

With her voice, it came flooding back: the panic; the gunfire; Max, with his cruel smile, stepping calmly from the crowd and leveling the pistol at him—and then the terrible, crushing pain, like someone put a fist through his chest. And the blood. So much blood.

He touched the skin above his heart gingerly. If this were a dream, this is the part where his fingers would come away red and he would remember he was dead.

There was nothing. No blood. He looked down. No wound. Not so much as a scar. He was bathed in sweat, but it was panic rather than pain. He took another moment to run an inventory of himself. Nothing hurt. Nothing ached. Despite the adrenaline pulsing through him, he almost felt as though he could hop out of bed and run a marathon.

"You're safe," she said again. "Just breathe."

He felt his own chest again. Whole and unmarked. "What happened?"

Even in the dim light, he could see the white of her teeth as she smiled. "I think you know," she said.

"He shot me."

"Yes."

"He shot me through the heart. I saw the gun, I felt it, I was dying—"

"Easy. Just breathe."

"Why?"

"Now, that is a very long story. The short version is you've just seen the true face of Simon Oliver and the men around him."

Words failed David for a moment. "No, I mean—I mean—why?"

"Why are you alive?"

David swallowed. He didn't really want to think of it like that. But he nodded.

"Because I saved you, David."

"The Water."

She nodded. "The Water."

"What's going on? Who are you? Who are you really?"

"Hush," she said. "Your body is healed. Your mind is going to take a little more time to deal with the trauma."

David realized he was shaking. "The trauma of being dead, you mean."

"If that's how you want to put it."

"I had a great big goddamn hole in my chest where my *heart* was supposed to be, what else am I supposed to call it?"

She just looked at him. He realized he was shouting. He struggled to take a deep breath. Then another. The hotel room smelled like jasmine and jet fuel.

"Sorry," he said.

"It's fine. As I said. You need a little more time."

"Can they find us here?" David rubbed his chest again. He was not particularly interested in seeing if he could rise from the dead twice in the same night.

"You're safe," she said for the third time. "No one will disturb us here. This hotel charges a great deal for privacy and security. And no one is even looking for us here."

"All right," David said. He slid back into the pillows, relaxing a fraction of an inch at a time.

She stood and crossed the room to the bed. He realized she was still wearing what remained of her gown from the party. The scent of cordite and blood still clung to it.

She recognized his discomfort immediately and slid out of the dress, tossing it far across the room. She drew the sheets back and straddled him.

Despite everything, he was already rising to meet her.

Before his mind shut down completely and his body took over, he had one last question. "Who are you?"

She smiled again, but this time it looked sad to him.

"Shako," she said. "My name is Shako."

WRAPPED IN THE SHEETS afterward, sweat cooling on their bodies, she told him the story.

A young Indian girl, Spanish conquistadors, and an impossible secret to keep. An inevitable betrayal. And then slaughter.

"I should have seen it coming," she said, fingers playing lightly over his chest. "I was young. It was the last time I was young."

# CHAPTER 23

FLORIDA
1528

SHAKO SAW THE Uzita die—everyone she'd ever known, her entire life—right before her eyes.

She forced herself to watch every moment from her hiding place in the trees, at the edge of the village. If she had arrived a little sooner, she might have warned her people. She was never far from the Uzita, even though she was no longer one of them. She could not bring herself to go too far.

Something between Shako and her father had broken when she pleaded for Simon's life. The rage that had spilled out of him vanished, only to be replaced with a grim and relentless disgust. He would not speak to her for days afterward. No one else did, either. She was an outcast living in their midst.

He tried to explain it to her once. It was late at night, and they were alone in the ceremonial house, the place where no one lived but the spirits. He brought her inside. Shako wondered if he would finally hear her apologies.

But Hirrihigua wanted to speak, not to listen. He wanted to explain.

Her father said that when he learned the invaders were coming—the first time they heard rumors of strange, pale men with exotic weapons and animals, arriving in huge boats at their shores—he knew that it would be a fight for survival. Whatever else those weird visitors were, they were men. And men always behaved in the same way. They took what they could and they would not be satisfied until they had it all. As chief, Hirrihigua had seen years where famine threatened the Uzita. He'd made hard choices long before Shako and her siblings were born. There were times when he could see their future extinguished by too many hungry mouths. In those times, he had led his people against neighboring tribes and taken whatever they had, so that his own children might live. He knew why people looked to conquer others. He knew that no one ever left his home without looking to take something back to it. If the strange men had come all the way across the world, farther than anyone had ever gone before, then they must, naturally, expect to take more than anyone had ever taken before.

Given the chance, he knew they would find the Water. And they would drink it, and then they would swarm across the land, undying and eternally voracious, consuming everything in their path.

Hirrihigua would not allow that. Like all of the other chiefs before him, he knew that the Water was too dangerous. He swore, as they did, to protect it—

which meant to keep the world safe from it, as well as keeping it from the world.

But he could not do that alone. This was why he'd promised her to Yaha. His tribe had to be stronger, had to be united, against the threat that was coming. Her happiness, her desires, they were small sacrifices to make for another generation of Uzita children. Shako hadn't seen it because she did not want to believe in anything more than the immediate future. She was young. That was her failing. That alone might have been forgivable.

But to lie down with one of the invaders? To reveal to him their secrets? To betray everything she'd been since the day she was born?

"You brought him into our world," he said. "You gave him yourself, and you gave him all of us as well."

In her father's eyes, she had become inhuman. There was no forgiving that.

She tried to speak, but he left her in the ceremonial house alone.

Her father's last words to Shako came in front of the entire village. He gathered them all to hear.

He told her to go. To disappear. She had separated herself willingly from the Uzita, and so she could no longer be a part of them. She cried and pleaded. He would not answer her, even when tears began to roll down his own face. The other men and women—even her own brothers and sisters—threw rocks at her when she would not leave.

Despite her father's order of exile, she could not bring herself to go very far. She lived in a small camp less than a mile away, hidden in a pocket of cypress and mangroves. Perhaps she still held out some hope of reconciliation, if not actual forgiveness. And there were those who left food out for her, and clothes, and other things she needed to survive. She learned to steal into the village in the dead of night, when her father's sentries would deliberately look the other way.

Then one morning, she heard the screams coming from the village.

She rushed back, but the noise and smoke told her it was already too late. Still, she had to see. She climbed into a tree and, hidden by the leaves, watched the Spaniards destroy her world.

She saw children stuck on pikes. One brother cut in half by the exploding weapons of the conquistadors. Her mother stabbed, over and over. And her father's corpse at the center of it all.

She saw Simón and his friends, too. Simón covered his eyes as he was dragged to safety, as if he could not stand to see what he'd caused.

His cowardice repulsed her. Every feeling she'd ever had for him curdled into disgust. She knew she was as much to blame for this as he was. But she would watch. She let the fires burn it all into her memory. Even as she wept, she would not allow herself to flinch.

She wanted to remember all of it. Every moment, every horror, and especially every face of every Spaniard.

As for Simón and the others, she would make each of them suffer. No matter how long it took. Because now she had nothing but time.

# CHAPTER 24

WASHINGTON, D.C.
1837

THE WHITE HOUSE smelled like an open toilet.

Simon had heard that the new president styled himself a man of the people. He'd heard about the inauguration that was open to every citizen and ended with most of the White House's furniture stolen or in splinters.

But he did not imagine that this president's common touch included the stink of feces in the air.

Simon had lived a long time already, and he supposed he should be grateful there were still some surprises left.

Max, at his side, made no comment, but kept a bright handkerchief soaked in perfume in front of his nose and mouth. It wasn't because of any foresight or planning on his part. He'd rarely been without it since returning to America on this trip. He said there was a special kind of smell that existed only here: "a mongrel breed of a new form of odor."

Despite the offense it caused everywhere they went, Simon found it difficult to reprimand Max for this. He was constantly appalled by the habits of these people himself. As poor as his family had ever been, they had held on to their dignity. They knew their place.

In America, any man felt comfortable speaking to them without a proper introduction and pressing his opinions on them. And once they heard that Simon and Max were from Spain, they were insufferably smug about their lack of royalty. In the pub where they had supper the night before, one man had even made a show of looking at Simon's breeches. "I was wondering if they got worn out quicker from all the bowing and scraping," the man had said, and the entire crowd had erupted in laughter.

Simon had considered killing the man but reminded himself that he had better things to do. There was a time when you could kill someone for insulting your honor, but he found people were growing increasingly intolerant of the practice. Times change.

He and Max were escorted up the stairs and into the presidential library on the second floor of the White House, and into the presence of the great man himself.

President Andrew Jackson.

Jackson sat behind a table covered with maps of Florida. His hair was white now, and his teeth were yellow, but the years had not bent him. His back was still ramrod straight, and the undeniable physical power that made men follow him was still there. Jackson looked up at them and dismissed their escort with a curt nod.

"Mr. President," Max began, smiling and courteous, "please accept our belated congratulations on your elevation to office. We must apologize that we did not send our regards sooner."

Jackson spat something brown and foul in the general direction of a spittoon. It hit the wall with a meaty sound instead.

It was not as easy as it once was to see Jackson. For all his talk of being a true democratic president, he'd learned to lock the White House doors in the past few years. The United States was still writhing in a financial crisis sparked by his shutdown of the federal bank, causing a massive explosion of credit and speculation, followed by an inevitable crash. There had been blood on the streets in the major cities as rioters screamed for food and jobs. Everyone wanted something from Jackson now.

Simon and Max had arranged for this meeting through the Freemasons. They were not members—Catholics were not allowed to join—but they had contacts within the organization that they used regularly. They'd found the Masons especially useful in forging new connections in the nascent United States, where it seemed nearly every man in public office was also a member of a lodge. They had paid their friendly Masons well. Under the Masonic code, Jackson would have found it difficult to refuse a request from them. But he clearly didn't like it.

"You've only got so much of my time and patience today, sir," Jackson said. "You want to waste it on pleasantries, that's your right. But I'd suggest you come to the point a bit quicker."

"The general is kind enough to be blunt," Max

said. "So we will return the favor. We are here to ask permission to bring a number of men and arms into Saint Petersburg, with an aim toward an expedition into the nearby jungle."

Jackson laughed, which caused him to hawk and spit again. "Seems to me I went to a considerable amount of trouble to remove you Spaniards from Florida the first time I was there. I don't know why I should let you back in now."

Jackson had claimed Florida for the United States in 1817, when he led U.S. troops against the Seminoles in Florida on the command of President Monroe. He'd slaughtered as many of the Indian tribes as he could find, and then kicked Spain out of the territory completely. Spain had been too weak to offer more than diplomatic protests. It was another one of the victories that helped him forge the legend that led to his election as president.

Behind his scented silk, Max frowned. He was losing patience with this jumped-up warlord, and Simon couldn't blame him.

"I believe we've already paid you well for passage into Florida," Max said. "Do you forget your promises? Or are you simply seeking more coin now that you've bankrupted your country?"

Jackson's scowl grew even deeper. "That's enough out of you," he said. "You get the hell out of here. I've never taken a single damned piece of Spanish silver, and I'll see you with pistols if you spread that slander around."

Simon sat down, since it was clear there would never be an invitation from the president. "More than a piece and more than silver," he said. "And while the general is a fierce dueler, I don't think he would be happy if he raised pistols against either of us."

Jackson glared at them both. And then the expression on his face changed as he looked—really looked—at them.

"Hell and damnation," he said quietly.

Simon smiled. "It hasn't been so long, has it, sir?"

Jackson's mouth remained open. They had last seen him when he was the territorial governor of Florida. He'd been a young man then. So had they. Now he was old. And they had not aged a day.

"Impossible," Jackson said. "I must have dealt with your fathers."

"Tell yourself that if you like," Simon said. "Either way, you were well paid for unlimited passage into and out of Florida."

It was an easy favor to grant. Florida was still too wild and too vast, and the United States too small to offer much in the way of government. Simon and the others did not feel any special loyalty to Spain by then; they'd become a power unto themselves. Having lived more than two centuries already, they had learned that countries were made up of men, and kings were nothing more than men on thrones. They thought they had more right to call Florida their property than Spain, or the fledgling nation known as America.

When Jackson left Florida, the Seminole tribes were mostly left to themselves. Simon and his men continued to move in and out of the area with little or no interference.

That had changed over the years, however. American settlers kept moving south, as did escaped slaves. Clashes between them and the local tribes gave Jackson the excuse he needed to send the army into Florida again.

However, the Second Seminole War was not going as well as the first. This time, the U.S. troops were not up against largely unarmed and unprepared tribes. This time, the Indians knew what was coming; they fought a guerrilla war against the invading forces, using their knowledge of the swamps and forests to hide and harass the American troops.

A company of 110 soldiers was attacked by the Seminoles. Only three survived. Shortly after that, more than a hundred commissioned officers resigned from the army, rather than go to Florida. Every attempt to find and punish the Seminoles failed. The Indians simply melted into the swamps and disappeared.

Simon and the Council were, admittedly, caught off guard by the conflict. They were long-lived, but they could be shortsighted. They didn't believe Jackson would mount a full assault with the United States reeling from a massive depression.

But Jackson took the presence of escaped slaves living in Florida, as well as the Indian tribes who defied him, as a personal insult. He wouldn't have a lawless refuge within the United States' borders.

Any pale face in Florida was now a target. Villages were burned. Settlers fled back north. The army retaliated by slaughtering whole tribes. No one was safe, and there was no end in sight. The entire war was rapidly becoming a quagmire, with Jackson second-guessing his commanders and changing generals at every disappointment and defeat.

As a result, the Council found itself cut off from its supply of the Water for the first time.

Simon and the others did not panic. They still had thousands of gallons of the Water in storage. But the lesson of Miruelo weighed heavily on them; after living so long, none of them had become any more reconciled to the thought of dying.

And there was another, more personal reason for Simon to return to Florida as well.

Jackson shook off his unease and put up his brave face again. Simon expected as much. Successful generals dealt with the facts in front of them, not the hidden truths behind.

"Even if you are who you say you are, I can't be held to promises made twenty years ago," Jackson insisted.

"Your word is only good for a limited time?" Max asked. "What a new and innovative concept of honor you Americans hold."

If looks could have killed, Jackson would not have needed to duel either Simon or Max right then.

"My compact was with your fathers," he said stubbornly. "Not you."

"You misunderstand us, General," Simon said. "We're not here to take something from you. We are here to offer you a solution to your war. One of the reasons your generals have been unable to deal with the natives is because they do not know the territory. Those maps you are looking at? They haven't been updated since you fought there. Your soldiers can't even find your enemies, much less fight them. We, however, have been in the territory countless times. We know the terrain. We know the tribes."

Jackson snorted. "The day I need help from a perfumed Spaniard to win a war, I truly will be damned. If that's all you're offering, go home. The United States will prevail, as always, without any European interference."

"Somewhat hard to prevail against warriors who can't be killed," Max said. "We've heard that the fiercest Seminole warriors have taken wounds that would end another man, but they show up again, and again, and again, as whole and healthy as ever."

Jackson looked startled for a moment, then regained his iron composure.

"Stories," he said. "One savage looks very much like another. It's easy to confuse them on the battlefield."

"I'm sure." Max smiled. "Even so, your men must be suffering from some fear, if they're spreading these kinds of ghost stories."

Jackson said nothing.

Simon rose and crossed to Jackson's desk. He leaned down and looked the man in the face. "Look at us, Mr. President. Do you really believe these are just stories? Or that we are the sons of the men who paid you twenty years ago?"

Jackson held Simon's gaze for a moment, then turned away. "And you propose to come in and save me? You might be sorcerers," Jackson said, "but there are still only two of you. Unless you have an army hidden up your sleeves, I don't see how you're going to do any better than my generals."

"Let us into Florida, and we can stop these unkillable warriors. We can end the problem at its source. And we will deliver you a trophy that will break the spirit of the renegades."

Jackson sat back in his chair. He finally met Simon's eyes again.

"Just how do you propose to do that, sir?"

Simon smiled. He knew he had the man now.

"We can bring you the Seminole Witch," he said.

AT FIRST SIMON THOUGHT it was just bad luck.

They would lose things. They used Narváez's money to finance a small expedition inland into America, searching for more gold and possibly more sources of the Water. It started on the same path they did in Florida, and then vanished without a trace.

They attempted a small armed settlement near the site of the Uzita village. That was sacked by Indian raiders, and only a few of their hired men escaped to tell them about it.

This was not surprising, or even unexpected. America was a dangerous place. People died. Simon and the others decided it was better to leave the Fountain unguarded, and let the savages do the work of eliminating any Europeans who might stumble upon the secret. They were still able to make trips in and out of the territory, and they could visit the Fountain whenever they needed to. Besides, they had hundreds of casks of the Water, and a few sips were all it took to keep them young and healthy.

Then in 1573, a shipment of their gold was hijacked by the English pirate Francis Drake. All of Spain's holdings and territories in the New World had become a machine that cranked out nothing but wealth by that time. Now called the Spanish

Main, the area produced gold, silver, gems, and spices, and then shipped it all back to Europe. The Council had extensive holdings throughout the Americas. They were shipping nearly twenty tons of the natives' gold and silver from a port called Nombre de Dios.

The shipment never made it out of port. Drake and his men stole it from the mule train carrying the treasure overland. They managed to escape despite hundreds of troops chasing them through the jungle.

This was the first time Simon heard the rumors. The Spanish troops reported that Drake had a native woman with him—a copper-skinned, dark-eyed witch who fought like ten men and had some sort of Indian magic that kept her from dying even when she was severely wounded.

Most people who heard the tales thought the soldiers were making up excuses for their own failure.

Only Simon knew differently.

Shako was alive.

Somehow, she had survived.

And she wanted revenge for her people. She blamed Simon and the others. Of course she did. He knew how it must have looked. She would have found her people slaughtered, and she would have known someone had been in the cave. She was out to kill them all, because they were the only ones left.

The other members of the Council were reluctant to believe him at first. Her own father had said she was dead. But Simon reminded them all that they should have been dead by now, too. Death was not as final as it should have been for anyone who knew the secret of the Water.

Over the years, they all saw the evidence. She picked at them, harassed them from afar, and stole from them. With Drake, she attacked their ships—and only their ships, no one else's. In Cuba, Aznar was stepping from a whorehouse where he'd done some particularly nasty things to a girl inside when an arrow buried itself in the door by his ear.

It wasn't until France in 1790 that Simon got an actual glimpse of her. She nearly killed him under the cover of a riot in revolutionary France. He escaped, barely. Francisco was not as lucky. His head was later sent to Simon in a wooden box.

They mourned Francisco, but they did not panic. They were protected, somewhat, by the fact that any Indian woman who showed up in most of the places they went stood out as a freak. She could not travel in the same way they could. They learned to avoid the places where she was safe, where she could hide or blend in. One of those, unfortunately, was Florida.

They still had plenty of the Water, and she was just a savage girl in the world they ruled.

Now, however, she planned to cut them off at the source. This was intolerable.

They heard the stories again. The Seminoles had a witch who led them, who fought more fiercely than any man, and who carried a magic potion that would heal any wound and restore the dead to life.

The rumors would have been enough to bring Simon, but when he'd learned that the Seminoles were massed around a certain area, repelling any outsiders, then he knew. Shako had come home, and she meant to deny him and the Council from ever drinking the Water again.

He had to break her hold over the territory, and if that meant breaking the Seminole rebellion, then so be it. They had suffered her attacks for too long. They would not be truly safe until she was truly dead.

Simon felt a slight pang at that, but knew it was necessary. He had to make the world a better place. If Shako stood in the way of that, then she had to die. No matter what he felt in the past.

"SHE NEVER MAKES IT easy, does she?"

Simon didn't reply, but he didn't think Max really expected an answer. He still remembered stumbling through the plants and trees of the jungle with an arrow through his leg, dying step by step, on his way to Shako and the Water the first time.

He hadn't expected that to seem like a pleasant stroll by comparison.

Jackson granted their request for free passage, but balked at their request to bring in their own paid mercenaries. He insisted that only U.S. troops would operate on Florida soil. They'd traveled overland to Fort Lonesome, where they were given command of three hundred soldiers, the men all either veterans or seasoned frontiersmen. They were not likely to drop from fever or exhaustion like the raw recruits who came to Florida for the first time and wilted in the heat. It was better than Simon expected.

He and Max were joined by Carlos and Aznar. They each carried a flask of the Water with them. Simon believed the four of them would be worth at least a dozen Seminole lives each.

They had been marching for five days since leaving the fort. They were currently camped barely a dozen miles from where they'd started.

The trail was difficult enough on its own: a winding track between the trees, too narrow and choked with roots for horses, occasionally leading through swamp and quicksand, clouded with swarms of biting flies.

But the Seminoles made it worse. Soldiers at the back of the line would vanish if they stepped off the trail to piss. Arrows flew from nowhere when the company would sit down to eat and make camp. They were attacked at night by screaming ghosts who ran past their sentries, slashing with knives and axes and firing rifles before they disappeared back into the darkness.

The troops Jackson had granted Simon were now sleepless, hungry, and frayed at the edges. They fought among themselves and took every order from the Spaniards with a reluctance that bordered on outright defiance.

They were losing, Simon realized, and they hadn't even had a real battle yet.

That was not to say they hadn't had some small successes. Last night they had managed to capture one of the Seminole raiders. He'd taken a bullet to the leg and was unable to flee with his fellow warriors.

They gave him to Aznar.

Simon checked the sun in the sky. Almost noon. Time to see what was left of the raider.

"See to the men, and have them begin breaking camp," Simon told Max. "Find Carlos. We're going to move soon."

Max nodded and left, while Simon gestured to Deckard, a veteran infantryman who'd been assigned to them as master sergeant. Deckard fell in step behind him, and they walked away from the camp.

Simon had no doubts where Deckard's real loyalties lay, but he was competent, and the other men would listen to him when they pretended not to hear Simon or the others. He'd proven crucial in keeping the march going.

But he was openly skeptical of their quest. "There ain't no witch," he'd said repeatedly. "Just a story the savages are telling to keep us scared."

He didn't have much faith in Aznar's ability to get answers from the Seminole, either. "You can't get one of them to talk," he said. "They don't feel pain the way white men do."

"All men feel pain," Simon said.

"We've captured them before. We've put questions to them, too, sharp questions," he said. "Not a one of them broke before he died."

They found the place where Aznar had set up to do his work. It wasn't too difficult. You could hear the screams.

Aznar stood over the Seminole warrior, drenched in blood up to his elbows and chin. It looked, at first glance, like a hunter had skinned a deer for meat and left the job half-finished. Aznar had flayed the

Seminole open down to the breastbone, his skin pinned back with nails to the tree where he was bound. The warrior must have sampled the Water at some point; there was no way he could be breathing otherwise.

"God Almighty," Deckard said, and turned away.

Aznar smiled at the soldier. "Oh, it would take more than this to get His attention," he said. "Believe me, I've tried."

Simon rubbed his eyes. He was too tired for this. "Aznar, stop trying to frighten the men. It's becoming annoying."

Aznar's smile faded, but only a little. In truth, he was becoming more frightening every day. As time went on, they were all changing, little by little, like stones being eroded under a stream. Simon supposed it was inevitable. They'd all had to give up certain beliefs as they remained alive while everyone around them died. They had all been forced to adjust, and to discard the habits that might have given them comfort as they navigated their new, eternal lives.

But Aznar seemed overjoyed to throw away any pretense to his former morality. He had grown to be the most vicious of all of them in a fight, secure in the knowledge that there was no wound that his enemy could inflict that wouldn't vanish with a sip of the Water. He acted without restraint, even when in public, even when restraint was necessary to keep normal men from guessing what they were. Some days Simon feared he was the only thing keeping Aznar from murdering and raping in the streets in broad daylight.

Still, he couldn't deny that Aznar's savagery had its uses. The Indian was broken. Simon could see it in his eyes. There was still contempt, still some defiance, but it would have taken inhuman reserve to remain silent while Aznar peeled back his flesh and showed him his own insides.

"He says they have a thousand warriors," Aznar said. "By which I take to mean they have perhaps a hundred."

"A hundred men who cannot die is still a formidable number," Simon reminded him.

"Oh, they die." Aznar stuck his knife deep into the Seminole's flesh. The man screamed, a hoarse and ragged sound. "Eventually."

"Stop," Simon said. "I want to know more."

Aznar sighed. "As you wish." He withdrew the knife. He listens to me now, Simon thought, but sooner or later, he'll want to turn that knife on me.

Simon shoved it aside. There would be time for Aznar later. There was always more time later.

Right now, he spoke to the Seminole in his own tongue. "The Witch," he said. "Where is she?"

Deckard muttered, "Maybe sometime you'll tell me how you learned to talk like a Seminole when you lived in Spain."

Simon shushed him, and turned back to the warrior. "Answer me truly, and I'll put an end to the pain. I swear it."

That brought a rasping laugh to the Seminole's lips. "I've heard promises from your kind before," he said. "I know what they're worth."

"I'm not one of the men who broke the treaties with you. I only want the Water."

"She said you would say that."

Simon tried to keep the hope out of his voice. "The Witch. So you have seen her."

"She's no witch. She is our Mother. And she has returned to wipe you from our lands."

Simon shook his head. Maybe the Seminole believed that. But he knew Shako could not. There were too many settlers, too many white men, too many guns, and more arriving every day. The United States was ever hungry for more land, more space, more territory. Shako couldn't hold them back from this meager swamp any more than she could roll back the sea. And she had to know it. All she was trying to do now was keep Simon from the Water.

"She's using you," Simon said. "She cannot stop us. All she wants to do is keep the Water for herself. Are you willing to die to keep her young?"

The Seminole tried to spit at Simon, but he'd been bled almost dry.

"I know who you are," he said. "And you are a liar."

"If you know who I am, then you know I will kill you."

"I've already been dead. I'm not afraid." His eyes were clouding. He didn't have much more time.

"Tell me where she is," Simon snapped, his patience at an end. He could have restored the Indian with one sip from his flask, but he suspected he'd need every drop for himself soon.

The Seminole lifted his head as much as he could. He smiled, although it was more like a grimace of pain.

"You won't have to look for her much longer," he said, his voice almost gone. "She's coming for you."

Then he rasped out one last breath and died.

SIMON WALKED THE SHORT distance from the camp to the spot where Aznar did his work. Aznar had his own tent. It made everyone breathe a bit easier to keep him at a distance. He seemed to like it better as well.

Simon carried two plates of the stuff the soldiers called supper. Ordinarily, this would have been taken to Aznar by the lowest-ranked man in the company. But Simon wanted to talk to Aznar. It seemed as if it had been decades since they had really talked. Perhaps it had been. He never liked Aznar, and they had not grown closer over time.

He worried he'd let things slip for too long with the former priest.

Aznar sat on the dirt by his tent in front of a small campfire. "Simon," he said, by way of greeting. He didn't bother to hide his surprise or his annoyance. Things like courtesy tended to evaporate after so many years together. Anything but basic honesty was exhausting over the long run. "What an honor. To have our august leader serve me himself."

Simon dropped the tin plate on the dirt next to the spot where Aznar sat.

"No one else was willing to come out here," he said. "The stink is too much."

He sat down across the fire, holding his own plate.

"It's not the smell," Aznar said, digging in to his food. "They're terrified of us, you know."

Simon thought of the casualties they'd taken so far, and the bloody fighting they had to do for every step of progress. "The Seminoles? Then they do a good job hiding their fear."

"I didn't mean the savages. I meant the soldiers. Living this close, for this long . . . We can't hide what we are. We go on marching when they're ready to drop. We don't get sick like they do. Our wounds heal while theirs fester. They know we're not like them. We scare them."

"We're foreigners. They don't like our accents. They don't like our looks. They don't like us. They don't suspect."

"Don't fool yourself. They know, even if they can't bring themselves to put it into words. We've left them behind, and they hate us for it."

"As long as they follow us. That's enough."

"They should be frightened of us, Simon. It's the smartest thing they could do. We will replace them. We're their death, whether they know it or not."

Simon looked at the gutted corpse, still roped to the tree, then back at Aznar, who ate his dinner as if sitting by a garden. He thought of a dozen ways to begin, discarded them all. Again, basic honesty was so much less tiring. He simply asked the question that was on his mind.

"What in the name of God happened to you, Juan?"

Aznar laughed, almost choked, then managed to swallow. "God has nothing to do with us, Simon. Not anymore. If He ever did."

"You would have called me a blasphemer for saying that once."

"You never would have listened," Aznar said. "You always hated me. Admit it."

Simon shrugged. He'd had a long time to learn to accept himself. He looked back on the man he was before he found the Water with the affection one might have for a wayward child. There was so much he simply didn't understand back then.

But Aznar was right: he'd never had cause to reconsider his initial judgment of the former priest. He saw someone who was never willing to risk his own life but was fearless with the lives of others, someone who would stand in judgment without knowledge or understanding, someone who spent the unearned credit given to him by the Church; someone who saw God's power as his own.

He didn't see the point of admitting this to Aznar, however. What he needed to know now was if one of his lieutenants was sliding fully into madness.

"Well. That was a long time ago. And I think we've both lost any right to judge the other by now."

"You think so?" Aznar's face turned dark. He continued eating, but now he looked more like a dog, ready to snarl at anyone near its food. "You still think you're better than I am." It wasn't a question.

"If I hate you so much, Juan, why have I kept you alive all these years?"

"You know the answer to that. At first you needed all the hands you could get. Then, later, you feared the others would rebel if you cut me off."

"And now?"

"Now I am too valuable to you. I do the things you won't dirty your own hands with," Aznar said.

"I'm a resource. A weapon. Nothing less, nothing more."

Simon didn't see much point in denying it.

"You were always wrong about me, you know," Aznar said. "I believed. I believed in God."

There was such sudden passion, such pain, in Aznar's voice that Simon was caught short. "What?"

"Is it that hard for you to conceive that you might have been wrong? You did not share my faith. So you assumed I was lying to myself in my robes."

Simon felt as if something shifted, all around him. Perhaps Aznar had a point. He had never considered that the young, sour-faced priest, all those years ago, might have been sincere.

"Did you ever consider how hard it was for me? I believed, Simon. I wanted to serve. I wanted to be a soldier, but that role, in my family, went to my brother. So I did what I could. I saw death everywhere. And still I believed: life everlasting, beyond this one, to those who were worthy. To those who would open themselves to the glory of God. It was never easy for me. I doubted. I lusted. I hated. But I had faith. Faith is never easy, Simon. Faith is belief in the absence of evidence. Faith is believing when everything in the world says you are wrong. Faith is designed by God to be tested. I believed. I had faith. And then you robbed me of it."

"You blame me for your lack of faith?"

Aznar laughed. He seemed delighted by Simon's lack of comprehension. "Who else? You took me to some pagan altar, and you sacrificed me. Humiliated me. Beat me. I thought I would die there. And I comforted myself with this thought: At last my pain is over. At last I will know God. I knew, Simon. I knew I was going to see our Father in Heaven. And then you gave me the Water."

Aznar paused. He was quiet for a long moment. "I thought that God would provide me life everlasting. Instead, it was you."

There was another long silence.

"Do you want me to apologize?" Simon finally asked.

Aznar seemed to shake off the silence, along with whatever thoughts haunted his eyes. The old gleam of malice returned. "For giving me all this?" He gestured all around them. "You must be joking. You freed me, Simon. From everything. From belief, from faith, from God. From Heaven and Hell. It took years, but eventually I learned. There are no rewards or punishments waiting for us. We broke the Covenant. I believed we were meant to suffer, to return to the dust, but that's not true anymore, is it? We can do whatever we want."

"As long as we get more of the Water," Simon said.

Aznar nodded. "True. I admit it would be quite a shock to find myself standing in front of Saint Peter at the gates after all this time."

"I thought you didn't believe anymore."

"I would hate to be proven wrong."

"You fear God won't forgive you?"

Aznar smiled. "I've done everything I can to earn His contempt. If there are unforgivable sins, I committed them. We both did, the moment we drank the Water. Of course, you drank it first."

"You can tell God I led you into temptation."

"That answer didn't work for Eve, did it? No, Simon. I have to rely on this being our only world. And the Water. I have nothing else. We have nothing else. Just survival. And whatever amusement falls our way."

He sopped up the last of his gravy with the hardtack roll that served as bread out here. Simon's dinner was still untouched.

"That's not true," Simon said. He wasn't sure why he felt the need to argue with Aznar, only that he did. "I still believe in the perfectibility of this world. This is why I still fight. I have not lost my faith. Perhaps mine was always stronger."

Aznar looked bored. "Perhaps your illusions simply take longer to die. Once your mind is set, it's like stone. That's a terrible habit for men who live as long as we do. It's going to cost you someday."

This was trying Simon's patience. "So why do you go on, Juan? Why bother? What keeps you going, if you truly have no faith anymore?"

"Why, I follow you, Simon. It's been entertaining so far. Isn't that enough?"

Simon stood up then. Aznar was still laughing as he walked away.

# CHAPTER 25

SIMON STARTED TO recognize the signs about a mile from the cave. It had been quiet the last night. No more raids. No more harassment on the trail. No lost soldiers.

It seemed as if a whole new forest of trees and saw grass had grown in the years since his last visit. But Simon could see that many others had beaten a path in the same direction, widening the trail enough for horses, making it easy traveling. There were burn marks in the grass from cooking fires and areas where the vegetation had been hacked to pieces.

The Seminoles themselves were gone. It was like she'd left her house with the door open for him. He was being drawn in deeper, he knew. He ordered Max and Deckard to the rear, in case the attack came from behind them.

"You think it's a trap?" Deckard asked.

"Of course it's a trap," Max and Simon both said,

almost simultaneously. They grinned sourly at each other. She had left them no choice but to spring it. They wanted the Water. There was only one way to go: forward.

The troops fell silent as they marched along the trail. No more talking or jokes or even complaining. They all listened to the sounds of the insects buzzing and the chatter and squawking of the birds.

We are lined up like ducklings, Simon thought. The Seminoles could break their column in a dozen places with an ambush.

The cave was almost in sight now. He saw the rise of the small hill that hid the rock, the beginnings of bare earth in the grass where the vegetation had been worn down by the presence of hundreds of others.

She had been here, but now she was gone. Simon didn't believe it, but it looked as if she'd left before he could get here. Would she really do that? Would she run?

"Spread out," he ordered the men. "Everyone off the trail, into the grass. Make as wide a net as we can, and keep moving forward."

This caused a few looks of dismay, but the men obeyed. They were experienced enough to recognize that while breaking formation was bad, staying in one place as a target was worse. They chose the least bad option, just as Simon had.

They crept closer, each man a point on a wide semicircle, walking the tall grass on the way to the hill and the clearing.

They were perhaps a hundred yards away when Simon began to believe Shako might really have fled. There was no sign of any other human life.

Then he heard the first scream.

Followed by another. And another. And another.

IT'S A MYTH THAT the eastern diamondback rattlesnake will shake its tail before striking. It does not warn its prey, and often makes its distinctive rattle only while launching itself to strike.

The buzzing sounds of the snakes' tails came from everywhere at once, drowning out everything but the screams. His men stabbed with their bayonets at the ground in a mad panic. Simon saw movement at his feet and looked down, barely in time to avoid the rattler's bite. There were at least three of the snakes within two feet of him. One slithered away while the other two reared up. He stepped back and felt something writhe under his feet. Something plucked at his pant leg, and then he felt the searing pain as the needle-sharp fangs pierced his skin.

The entire area was infested, he realized. There had to be hundreds, maybe even thousands, of them. They were biting everything that moved. Some men were already down on the ground, bitten multiple times, their skin already swelling from the venom.

For a split second, Simon was utterly lost. The snakes would never gather like this on their own.

Then the grasses in front of them erupted. Seminole warriors appeared from their holes, tossing away the carpets of saw grass they'd used to hide themselves.

A few had bows and knives, but most carried rifles. They opened fire on the U.S. troops, who were still trying to stab the snakes on the ground.

The first round of shots took down roughly half of Simon's men.

He missed being shot only because he was already bent over, pulling the snake's fangs from his pants where they were stuck like fishhooks.

Bullets flew past his ears. He could feel the heat.

On top of the hill, he saw her. She stood there, arms at her sides, without even a weapon. As if nothing would ever touch her. He could not see her face, but Simon imagined she had to be laughing at him.

Of course it's a trap, he'd said.

The rage took over then, and he ran forward, bayonet fixed to his rifle. A Seminole warrior rushed to meet him. Simon stabbed him directly under the breastbone and pulled the trigger. The bullet tore through the man's back.

He yanked his bayonet from the corpse and pulled out his pistol to aim at the next warrior who came at him. He shot that man in the face. Then he stabbed the next man and the next. He was a demon, screaming obscenities, slashing with his sword when the rifle and bayonet were stuck in the ribs of another dead Indian. He felt a bullet punch him somewhere in the side, but it was not enough to stop him. Nothing would stop him.

He saw that he was not alone. On Simon's left, Carlos was an elegant dancer, slicing his way through the Seminoles with his sword, weaving among them, never once where they were putting their own blades and bullets. On his right, Max and Aznar were in a scrum of U.S. infantry, the men who'd somehow survived the snakes, and they were fighting the Seminoles hand to hand, face-to-face.

Simon saw an open spot of ground and ran for it.

Shako was no longer on top of the hill.

He knew where she'd gone. She was in the cave. He ran to catch her.

The blow from a war ax rang against his skull. He'd turned with it, but he still felt the blood rush from his scalp and saw stars in the air.

The Seminole rose up above him, and Simon realized he was on the ground. The warrior brought up his ax to deliver the final blow, but he was so slow. So slow compared to Simon. Simon already had his other pistol out, and fired. He could not miss at that range. The bullet went through the man's mouth and out the back of his head.

Simon was back up and running before the body hit the ground.

There was no one else in his way. He reached the mouth of the cave.

He stopped. His vision blurred. He was losing blood fast. It didn't worry him. He had his flask, safely tucked in his hip pocket. All it would take is a sip, once this was over, and he had no doubt he would end it quickly when he saw Shako. Now he understood that she truly meant to kill him, and any tender feelings he once held for her burned up completely in his rage.

He stopped. He had to. For a moment, he couldn't understand what he saw.

The mouth of the cave was clogged with barrels, one after another, leading down into the dark.

It was so odd, it made him pause, even as he heard the battle and screams continue on the other side of the hill.

"Simon," her voice called.

He turned. She was only a dozen yards away. He must have lost more blood than he thought. He hadn't even seen her.

The venom, he realized. It was working fast. His vision was narrowing to a tunnel. He needed a drink. But first he needed to make her pay.

He staggered forward, sword in one hand, knife in the other. It was not the knife she'd given him. He'd replaced the handle and the blade. That made it new. That made it his.

Simon was trembling now. He was not thinking clearly. He knew it. But he could do this. He could finish this now.

She held up a small, burning wick. She had nothing else.

"Don't die yet, Simon," she said. "I want you to see this."

She dropped the wick on the ground. A trail of oil and black powder, leading to the cave, began to burn and spit immediately.

Simon finally recognized the smell that was burning his nostrils. It had blended with the other scents of gunpowder and smoke.

Oil. A lot of it. The barrels must have been soaked in it. They would go up like dry tinder. And inside them . . .

He put it together just before the fire reached the first barrel.

He could see Shako clearly, even though everything else was going dim. And yes, she was definitely smiling.

She turned and ran. He did the same.

The explosion picked him up like a giant's hand and pitched him through the air. He bounced once or twice. He couldn't tell. Rocks and dirt fell like a rain shower, half-burying him.

He couldn't hear anything. He was blinking, desperately trying to clear his eyes.

He felt too weak to raise his head, but he knew he had to see. She'd gone to so much trouble to show him, after all.

The mouth to the cave, the cave itself, the hill and the tree above—they were all gone. Just gone. The cave had collapsed in on itself, leaving a wide, deep depression in the earth.

Shako was gone, too.

Max found him a few moments later, took his flask from his pocket, and forced him to drink.

It didn't matter. She'd already killed them all.

LATER, THEY COUNTED THE DEAD.

Nearly two hundred of the U.S. troops were killed, either by snakebite or by the Seminoles. The rest were wounded. Simon had no idea how long they'd live once they returned to civilization, even if they made it back. No matter what, they were done as soldiers. Those who, somehow, survived the snakebites—they must have gotten less venom than the others—were barely able to stand. Their limbs would be weak until the day they died, their bodies damaged on some fundamental level. Those who stood against the Seminoles were all cut or shot or both. And every soldier was taking home a piece of the cave with them. The blast had sent splinters of rock flying faster than bullets in every direction. Everyone got at least one chunk driven into his skin.

No one escaped unscathed.

Shako left behind about fifty of her soldiers, killed either in the battle or in the massive explosion. The rest of her people, however many there actually were, were gone.

Shako herself had vanished. Carlos suggested that perhaps she died in the blast as well, but none of them really believed it.

They sat within sight of the ruined hill, waiting for the survivors to be ready to march. Deckard, who'd been spared the worst of the battle in the rear, was doing his best to get the troops prepared. No one wanted to be here when night fell, and the wounded needed medical attention. Anyone with two working legs would help carry a stretcher. The men were on the point of open rebellion now. Not only had the Spaniards led them into a humiliating defeat, they'd been forced to leave a number of bodies in the grass, because the snakes were still there and more agitated than before.

"She must have spent months gathering them," Max said, not for the first time.

He and Simon and Carlos and Aznar were all sipping from their flasks, watching Deckard threaten and cajole the men. This would probably not help the soldiers' morale, but they were tired, and they needed to heal as well. Shako had come very close to killing all four of them in one stroke. Worse, that did not even seem to be her main intention.

"She wants us to suffer," Aznar said. "She knows

our dying will be slow and painful without the Water. She wants us to endure that."

Simon shook his head. "No. That wasn't her aim."

They all looked at him with disbelief. Aznar practically spat at him. "You are still going to defend her?"

Simon should have punished that disrespect, but he was too tired. Instead, he said, "She didn't care what happened to us, as long as we saw that we'd lost the Fountain. This is all a distraction. Her people, her followers—they're gone. She wanted to save them. From us. I will lay odds they are so deep in the swamp now we never see them again, no matter how long we live."

"However long we live," Max said, "is much shorter now, thanks to her."

"We are not dead yet," Simon said, standing up. He saw Deckard approaching. It was nearly time to be on the move.

"Simon, the Fountain is gone."

"And we have thousands of gallons of the Water left," he said. "We have a long time left to us. We can still accomplish our goals. The world is not perfected yet. We are not done."

He looked at each of them in turn. "Perhaps we are no longer Immortals, but I refuse to lay down and die here. We still have centuries. If that is not enough, then we are not the men I thought we were. We can still achieve greatness if we do not weaken."

He saw the words strike home with each man. They all nodded.

Deckard waited for them.

"Now get up," Simon ordered. "We have many miles to go, and our work is only beginning."

They rose and began walking to the troops, calling out to some of the soldiers, assuming commands. They stood straight and tall again. The miracle of the Water. You'd never know any of us were injured, Simon thought.

Nothing was certain in this life. There were still wonders to be discovered. Perhaps they would find another source of the Water.

Perhaps someday they would even learn the secret for themselves.

Wouldn't that be something.

Simon slung his rifle over his shoulder and began the long march back.

THE BATTLE, WHICH WAS never recorded in any history book, turned out to be a pivotal one in the Second Seminole War.

The Seminole Witch vanished, never to be seen again, as did her band of warriors. Without her, any tactical advantage the Seminoles had was overwhelmed by the number of troops and weapons that President Jackson poured into Florida. The Seminoles fought a brilliant guerrilla campaign, but in the end were broken by the massive force. Along with the majority of Indian tribes in the United States—most of whom had lived peacefully alongside the white settlers for years—they were rounded up and sent west to reservations along what became known as the Trail of Tears, a thousand-mile trek that most of the Indians were forced to make on foot. As many as half of them died along the way due to exposure or starvation.

A handful of Seminoles went into the swamps, so far and so deep that no government troops could reach them. By the end of the Seminole War, which cost fifteen hundred American lives and $20 million, the army was tired of trying. They were allowed to stay hidden.

The Seminoles remained the only Indian tribe never to surrender to the U.S. government.

It was not until after World War II that the Seminoles were finally officially recognized again in Florida. They won back a fraction of their lands in court and eventually built casinos on them.

Simon, watching this over the years, was not surprised. He had long since learned that his ability to predict the future was limited at best.

There was only one thing he knew for certain. It had been foolish and stupid, but there was a small piece of him that hoped he could make Shako see things his way. That she might put away her crusade against him and rediscover something of the feelings they had once shared.

It was idiotic, he learned that day. Aznar, as much as Simon was loath to admit, had made a good point. Shako wanted them to suffer before they died.

Whatever he believed they'd shared, that was dead and buried, years before. However long he lived, there was no changing the fact that he and Shako were enemies, and their own war would end only when one died.

And he would not give up his life so that she might live. He still had too much work to do.

# CHAPTER 26

TAMPA, FLORIDA
NOW

SIMON WAS STILL furious as he and Max went to meet the scientists.

This was Max's punishment. No matter how much Max protested, no matter how obvious it was that it was the only way to keep Simon alive, Simon still clung to his insistence that even his stupidest orders were to be followed, no matter what.

The days after the disaster at the party—or the Ballroom Blitz, as one of the wittier reporters at the local TV station called it—were nothing but tooth-grinding humiliation for both of them.

At heart, Max knew that Simon still believed himself a soldier. His earliest training had been for war. He'd learned patience and strategy over his long, long life, but when attacked, his basic instinct was to respond in kind. He never changed. It was like trying to talk Napoleon out of marching on Russia. That hadn't gone well, either.

Simon found himself answering questions from the authorities. First the local police, then federal officials, and then again from the people put in charge of the joint task force that combined both. There were a lot of rich people among the dead, wounded, and frightened, and this demanded a massive response. (Some things really had not changed since they were young; no one strikes at the nobles without paying for it.)

Now all Simon wanted was a target, someone on whom he could vent his frustration. Max was elected. So Simon brought him along for this chore.

They entered the conference room. The young men and women who'd assembled to meet them all wore their white lab coats. They were scientists, like David. Some of them had worked on Revita, and other pills and wonders that Conquest had discovered and sold while trying to crack the secret of the Water. Some were close to brilliant.

But David outshone all of them, like a sunrise blazing against a candle. He'd spurned their help in most cases, and treated them like grad students and assistants the rest of the time. He hadn't done it to be cruel, Max believed. It was just the native arrogance of a genius. David wanted to do everything himself, because if someone else could do it, then, by default, it wasn't worth doing.

That ruthless process of elimination had created more than a little resentment between David and his so-called colleagues. David's massive salary and access to Simon hadn't helped. Neither did the discovery that Revita would cause cancer in one in ten of its users. Simon didn't care. They had plenty of things to do to keep them occupied with the rest of Conquest's medicines. He'd believed in David, because he believed it was possible for a single genius to succeed where the crowd of ordinary men would fail.

Now David was gone, and they were forced to turn to these ordinary men and women to learn what the fallen star had been doing all those months.

Max expected at least a little triumph from the assembled white coats. They were being recognized while the boy wonder had vanished.

But the Conquest scientists were not showing him anything like victory. They sat around the table, looking away from him, staring at the walls or into their coffee cups. Some of this had to be shock—many of them had been at the party, and probably still heard the echoes of the gunfire before they went to sleep—but it was something else as well.

Max recognized it instantly: they were embarrassed.

Simon looked around the whole table, waiting for someone to speak. His anger was evident. No one wanted to be the focus.

"Well?" he said.

Silence. Finally, one of the men in the white coats cleared his throat. His name was Quentin Reed, and he was an exceptional scientist in his own right. Before he came to Conquest, he had a list of publications that filled twenty pages when printed out. He'd done work on HIV and blocking viral contamination of healthy cells by using monomolecular barriers. It was all groundbreaking, but in an ordinary way. None of his work was the quantum leap forward that David Robinton was capable of, and deep down, Max suspected Reed knew it.

But if there was anyone who could take David's recipe and start baking with it, it would have to be Reed.

"We need more time," Reed finally said.

Wrong answer. That was obvious from the look on Simon's face. "Do you, now," he said flatly.

"You have to understand. Robinton didn't let any of us into his work. Not very deep, anyway. We're looking at most of this for the first time. And sure, we can understand the basics, we can see where he started, but we're having trouble making some of the leaps he did."

Simon stared at Reed for a long moment. "How long?"

"It's not a problem," Reed said quickly. "We're very close."

Someone else at the table muttered at that. Reed shot them a hard look. "We're very close," he said again. "You have to understand, we've got the bare bones here. But to get you a finished product, that's going to take longer."

"Robinton had a finished product. I saw it. He showed it to me."

"Well, yes," Reed admitted. "But we've only got the formula. Not the samples. He didn't leave any samples."

"And the formula isn't enough?" Simon's voice was dangerously soft now.

"No, no, that's not what I'm saying," Reed said. "We can do it from formula."

That seemed to be too much for another one of the white coats. A woman at the other end of the table spoke up. "Oh, bullshit, Quentin. You looked at his notes as long as we did, and you were just as confused."

"Shut up, Michele," Reed snapped back.

But the dam had broken now. The white coats were squabbling. "I've never even *seen* anything like that kind of synthesis."

"—fucking *hydrogels*? How are we supposed to—"

"Do you know what would happen to a test subject if we got even one thing wrong? We're talking an indictment, not a lawsuit—"

"Shut up, shut up, shut up!" Reed shouted.

They all quieted down. Except the one called Michele.

She looked right at Simon and Max. "Listen. Bottom line: this is frontier biotech, and we can barely read the map. We're starting from where he left off. But we don't know what he did to get where he went. What David Robinton did was out-of-the-ballpark, next-level stuff. He came up with three or four ideas that would have been enough to take us five years ahead of everyone else on the way to the finished product. As for the final result, I'll admit it, even if Quentin won't. There's stuff in there I've never seen before. Even with instructions, we have to go back and learn how to do it all over again. And we're making a lot of mistakes. It's not like assembling an IKEA desk, either. This is more like learning how to repaint a Van Gogh."

Reed swore at her. "You're being overly dramatic, Michele."

"Am I? Then show him your work, Quentin. Show us all how it's done."

Simon ignored the bickering. "How long?" he asked again.

"A year."

"A year?"

"Minimum. If you don't want to kill everyone who takes it."

Reed was still talking. "You just have to roll back the product launch, right? It's not fatal, right?"

Fatal. Max almost laughed at that. They still thought Simon was worried about release schedules and stock prices.

"Let's say it is fatal," he said. "What would you say if I needed it inside six months? Life or death."

The white coats exchanged worried looks. No one spoke. Then Michele found the courage again.

"Six months?"

"Three would be better."

"Life or death?" she asked.

Simon nodded.

"We just can't," she said. "There's no way. If three months is life or death, I'm sorry, sir. You're dead."

SIMON WAS STILL GIVING Max the silent treatment as they rode the elevator down to the subbasement.

It was time to refill the bottles. They had all used a lot of Water to heal from Shako's attack. Peter still had a scar.

"So, it's going to take time," Max said. "We still have the formula. We have time."

Simon didn't respond.

"I'm saying we still have options. There's no reason to panic."

Again, nothing.

Be that way, Max thought.

Ordinarily, Simon refilled their flasks and bottles with the Water by himself. Max wondered exactly how this was meant to teach him a lesson, and Simon wasn't saying anything more than necessary.

When the elevator doors opened, the cold air hit Max in the face. The basement was always cold, even when it was scorching and humid outside.

It had been difficult, digging into the swampy Florida ground all those years ago, and nearly a century of maintenance and upgrades had cost them as much as it would have to build a skyscraper. But this cellar was now better built than the White House's fallout shelter. It had systems and pumps maintaining fresh air and perfectly balanced humidity. It was the storehouse of the greatest treasure the world had ever known.

This was where they kept the last of the Water.

Over the years, they had stored it in various places, at first in the wooden casks that they'd made themselves with the broken planks from their shipwrecked landing in Florida. Then they had transferred the water into barrels crafted by the best coopers they could find in Cuba and Mexico. Years later, the water was transferred again, like old wine into new bottles, or in this case, into airtight steel drums.

When those began to rust, Simon had the Water drained into specially designed containers made of high-tech ceramics and million-year, nondegradable plastics. They could be dropped from a height of nine stories without breaking, and would not lose so much as a molecule to evaporation.

Then he and Max moved them back into the Vault.

Max, as Simon's right hand, knew its location. It was a secret to the others. But only Simon knew the combination to the door. Simon usually handled the Water personally. Max tried not to take it as too great an insult that he was rarely allowed access to this holy of holies.

Simon pressed the buttons, and the heavy steel slid back noiselessly into the walls.

Max got his first look inside in several years.

And felt like he was dying.

It was almost empty. There was one barrel.

"It's only half-full," Simon told him. Then he laughed. "Or half-empty, depending on how you look at it."

Max found he was having trouble breathing.

"You were saying something about not panicking, Max?"

Max swallowed. "How . . . how did this happen?"

Simon laughed at him, genuinely amused. "It's been a long time."

Max put a hand on the cold, metallic wall to steady himself. He was looking at death: not just the death of his dream of moving forward, of evolving past their current state, but true death. The end of a life that, he realized now, he had not ever really believed was capable of ending.

He felt sick. He felt like he was about to fall to the floor.

"Oh my God," he said. "Why didn't you tell me, Simon?"

"I'm telling you now," Simon said. "Do you finally understand? We are out of options, Max. This is the reality. We either succeed with David or we die without him."

Max managed to pull himself together. He wiped the cold sweat off his forehead and stood up straight. "You're right, of course," he said.

Inside, however, he couldn't stop his mind from spinning as he looked at Simon.

How many times have I protected you and kept you from your own bad decisions? Too many to count. Still, through it all, I've always trusted you to find the right path.

But now, for the first time in centuries, Max was filled with doubt.

Maybe Max could not save Simon after all. At this point, he was wondering if he'd even be able to save himself.

# CHAPTER 27

GULF COAST, FLORIDA
NOW

DAVID HAD ASSUMED they would be fleeing the country in disguises or hiding under the deck of a ship like smugglers.

Instead, he found himself watching the sun reflect off the Gulf of Mexico from the passenger seat of a cherry-red Mustang convertible.

"This doesn't seem very smart," he said again. "For a couple of people who are supposed to be hiding, we seem pretty conspicuous."

From behind the wheel, Shako laughed at him. Again. "You've got the same habits of mind as they do. People who are in hiding are supposed to hide. We're supposed to be scared, scurrying beneath the floorboards. Fugitives aren't supposed to be out in the open, enjoying themselves. So you could at least try to look happy to be here."

"Sorry. It's hard not to imagine a big target on top of my head right now."

"The Council is powerful, David, but not omnipotent," she said. "They cannot watch every airport and dock and pier and boat on both coasts of Florida, or every car on the road. They do not have access to spy satellites. And even if they did, they would need to know where to start looking. The world is still bigger than they are."

"You seem pretty sure of yourself."

"I've been doing this a long time, and I know them pretty well," she said. "Anyway, you're probably still a little nervous from being shot."

David realized he was rubbing his chest underneath his shirt again, and stopped.

She smiled at him, even more dazzling than the light from the Gulf. "Much better," she said. "Try to enjoy the ride."

Easier said than done. His head was killing him. Ever since they'd left the hotel and started driving east along the Gulf, David had felt under assault from all his senses. Despite his black wraparound shades, the sun pierced his eyes. He could hear the stereos in the highway traffic, despite the wind and noise. He could taste the different hydrocarbons from the exhaust, each one a bitter flavor on his tongue.

And when he was not in pain, he felt stupid and stoned. He didn't like drugs, had never really done many of them in college, but now he found himself staring at things like a drooling hippie moron. He lost himself in the deep red of the car's paint job for minutes while Shako packed the trunk. A breeze over the hairs of his arm set his whole body shivering with delight. He tracked a flock of gulls through the air, memorizing its route instantly, becoming lost in the intricacies of the swarmlike behavior as it flew.

Shy—no, Shako, he reminded himself—noticed, and sympathized. "It's not easy the first time," she said. "The world becomes so much richer. So much sharper."

David looked at her. "This is what it's like for you all the time?"

She nodded. "Most of the time."

"How do you deal with it?"

Her smile again. "Years of practice."

After waking in the hotel room, David had examined himself thoroughly under the bathroom lights and in the mirror. The first thing he noticed was that the front tooth he'd chipped in sixth grade—playing tetherball with a friend, the half-deflated ball caught him in the lip—was whole and perfect again. His hairline had edged down slightly, filling in the thinning patches. A jagged scar on his inner arm, a souvenir from falling under the cleats of another player in a college soccer game, had vanished.

David knew that eventually the effects of the Water would wear off. He'd seen it in all the test subjects. At a certain point, aging began again.

Right now, he wasn't sure if he was anxious for that or dreading it.

There was a question that kept nagging at him. "This is really how you've spent your whole life?"

She eyed him sharply from behind her sunglasses. "What's that supposed to mean?"

"You've had literally hundreds of years, and you've spent them trying to kill six men."

"There were eight when I started."

David shrugged. "Not a real impressive score."

David was suddenly thrown against his seat belt as Shako hit the brakes and skidded across traffic. They came to rest on the shoulder, burned rubber and the wailing horns of other drivers in the air around them.

Shako was very close to him, speaking very precisely.

"You have no idea," she said coldly. "You barely have any idea what a woman has to go through now. Then, I was considered something subhuman. Property at best. I was not allowed to hold money or a weapon or to reveal that I knew how to read or speak anything but my native tongue. I had only myself. They had the entire world, and the way it worked, to keep them safe. I used everything I had, including time. I knew the world would change, however slowly. Everything I built cost me, but I knew it would eventually be worth it."

David was still reeling from the adrenaline and the sudden stop. He knew the better thing to do would be to shut up. But part of him would not accept that this woman—who carried so much more than he could ever know, let alone understand—was not the same woman he'd spent the last half year with. So he said what he felt.

"It seems like such a waste. That's all."

For a split second, he thought she'd strike him. He wondered if she'd stop at just one blow.

Then she seemed to physically take control of herself.

"I told you what I had to watch," Shako said at

last. "What I had to endure. Imagine losing every single person you knew. Every member of your family, your extended family, your neighborhood, your city. All of them, murdered before your eyes, because of someone you thought you trusted. Because of your mistake. Can you honestly say that you would not spend eternity trying to make that right?"

"You call this making it right?"

"You don't get to judge me, David."

"That's not what I meant. You could have changed the world in any number of ways. All of you could have. But instead you're locked into this cycle of revenge."

Shako looked at him with undisguised contempt. "You wouldn't say that if it was your family. I know you, David. You lost your sister, and you've spent your whole life curled around that fact. Every thing you've done has been for her. You're not that different from me."

"I've worked to save people's lives," David said. "That's different. Maybe I'd feel like you if Simon killed someone I know, but—"

Shako laughed.

"What's so funny?"

"Did you really think your father was driving drunk?"

David listened to the cars flying past on the road, to the rush of displaced air, for a long moment.

"What?"

"Your father was working for a subsidiary of Conquest's on a way to cure diseases like your sister's. Simon and the Council saw some value in it.

They allowed him to see some of their research on the Water. Your father was brilliant, David. Almost as smart as you. He began to put it together. He became a threat. So they arranged an accident for him and your mother."

"No," David said flatly. "That's too much of a coincidence. I don't accept that. And I don't need it. I've already told you, I'm with you against Simon, I don't need you to make up some—"

She cut him off. "I don't need to make anything up. I wouldn't make the effort. Max sent a cleaning crew who took your parents, put them in a car and soaked them with bourbon, and then ran that car off a cliff. That was how you initially came to their attention. They saw your test scores and decided to keep an eye on you, just in case, ever since."

David felt as though her words had actual physical force behind them. He kept seeing the closed caskets. Hardly enough to bury, one man at the funeral had said, not knowing or caring that David was close enough to overhear.

"How do you know this?"

"I know almost everything they've done in the last two hundred years. This is hardly the worst thing."

"Why didn't you warn them? Why didn't you stop it?"

"I was on the other side of the world at the time."

"But if you weren't? If you'd been around?"

"It doesn't matter," she said. "This is a war, David. People die."

David looked away from her.

"Now it matters, doesn't it?" she said. "When it's the people you care about."

"Why did you tell me this?"

"Because you need to face the truth," she said. "Your sweet little girlfriend Shy does not exist. She never did. She was a mask I wore for a short time, like many others I've worn and forgotten. She was a tool—a means to an end—just like you are. Simon and his men make the world uglier every day as they fashion a little bit more of it into their own image. But even if they didn't—even if they had spent every moment of every hour since they killed my people doing their best to build paradise—I would still kill them. They destroyed my life. They murdered my family. And they used me to do it. There is no forgiveness for that and no amount of redemption that will save them from me."

David didn't respond.

Shako put the car back into gear and rejoined the traffic, moving relentlessly down the highway once again.

DAVID'S MIND WOULD NOT accept it. She was old. Impossibly old. In doing his research, David had spent many hours in nursing homes and hospitals with the elderly. There was a whole suite of specific odors and sounds he associated with the weight of years: the failing of bladders and body parts, the creaking and farting and sighing and groaning as all the pains and problems accumulated in bodies that could no longer keep from breaking down under the strain.

But nothing about Shy—Shako, he kept reminding himself, Shako—hit those triggers in him. He looked at her and saw a woman younger than him, who moved with a fluid, athletic grace.

The only place he glimpsed her age was in her eyes. There were times he caught her looking at him, as if from a great distance, and he felt like a small animal on the ground being hunted by a bird of prey.

There was a ruthlessness there. He'd seen something similar when Simon had threatened the senator.

It reminded him that Shako was basically an alien being, a time traveler, and he was just one more brief life in the thousands she'd already seen flicker out over the years.

She'd basically admitted she was using him. She had her own plan, and David's life and happiness did not matter much in her endgame. He had to guess, of course, because she wouldn't tell him what she was doing. She'd lied to him about everything, including her name. There was no reason to trust her.

But it did not stop him from wanting her.

If anything, he wanted her more now. He was ashamed of himself. She'd been lying to him about her life, about his own place in it, and the entire history of the world, actually—and yet every time he came near her, he was nearly dizzy with lust.

The first time anyone drank the Water was intoxicating, she told him. His body was undergoing a new burst of strength and speed and power. And it was like being given the testosterone levels of a fifteen-year-old boy again. Not to mention the fact that he'd nearly died. No wonder you want to take the new car for a spin, she said. She was laughing at him, that distant look in her eyes.

She met him more than halfway. They checked into a hotel room near the Atlanta airport and did not sleep for the entire twelve hours before the flight Shako had arranged. Every time they disconnected, sweaty skin still clinging wetly as they fell back onto the bed, panting, every time all he had to do was look at her again, see her breasts rising and falling as she breathed, see her eyes dancing as she looked back, and he would find himself growing hard again and then he was grabbing at her.

She was on top of him, grinding herself down on his hips as if squeezing every last drop from him, when she looked at the clock and stopped abruptly.

"It's time to go," she said, and made her way to the bathroom, where she washed and changed quickly.

David, despite the upgrade the Water had given him, took a while to get off the bed.

He wondered briefly what would happen if he just lay there, if he refused to get up. He didn't suffer from the illusion that she would come back to bed and join him, that they could hide out here forever. He knew she had a plan, and he knew she would not share it, not until she was ready.

But what if he said no?

It was an interesting question, but ultimately a pointless one.

He got up and got clean and got dressed. He was lost, and he knew it. Shako was his only guide. He would follow her anywhere.

SHE HAD A PASSPORT with his picture but not his name. The polite customs agent barely glanced at it. They didn't have to stand in line; the agent came to them as they waited in the lobby of the executive terminal. Once more, David experienced the power of flying on a private jet. They were comfortably seated when a steward asked what they'd like for dinner. Shako selected steak and lobster for them both.

Then the plane began to taxi down the runway, and the pilot told them it would be a little less than five hours before they arrived in Colombia.

David tried to relax and enjoy the ride.

# CHAPTER 28

SIMON TRIED TO tamp down his anger again as he left the conference room, and failed.

He'd lost track of the alphabet soup of agencies that swept into the city and demanded his time: FBI, DHS, NSA, DEA . . . He wondered if they got a group discount on their hotel rooms. There was already talk of a civil action as well, a possible congressional investigation.

For his part, he hid behind his lawyers' fine suits and eight-hundred-dollar-an-hour manners, and claimed ignorance of everything except his own name.

For all their questions, he knew the real answer behind all of this: betrayal. It was something he knew quite well, and the rage it inspired seemed to grow stronger the longer he lived.

First, there was Max's idiotic move, shooting David. He could bleat and moan all he wanted about how it was meant to protect Simon, about how he was trying to save him, but it was still a betrayal. He'd given his orders. David was not to be touched until Simon said so, until the replacement for the Water was completely ready. Max had overstepped his bounds. Simon would have to find some way to punish him for that.

Next came the question of how Shako had gotten past his security. This was more housekeeping than an actual matter of pride. She'd always managed to find a way to get close to him, no matter what defenses he might have in place. But he needed to know where the hole in the wall was before he could fix it. He set Max and Peter to the task of questioning the security personnel away from the police and the federal agents, under the guise of "getting the story straight." In fact, he wanted to know who had helped her. One of them had to have been bought by her; she should not have gotten through the front door.

Finally, there was the only betrayal that really mattered: David.

She had been with him. He had been holding her hand, and they moved together with an ease he still recognized and envied after almost five hundred years.

He was hers. And she was his. He wanted to believe David was her pawn, but he knew in his heart it was more than that.

She would have left a pawn behind to die. Instead, she saved him.

He had to admit he considered David more than a pawn as well. Never an equal, really, because he didn't think anyone with less than a century of life could approach him as an equal. But he respected David. Respected his morality, and his intellect, and his idealism. He believed the boy had wanted to change the world for the better. Simon was not above using that, but he respected it. He'd been willing to make him one of the Council. Simon had been prepared to call David a brother and a friend.

And David had been fucking Shako the entire time.

He realized he was grinding his teeth again. With a conscious effort, he put that aside. He willed himself to be calm.

Max waited for him when the elevator doors opened. Max looked weary and beaten. The hang-dog expression on his face only irritated Simon even more.

"Any word from the scientists?"

"Some," Max said.

"What do they say?"

"What do you think?" Max shrugged. "No help."

"Of course not. The only man who can help us is with her now. Thanks to you."

Max said nothing. Simon would not have that. He wouldn't have silence now, after so many years of unwanted advice. "What?"

"It seemed to me he was with her long before that."

"Are you trying to be funny?"

"Believe me, Simon. Nothing about this is funny."

"Have you found her yet?"

"We have our contacts in the FBI and the NSA. They're looking. Along with every policeman in the state. But she's had a lot of experience hiding from us."

"Look harder."

"You always seemed to know where she was before."

Simon stopped in the hallway and stared at Max for a moment. Was he trying to enrage him? Where was this coming from?

"You are trying my patience, Max."

Max looked even more exhausted. "For that you have my sincere apologies, Simon."

"If you are looking for someone to blame for our current situation, perhaps you should start with the mirror. Or do I have to remind you that you put a bullet into our only chance of survival—"

"Simon, please," Max hissed.

Simon realized he was almost shouting. There were employees nearby, people in their cubicles and offices, all listening to the boss on his rampage.

Simon got himself under control.

"Perhaps the boardroom is a better place to continue this discussion," Max said quietly.

Simon scowled but nodded. They took the elevator to the top floor and opened the heavy, locked doors.

Simon entered and then froze in place.

Peter and Sebastian were seated at the table in their usual places.

But there was someone in Simon's chair.

Aznar smiled at him.

"Hello, Simon," he said. "It's so good to see you again."

# CHAPTER 29

BERLIN, GERMANY
1945

AZNAR WAS CADAVER thin when the soldiers brought him out of his cell. His POW uniform hung on him like a scarecrow's rags, and his face showed fresh bruises and welts.

For all of that, he walked proudly, his head up high. The two Allied soldiers who escorted him held his arms gingerly, as though they were touching a soiled rag.

Simon rose from the chair where he'd been waiting. It had taken many, many favors to get him into the provisional offices of the Allied command. In one pocket, he held all the passes signed by different generals he'd used to reach Berlin. He wondered again if it was truly worth the effort to do this face-to-face.

Simon had spent most of the war in Spain, and like Spain, the Council was officially neutral but sided with the Nazis in every way that mattered.

Still, Simon and the others had never given up on any of their investments in the United States. They weren't alone in that. Many of the biggest German industrial firms maintained strong ties with America even as their soldiers were killing Americans on the battlefield.

Simon had lived too long to put all his money on one fighter.

Aznar was the Council's official representative to the Nazi leadership. He'd even been given a uniform and his own personal escort. At the time, Simon had assumed it was because the Nazis appreciated the financial help the Council had given them during Hitler's march to power.

Then, as the war ground on to the Nazis' inevitable defeat, a friendly colonel on Eisenhower's staff had given Simon some of the photos taken as the Germans retreated farther and farther back. Photos from places named Treblinka, Auschwitz, and Dachau.

Simon, who thought he'd become untouchable over the years, looked at them and felt his stomach turn. In that instant, he knew what Aznar had been doing while serving the Nazis. He withdrew all financial support from the Nazis and their related regimes. He pressed his contacts in Spain's fascist government to do the same. It didn't take much effort. Everyone saw the writing on the wall. The war was almost over; the Thousand-Year Reich ended up lasting five.

The Americans got Aznar just before the Russians stormed Berlin, and a good thing for him, too. The Soviets would have tortured him, and eventually Aznar would have bargained for his life with the only asset he had remaining: the secret of the Water. (The Council had no real connection with the Soviets, which was an oversight Simon would have to correct. He never expected the Bolshevik revolution to last, or that the starving Russian peasants would become one of the victors in the bloodiest war the world had seen yet.) The Americans beat Aznar and starved him, but the Council, with its influence, was able to keep him alive.

Which is to say, Simon kept him alive. Again.

He suddenly felt very heavy, as if all those deaths Aznar had caused were suddenly heaped on his shoulders.

Aznar seemed just as happy as the last time Simon had seen him. If he knew how close he'd come to real death, he didn't show it.

The American soldiers removed Aznar's shackles and handed him over to Simon. They did not ask for any paperwork. There was to be no record of this.

"You can go," Simon said. They seemed only too happy to oblige.

Aznar gave Simon his usual beatific smile. "I don't suppose you have anything to drink?"

It was too much for Simon. He backhanded Aznar halfway across the room.

Aznar knocked over a chair and came to rest against the wall. He struggled to stand for a long time, and then finally remained on the floor.

It wasn't from weakness. He couldn't rise because he was laughing too hard.

"You think this is a joke?" Simon demanded.

"You don't?" Aznar replied, wiping the blood from his split lip.

"I know what you did. The camps. The experiments."

"I saw a chance to expand our knowledge, perhaps even duplicate the Water. If I'd succeeded you'd be kissing my feet now." He looked at Simon, saw the rage there. "Well, no, never that. You have never given me my due respect. That would be too much to ask."

Simon felt the urge to beat him again, to beat him to death this time, to throttle the life from him. He clenched his fists and forced himself to stand where he was. "Those were not soldiers. They were civilians."

Aznar shrugged. "What of it?"

"'What of it?'" Simon spat back. "You slaughtered women and children."

"And not for the first time, either. You've grown so squeamish over the years, Simon. We once caught babies on our swords."

"No. I never did. There are limits, even in war."

"There are no limits. Not in war, not anywhere on this planet. We are free to do whatever we want, Simon, without the fear of death. There is nothing holding us back."

"What are you?" Simon asked. "This was inhuman."

"Inhuman? You're right," Aznar said, finally getting to his feet. "I am not human. And neither are you. Humans are here to amuse us, to serve us, and to die for us. We left humanity behind a long time ago. It's time for you to stop lying to yourself."

Simon looked at Aznar's face. Suddenly, he was sick of it.

He opened his coat and took out a wallet filled with cash. He threw it on the floor at Aznar's feet.

"This is the last thing you will ever receive from us. The Council is done with you."

That finally cracked Aznar's good humor. "What?"

"You heard me. I have tolerated you for too long. We've lost far better men than you. It's time for you to join them."

To his credit, Aznar did not beg. He sounded almost regal when he said, "You cannot do this. The others have a say."

"The others have already decided. They left it to me."

"We live and die together. That was our oath."

"What does an oath mean to someone who's not human?" Simon said. "You believe you've gone beyond morality, beyond limits? Then go. Be on your way. See how far you get without the Water."

Aznar's face twisted into the ugliest mask of rage and hatred Simon had ever seen. For a moment, Simon thought he would be foolish enough to attack, to give Simon the excuse to put him down once and for all.

But then the trembling stopped and the smile returned. "You should have done it. You should have killed me here and now. But you can't, Simon. You are still clinging to the illusion of humanity."

"Good-bye, Juan. We will not meet again."

Simon turned his back on Aznar and walked to the door. He was done.

"You're wrong, Simon," Aznar called after him. "I will see you in Hell, if not before."

"You don't believe in Hell," Simon called over his shoulder.

"No," Aznar agreed. "But you will."

# CHAPTER 30

TAMPA, FLORIDA
NOW

SIMON MIGHT HAVE fought them, but he hesitated for a split second. That was all they needed to take the choice away from him.

Peter and Sebastian were over the table in a heartbeat. They pinned Simon's arms. Aznar disabled him with a single punch to the gut that felt as though it touched his spine.

Simon dropped to the floor, gasping and heaving.

Aznar kneeled down beside him and said, "There has been a change in management, my old friend. You've been retired."

Simon glared at him from the floor. "You're going to die for this, Juan."

Aznar tsked at him. "Stop. You were never a very good villain, Simon. Your heart simply wasn't in it. Believe me, I'm much more suited to the job."

"Stay down, Simon," Peter warned. "If you want to live, stay down."

"Traitors," Simon spat.

Sebastian kicked Simon in the ribs. "Traitors? You call us traitors?" He had to be restrained by Peter from kicking Simon again. "We know how much Water is left. What were you planning on doing, Simon? Were you going to let us die?"

Simon didn't answer, but turned his eyes on Max. Max sat there, unmoving, watching, as he had the whole time. He didn't look away from Simon's accusing glare.

There was no point. He was guilty. He had betrayed his best, his oldest, friend. A man he would've died for a hundred times. More important, a man he had lived for.

And he would do it again in a heartbeat.

MAX HAD RECEIVED AZNAR'S call late at night, and found him hiding behind a Dumpster outside a convenience store at 3:00 A.M.

Half of Aznar's body looked caved in, and he was bleeding freely. He'd fallen nearly six stories, something that might have been fatal without their enhanced durability and strength. He did not have to explain, beyond her name: "Shako."

Max considered letting him die right there, but he did not believe Aznar had outlived his usefulness yet. Especially if Shako was this close to them. Max gave him his emergency flask. Aznar emptied it completely.

Aznar lived, but it presented Max with a serious question. How was he supposed to tell Simon that Shako was in Florida again without revealing Aznar's involvement?

In the end, he'd decided to keep the secret hidden and rely on the security they already had. It had kept them safe for years, after all.

The slaughter in the ballroom showed him how grievous his error had been. He did not suffer much guilt for it, however. He'd made mistakes that cost lives before. He could live with that, as long as he believed it was another turn, no matter how twisted, on the way to a greater good.

But then Simon showed him the vault, and the nearly empty, final barrel of the Water.

At that point, he realized he'd been doing the same thing he counseled Simon against: he was deluding himself.

Simon had taken them all down the wrong path. Max had let himself think it didn't matter how long the journey took, because they were functionally immortal.

Only when he saw how little Water remained did he remember that "functionally" immortal was not the same thing as actually living forever. There were no guarantees. Any one of them could die at any moment, despite the great gift they had been given. They had all wasted so much of their time.

Simon had wasted so much of their time.

So Max went to the cheap motel where he'd hidden Aznar and told him the truth. Then he and Aznar went to the others and told them as well.

Things moved rapidly from there.

They went to the basement and divided up the

last of the barrel. (Did Simon think Max really wouldn't notice the combination on the vault? Another insult.) Aznar drank his share of the Water immediately. He said he'd need all his strength for this.

Sebastian and Peter looked to Max to lead them at first, but he was too heartsick. He stayed quiet and meek, and Aznar shouldered him aside to fill the empty space.

That was fine with Max. He realized that some part of him must have been planning for this all along. Max kept Aznar alive all these years because, in his heart, he knew he did not have the strength to do what must be done: to push Simon aside if things ever got dire enough.

Aznar was not really strong enough to lead, but he was cruel and hateful enough to take Simon's place anyway. He would act out of revenge and spite and malice.

Max would have to live with that because Simon could not be allowed to continue on this course. Suicide was one thing. That was a personal choice, and as repugnant as Max found it, he would not have stood in Simon's way if he'd chosen it. But he was deciding on death for all of them. He was murdering them all as surely as if he held a gun to their heads and pulled the trigger. It was painful to admit, but there was no longer any time for self-delusion. Max had trusted Simon for half a millennium. He had waited patiently for Simon's great plans to come to fruition. He had believed that Simon would find a way to solve any problem.

Now he knew he'd been wrong for centuries.

Simon had gambled and lost. There was no longer any time. They should have chained Robinton to a stool in the lab and forced him to work. They should have killed Shako years ago. They should have searched harder for a new source of the Water. There were so, so many things that should have been done.

They were facing a very final deadline, and they were left with only one option: recover David and force his formula from him. Max knew he still loved Simon too much to be the man who would knock him from his throne. He would not let Aznar kill him, no matter what else happened. But neither would he let Simon fail them all again.

They were simply out of time.

THEY TOOK SIMON OUT of the room, chained hand and foot. Simon wasn't struggling anymore, but they knew better than to trust him. They would bundle him down an empty corridor, to a waiting elevator, where a well-paid team of discreet security professionals would take over.

Max sat alone in the boardroom for a moment.

"You should have told me how much Water was left, Simon," he said to the empty room. "You should have trusted me."

Then he got up and went to join the others.

The time for regrets was over. And so was Simon's reign.

The Council of the Immortals was under new management, starting now.

# CHAPTER 31

PUERTO TRIUNFO, COLOMBIA

CARLOS BELIEVED IN the power of myth. He allowed everyone to think he traveled the world, skipping from one safe house to another, never sleeping in the same room twice. To his underlings, rivals, and enemies, he was the man who could be literally anywhere.

Carlos sincerely doubted he would inspire such fear and respect if they knew most of his world consisted of a couch and a flat-screen TV.

He lived in the same villa outside Cartagena, Colombia, where he had spent much of the past two hundred years. It had been renovated and rebuilt a dozen times, so that now it was a fully modern palace with thirty-six rooms, a helipad, and an Olympic-size pool. Not that Carlos had seen much of it. He lived full-time in his own bedroom on one of the upper floors.

He had once been the skinniest and fastest of the conquistadors, his body like a knife blade honed by his constant fencing practice. Now he weighed close to four hundred pounds. He had been a blurring-swift terror in a fight, able to duel three or more opponents at once. Now he lumbered from the couch to the bathroom to the bed. The Water had kept him alive despite literal decades of gluttony, but it couldn't keep him thin.

When he was a boy, there was never enough to eat. He was well-off by the standards of the time. He never starved. He never suffered from the famines and shortages the same way that the peasants did. (Sometimes Carlos reflected on how much things changed. "Peasant" used to be a simple statement of fact. Now it was an insult.) But he was always hungry. There was never enough food to be truly full. To be truly sated. He was so skinny because he burned with nervous energy. It made him fast, but it also left him feeling empty much of the time.

To him, the greatest wonder of the new world was how much there was to eat. All it cost was money. It would have shocked and amazed these soft moderns to learn that once there was a time when it didn't matter how much gold you had if there was a bad harvest. There were limits back then. There were things money could not buy.

Not anymore, though. He could have anything he wanted. Food from literally all over the world, any kind of meat or fish or sweet or cake. All it took was money. And he had plenty of that. People gave it to him in bales that filled shipping containers for the powder he harvested from the coca fields. It still seemed like a sin to him, to waste all that good land on drugs. But not so much of a sin that he turned it back into farmland. After all, nobody would pay him nearly as much for corn.

So, without any restraints on his time or his appetites, he stayed home and ate, while his myth did the hard work of maintaining discipline in his empire, in the world.

That was enough for Carlos. He had seen the world. He'd seen enough of it.

When Simon first told them, "I have a way you can live forever," Carlos leaped at it, like they all did. It wasn't until much later that he realized no one ever asks themselves why they would want to live forever. As a young man, with a limited imagination and not much more experience, he thought it would be an endless pursuit of pleasures—a constantly renewed menu of all the little joys that make life worth living. But he found, after the first century of his life ticked over, even pleasures could grow dull.

While some of the others, like Simon, were happy to keep running in place with the endless changes of days and weeks and years, Carlos found it all too tedious. There was just so much trivia. What clothes to wear with the changing fashions. What language to use, as the influence of nations rose and fell. (He'd once spoken French for diplomacy, German for business, and English as little as possible. He was not going to learn Mandarin now, not at his age.) He'd traveled by ship, by train, and by airplane, and endured the thousand little indignities that seemed to survive no matter how advanced the methods of transport.

To live forever, you have to have something to live for, Carlos realized, far too late. Simon lived for his dream of a conquered world. Max lived for Simon. Sebastian lived for the next woman, Peter the next challenge, and each sustained his brother in the low times. Aznar lived to kill.

As for Carlos, all he wanted now was to be comfortable. Aside from a few trusted lieutenants and his servants, no one knew how fat and slow he'd become, distorted and made grotesquely huge by a constant train of food brought to him on serving platters day and night.

Of course, there had been one occasion when one of those trusted lieutenants thought all the flab had made Carlos soft. The man's name was Emilio, and he arranged for a hit squad to enter the villa and kill the bodyguards he hadn't been able to bribe.

Carlos had heard the gunshots from below while watching "The Slugger Attack" at 3:00 A.M., snared from Taiwan by his satellite dish. If he'd been watching *Die Hard* or *Lethal Weapon*—they were his favorites—he might not have heard a thing. But he had the sound down low because he didn't understand the language anyway.

He heaved himself from the leather couch as fast as he could. Which was not very fast. His brow popped with sweat at the unaccustomed exertion, and he'd made it only a few steps toward his gun cabinet when the door burst open and the first assassin rushed in.

The hit man's eyes were wild and he immediately fired a three-round burst from the H&K he carried, hitting Carlos right in the chest.

He probably thought he'd just killed the king, which was why he let out a whoop and raised his arms—including the one with the gun—into the air in triumph.

Only Carlos had not fallen down.

Carlos's bulk was wrapped around a still-small frame. The bullets had plowed into an ocean of flesh without hitting anything vital. The Water went to work at once, closing off blood vessels and rebuilding damaged tissue.

By the time Carlos got his gun, the bleeding had almost stopped. The assassin gaped the entire time, unable to believe the evidence of his own eyes. Carlos aimed carefully and fired twice with a long-barreled Magnum .44. (He also loved Dirty Harry movies.)

He hit the assassin in his legs, shattering both, knocking the man to the floor.

The would-be killer was slipping rapidly into shock and would have bled to death, but Carlos didn't allow that to happen. Emilio's other hired guns made their way up the stairs just in time to see Carlos finish clubbing him to death with his massive fists.

Carlos again heaved himself to his feet and faced the gunmen. They looked down at the fragments of their companion's skull on the tiled floor.

Then they looked at the wound on Carlos's chest, which finished sealing itself shut right in front of their eyes.

They screamed like children. Carlos had to admit he was quite pleased and flattered by the sound.

They fired their weapons indiscriminately, pure panic causing them to spray bullets around the room like water from a hose. They managed to hit him only twice more before he lined up his shots and fired, killing them all.

Carlos moved slowly but steadily to the locked safe where he kept the Water. He left bloody fingerprints on the combination dial but got it open without too much trouble. The jug—perfectly sealed to prevent evaporation—sat in a specially cooled chamber behind the heavy door. He cracked it open and took a long swig: more than six months' supply in a single gulp.

But he could still hear men moving through his home. The slight squeak of a leather sole on the tile of his staircase. The next group would be a bit more careful. Which meant Carlos had work to do.

He went through the house methodically, an H&K in one hand and the jug of Water in the other. In the end, there were twenty-three hired men who died that day. He was shot eleven more times, most of the bullets burying themselves harmlessly in his fat, although one stray ricochet smashed him in the temple, causing a bloom of blood and bone.

He found Emilio in the kitchen, hiding in the walk-in freezer. He also found the bodies of the household staff, who had been killed first, presumably to keep any of them from warning him.

Carlos dragged Emilio out of his hiding spot, then kneeled to face the man, who cowered on the floor, babbling apologies and begging for his life.

Emilio, even while begging, could not take his eyes off the wound on Carlos's head. The ricochet had penetrated his skull and the sinus cavity beneath it, but went no deeper.

It itched. Carlos dug around inside with a finger. After a moment of probing, he removed the deformed fragment of lead. He examined it, then tossed it away.

The jug was almost empty. Carlos drained the last of it, and the bloody corsage on his forehead began to disappear.

Emilio trembled silently as it was replaced first by a new piece of smooth white skull, then by pristine, unwrinkled flesh. Then he began to wail.

Carlos slapped him once with his fat, open palm, just to shut him up.

He asked only one question: "Do you understand now?"

Emilio nodded so hard Carlos feared his head would snap off.

"Good. I don't want to have to have this conversation again." He waved a hand toward the bodies lying all over the Saltillo tiles, the once-pristine furniture. "Now, get rid of this garbage before it stinks up my house."

Emilio leaped up and ran toward the first body.

Carlos, meanwhile, tottered toward a nearby chair. "But first," he said, "bring me something to eat."

Emilio looked relieved and then confused. "Sir?"

"You're the cook now. And you'd better be good. I'm starving."

Today, if anyone ever so much as grumbled about Carlos's leadership, there was always Emilio, the cook, standing there in the kitchen, willing to tell anyone who'd listen about the demon hidden behind all that fat. Emilio held him in almost religious awe now. The thought of another betrayal was too frightening, too impossible, for him to ever seriously consider again. Because how do you kill a man who won't stay dead? How do you ever escape the wrath of a man like that?

The answer: you can't. Because he is not really a man at all.

For everyone outside of Carlos's immediate circle, there was the power of myth. And for everyone inside it, there was the truth, which was far more powerful.

No one had tried to knock Carlos from his throne since.

CARLOS YAWNED AND STRETCHED and scratched. He pressed the remote, which rang a buzzer in the kitchen, signaling that he wanted more food.

No response. No one came hurrying up the stairs to take his order.

He pressed another button on the remote, which turned on his intercom. He called for his guards.

Again, no response.

Now he was forced to move. He was not afraid at this point, only irritated. He hated to interrupt the *Gilligan's Island* marathon to have to kill a bunch of people.

He lumbered down the stairs, his .44 in one hand and an Uzi in the other. They looked like toys in his big paws.

On the first landing, he found his guards, lying there with their throats cut. He stepped in their blood and kept going down.

On the main floor, he found the front door wide open. He was not so foolish as to call for the guards on the perimeter of the house now. He knew they were already dead.

He heard something from the kitchen.

Tracking sticky red footprints, he walked in that direction, the guns held in front of him.

He did not have the agility to leap and roll gracefully into the room. He just kept walking, depending on his bulk to survive the first few bullets as he had in the past.

Carlos prepared to sweep the room with both guns, emptying the chambers at the first sign of movement.

Instead, he froze.

Shako sat at the kitchen counter, holding a combat shotgun with a barrel that looked as wide as a coffee cup. She held it aimed at his head.

There were some wounds that even the Water would not bring you back from, and having your head removed by the slug from a Street Sweeper riot gun was one of them.

Carlos lowered his guns but did not drop them.

He saw the other two men with Shako. The first was his cook, Emilio, who was trembling, tears running down his face, as he stirred eggs in a bowl furiously.

The other, a young man, sat at another stool with an omelet fresh from the skillet on a plate in front of him. Carlos could still see the steam rising from it.

It took Carlos a moment to recognize the man from his pictures. It was David Robinton.

"Hungry?" Shako asked. "Emilio wanted to send you something when you rang, but we convinced him the walk down the stairs would do you some good."

She spoke in Spanish. If Robinton understood, he didn't show it. Carlos replied to her in the same tongue.

"Shako," he said, by way of greeting. "You look the same."

"You don't."

He ignored that. In English, he said, "Dr. Robinton. You should really try the omelet. Emilio makes them with peppers and cilantro grown right outside in the garden."

The scientist didn't respond to that any more than he did the Spanish. He showed no interest in his food. Carlos suspected the guns killed his interest in breakfast and conversation.

He switched back to Spanish. "Are you here to kill me, Shako?"

She looked disappointed. "I've known where to find you for years, Carlos. It's not like you move around much."

"True. So why are you here?"

"We have a proposition for you. How would you like to live forever?"

"I've heard that before."

"Simon's supply of the Water is almost gone. We are offering you the only alternative."

"There's always your supply."

"Mine is almost gone as well. But fortunately

Simon found the one man who could create a replacement. Simon lost him. I have him now."

Carlos looked at David carefully. He did not appear to notice the proprietary way Shako spoke about him. "And he's willing to do what you say?"

Shako smiled. "What do you think? Stay with Simon, and he can offer you only death. If you want to go on eating your way through the years, you'll join us."

"And what do you require of me?"

"Drop the guns," she said, "and we'll talk."

A genuine smile crossed Carlos's face for the first time in decades. He felt something he thought long dead inside him: curiosity. At the very least, this should be worth missing *Gilligan*.

He dropped the guns.

DAVID WAS SURPRISED TO find that a drug lab actually made a fairly decent genetics research facility.

Carlos's employees, like all of Silicon Valley and Wall Street, were always on the lookout for the Next Big Thing. Once the cartels discovered that the addition or subtraction of a few molecules could result in a formerly illegal drug instantly becoming an entirely new—and legal—substance, they began investing in high-tech equipment.

Carlos had accepted Shako's offer quickly, and immediately began treating them both as valued guests. He gave them huge, airy rooms and servants to see to their every need.

Still, it was not exactly elegant. Aside from Carlos's screening room—where the fat man spent most of his time—the furniture and fixtures, while expensive, all looked as if they were purchased in bulk, then left to rot. The couches were white leather, scarred with cigarette burns and stains. Turning on a lamp or a faucet or flushing a toilet was a 50/50 proposition at best.

But Carlos was never less than a gracious host. They ate with him every night in a dining room that could have seated twenty, and were served gourmet meals by Emilio, who walked like he was constantly expecting a blow to the head.

"It doesn't really seem like he wants to kill you," David said to Shako once.

She gave him an icy smile. "He wants to live more than he wants to see me die," she said. "That's why you're here."

The deal was simple: in exchange for his loyalty and support, Carlos would get David's cure. David would be given everything he needed to make it, and they would be protected from the other members of the Council by Carlos's army of drug warriors.

As a result, David had several assistants, high-powered microscopes and lab equipment, and a clean room that was better than many of the ones he'd worked in while in grad school.

His guide around the lab was Rajiv, a cheerfully amoral young man with a bachelor's in pharmacology and a master's in molecular microbiology (vocational) from the University of Mumbai. Any equipment the lab didn't already have, Rajiv promised he could have shipped and installed within forty-eight hours.

He was as good as his word. Within a week, the process of re-creating the hydrogels was well under way. David had only to watch and step in at a few crucial places. Otherwise, it was all working even better than the first batch.

His work was easier, but that came with a downside: he also had more time to think.

Shako.

He sometimes wondered how much of her story was true, and how much had been crafted specifically for him.

Carlos liked to talk. And while not exactly friendly, the big man seemed to like having an audience for his stories.

Shako could not stand to be in the same room with him, so she would leave as soon as possible. But David listened, and with a few questions, prodded Carlos into talking about his shared history with Shako.

Much of what she'd told him was supported by Carlos. But even so, it was disturbing. The force of will, the hatred, necessary to sustain a centuries-long campaign against these men was terrifying to David. Logically, he knew that his own moments with her were insignificant by comparison.

The more David thought about it, the colder it left him. When he approached it like one of the problems in the lab, the answer kept coming up the same. He was a means to an end for Shako, and nothing more.

She had been using him, after all. For something far larger than he could have ever imagined. But using him nonetheless.

He wondered if he could live with that. He'd been dragged into this war against his will, and he wasn't sure if he wanted to fight it. He wondered what would happen if he said no to any one of Shako's requests, if he tried to walk away and go home now.

Again, he reached an answer he didn't like.

At the moment, he seemed to have no choice. And, stupid as it might have seemed, he still wanted her. He wanted to believe she loved him, and that it made everything else small by comparison.

That all changed when the messenger arrived.

THE MAN WAS ESCORTED into the foyer by several of Carlos's guards. He was well dressed, polite, and unarmed.

"You know him?" Shako asked. She and David had been summoned by Carlos to see the messenger as well.

Carlos nodded. "He's been here before. Simon sent him."

A rapid-fire conversation in Spanish between Carlos and the messenger followed. The messenger opened a bag—very slowly—and withdrew a flat black rectangle. It took David a moment to recognize it. It was a videotape.

The messenger was allowed to leave. Carlos took the tape up to his room. Shako and David went with him.

The tape went into an antique VCR. The sound of it whirring to life brought back deep memories from David's childhood, when he would watch rented movies with his sister to pass the time.

"Who still uses videotape?" he asked.

"Quiet," Shako and Carlos both hissed in response.

At first there was only a black screen and the sound of something bumping up against the camera's microphone.

Then images began to appear. A peaceful main street of a small town. From the trees, David knew it was Florida. Video of children in a park, running and playing. Old people in lawn chairs outside their home. Cars in the parking lot of the local supermarket. A school. A small hospital. The shaky handheld footage would stop and start as the camera was turned on and off between shots.

Finally, a lingering view of the local post office. The sign out front read Cypress Grove.

Carlos laughed once.

Shako didn't say anything, but David saw her jaw clench slightly.

Then a man appeared on the screen. David didn't recognize him, but Shako and Carlos both did.

"Aznar," Carlos said.

"Hush," Shako ordered him.

"Shako," the man called Aznar said. "I suppose this will find you with Carlos. If you haven't already killed him. And Carlos, if she hasn't already killed you, you'll wish she did. That's all I have to say to you, you piece of shit."

Carlos laughed again.

The tape went on. "Shako, this has all gone on too long. The world is growing too small. I wanted to let you know that things have changed. Simon is no longer in charge. We are no longer willing to tolerate your existence as he did. We are done suffering you. So this is the only offer I am going to make. Come back to the United States, bring Robinton with you, and I will make your end quick and painless. If not, I will murder every single person in this little backwater town. You know I can do it. I am here already. So make up your mind, Shako. Or lose another village."

The screen went blue. The tape was over.

"What the hell was that about?" David asked.

"Cypress Grove," Shako said. "It's a small town. Mostly Seminole. Not far from where all this began."

"Simon has lost the throne," Carlos said.

"They're desperate. They never would have accepted Aznar's return if Simon still had any hold on them. Their supplies must be lower than I thought. They're panicking. Typical cowardice from your kind."

"No offense taken," Carlos said.

Shako ignored him.

"So, that was Aznar," David said. "You told me about him. He'll really kill them all?"

She shrugged. "He'll try. He's done worse."

David thought he was beyond surprise by now. He was wrong. "He would try to kill a whole town? Actually murder every person in it?"

"Oh, I'm sure he'll have help," Carlos said. "But yes, it's quite feasible. You have an isolated population, only one or two entrance roads, jam the radio waves, cut phone lines, and take out the local police first. Then you go house to house, sweep out the residents . . ."

"That's enough, thank you," Shako said.

"He asked. I'm just telling him how it's done."

"We have to go back," David said.

She gave him a cold look. "You think I should surrender myself to them?"

"Or stop them. Those people—"

"—can take care of themselves," Shako said. "I will not come running when Aznar snaps his fingers."

David was suddenly incensed. "They didn't ask for this. Those are innocent people. If there's any chance our going back can save them, then we should go back."

"Do you think I'm only protecting myself? He'll kill you. Not as quickly as he'd kill me, but he'd get around to it, once you were no longer of use," Shako said.

"We'll think of something. We'll find a way to beat him."

"We?" Shako smiled. "There is no 'we' here, David. This is not up to you. I have one advantage over them, and that is the fact that you are not with them. I will not give that up. If they want to survive, they have to come here and get you, and I'll kill them when they arrive. Or they will die when the Water runs out and they turn to dust. Either way, they will not continue to hide like roaches in the cracks of history."

"Again, no offense taken," Carlos said.

She ignored him again. "Either way, they will die. That's all that matters."

After all he'd heard about Simon and Shako's five-hundred-year war, David tried not to be shocked by the callousness of it. He failed.

"And to hell with anyone who gets caught in the middle?"

"They can take care of themselves. I told you that once. Now we are done discussing this," she said, and left the room.

Carlos turned to David from his chair. "Want to watch some TV? There's always a game on somewhere."

David didn't respond. Until that moment, he hadn't seen it. He hadn't wanted to see it. From a five-hundred-year-old perspective, Shako and Simon barely even registered normal people anymore. Like ants under their feet.

"Come on, boy, don't pout," Carlos said. "It's not like you're going to run off and save those people all by yourself."

"No," David admitted. "Not by myself. You're going to help me."

It was time to start making his own decisions again. It was time to remind Shako and Simon both what it meant to be human.

BY THAT NIGHT, EVERYTHING was ready.

David went to Shako's room. They had been sleeping apart for days now. David thought it helped him keep a clearer head.

She stood at the window, looking for something. She didn't turn around when he entered, but she knew he was there.

"What?" she asked. "You've come to forgive me?"

"No," David said.

When she turned, she saw that David wore a light

summer suit—one of the many gifts from Carlos they'd both been given—and a briefcase locked to his wrist by handcuffs.

"That's an interesting ensemble," she said. "Taking a trip?"

"Hopefully we both are. I came to ask you for something."

She waited.

"I want you to come with me. Help me save those people in Cypress Grove. We go there, get the police, the National Guard, whatever it takes. Protect them from Aznar."

She simply said, "No."

"You're really willing to let innocent people die for your vendetta?"

"Everyone is willing to sacrifice others for their goals, David. Even you."

"I would never—"

"Elizabeth. That little girl. She trusted you."

David was caught up short.

"I saved her."

"You could have killed her."

"But I didn't."

"You were willing to take the risk. And you put her life at risk again. Did you ever bother to check on her again after you used her as an experiment?"

"I— There was a lot going on. With you. With work. I knew she was taken care of at the hospital."

"You made her a target. The Council does not want anyone to know their secrets. Even little girls."

David went pale. "Oh my God. Did they—?"

"No," Shako said. "But only because I was there

to stop them. So spare me your moralizing, please. You used her and you nearly killed her. Twice."

David put a hand on a nearby chair to steady himself. He sucked down a deep breath.

"You're right," he said. "I fucked up. All the more reason I should do the right thing now. And so should you."

She laughed. "Go away, David," she said. "You don't know what you're talking about."

He looked sad. Then he stood up straighter. "Here's what I know," he said. "I know that I will not let anyone else die for this. Not if I can help it."

David put the briefcase down on a table, then popped it open. Inside, cradled in impact foam, were a half dozen miniature jet injectors, smaller versions of the kind used for mass vaccinations. They were loaded with plastic vials, filled with clear liquid.

"I've made six doses of the hydrogels. They're all in here. I've promised them to Carlos."

Shako was instantly on edge. She shifted her weight, moved forward onto the balls of her feet. Ready to fight.

"But only if he takes me back to stop Aznar."

She put one foot forward, light as a ballerina. "I can't allow that," she said. "You are too valuable. Aznar cannot get his hands on you. He will break you, David. He would torture you until you gave him anything he wanted. I cannot risk that. Do you understand what I am saying? *I will not let you go to him.*"

"Why did you save me, Shako?"

That stopped her. "What?"

"You could have let me die in Florida. I had a bullet hole in me. All you had to do was wait a minute. Then you could have gone after Simon. You could have gotten them all, probably. You'd be that much closer to that vengeance you've wanted for so long. So why didn't you?"

Shako didn't reply.

"Here's what I think. I think you're not inhuman, as much as you'd like to be. I think the others have become less than they were, but you've become more. I think you still believe in something more than what it takes to keep life going and what it takes to end it. I'm a scientist. I couldn't name whatever that thing is. It doesn't show up on any test. But I believe in it just the same. I have to, because that's the thing I've been trying to preserve. Not just the mechanical pieces of the body. But the thing inside. The thing that tells us why we live. I hope there's a part of you that feels the same way."

She still didn't say anything.

"Idiotic, I know," David said quietly.

"Yes," Shako finally said. "Yes, it is. But only because you're right. I didn't want anything between us, David. Not anything real. I have trained it out of myself. Or at least that's what I thought. But when you were dying, I found some spark of something that was supposed to be dead."

For a moment, David's face lit up with hope.

"And I was wrong. It is an illusion. It's meant to keep us alive and procreating, nothing more. We chase after each other in search of some animal comfort, and we dress it up in words. It's a powerful lie, but it's still a lie. I believed it for a moment.

I admit it. I could not bear the thought of a world without you in it. I've lost many, many people over the years. I thought I couldn't bear to lose another. I was wrong. I should not have saved you. And I would not make the same mistake again. As much as I'd like to pretend otherwise, David, there's nothing outside of survival and death. I can live without you. I can live without anyone. That's the truth. So please do not test me on this. It won't end well for you. But it will end."

David looked as if something had broken inside him. He closed his eyes briefly. Then he stood taller.

"I can't tell you how sorry I am to hear that," he said. "All right. Come on in."

The door behind David opened. Carlos's men, all experienced killers, filed in quickly, each carrying an Uzi. A little retro for most modern drug dealers, who preferred the H&K or military surplus AK-47s now, but still brutally effective at unleashing a swarm of bullets in close quarters.

Carlos entered after them, his Dirty Harry .44 stuck in his enormous waistband.

Shako could either leap at David or try to escape.

She pivoted, ran, and tried to hurl herself through the window.

The glass did not break. Instead, she hit hard and bounced off, back into the room.

It might have been funny if David hadn't seen the shock on her face, compounding the betrayal.

"Bulletproof glass," Carlos explained. "You're not leaving that easily."

Carlos's men approached her carefully, guns up. Shako crouched, ready to attack in any direction.

They never got close enough to let that happen. At eight feet away, they formed a circle. They dropped their guns and lifted Tasers and fired in one smooth motion—the darts and cords lancing out and snagging in her skin, hitting her with hundreds of thousands of volts at once.

She went down on her knees, shaking uncontrollably. But she was still conscious.

"Hit her again," Carlos ordered.

"You said you wouldn't hurt her," David reminded him.

"At this point, I want to make certain she doesn't hurt me. Or you," Carlos replied. "Again."

They loaded Shako with more electricity. She flopped like a fish.

"Once more, just to be sure," Carlos said.

"No!" David yelled, but they didn't listen. This time, Shako barely moved. David thought he smelled a greasy odor like grilled meat.

"All right," Carlos said, satisfied. "Tie her up and get her to the plane."

David wheeled on him. "This is not what we discussed."

Carlos removed his gun from his pants but didn't point it at David. Not yet. "Do you trust her to stay here while we go back to the States? Of course you do, you're an idiot. But I know her. She would be after us as soon as she could. She might even arrive before us, knowing her. I won't have that. She comes along."

David grimaced. He had little choice here, now that the ride had started and everyone was locked into their seats.

"All right," he said. "But any harm comes to her and you lose any chance of more than what I've got in this case."

"Yes, yes, yes," Carlos said, waving the gun around. "Now. Can we please go to the plane?"

THEY FLEW IN A private jet again, but this time Shako rode in the cargo hold.

It was pressurized, so it didn't kill her, but the temperature soon dropped below zero. By the time they landed, she'd be lucky to stand, let alone fight.

She tried to conserve what warmth she could, and cursed David in her mind.

He didn't understand. Of course he didn't understand. She didn't explain. And then, when she tried, he heard exactly the wrong message.

Some genius. Always trying to avoid the inevitable. Always trying to save people.

She huddled and curled into herself on the cold steel floor.

Instead, he'd probably just killed them all.

# CHAPTER 32

TAMPA INTERNATIONAL AIRPORT
FLORIDA

THEY LANDED LATE at night. David was sleeping when Carlos's man poked him with the barrel of a MAC-10. The plane was taxiing inside a hangar. He hadn't even felt the jet touch down.

He rubbed grit from his eyes as he stepped out of the Gulfstream. It took David a moment to realize there was a party of men waiting for them in the hangar.

Max was there. So were Sebastian and Peter. And a bunch of guys with guns. And one man standing in front of all of them.

David recognized him from the videotape. Aznar.

Simon was nowhere to be seen.

David looked wildly at Carlos, who emerged from the jet sideways, angling his bulk through the airplane's door.

He saw the guns and Aznar.

"You," he said.

Aznar smiled broadly. "Me," he agreed.

Carlos shoved David aside, moved with surprising speed down the stairs and across the floor. He stopped in front of Aznar and they glared at each other.

Carlos pulled out his .44. He pointed it at Aznar.

The guards on all sides tensed up, weapons ready.

Then Aznar threw up his hands and bellowed, "Let's get ready to *rumble*!"

They both burst out laughing and embraced.

Oh shit, David thought.

They were giggly as schoolgirls when they turned to face him.

"My apologies, Dr. Robinton," Aznar said. "My name is Juan Aznar. It is a pleasure to finally make your acquaintance."

David said nothing. That sent Carlos into more fits of laughter.

"I think he's actually surprised."

"It's hard to remember being that young," Aznar said.

David pointed to the briefcase, still handcuffed to his wrist. "I thought you wanted this."

"We do," Aznar said. He turned to Carlos. "May I?"

Carlos handed over the gun. "Of course."

Aznar snapped his fingers, and his men moved in response. Shako was unceremoniously dumped onto the concrete floor out of the cargo hold. Even though she was shivering violently and barely able to stand, she still lunged for the closest thug.

He stepped back, sliding in his elegant shoes, and hit her with the butt of his weapon.

Then they dragged her over to Aznar and made her kneel. He pointed Carlos's borrowed pistol at the base of Shako's neck.

"The briefcase, please," Aznar said.

David hesitated.

Aznar rolled his eyes and pulled the hammer back on the pistol. "Do I really have to count to three?"

David shook his head. He took the key from his pocket and undid the handcuffs.

"David, don't," Shako called from the floor.

"Quiet," Aznar hissed. "I've heard more than enough from you for ten lifetimes."

David handed the briefcase over to one of the guards.

"Excellent," Aznar said. He took the case from the guard, then nodded. Shako was picked up by three other men and carried to one of two identical white vans. Aznar waved the gun vaguely in David's direction.

"You too, please. Into the next van."

"You've got what you wanted," David said. "You can let us go."

That got him nothing but more laughter. "So young," Carlos said.

The cuff that had held the briefcase was locked to David's other wrist and he was escorted past them on his way to the van. He gave Carlos a hard look. "So, this is what your word is worth."

Carlos laughed, his flab moving under his skin like seismic waves. "Oh. You child. Did you think

I'd betray someone I'd known for centuries in favor of a boy I've known for a few weeks?"

"You seemed pretty happy with the deal when you thought it meant you'd be the only one left with the formula," David shot back.

Carlos opened his mouth to say something, but Aznar spoke up first, his face thoughtful. "You know something?" he asked. "That's an excellent point. You didn't contact anyone when this boy and Shako first showed up on your doorstep."

The amusement left Carlos's face instantly. "Juan," he said. "Surely you know that I would never—"

"Why not?"

"I told you about them as soon as your message arrived."

"But not a moment before. Did you think you could outlive us? You wanted all of the boy's formula for yourself?"

Carlos began to look a bit nervous. "No, of course not. I was simply waiting to see how best to manage the situation. They were in my home, Juan. I had no alternatives."

Aznar looked impatient at that. "You're a drug lord, Carlos. You have a thousand men with guns. How did they survive until we sent our message? Did they plant a bomb somewhere in all those folds of fat?"

Now Carlos looked angry. "Have a care, Aznar. They're here now. I brought them to you. No one else. To you. That should tell you all you need to know about my loyalties."

"Yes," Aznar said. "It does."

Then he put his gun just under Carlos's right ear and pulled the trigger.

The 240-grain slug punched through Carlos's skull and blew a fist-size hole out the other side of his head. David saw the drug lord's eyes literally pop from the sudden pressure of a bullet moving at fifteen hundred feet per second through his brain.

Carlos's body fell like a slow-motion landslide to the ground, first at his knees, then at his massive waist, and finally his torso and his ruined head. It seemed to take hours.

Carlos's bodyguards were caught completely flat-footed. One of them belatedly put a hand into his waistband for his own weapon.

Aznar turned the .44 almost casually toward him. "The moment to be a hero has passed," he said.

The man slowly moved his hand away from his body.

"Good," Aznar said. Then he aimed the .44 down at Carlos's head and emptied the rest of the chambers. What was left looked more like a stain than anything human.

"That ought to do it," Aznar said. He turned to the guards again. "You can work for us now, if you like. Or die. I don't really care much one way or another."

Carlos's former employees were not complete idiots; they chose to live.

David stood there, his ears still ringing, looking at the remains of Carlos's head. Aznar dropped the empty pistol and gestured grandly toward the van.

"That was one of my oldest friends, David. And I don't even know you. Keep that in mind."

David walked over to the van.

The doors were opened for him. In the brief moment that light penetrated the dark interior, he saw another body, also handcuffed, sitting awkwardly against the wheel well.

Simon.

Simon blinked in the sudden glare, and his eyes fixed on David.

"I believe you two have a lot to discuss," Aznar said.

David was shoved inside. He saw Carlos's men struggling to get the massive body of their former boss into the plane's cargo hold.

The doors slammed again, and everything went black.

# CHAPTER 33

SIMON AND DAVID couldn't see each other, or anything else. The interior of the van was completely dark and sealed off from the driver's cabin.

Somehow it made it easier to talk, without having to look at Simon's face.

"You seem pretty calm," David said. "Is this where the Illuminati come bursting in to save you?"

"Illuminati?" He laughed. "A wet dream for those who cannot take responsibility for their own actions. I've been to the Bilderberg conference, sat on the Council on Foreign Relations and the Trilateral Commission, and spent a weekend at the Bohemian Grove. They're all the same. Very rich and important people suffering under the illusion that they know how things work, who are just as surprised by what's on the news as everyone else. Believe me. If there were any secret masters of the world, I'd have met them by now."

"Maybe you just don't meet their standards. I certainly expected more. Five hundred years old and you're in the back of a van with a mere mortal like me."

Simon laughed again. He seemed relaxed, even happy. He spoke as if it were a relief to finally drop the many masks and disguises, as if he'd been suffocating underneath all of their layers.

"Oh, David. You're so young. It took me almost a century to see it myself. Humans are herd animals. They are slow, but they move like glaciers across continents, inevitable and unstoppable. All I've ever tried to do is steer them. And even unlimited wealth and endless life are small tools against the shortsightedness and greed of millions of your kind. It's like reincarnation. Which is an utter fantasy, by the way. I've lived a very long time and never met anyone twice. But I'm sure you've noticed that everyone who believes in it always claims they were royalty or a hero or nobility in a past life. No one wants to be a peasant. The fact is, the world has always been too big for one ruler. Most of the time, history is just a thing that happens to people. We have worked hard to make a difference, but there were only eight of us. Our time and resources were limited, compared to the task at hand. We couldn't be everywhere at once. And we made mistakes. Do you have any idea how long I spent winning the loyalty of the king of Belgium? I wish there *was* a way to control every variable, to run the whole world from behind the scenes, to make it as simple as the conspiracy theorists say."

"Yeah," David said, voice dripping with contempt, "it's a damn shame, all those people living their lives without your permission."

Suddenly Simon's good humor dropped. "My way is *better*," Simon hissed. "Look at how you people behave if left to your own devices. You don't even have to pick a genocide. They are all depressingly similar. Instead, just watch a single man in a car on the freeway when he suddenly realizes he's got to make an exit. He will cross five lanes without looking, endanger dozens of lives, maybe even cause a massive pileup that backs up traffic for a day—all because he can't possibly wait for the next stop on the road. Literally billions of dollars have gone into making cars safer, to designing airbags and crash safety, and improving roads to funnel people where they need to go. And one man can destroy all that in a split second of stupidity and selfishness."

"And what have you done? From what Shako tells me, you've started enough wars and genocides to qualify as a horseman of the Apocalypse yourself. Five hundred years of corpses. You want to take credit for that?"

"You have no idea."

"I've seen enough."

"You have no idea," Simon said again, "what the world was before you were in it. You still weep for your sister? When I was born, nearly half of all children died before they were five years old. Just having a baby could be a death sentence for women. People poured their shit in the river and then drank the water. They starved when the winter was bad or when the summer was too hot, and every few years, some plague or another would rip through them and the corpses would pile dozens high in the street.

"And you have the nerve to complain? You soft, overfed toddler. You grew up on land that was paid for with the blood of millions. You think the natives just walked away from it? They had to be forced at gunpoint. I know. I held the guns. Your buildings, your institutions, your colleges and universities were built with dollars from slavery. Your country grew fat and happy while millions of men, women, and children were bought and sold like cattle. The bloodstains are so deep in the fabric of your nation you don't even see them anymore. All you get is the reward: a limitless future, a vast nation, unlimited possibilities, from sea to shining sea."

David felt as though he had to speak up for himself. "I didn't do any of that."

"You didn't have to," Simon shot back. "I did it for you. Me and everyone like me. We did the hard things. We did the vicious things. We did it for the future. You want to blame me for the way the world is now? I will take it. I admit it is not what I had planned. But I will take credit for every forward step, every small, bloody inch of progress, because I had to claw each one with my fingernails."

"You've killed thousands of people."

"Oh, more than that," Simon said. "Many more. I have slaughtered my way across continents and built machines of death and paid politicians to wage wars. But every time, I did so knowing that there was something better that could come out of the bloodshed. For every corpse on my conscience, I've saved a thousand lives. The world is better now than it once was. And I will take credit for that."

David was silent for a moment. "And yet Shako still wants to kill you. I guess she just can't see the bigger picture the way you can."

"You don't understand us," Simon said. "Our first lives were like our childhoods. Everything was so vivid and new. We didn't know how long our lives would be. So of course we carry the wounds and scars deeply. The same way you still probably tear up at the thought of your first puppy. The same way she and I still love each other."

David laughed out loud at that. "You think she loves you?"

"I know she does."

"That's funny. Because when we were in bed together—"

Something like a growl escaped Simon's throat. "Be very careful, David."

"Sorry. Didn't realize how sensitive you are. When we were in bed together, *fucking*— Too offensive? Want me to stop now?"

No response.

"Shako never mentioned loving you. Lots of talk about killing you. But nothing about love."

"You still don't understand. You're a pet to her. At best. A toy."

"Maybe so," David admitted. "I'm smart enough to admit that, even if it stings. But at least I don't fool myself into thinking I'm a god."

Simon laughed bitterly. "There is no God. But if there were, I'd be far closer to him than to you. After all, I changed *your* life."

"Because you gave me a job?"

"Because I killed your parents."

David went silent in the dark.

"All your pillow talk, and Shako didn't tell you that? I'm surprised."

"She told me," David said quietly.

"I see. You didn't believe her. Well. I can't blame you. She'd already told you so many lies. How are you supposed to know what to believe? If it gives you any comfort, it wasn't anything I enjoyed. It was another sacrifice. Your father was a brilliant man, David. Truly. But he was as limited in his morality as you are. He couldn't see the greater good."

"Simon," David said, "go fuck yourself."

Simon sighed heavily. "You see? You're simply reacting on a genetic level. Responding to the loss of your parents, your sister. A slave to your instincts to protect the animals that have the closest similarity to you. This is why we do not have children. As soon as you are tied to their future, rather than your own, you are lost. You become part of the herd. The world cannot survive such sentimentality. That is what separates me from you, and all those like you. I can see the end. The rest of you are fatally distracted."

"You're right," David said.

Surprise filled Simon's voice. "I am?"

"Yeah. I wasn't sure if Shako was telling me the truth. Now I know. And you're still utterly full of shit. Five hundred years and what have you really done? You might think you're not a part of the herd, but you're just as selfish and shortsighted. Look at everything you could have done better. You could have cured any disease. You could have revealed the Water to the world years ago, made it into an international resource. You could have fed the starving and housed the poor. You could have taken your wealth and built cities on the moon, for Christ's sake. You could have been walking among the stars by now. You could have done anything."

Simon snorted. "You think the world works like that. You're not so bright after all."

"Maybe you're right. But I know you've had five hundred years, and all you've done is live the same pointless, stupid life over and over again. You've fought the same petty little squabbles, trying desperately to hang on to something you stole in the first place. All because you're too frightened to face the truth. Everybody dies sooner or later, Simon. With or without the Water. Everybody dies. And so will you."

"Is that your idea of a threat?"

"No. It's a fact. You've lived a long time, but it's going to end soon. I'm going to kill you. Count on it."

Simon sat with that for a long time. David thought perhaps the other man was finished talking. Then Simon spoke up again.

"You're right, David. Everyone dies," Simon said. "But I'm willing to bet I'll outlive you."

The van came to a halt. They had arrived.

THEY TOOK THE TOP three floors of the casino's hotel. They put it all on Simon's AmEx Black, which Aznar found hugely amusing.

They explained to the hotel management that this was all for a top-secret visit by a celebrity, very hush-hush, someone you'd definitely recognize, but please, keep it to yourself.

The Council now milled around in one of the top-floor conference rooms.

David was downstairs in one of the hotel rooms, but Simon sat in a chair at the back of the room, hands cuffed.

"I'm not sure why I'm here," he said, when Aznar came close. "If you're looking for a consultant for your plan, I don't think you can afford my fees."

Aznar turned and slapped him.

"Shut up," he said. "You're only here because Max insists. But that doesn't mean we can't hurt you."

"Why don't you just kill me and get it over with?"

Aznar leaned in close, with a smile that reached all the way to his eyes. He looked around to make sure no one else was listening.

"Because I want you to see how easily I can accomplish everything you've always failed to do, of course," he said. "In less than a week, I will secure the Council's future, eliminate its greatest enemy, and solve the problem of the Water. Then I'll kill you. I should have thought that was obvious."

Simon considered that. "I never liked you, Juan."

"The feeling is mutual, Simon."

"Can we please discuss Shako now?" Max asked, calling Aznar away from his fun.

She was still in the back of one of the vans. Max wanted to interrogate her immediately and force the location of her supply of the Water from her.

It was Aznar, surprisingly, who objected.

"Don't get me wrong," he said. "I'm happy to torture her. I will gladly begin slicing strips from her skin if you want. It just won't do any good."

Max didn't believe it. "Surely you have more faith in your own skills."

Aznar rolled his eyes. "I've been fighting her, harder and closer, than you or Simon ever have. In Kosovo, I saw her pull a chunk of shrapnel out of her own abdomen and use it as a knife. I hate her more than you can understand, Max, but I know exactly what she is capable of. She will resist. We could remove her spleen and show it to her, and she would still resist. It's who she is."

"So, what do we do?"

"Keep her alone. Do not allow any of the men near her. Not even within arm's length, even to feed her. Lock her in a cage and keep a gun on her at all times. Any one of our men who tries to touch her will die, and she will use the opportunity to escape. You know it's true."

"Oh, come now," Max said. "She's not a wild animal. She's still no more than we are."

"Really? Have you not spent the last five centuries hiding from her? Was that just me, then?"

Max made a face, but Aznar could tell: he'd won the argument.

"What if she doesn't have any more?" Peter asked. "What if it turns out Shako has run just as dry as we have?"

"Then we have David," Max answered. "And he will give us whatever we want to avoid anyone else getting hurt."

"Or maybe you'll just kill us and take what's left for yourself," Sebastian snapped. He'd been angry since Aznar had killed Carlos.

"Carlos forgot his place," Aznar reminded him. "Don't forget yours, and you'll be fine."

Peter hoisted the briefcase they'd taken from David at the airport. "Why don't we just take our medicine now? Then we don't have anything to worry about."

"You trust Robinton that much?"

"He didn't know Carlos would deliver him to us. You saw the look on his face."

"He's not an idiot. Maybe he planned for this. Maybe there's some kind of poison," Aznar said. "It's what I would have done."

They all thought about that for a moment.

"Bring him in," Aznar said to one of his men. "There's one way to know for sure."

"And what about Shako?"

Aznar already had the answer in mind. "She said she was willing to see her people die again," he said. "So let's call her bluff. Let's show it to her."

THEY RELEASED DAVID FROM his cuffs.

Shako watched from a chair. She had come quietly from the parking garage with three of Carlos's men. It made Max nervous, but all three men were already standing next to her with guns, so he didn't know what else to do about it.

Aznar had the briefcase open on the long table and the injection guns out.

He summoned David over to the table.

"We're anxious to try your miracle cure, Dr. Robinton," Aznar said.

David stared him down. "You've made it pretty clear you don't need my permission."

"Well, this is our problem. We're not sure that it's entirely safe. We suspect you might have done something that could actually harm us rather than help us."

"That's not very trusting of you."

Aznar smiled. "We live in cynical times."

"So what? You want a guarantee?"

Aznar took one of the injectors from its foam cradle. "I want you to try it first."

David didn't say anything. He took the gun, popped the cap off, and shot himself in the arm without hesitating.

He handed the gun back to Aznar. "Feel better now?"

The others waited. Nothing happened.

One by one, the Council took the guns from the table and injected themselves.

They waited again.

"It doesn't feel like the Water," Aznar said, smacking his lips, as if trying to rid himself of the aftertaste.

"Simon said it would be different."

"I told you, Max," Simon said, from his chair at the back. "It's not the same thing."

"That's true," David said. "I couldn't duplicate it exactly. But it works. Aznar should be able to tell you. He saw the girl I gave the first dose."

Aznar nodded. "I did. She was recovered. Healthy."

Another moment passed.

"I'm feeling a bit parched," Simon said from his chair. "And I notice there's one dose left."

"No, Simon," Aznar said. "Let's see you get old and gray for a change. See how you enjoy it."

He took a step closer to Shako but still kept a respectful distance.

"Pay attention now," he said. "This next part is especially for you."

THEY GATHERED ALL THEIR hired guns, Carlos's people and Conquest's. Altogether, they had fifteen men.

Simon and David and Shako were at the back of the room, uncomfortably close, their hands all tied. Shako had David's cuffs around her ankles now as well. David was tied with a set of plastic zip-cuffs.

They waited. They had no choice.

Aznar stood at the front of the room and addressed his men like a general.

"Gentlemen," he said. "Five miles down the road from this casino is a small town called Cypress Grove. We are going to kill every man, woman, and child who lives there."

The men Conquest had hired looked around, as if to see if someone was filming this for some obscene joke. Carlos's men did not move. It was not the worst thing they had ever been asked to do.

No one objected.

"We will take out the cell-phone towers first, then the phone lines coming out of the town. You'll all be given maps. We will begin at the police station. There shouldn't be much of a problem after that. This is Florida, however. Most of the homes will have at least one gun. But they won't be ready for us. No one is ready for something like this."

He looked at the back of the room.

"Do you hear me, Shako? Do you understand? We are going to kill them all. Just like we did before. Unless you cooperate. Unless you tell me where I can find the rest of your Water."

She said nothing.

"You're a cruel woman, Shako," Aznar said. "I wonder how many people will have to die before we can soften that hard heart of yours. Perhaps we will start at the elementary school."

There was a knock at the door. Aznar looked annoyed. He'd just been warming up.

One of Carlos's men cracked open the door. A young man wearing the uniform of a hotel waiter stood there.

"The management wanted to know if you would like some complimentary champagne."

Then his eyes widened as he caught a glimpse of the room. "Whoa. That is a serious number of guns, man."

"Bring him inside," Aznar barked.

The *sicario* yanked the boy into the room and shoved him to the carpet, Uzi barrel nudged close to the back of his neck.

Shako sat perfectly still.

Aznar's eyes flashed at her. He crossed the room to the boy. The kid could not have been much more than nineteen, built like a jock but still baby-faced. He was Seminole, his smooth skin a darker version of Shako's own.

Aznar waved away the gunman and brought out his own weapon. He pointed it at the boy's head. "Tell me, young man. Do you live in Cypress Grove?"

The kid looked up, eyes wide. "What?"

"Simple question. You work here part-time? Is this how you make a little extra money after school? Serving drinks to drunken palefaces as they gamble away their Social Security?"

"Yeah," the kid said. "I mean, yeah, I'm from Cypress Grove."

Aznar beamed. "Well, then. I think we can begin. What do you say, Shako? Are you willing to save him? Tell us where to find the Water now, and you stop it all."

Her voice was ice cold. "You won't spare him. Not even if I tell you."

Aznar shrugged. "Then it looks like we've found our first victim." He aimed the gun.

The boy began to yell. "No, no, no, man," the kid said. "I'm not!"

Aznar lifted the gun, amused. "No? You're not? This isn't really up for debate, son."

Then the fear seemed to drop away from the kid. He actually smiled.

"No," he said. "I'm not that. I'm the distraction."

There was just enough time for a ripple of unease to spread through the room.

Then everything exploded.

THEY WERE UP ABOVE the ceiling. They were all Seminole.

They dropped straight through the tiles, moving incredibly, impossibly fast.

They fell among the gunmen and started laying waste to every body within reach.

They were unarmed, for the most part. The oldest of them was the same age as the waiter. They were kids. Teenagers going up against a roomful of hardened killers.

It was no contest.

One boy punched a *sicario* in the throat, turned and snapped the neck of the man next to him. A Conquest thug aimed his gun at the boy and immediately had it taken away, his arm folded back and broken by a girl half his age. Another young man faced off against an experienced Colombian enforcer and knocked the man across the room with a front kick, breaking his spine.

Aznar screamed in rage. He aimed and pulled the trigger of his hand cannon. He blew a chunk out of the wall.

The waiter leaped up to face him. Aznar was fast enough to bring the gun around and pistol-whip the boy across the face.

Then Shako stood and, with a sudden, unbelievable strength, snapped the chains of her cuffs.

Aznar looked as if he couldn't believe it. He brought his gun up to aim it at her. But she was no longer where he was aiming. Instead she was coming up on his side, moving too fast.

She leaped and brought her heel against the side of his head.

There was a sickening crunch.

Aznar's mouth was still wide open, even though

he didn't make a sound. The gun dropped from his hand.

He seemed to fall in slow motion.

Shako landed and then leaped again. She came down on his neck.

Even with the gunfire, the slick pop-and-crack could be heard through the room.

Aznar lay on the floor, his head now at an unnatural angle to his body.

Then it was over.

Aznar looked up, mouth working but making no noise, as Shako towered over him.

"No," he said. "Not like this."

"Were you expecting more?" Shako asked him as the light began to dim in his eyes. "Your mistake. You always thought you mattered more than you did. But you were not my greatest enemy. You were a cockroach. Hard to kill, but in the end, just another insect. There is no clash of champions. There is no final battle. There is just you, dying, alone."

Aznar began to choke. Shako made a face and stepped on his throat.

A moment later, there was nothing but silence.

Simon and David were still seated, slightly in shock, mere witnesses to all the carnage that had been delivered with such precision.

The men of the Council were all surrounded by at least three of the Seminole youths. They were kids. But they moved with superhuman grace and power.

Simon recognized it at last. They had all drunk the Water.

Shako pointed at David.

"Cut him loose," she said.

"Yes, *Cvcke*," one of the boys said, and went to David with his knife to cut his hands free from the zip-cuffs.

Simon recognized the word. It was different from the Uzita language, altered by centuries and different tribes, but still had the same root.

"*Cvcke?*" he said. "Why would they call you Mother?"

Shako said nothing.

David stood up, looking weak and unsettled. Simon wondered if he'd been hurt, but there were no visible wounds.

He'd figured it out first.

"Because she is their mother, Simon," David said. "She's the mother to all of them."

# CHAPTER 34

FLORIDA
1528

WHEN THE SLAUGHTER of the Uzita was finally done, Shako slipped from the tree and quietly escaped back into the brush. She knew she had to move quickly if she wanted to survive.

She raced back to her camp and took everything she could carry. Then she went to the cave.

At the Fountain, there was no time for ceremony. The power was not in the words, she knew. It was in the Water. And she was beyond forgiveness anyway. She filled several skins with the Water. Then she leaped into the pool herself, drinking deeply as she swam, letting the Water soak into her, saturate her, fill her up inside and out.

Her old self had died with the rest of her village. But when she emerged from the pool, she was reborn. Physically, she was stronger and smarter and now more durable than perhaps any human being had ever been.

She finally understood what her father had been trying to say. The future demanded hard choices at times. She carried that future now, and keeping it safe meant giving up on revenge, at least for a while.

Hirrihigua would not let her return to the tribe because she was carrying Simon's child. She was tainted in his eyes, and so she was exiled. She never strayed too far, because she'd always hoped to be accepted back someday. She'd hoped her father could find a way to forgive her.

So she was nearby when Simon and his kind killed them all.

She knew she would need every gift, every advantage, for the purpose of her new life. She would hunt down everyone who participated in the slaughter of her people and make them pay in kind.

First, however, she ran. She ran because she was still outnumbered, and she didn't yet know how to kill them all. She had to plan.

But, most important, she could not let the last of her tribe die.

She had to find a safe place to have her child.

SHE TRAVELED NORTH. SHE found other tribes there, who were far away from the ships landing on the southern coasts. At first she was greeted with suspicion. But then they saw what she could do. Her strength was greater than their most powerful men. She could heal the sickest of them, although she saved that for the young and the children. She carried steel, which most of them had never seen before. And she had all the secrets of the Water

Clan to teach them, learned when she was still just a girl with the Uzita. In time, she held a place of reverence among her new people.

Her son, when he was born, was treated like a prince. He would become a great leader, even if his skin was much paler than anyone had ever seen before, and his features far more delicate than the other boys'.

The other members of Shako's new tribe assumed it was because he'd been touched by the same strangeness that allowed Shako to live without aging and to do so many other things.

In a way, that was true, Shako supposed. He was growing in her belly when she sank into the Water and came out again. But she recognized other things in her son that had nothing to do with her. His intellect, his ambition, and his talent for war—all of those were gifts from his father.

She didn't discourage him in any of those things. She knew what was coming. And her new family needed a warrior to lead them and protect them.

When her son was almost twenty, she left them all behind. This was only a short stop for her, a place and a time to rest. She had her own tasks ahead.

But she never forgot them, and they never forgot her. Even as they moved south, into the lands once occupied by the Uzita, the Apalachee, the Timucua, and the Mocoso. Most of those tribes were dead now, killed by either the Spaniards or the diseases the Spanish brought with them. The stragglers and survivors were welcomed by Shako's people.

Eventually, this band of Creek forged their own identity. They traded with and occasionally fought the Europeans who kept coming to Florida. The Spanish were always slightly afraid of them.

They called them the Seminole, a corruption of the Spanish term for "runaway," or "wild one."

And among them, there was always a select group of the finest warriors, young men and sometimes women who represented the tribe's future. In secret, they would travel to a place in the wilderness. There they would be taken down a path that led into a tunnel, a tunnel that opened into a cave the size of a warehouse.

At the center of this cave was a spring that fed water into a pool that glowed an eerie blue.

The young men and women would drink of the water and be made better than they were before. Then Shako would train them and send them back to their homes, where they would serve in secret: the fiercest warriors, the finest protectors. Generation after generation, they received just enough of the Water to make them strong, to make them superhuman. But she never allowed them enough to tempt or corrupt them. She made certain they were smarter than she was.

They called her Mother, for they were all her children.

# CHAPTER 35

THEY WERE TEENAGERS. Boys and girls. But they moved with practiced ease and grace as they went among the dead, gathering their weapons, sliding clips and bullets from the guns and tossing them into a pile at the center of the room.

No matter what they looked like, they were warriors. Shako's secret weapons.

"These are . . . our children?" Simon asked, incredulous.

"No," Shako corrected him. "They are my children."

"I never knew."

"Would it have changed anything?"

Simon couldn't answer that. She turned away.

Shako went to David and held him. She tried to kiss him, but he kept her at arm's length.

"You might have told me," he said.

"I'm sorry," Shako told him. "I couldn't risk them

knowing about this. There was no way to explain. But you see? They would have been able to take care of themselves. It's what I raised them for."

"I understand now, I get it," David said. He looked very pale now. "I just really wish you'd told me."

Then he collapsed, a fresh red spatter of blood appearing on his lips as he began coughing.

A second later, Max, Peter, and Sebastian all hit the floor as well.

DAVID'S FORMULA, WHEN IT worked properly, introduced synthetic DNA that replaced the repair-and-excision sequences that kept errors out of the genome. Put simply, it cut-and-pasted new DNA that was flawless in place of the DNA that was old or damaged.

But that same process could be used to simply slice the DNA to ribbons, without replacing anything. It could, in theory, unwind the double helix and break down the DNA itself, causing cell disintegration on a massive scale.

Eventually, organs would fail. Tissues would break down. The human body would not know how to repair itself from the billion small tears and cracks that arose every minute of every day.

David figured it would take thirty minutes to an hour for the effects of a process like that to become apparent.

He was off by about ten minutes. He must have misplaced a decimal point somewhere back in Colombia, but it was a moot point now.

He and the others were all dying, falling apart at the fundamental level.

IT UNDID THE WORK of the Water. It was, in a way, a cure for immortality.

The men of the Council suddenly got very old, very fast.

Their skin withered and shrank and folded in on itself like a peach rotting in time-lapse photography.

Max screamed in pain.

Simon thrashed against the cuffs holding him, tried to stand up with the chair still attached. One of the boys shoved him back down.

"Please," he yelled at Shako. "Let me—please. If you ever felt anything for me. Don't let him die alone."

Shako thought about it for a long moment.

In that time, the men on the floor shriveled before their eyes. It was not a quiet process. They all screamed now, as their muscles shrank and bones popped audibly from tendons. Their skin cracked and wept and bled.

Their eyes clouded over, years of macular degeneration blinding them in seconds. Their teeth fell out of their gums.

Simon could smell them, a rank foulness rising as their bodies rotted from the cells up.

"Please," he said to Shako again. "Let me go to him."

Shako eyed him coldly, then looked at Max, who was curling up into a ball now, his fine suit soiled with blood and fluids, hanging on him loosely as he boiled away to nothing.

Centuries of damage and disease and injury, all concentrated into a few brief minutes, all falling down on him at once.

"You want to comfort him?" Shako asked. "Give him some solace in his last moments? Ease his pain? Hold his hand?"

Simon was prepared to beg. "Yes. Please. I owe him that," Simon said.

Shako took a step closer to Simon, blocking his view of all three of them.

"No."

That was all. One word.

Their bones cracked under their own weight. Max screamed once more.

And the three immortal conquistadors died, leaving Simon alone in the world, the last of his kind.

Shako stepped away, and Simon could see them again. One last spasm had turned Max's head. His skin was wrapped tight around a skull. It looked as if his jaw was open in an eternal scream of agony.

Simon looked at this for a long time before he realized that tears were running down his face.

No one cared. They were doing their best to save David.

One of the children—one of his descendants, Simon realized with the same shock as before—had a paramedic's kit. He was trying to inject something into David's arm. He couldn't find a vein.

Useless, Simon knew. There was only one thing that could save David now. Shako had to know it, too. So why was she hesitating?

"There is another source of the Water," Simon said.

"Yes," Shako said.

David had lapsed into unconsciousness. He was younger than the others, but he would not last much longer. It was obvious.

"Then what are you waiting for?" Simon said. "Take him there. Save him."

She looked at him. "And start all this over again?"

Simon sat for a moment. Then he spoke again. "Whatever I did to you, that was my fault. Not his. We brought him into this. First me, then you. All he has ever tried to do is the right thing. You can't let him die for that."

"You're wrong," she said.

But then she spoke to the two Seminole youths and had them pick David up.

"I can't let him die, but that's not the reason."

She told one of the others to bring around a car. They needed to move quickly.

"We're going to the cave," she said. She pointed at Simon. "And he's coming with us. I want him to see this."

# CHAPTER 36

THE TRIP WAS easier than it had been a hundred fifty years before, but it was still not easy.

The Range Rover that Shako drove—David rapidly deteriorating in the back, held by her two young warriors—ate up a lot of ground at the edge of the swamp. Still, it sank in muck to the axle when they tried to cross a field of mud flats near the river.

They went on foot from there. Simon was not bound, or even watched that closely. He wondered if he had won some small amount of respect from Shako for speaking for David's life.

Probably not. More likely, she was just too worried about David to spare any more thought on him.

They covered the distance as fast as they could on foot, winding down trails between the trees, headed into the thickets. A hidden trail emerged from behind the overgrowth; Simon found himself placing his feet on stone steps half-buried in the mud, then turning into a seeming wall of vegetation to discover a tunnel carved into the branches.

For years he had suspected there was something still here. He swore he could almost feel it in his blood, the last remnants of the Water in his system vibrating in tune with a hidden spring somewhere underground. But they had never been able to find anything, in all the years they looked. Their attempts to claim the land were blocked, always by the remnants of the Seminole tribe. In the nineteenth century, his scouts were cut down by arrows and axes. And then, in the twentieth century, once the Seminole were recognized by the courts again, Conquest found itself cut off by lawyers paid for by the newfound wealth from Indian casinos. He was never able to purchase so much as an acre of Seminole land, and Simon eventually dismissed his feeling as foolish hope.

Now he knew he was right.

It was almost dawn when they found the small waterfall. Shako turned abruptly, almost into the rock face of the hill, and then simply vanished.

The Seminole boy and girl did the same, David supported between them, and Simon saw it. A dark fissure in the rock running eight feet high but only a few feet wide.

Carlos never would have fit through here, he thought, and turned to the side to ease through.

He stumbled immediately. It was pitch-dark, and the drop was sudden and steep.

The Seminole girl kept him from falling when he bumped into her.

In a few moments, his eyes adjusted. There was

a slightly phosphorescent lichen on the cave walls that glowed enough to allow a dim view. The others moved swiftly, finding their footholds from memory. He moved as fast as he could behind them, feeling each step along the way.

Eventually, as they went deeper, the path grew wider. The rock and earth above him was cross-braced with old timbers, and holes were punched at the end of one cave to create entrances into the next.

He realized the timbers were not for support. They did not keep the passages open. Rather, they held back tons and tons of debris that had been shifted from the passage up to the ceiling. If the braces were to fall, the entire tunnel would collapse in on itself.

A safety measure, Simon figured. One of Shako's ideas, no doubt.

They came to the final chamber. Now Simon saw the blue glow. It felt calm and welcoming. He stepped through the last passage, which was fashioned like an archway, with rough-hewn bricks curving over the top, where they met at a keystone.

That's where he saw the bodies.

Their skin was as fresh as if they'd died yesterday. Simon felt the moisture in the air. The Water, the condensation, it must have acted as a preservative.

They all lay on the floor of the main chamber, at various spots around the eerie, glowing pool. They were on their backs, wearing clothes from hundreds of years before. There were chiefs in their full ceremonial finery, and some men wearing only loincloths. There was one body that looked

Aztec, wearing long-decayed feathers and tarnished gold. There was even something that looked more ape than man, a hairy hominid with a face almost simian except for its disturbingly human eyes, open and staring at nothing.

He was about to ask how they died when it became obvious.

They were all suicides.

Some had slit their wrists, the blood long since run out but the neat slashes still open. Others had cut their own throats. One man, who must have had inhuman determination, had slowly wrapped a leather cord around his own neck and then twisted a wooden handle through it, over and over, until it tightened and strangled him. His face was mottled and bloated, but Simon could still see the hint of a smile on his lips.

"What is this?" he demanded.

Shako looked up from where she was hovering over David. She had a plastic bottle in one hand. She was trying to get him to drink. It wasn't working.

"This is exactly what it looks like," she said. "This is what I wanted you to see."

"Immortals," he said.

"Every one who used this pool before us. Strangers and travelers who stumbled upon it. My ancestors. Others, far older than them. Every one who lived long enough to know they were tired of it. There's more to life than simply not dying."

"My God," Simon said. "The years in this place. And they all just gave up?"

"We're not meant to be like this," Shako said. "None of us."

Simon felt somehow cheated. Another secret she'd kept from him. And always a moral at the end of the story.

"Then I suppose you should let him die," he said, pointing to David.

"I told you already," Shako said. "I'm not going to let that happen."

"It doesn't look as if it's up to you."

The Seminole boy was trying to get David to swallow the Water, too. It still wasn't working. He shook his head. He looked up at Shako helplessly.

Shako picked David up in her arms. His flesh was practically dissolving now, sliding off in chunks as he was undone from the inside out. Water and blood dribbled from his mouth. If he was breathing, it was so faint that Simon could not see it.

But he could see Shako's tears.

She lifted him and carried him to the edge of the pool. And then she dropped him.

Simon crossed the cave to stand with them and watch the surface.

The pool was not large, but it was surprisingly deep. The blue glow was all they could see on the surface. Below that was nothing but darkness.

They waited. Nothing.

The surface became still, the ripples from David's body slowly flattening, then disappearing altogether.

The pool was once again as flat as a pane of glass.

Now? Simon wondered.

Shako and the boy and the girl were completely fixated on the Water.

Simon reached under his shirt and found the

knife. So many years. So many times he'd replaced the handle and the blade. But it was the same knife. The one Shako had given him.

The only truly unselfish gift he'd ever received in his long and twisted life.

He prepared to draw the weapon. The boy was closest, so he'd get the blade at the back of his neck, right at the soft spot where the spine met the skull. Simon would pull it out and slice it around into Shako's side. It would not be a fatal strike, but it would probably puncture a lung, which would keep her down long enough for him to use his fists to beat the girl.

Shako had brought him here to show him. He'd seen.

He'd seen a chance to make it all right again, to start over. A whole new source of the Water. A whole new beginning.

He gripped the knife.

Then something burst from the pool, gasping and blindly clawing for air.

Simon flinched back, startled. The boy reached out and grabbed one of the flailing hands. Shako grabbed the other. The girl put her hands around Shako's waist, and they pulled, all together, yanking the flailing swimmer free, straining as if they were meeting resistance, as if the pool did not want to let the body go back to them.

With a final tug, they heaved David onto the stone floor.

He lay on his back, choking. The boy turned him over, and pure blue Water poured from his lungs as he gagged and vomited it out.

Shako was kneeling next to him, her iron control finally broken, weeping and saying prayers in Uzita, a language Simon still recognized, if only from his dreams.

Simon wanted to give them a moment. But he couldn't.

There was still so much to do, and so little time.

He grabbed the knife again and stepped forward.

And was slammed back into the wall of the cavern so fast that he could barely see what had hit him.

He tried to bring the knife up to stab his attacker, and felt it plucked from his hands effortlessly, his fingers snapping like twigs as he tried to keep his grip.

Frighteningly blue eyes stared into his out of a face that was David's but was as cold and still as stone.

Simon saw the knife spin in David's hand, and then watched, helpless, as David drove it, blurring fast, into his chest.

It hurt, but more than that, it went deep. So deep that it scraped against something and then severed it completely. Simon felt it like a string being cut in him. His arms and legs spasmed once and then went dead. The knife was still buried in him, wedged between his ribs, angled with a surgeon's precision down and back into his spine.

David lifted him as though he was nothing. Simon stared into those deep blue eyes and saw nothing human.

"David," Shako's strong voice said. "No. Stop."

David blinked. The blue vanished, returning to his own, normal coloring.

He looked confused, like a sleeper woken from a nap. And the strength fled him. He dropped Simon on the floor of the cavern. Shako came to him and pulled him away.

Simon kept trying to reach the knife. His arms would move only half the distance. He could not seem to bend past his waist.

He fell back.

Shako stood over him, her arm around David, who was still dripping wet, still looking confused and frightened.

"I showed you," Shako said. "I tried. I still held out some hope. But you didn't want to see. You never understood."

Simon was filled with a sudden bottomless rage. "No," he hissed at her. "I have lived too long. To let it end like this."

She reached down and, surprisingly gently, stroked his hair from his face.

"You're right," she said. "You have lived too long. But everything ends. Sooner or later, everything ends."

She rose and took David's hand. "What you have to find is the one thing you cannot live without," she said.

David did not speak. He shivered, as if struck by some bone-deep chill. He looked at everything with a kind of horror and awe.

Shako fit herself under his arm and led him away.

The Seminole boy and girl looked at him for a moment longer. Then they, too, walked away.

Shako paused at the passage out of the cave. Simon could just see her there if he turned his head. The boy and girl supported David while she reached above her head to the keystone at the top of the arch.

She slid it from its place. Then they all turned and left him.

The first block fell a moment later, gravity overcoming inertia, sliding slowly at first, then gathering momentum. The second fell after that, and then the next, and then two or three at once, and then the archway collapsed completely.

The chain reaction began at once, as smaller stones dropped out of the places where they supported the larger stones. First one or two, then dozens at a time.

Within a moment, the rocks fell like rain, and the tunnel was crushed under the weight of tons of stone.

DAVID AND SHAKO AND the youths were at the surface by then, watching. They heard the grinding sound of rock breaking far below, and saw a dust cloud rise out of the cave's hidden entrance.

David was still not entirely sure where he had gone, or how he'd come back. He had a deep, nightmarish sense of being swallowed, being absorbed like a drop of water in the ocean, becoming part of a current that flowed through vast reaches over and through the earth. He grasped, if only for an instant, how small a part of the whole he carried. And then he had been violently cast out again, where he found himself holding Simon off the ground.

He looked at Shako and decided it did not matter. They were alive. They held each other tightly.

This day was a gift. And so were all the others that would come after it, however many they had left, wherever they would reach an end.

# EPILOGUE

SAINT PETERSBURG, FLORIDA
ONE MONTH LATER

*"Anything eternal is probably intolerable."*
—CHRISTOPHER HITCHENS

HERE HE COMES," Jenny said. "Same time, every day."

"Back off, he's mine," Mia told her. Jenny laughed, but Mia was not entirely joking.

They were behind the reception desk of Three Graces Nursing Home, watching the young man walk up the steps to the front doors.

He'd visited every day since he'd brought the old woman here. It was more a nice gesture than anything else. The old woman was too far gone to notice anyone. Her eyes were clouded with cataracts and she was mostly deaf as well. Not that she would have been able to respond. She was well on her way to the final stages of Alzheimer's, unable to drag herself from old memories long enough to focus on anything in the present day. When Mia dressed her and bathed her every day, it was like handling a fragile paper doll.

No one was quite sure what her relation was to the guy, David Robinton. He looked nothing like her. He sat with her quietly, or sometimes read to her, or occasionally pushed her wheelchair on the paths around the manicured lawns of the facility.

Mia and the other nurses had taken an interest in him. Three Graces was amazingly quiet. Most of the patients were there to wait comfortably for the inevitable. Every few weeks, another one was taken away in the ambulance that always came to the back entrance and never used its lights or sirens. So David was a mystery she and the other staffers could use to pass the time. He was ridiculously good-looking, but that wasn't all. Three Graces was not cheap. It was more like a high-end hotel than a hospital. There was no stink of urine or death, like some of the holding pens where Mia had worked before. The halls were spotless, the walls dotted with nice prints of Cézanne, Chagall, and Monet, and the rooms had fresh flowers every day. A singer came into the atrium and played a grand piano every afternoon. She knew that whoever he was, David was probably quite wealthy. And, on the forms he signed, she saw that he was a doctor of some kind.

She kept an eye on him while he visited. She was supposed to stay close to the patients, especially when visitors were around, to make sure that they didn't need anything or have any medical emergencies. And if that gave her a little more time to talk with the nice, handsome, rich, young doctor, well, that wasn't a bad thing.

Today, he didn't leave the old woman's room. She checked on them several times, and he only sat by her bed in the chair. She didn't seem to notice he was there.

After an hour, he walked by the front desk to sign out. Mia came around the desk and stood close to him. He rubbed his eyes, wiping away the tears that had formed there. She saw that a lot.

"Same time tomorrow, David?" she asked.

"Same time," he said.

"Good. It gives us something to look forward to," she said. She leaned in closer. "It gets incredibly dull here. You're the most exciting thing that happens all day."

He laughed politely. "I'm not exciting. Believe me. I prefer the peace and quiet."

"Oh, it's good for the old people, sure. But after a twelve-hour shift, I could use a little more noise."

And this is where you ask me what I'm doing after work, dummy.

But David just said, "See you tomorrow."

She tried one more time. "It's so nice of you to visit—your grandmother, I guess?"

David smiled at her and showed her his wedding ring. He didn't say anything. Then he walked away, and out the door.

Mia was blown away. You arrogant bastard, she thought. Maybe she was flirting with him a little, but for him to assume that she was going to leap on him and desecrate his marriage vows right in broad daylight, that was truly a spectacular amount of ego.

She tried to shake off her irritation. It was time to deliver the meds.

She went to the old woman's room first. Mia still had no idea how David was related to her, but now she didn't care. She didn't need to worry about someone that full of himself, that was for sure.

She never noticed that the old woman was wearing a wedding ring that matched David's exactly.

Instead, she asked herself the same question she always did as she helped the old woman choke down her pills:

What kind of a name is Shako, anyway?

## ACKNOWLEDGMENTS

As always, many thanks are due to Alexandra Machinist, my brilliant agent. Thanks as well to my peerless and patient editor Rachel Kahan; Tom Jacobson; Monnie Wills; Dr. Kira Chow, for her read of the manuscript and medical advice; and to Kerri Keslow, for the use of the names of her sons, Parker and Weston.

This is a work of fiction. However, there was a survivor of the ill-fated Narváez expedition named Juan Ortiz who lived among the Uzita. Ortiz was reportedly saved from a horrible death when the daughter of the Uzita's chief pleaded with her father to spare him.

The search for a cure for aging—a biological fountain of youth—is also very real, as detailed in Jonathan Weiner's excellent *Long for This World: The Strange Science of Immortality*. It describes the work of Aubrey de Grey and other gerontologists who seek to solve what de Grey calls the Seven Deadly Things, the ways in which our bodies break down and age and betray us. For anyone investigating the possibilities of an engineered immortal lifespan, that book is the place to start.

The horrific toll of the ongoing drug war in Ciudad Juárez, Mexico, is described in Charles Bowden's remarkable book *Murder City: Ciudad Juárez and the Global Economy's New Killing Fields.*

The number of deserters and resignations from the U.S. Army during the Second Seminole War, as well as other facts about the Seminole wars, are taken from Howard Zinn's *A People's History of the United States: 1492 to Present.*

Shako and Simon's language lesson is not in Uzita but in Creek, which I took from http://native-languages.org, the website of Native Languages of America, an organization dedicated to preserving Native American languages. The websites for the Creek Language Project at the College of William and Mary (http://lingspace.wm.edu/lingspace/creek/) and the Seminole Tribe of Florida (http://www.semtribe.com/) were also helpful.

Any errors are mine alone, as are any alterations I've made in history and geography.

Read on for an excerpt from

CHRISTOPHER FARNSWORTH'S

next action thriller

# KILLFILE

*Coming August 2016*

I KNOW WHAT YOU'RE thinking. Most of the time, it's not impressive. Trust me.

Dozens of people move around me on the sidewalks in L.A.'s financial district, all of them on autopilot. Plugged into their phones, eyes locked on their screens, half-listening to the person on the other end, sleepwalking as they head for their jobs or their first hits of caffeine. The stuff inside their heads can barely even be called thoughts: slogans and buzzwords; half-remembered songs; the latest domestic cage match with whoever they left at home; dramas and gossip involving people they'll never meet in real life. And sex. Lots and lots of sex.

*<can't believe she tweeted that going to get her ass fired> <meeting at 11:30 lunch at Chaya after> <bastard tell me where to park that's always my spot> <damn those are some tits wonder how she'd*

*look in high heels and bent over> <she woke me up daily don't need no Starbucks> <I know right?> <like it would kill him to do the dishes once just once in his life> <not bad I'd fuck her> <who's got the power the power to read uggggbhh stuck in my head again> <forty bucks just to get my car to pass an emissions test thanks Obama!> <OMG did u see that thing on BuzzFeed LOL> <so that's $378 with electric and shit shit shit about $200 in the checking account and Matthew's got that dentist appointment please God don't let him need braces> <Lakers have got to dump Kobe if I was coach I tell you man seriously what are they thinking>*

That's what I live with, constantly, all around me like audible smog.

Most of the time, it's just annoying. But today, it makes it easy to find my targets. They're fully awake, jangling with adrenaline and anxiety. They stand out, hard and bright, a couple of rhinestones glittering in the usual muck.

I cross Fifth Street to the outdoor courtyard where the first guy is waiting at a table, empty Starbucks cup in one hand. I'm supposed to see him.

The one I'm not supposed to see is watching from a half a block over and twenty stories up, on the roof of a nearby building. I can feel him sight me through the rifle scope. I backtrack along his focus on me, reeling it in like a fishing line, until I'm inside his head. He's lying down, the barrel of the gun resting on the edge of the roof, the cool stock against his cheek, grit under his belly. His vision is narrowed to one eye looking through crosshairs, scanning over all the people below him. If I push a little deeper, I can even see the wedge he placed in the access door a dozen feet behind him. He taps his finger on the trigger and goes over his escape route every five seconds or so.

They're both nervous. This is their first kidnapping, after all.

But I'm in kind of a bad mood, so I'm not inclined to make it any easier. I get my coffee first—the line is a wave of pure need, battering impotently against the stoned boredom of the baristas—and then walk back out.

Time to go to work.

I take the open seat across from the guy at the table. I dressed down for this meeting—black jacket, white oxford, standard khakis, everything fresh from the hangers at Gap so I won't stand out—but I still look like an insurance salesman compared to him. He's wearing a T-shirt and baggy shorts, with earbuds wired into his skull beneath his hoodie. Nobody dresses for business anymore.

"Seat's taken," he says. "I'm meeting someone."

I put down my coffee and tap the screen on my phone. His buzzes in response immediately.

He looks baffled. He doesn't get it. I try not to roll my eyes. In real life, there are no Lex Luthors.

"That's me," I tell him. "I'm your meeting."

*<how the fuck did he know?> <he was supposed to call first> <doesn't matter> <don't let him see it> <stick with the plan> <stick with the plan>*

He covers pretty well. He doesn't ask how I knew him, even as he fumbles to shut down the phone. It's a burner. That headset in his ears? It leads down to his personal phone, keeping a direct line open to his buddy up on the roof. If this conversation doesn't end with them substantially richer, he only has to say one word and his friend will blow my head off my shoulders.

So he still thinks he's got the upper hand in this conversation.

"Fine," he says. "Let's get to it."

"What's your name?" I ask.

"We don't need to get into that." *<Donnie>* "All I need from you is the bank transfer. Then the girl can go back to her rich daddy."

I'm already bored. Donnie here has gotten all his moves from TV and movies. He's an amateur who thought he'd stumbled into his own personal IPO when he met my client's daughter in a club two nights ago.

At least I can see why she went with him. He's got catalog-model good looks and, from what I've learned, a ready supply of drugs that he sells at all the right places. She probably thought he was no worse than her last two boyfriends.

But as the gulf between the One Percent and everyone else grows wider, kidnapping idle rich kids has become a minor epidemic in L.A.

Guys like Donnie and his partner—can't quite snag his name yet, but he's still there, watching through the scope—lure one of the many Kardashian or Hilton wannabes away from their friends, drug them up, then lock them down until they get a ransom. The parents pay, and the kids usually come home with little more than a bad hangover. The police are almost never involved.

You haven't heard about this because the parents know people who own major chunks of stock in CNN and Fox. They don't want the idea going viral, and they know who to call to kill a story.

But they also know who to call when they want something like this handled.

My client, Armin Sadeghi, is a wealthy man who had to flee Iran as a child when a group of religious madmen took over his country. That sort of thing leaves a mark. He doesn't particularly trust the police or the government, especially when it comes to family.

"We need to make sure she's alive and unharmed," I say, sipping my coffee.

"She's fine," Donnie says. *<drugged out of her head>* *<Christ, I've seen guys twice her size OD on that>* "But she won't be if you don't give me what I want."

I get a glimpse of Sadeghi's daughter, skirt bunched up over her waist, snoring heavily, face-down on a soiled mattress. Well, at least she's alive.

"So here's how it's going to work," he begins.

I cut him off. "Where is she?"

"What?" The location appears behind his eyes like it's on Google Maps. A hotel stuck on Skid Row, one of the last pockets of downtown to resist coffee shops and condos.

I lift my phone and start dialing. He looks stunned. "Sorry, this won't take long."

"What the hell do you think you're—"

I hold up a finger to my lips while the call connects to Sadeghi. When he picks up, I tell him, "She's at a hotel in downtown Los Angeles," and recite the address from Donnie's memory. He's got a group of well-paid and trusted security personnel waiting to retrieve his daughter.

"Hold on a second," I say as he's thanking me and God, in that order. "What room?" I ask Donnie.

It pops into his head even as he says, "Fuck you."

"Room 427," I say into the phone. "You can go get her now."

I disconnect the call and look back at Donnie. His confusion has bloomed into bewilderment and anger. "How the hell did you do that?" he demands.

He's desperately trying to maintain some control here, torn between running to the hotel and doing some violence to me. I can feel his legs twitch and his pulse jumping.

I can sense the same anger, the same need to do harm, coming down from above. The scope is still on me.

"I know your buddy can hear me," I say, as calmly as I can. "What's his name?"

"Go fuck yourself," Donnie says. <*Brody*>

With that, a jumble of memories sort themselves into a highlight reel of Donnie and Brody, both of their lives coming into sharper focus. Donnie: the club kid, the dealer. Brody: one of the thousands back from the military, no job, no real family, no marketable skills outside of combat training. A partnership forms. Donnie likes having a badass on his side. Brody likes being the badass. They both like the money.

I hope they can both be smarter than they've been up until now.

"All right. Donnie. Brody. You need to recognize that this is over. You can walk away right now, as long as you never get within a thousand yards of the girl or her family again."

I boost the words with as much authority and power as I've got, pushing them into their skulls, trying to make them see it for themselves.

Donnie hunches down. Even if I weren't in his head, I'd see that he's gone from angry to mean. I'm maybe five years older than him, but he's hearing his parents, every teacher, and every cop who ever told him what to do. His anxiety has a sharp and jagged edge now, like a broken bottle in the hand of an angry drunk.

"Yeah?" he says. "And what if we just kill you, instead?"

Not my first choice, admittedly. Out loud, I say, "You spend the rest of your lives running. And you still won't get paid."

I can sense some hesitation from Brody twenty stories up. But he keeps the rifle pointed at my head.

This close up, a little empathy for these morons seeps in around the edges. Neither of them was raised by anybody who gave anything close to a damn. They're scared by my spook show, torn between the need to run and the need to punish. It could go either way. I push harder, trying to steer them onto the right path. I'm working against years of bad habits and ingrained attitude.

But surely they are not stupid enough to try to kill me in the middle of downtown Los Angeles in broad daylight. They just can't be that dumb.

I try to help them make the right decision. <*Go home*> I send to them, as hard as I can. <*Give it up. Be smart. Please.*>

Donnie stands up. "Fuck it," he says.

I relax, just a little.

Then he makes his choice, like a motorcycle veering suddenly down an off-ramp.

"You tell that bitch and her old man we'll be seeing them," he says. "Never mind. I'll tell them myself."

Triumph spreads through his head like the shit-eating grin on his face. I don't know exactly what he's got in store for the Sadeghis. All I see in his mind is a knife and bare flesh.

And blood. Lots of blood.

"Do it," Donnie says. Talking to his partner, not to me.

I feel Brody begin to squeeze the trigger.

Idiots.

I see it so clearly through Brody's eyes. The weapon, a Remington 700 Police Special he bought online, comes alive in his hands. There's a brief flash memory of test-firing it into dunes in the Mojave. He calculates distance and velocity and timing all by reflex. Brody was a good soldier. He breathes out and the rifle bucks slightly as he sends 180 grams of copper-jacketed lead toward my skull, still neatly framed in the crosshairs.

There's a small explosion of blood and bone and my body pitches forward, dead as a dropped call.

But when Brody looks up from the scope, he notices something off. My body is in the wrong place. He can tell, even from that distance.

He puts his eye back to the scope and sees me there, still alive, coffee still in hand.

Donnie is on the ground, arms and legs splayed out at unnatural angles.

Brody feels something sink inside, like a stone dropping into a pool. He jumps to his feet, rifle in hand, and runs toward the door and the escape route he'd planned.

I can see it as clearly as he does, riding along behind his eyes.

Something strikes his shin just above his foot and he goes flying forward. And instead of pitching face-first into the gravel-topped surface, there's nothing.

It takes him a moment to realize he's tripped over the edge of the roof. He sees clearly again and realizes he's in midair, hands and legs windmilling uselessly, touching nothing but sky.

He was sure he was running toward the door.

Then he's aimed like a missile at the pavement below and the pure, animal terror kicks in. The ground rushes up to meet him at thirty-six meters per second and he screams.

I was far enough into Brody's head to cut and paste his perceptions, editing his vision before it got from his eyes to his brain. I put an image of my own head over Donnie's for the shot. When Brody got up to run, I flipped his vision of the roof, made him think the door was in front of him.

I get out of his mind before he hits the ground, but I can still feel the echo of his fear.

I tamp it down and concentrate on going through Donnie's pockets. A little brain matter and a lot of blood leak from the exit wound. His eyes are empty.

Someone comes up behind me. "Oh my God, what happened to him?"

I hit them with a blast of pure panic and disgust—

not too hard at this point—and yell, "Call 911! Get an ambulance!"

They bounce back like they've touched an electric fence.

I find what I'm looking for: Donnie's phone and the hotel room key.

Before anyone else can stop me, I walk away. Not too fast, not too slow.

Around the corner, I have to stop and put my hand on the closest wall to stay upright.

The deaths hit me.

I was too close to both of them. Donnie's last moments weren't too bad: a feeling of victory suddenly cut short, a sharp pain, and then blackness as the bullet tore a gutter through his brain and emptied him of everything he was.

Brody, however, had a good, long time to realize that he was going to die. He took a second breath to keep screaming.

I manage to keep my coffee down. I pull myself together and file both deaths away, in the back of my head, for future reference.

Then I call Mr. Sadeghi again. No, he hasn't sent his team to the address yet. They're still getting ready.

"Never mind," I tell him, looking at the hotel room key. "I'm closer. I'll pick her up and have her home within the hour."

I can't read what's going through his head over the phone, but the relief in his voice sounds genuine. Parental bonds are tough to break, or so I'm told.

I hear sirens. The police will be here to collect the

bodies soon. My bet is that they'll call it a murder-suicide, a couple of small-time scumbags settling a business dispute.

I wonder if I did this on purpose. If I was just so offended by their arrogance and their casual cruelty that I pressed their buttons and boxed them into this ending.

But it doesn't work like that. My life would be a lot easier if it did. They could have just walked away when I told them. I can push, I can nudge, I can mess with their heads, but despite all my tricks, people still find a way to do what they want. Their endings were written a long time before I ever showed up.

Or maybe that's just what I tell myself.

I get my car and head toward the hotel.

*NEW YORK TIMES* BESTSELLING AUTHORS

# JAMES ROLLINS

AND

## REBECCA CANTRELL

***The Order of the Sanguines***

## THE BLOOD GOSPEL

978-0-06-199105-9

An earthquake in Masada, Israel, reveals a subterranean temple holding the crucified body of a mummified girl. A trio of investigators sent to the site is brutally attacked, thrusting them into a race to recover what was once preserved in the tomb's sarcophagus: a book rumored to have been written in Christ's own hand.

## INNOCENT BLOOD

978-0-06-199107-3

Now, an attack outside Stanford University thrusts Erin back into the fold of the Sanguines. As the threat of Armageddon looms, she must unite with the eternal spiritual order and a terrifying power to halt the plans of a ruthless and cunning man determined to see the world end—a man known only as Iscariot.

## BLOOD INFERNAL

978-0-06-234327-7

As an escalating scourge of grisly murders sweeps the globe, Erin Granger must decipher the truth found in the Blood Gospel. With the Apocalypse looming, Erin must again join forces with Army sergeant Jordan Stone and Father Rhun Korza to search for a treasure lost for millennia, a prize that has fallen into the hands of the forces of darkness.